**Praise for Bertrice Small
"THE REIGNING QUEEN OF THE
HISTORICAL GENRE"***
and Her Novels

"Bertrice Small creates cover-to-cover passion, a keen sense of history, and suspense." —*Publishers Weekly*

"Small fans . . . know what to expect . . . a good story."
—*Library Journal*

"Ms. Small delights and thrills." —*Rendezvous*

"An insatiable delight for the senses. [Small's] amazing historical detail . . . will captivate the reader . . . potent sensuality." —*Romance Junkies

"[Her novels] tell an intriguing story, they are rich in detail, and they are all so very hard to put down."
—The Best Reviews

"Sweeps the ages with skill and finesse."
—*Affaire de Coeur*

"[A] captivating blend of sensuality and rich historical drama." —Rosemary Rogers

"Steamy . . . a work of grand historical proportions . . . a must read!" —*Romantic Times* (top pick)

"Brimming with colorful characters and rich in historical detail, Small's boldly sensual love story is certain to please her many devoted readers." —*Booklist*

BERTRICE SMALL

THE BORDER LORD AND THE LADY

A SIGNET ECLIPSE BOOK

SIGNET ECLIPSE
Published by New American Library, a division of
Penguin Group (USA) Inc., 375 Hudson Street,
New York, New York 10014, USA
Penguin Group (Canada), 90 Eglinton Avenue East, Suite 700, Toronto,
Ontario M4P 2Y3, Canada (a division of Pearson Penguin Canada Inc.)
Penguin Books Ltd., 80 Strand, London WC2R 0RL, England
Penguin Ireland, 25 St. Stephen's Green, Dublin 2,
Ireland (a division of Penguin Books Ltd.)
Penguin Group (Australia), 250 Camberwell Road, Camberwell, Victoria 3124,
Australia (a division of Pearson Australia Group Pty. Ltd.)
Penguin Books India Pvt. Ltd., 11 Community Center, Panchsheel Park,
New Delhi - 110 017, India
Penguin Group (NZ), 67 Apollo Drive, Rosedale, North Shore 0632,
New Zealand (a division of Pearson New Zealand Ltd.)
Penguin Books (South Africa) (Pty.) Ltd., 24 Sturdee Avenue,
Rosebank, Johannesburg 2196, South Africa

Penguin Books Ltd., Registered Offices:
80 Strand, London WC2R 0RL, England

Published by Signet Eclipse, an imprint of New American Library, a division of
Penguin Group (USA) Inc. Previously published in a New American Library
trade paperback edition.

First Signet Eclipse Printing, December 2010
10 9 8 7 6 5 4 3 2 1

For Kathryn and Kenneth Rubin, with love from Moi—
Happy Anniversary!

Chapter 1

"*I* will not raise his bastard, Papa," Luciana Maria Pietro d'Angelo said in a hard voice. She was a pretty girl of seventeen, petite, with skin the hue of ivory, and long, thick hair the deep black of a starless night sky. The hair was carefully contained in a golden caul. Her face was a perfect oval, her nose straight but not too long, her mouth generous, and the brows above her chestnut brown eyes were delicately arched.

"Madonna, do not use such crude language," her elderly female companion said nervously. "You are to be a contessa."

"Nevertheless, I *will not* raise his bastard," the young woman said, stamping her small leather-shod foot. The elegant fingers of one hand plucked irritably at the scarlet silk damask of her gown.

"*Fiore mia,*" Master Pietro d'Angelo said soothingly, "as your dear mama is not here to instruct you in the behaviors a wife must accept, it is up to me to do so. As a wife you are required to do what your husband asks of you even when you find it distasteful. The Earl of Leighton honors you with his name and his title, Luciana."

"The earl wishes nothing more than a rich wife to shore up his fortunes, and to give him a male heir," the girl replied bluntly. "Do you take me for a fool, Papa, that I do not know why my hand in marriage has been sought by this man? There are many who would have me to wife," she said boastfully.

"Not in Firenze," her father reminded her stingingly.

Luciana flushed, and the reddish purple staining her delicate skin was not a flattering color.

"I know there are others who would have had you here, *fiore mia,"* her father said, "but Robert Bowen, while poor, is of ancient lineage, and more important, he is an honorable man. He will respect you, *cara,* and treat you well. Do you think I would give you to just anyone? Soon I must return home. I want to know you are in safe hands."

Safe away from Firenze, the merchant thought to himself. *Then perhaps you will not end as your poor mama did.* His daughter was so like his late wife, and yet she wasn't. Carolina had been beautiful and impetuous, but she had not their daughter's intellect. Would that intelligence save his child? He prayed it would.

"I do not question your choice, Papa," Luciana said in a softer tone. "But this Englishman needs my dower more than I need him. I can see he is a prudent man who will not squander the wealth I bring him."

"And you will advise him to invest some of that coin so his wealth may grow, my clever daughter," her father said.

"I will encourage him, Papa. He must not take risks that he shouldn't, but you must assure him my advice is good though I be a female," Luciana said, smiling.

"Ahhh." Master Pietro d'Angelo sighed. "If only your brothers had your business acumen, *fiore mia*! What a merchant you should have made! And Firenze would be all the richer for it. Aye, I will tell your lord to listen and heed you in these matters." *But how candid should I be with him about your mama's fragile emotions?* he wondered silently to himself.

A servant entered the hall to announce the arrival of the Earl of Leighton.

"Bring him in at once!" Master Pietro d'Angelo said. "Do not keep His Lordship waiting, Paolo." He turned to the two women. "Go with Donna Clara, Luciana. Leave the hall. *Presto! Presto!*"

"Remember, Papa, I will not raise his bastard," the girl said as she departed.

But though Donna Clara urged her charge from the hall, Luciana had decided that she would not go. To her companion's distress the girl secreted herself behind a carved screen at the back of the hall where she might both observe and listen.

"He is handsome enough," she whispered to Donna Clara as Robert Bowen, the Earl of Leighton, entered, coming forward to greet her father with an elegant bow. "And neither too old nor too young. He can still father children on me." Her brown eyes silently admired the earl's lithe figure. The dark blue velvet fabric of his coat was showing wear, but Luciana was pleased to see the dragged sleeves were lined in a medium blue silk brocade. He obviously had style, but not the means to indulge it.

"If your papa says you will marry him, it will make no difference if he is ancient or crooked of back, Madonna. You must do as you are bidden," Donna Clara said primly.

"Hush, old crow!" Luciana scolded her companion. "I want to hear what is said." She leaned forward, listening eagerly.

Master Pietro d'Angelo welcomed his guest, inviting him to sit, signaling to his servants for wine and cakes. "And now," he said when they were both settled, "we will finalize the arrangement for your marriage to my daughter, my lord. There are but one or two small details to settle. Luciana's dower is sufficient?"

"It is more than generous, Master Pietro d'Angelo," Robert Bowen answered. "What *small* details?" The earl's blue eyes were slightly wary of some last-minute change to be made in a contract he had already agreed upon.

"A trifle, my lord, to be sure," the merchant replied, seeing the suspicion blooming in his companion's look. "Luciana is a carefully raised virgin with the delicate sensibilities of a true Florentine gentlewoman. I beg that you not burden your bride with the care of your bastard," Master Pietro d'Angelo said nervously. Damn his daughter for putting him in this position, but he knew his wench too well to argue with her on this point. Better he beard the earl, who was certainly more reasonable and would understand. But even if he didn't, would he be desperate enough to agree? "I have been informed that the child is as dear to you as my Luciana is to me. But my daughter is young and romantic. She wants all of your attention, as any bride would. She wants to bear you your heir, and cannot help but be jealous of another woman's child." He paused, looking hopefully at the earl.

Robert Bowen felt a bolt of irritation. Then, remembering that the girl's fat dower would rebuild his family's ancestral home, which had fallen into disrepair when early earls had spent what small income they could wrest from the estate going on Crusade, he let common sense overrule his pride. Unlike other knights, his ancestors had not returned carrying the treasures of the east with them. They had returned injured, unable to be of further use to anyone, let alone their families. Or they had not returned at all, leaving widows and children to carry on at Leighton Hall. Now Robert Bowen, current and possibly last earl of Leighton, must marry the daughter of a wealthy Florentine merchant in an effort to restore his family's fortunes, and gain sons. He would have to wed the wench if she were a toothless idiot.

He drew a deep breath. "My daughter, Master Pietro d'Angelo, is not a bastard. Because I was to wed her mother, who tragically died in childbirth before our union was formally solemnized, I requested that Cicely's birthright be recognized by both Holy Mother Church and English civil law. When she was three, the papers arrived from Rome attesting to her true birth as my legitimate daughter. And English law accepted my petition just prior to her first birthday. Lady Cicely Bowen is no bastard."

Dio mio! He was going to have to say something to justify his daughter's stubbornness. He lowered his voice so no one else in the hall might hear him, and leaned forward. "My lord, I beg you to understand. My deceased wife, Carolina, was a woman of the most delicate, the most fragile sensibilities," he began, struggling to find just the right words in English to explain. "If something distressed her, she would alternate between a deep despair, weeping for hours until she was weak, and being so exhausted she would lie abed for several days. Or worse, she would fall into a ferocious rage that was difficult to calm. It was much like a great storm that had to blow itself out to sea. Because she was such a good wife to me, I tolerated these foibles of her female nature. Our daughter, while possessing the intelligence of a born merchant, also has her mother's sensitive and refined nature. You will not be able to change it, I fear."

There! It was said. He held his breath, awaiting what the earl would say now. Would he decide to nullify the marriage contract? Or would Robert Bowen choose to overlook this weakness in his daughter's character because of his own needs? The Florentine merchant gambled that the latter would be the earl's choice. He was therefore relieved when the earl responded as he now did.

"For the sake of Luciana's fragile sensibilities, I will indulge these delicate emotions for as long as it takes for her to overcome them. I will compromise with your daughter, Master Pietro d'Angelo," the earl said. "I will domicile Cicely and her nursemaid, Orva, in a large cottage at the far end of my gardens. Then Luciana may come to know Cicely. She will like her, for she is a charming little lass. When that time comes my child will return to the main house."

"It is an equitable arrangement," the merchant

agreed, nodding. He had suddenly realized as the earl spoke that his tolerance would extend no further. But at least Pietro d'Angelo's conscience was clear. He had disclosed his daughter's weakness.

There was no need for the earl to know that his wife, Carolina, had died by her own hand. Only he and Donna Clara knew the truth of Carolina Pietro d'Angelo's demise. The priest had been told that she had been sleepwalking when she fell from the balcony of her bedchamber. The Church did not need to know that Carolina had, in a moment of weakness, taken a lover and, when she found herself *incinta*, had taken her life rather than shame her husband and their family. Master Pietro d'Angelo never knew the identity of the man who had seduced or been seduced by his wife. No gossip had ever emerged.

Hidden behind her screen, Luciana had heard the last words spoken between her father and the earl. She hissed angrily. But then she allowed her anger to ease. Once she was Robert Bowen's wife she would have a stronger position in his life. At least the brat would not be under her feet.

"He is a *real* man, your husband-to-be." Donna Clara cackled softly. "You will not twist him about your little finger as you do your father and brothers, Madonna."

"Aye, I will," the girl said in a hard voice. Was she not young and beautiful? And would not the earl want to please his bride? He would do whatever she desired of him. Men did not refuse her. She would wrap him about her finger and he would be her slave! Her mouth twisted in a small smile as she already savored her triumph. She was free now of Firenze, and free of her overprotective father. She would soon be the Countess of Leighton, a great English lady. And her husband would love and adore her because she would make him!

Donna Clara sighed. "Aye, you probably will. Men are fools." Then she said, "What a coup for your father, who brought you to London to protect you from the unwelcome rumors surrounding your association with Signore di Alba. Now he may return to Firenze proud to announce your marriage, and to tell all who will listen that his daughter is a contessa! Finally your younger brothers may make respectable marriages within the great houses, thus strengthening the *famiglia* Pietro d'Angelo. Remember what they say in Firenze: 'A man without wealth is also a man without esteem.' Ah, if only you had not involved yourself with di Alba!" the older woman lamented.

"Nothing happened with di Alba," Luciana half lied. "I was only amusing myself while I waited for Papa to make a great match for me."

"I believe you," Donna Clara said, although she was actually not certain. Still, if the girl had ruined herself, it was Donna Clara who would be blamed. She was a poor relation, and needed to retain her standing within Master Pietro d'Angelo's household. What would happen to her if she were driven away? Better she follow the girl's lead. "Signore di Alba was a knave. He hoped to force your papa into a marriage alliance by making you appear undesirable to a more desirable family."

"He was poor," Luciana said scornfully. "Why would I marry a poor man when so many rich men sought after me? Di Alba was a fool. A handsome fool, but a fool nonetheless."

"You were foolish too to ever involve yourself with him, Madonna," Donna Clara scolded the girl gently. "And now you must wed in England. The earl is a poor man too, but he is noble, and I am told he is respected. You will be a contessa. He will gain wealth, and your children will be nobility. 'Tis a good arrangement, and one made many times before through the ages."

A servant hurrying from the hall stopped when he saw the two women in the shadows, saying, "My master has sent for you, Madonna. Shall I tell him you are here?"

"*Buffone!*" Donna Clara snapped, reaching to cuff

the servant, who ducked the blow. "Say the signorina will join the gentlemen shortly." She turned to Luciana. "Come, *bambina mia*. Let us freshen your hair and gown so the earl will be pleased to see you."

"Nay, he would show pleasure if my eyes were crossed and my teeth crooked," Luciana responded dryly. She stepped from behind the carved screen and made her way forward. Reaching the two men, she swept them a graceful curtsy. "Papa. My lord." She greeted the gentlemen in a deceptively soft voice, her eyes modestly downcast as she moved to take her seat on a stool by her father's side.

But the Earl of Leighton took her hand and drew Luciana to him. "Your father has spoken to me of your concerns regarding my daughter," Robert Bowen began. "I understand. But you must know and accept that my child is legitimate. As such she will stand among my legal heirs. If you do not give me a son, she will inherit my estate one day. But I expect you will give me several sons, Madonna Luciana." The blue eyes looked down into her brown ones.

"You will walk with the earl," Master Pietro d'Angelo said to his daughter. "You should know each other better before the marriage is celebrated."

Robert Bowen tucked the girl's dainty hand in his arm and led her off.

When they were out of earshot Luciana said, "I am glad you will not make me share you with your daughter."

"Her name is Cicely," the earl answered quietly.

"I do not care," Luciana replied. "I shall never see her."

"Nay, you do not have to if you choose not to," the earl told the girl. "You will be far too busy, lady. Your rich dower and your late mother's reputation for fecundity make you worthy to be my wife. I will keep you on your back with your legs open to me until you prove fertile. I want sons, lady, and I mean to have them on your body."

He pushed her into a darkened corner of the hall. Then, taking her oval face in his two hands, he kissed her lush mouth with a hard, fiery kiss.

Luciana's heart beat rapidly as one of the earl's big hands moved to clamp about her waist while the other reached down to squeeze her left breast hard through the fabric of her gown. His fingers found the nipple of that breast stiff with her arousal, and he pinched it several times.

"I know the rumors about di Alba," he growled into her ear.

Luciana moaned against his demanding mouth. "Falsehoods!" she protested.

The Earl of Leighton laughed knowingly. "We shall see, lady," he said wickedly as he bit down on her ear-lobe. "I am no fool. If you do indeed possess a tiny heart-shaped birthmark upon your left thigh I will know 'tis you who are the liar, and not di Alba." His lips moved teasingly across hers again.

The girl grew pale at his words. "I am still a virgin," she insisted to him. "I swear it by the innocence of the Blessed Mother! *I am a virgin!*"

"That too I shall soon learn, lady," he told her cruelly. Robert Bowen laughed again. "Do not fear, Luciana. It is your wealth that attracts me, not your virtue. But be warned: From this moment forth I will expect you to remain faithful to me alone. Should I ever discover you have not been faithful I will kill you with my bare hands, and be lauded for it. Do you understand me? You may whore no more." The blue eyes had turned icy with warning as they looked down into her face.

"*Sì*, my lord," Luciana whispered. "I understand, but I swear to you that no man's cock has entered my body, and none will but yours." *Dio!* They had always said that the English were a cold race, but this Englishman certainly was not. He excited her! She felt the moisture pooling between her nether lips. She was already half in love with him, and trembled in his strong arms. He would share her with no other man, but she would share him with no other female. Even his little daughter!

The earl was not certain how truthful his intended was being with him, but he did believe she was an honorable woman. Whatever had happened before she came to England would not happen again. He had learned by chance from a friend returned from Italy of the stories being bruited about Firenze by one Signore Vincente di Alba regarding Luciana Maria Pietro d'Angelo. Some gossips even said her father had spirited the girl away because she was with child. Robert Bowen knew that not to be true, for the Pietro d'Angelos had been in London for over a year now. His friend had also told him that Signore di Alba was heavily in debt, and had convinced his creditors that he would soon have a wealthy wife when Master Pietro d'Angelo returned with his daughter.

"Do you believe me, my lord?" Luciana said softly, gazing up at him with doe eyes. She pressed herself against him.

The earl laughed softly, recognizing her budding lust. "Soon, little one," he promised, stroking the top of her silken head. "We shall not tarry on our way to the altar."

Several days later the wedding contracts were signed in her father's London hall, the priest from Westminster who had drawn them up overseeing the formality. The spiritual blessing would be given and the ceremony celebrated shortly afterwards. Then the Earl of Leighton would take his bride home to Leighton Hall in Gloucestershire, where her duties as mistress of his house would begin as she prayed for sons.

Luciana was almost weak with her excitement. She took Donna Clara aside. "You are certain I am still a virgin?" she demanded of her companion. "The old witch knew what she was doing?"

"Her examination showed his fingers had slightly torn your maidenhead, but that it was still intact, Madonna," the older woman said. "But to make sure your bridegroom is fully satisfied we shall begin this day to treat your sheath and its opening with alum to shrink it. It will make it difficult at first for his cock to penetrate into your body. He will be so aroused by it, and by your cries of innocence, he will not notice that your maidenhead gives way easily. And there should be some blood. But you shall also secrete a small chicken's bladder of blood to break in your bridal bed so the earl will have no doubt as to your virtue, *bambina mia*."

"If my passage is tight it will hurt," Luciana complained. "I felt his cock through my gown as he held me. He is a large man."

"You must bear a little pain, Madonna, so your husband will be content in his mind that he is the only one to have trod your love path. Better that than a lifetime of suspicion," Donna Clara reminded the girl.

"My father says you are to remain in England with me," Luciana noted.

"I am pleased to do so, for I am devoted to you, Madonna, and not just because we are linked by a small blood tie. I will always keep your secrets," Donna Clara said softly, "and I will always see to your best interests."

"Old crow," Luciana said affectionately. "Still, I am glad you will be with me, but you must begin to treat me with more respect now that I am to be a great lady." Secretly she was relieved her longtime companion was remaining. Donna Clara was often the voice of reason for the girl, and Luciana was intelligent enough to realize it. She would have someone with whom to speak her native tongue, and who could advise her wisely.

The Church's blessing of the Earl of Leighton's marriage to Luciana Maria Pietro d'Angelo took place on a bright May morning. A feast was held afterwards, the invited guests coming from the community of wealthy foreign merchants in London, as well as several of the earl's acquaintances. The newly married couple would remain the night in her father's house. Less than an hour after the bridal pair had been formally put to bed Luciana's genuine screams of agony as her bridegroom's cock penetrated her could be heard briefly in the hall where the guests lingered. There were nods of approval in Master Pietro d'Angelo's direction, and he smiled and nodded back in return. The rumors set in motion by Signore di Alba would now be put to rest, and he could return to his beloved Firenze to tell all of his daughter's brilliant marriage to an English nobleman.

Upstairs in the bridal chamber the earl fingered the heart-shaped mark on his bride's smooth, plump thigh. "How did he know?" Robert Bowen asked her.

"A group of us went riding from the city one day. It was hot. We stopped to cool ourselves by wading in the shallows of the river. I raised my skirts too high," Luciana lied as she kissed his mouth.

And Robert Bowen chose to believe her, for her passage had been so tight he could not believe any other man had ever gotten into her. And the tears of anguish upon her pale cheeks as he entered her were certainly real. His cock had met enough resistance in her maidenhead that he now believed for sure in her virginity, and there had certainly been a goodly show of blood. She had gained no pleasure from this first joining, he knew. But he would see she did in the future.

They had planned to leave London the following day, but the bride was unable to ride, being sore. He had used her thrice on their wedding night, and by the third time she had learned the delights of pleasure. She was open to passion, the earl was pleased to find. He would have no need for a mistress for the interim. Finally, three days after they wed, they rode forth from the town. Master Pietro d'Angelo had promised to pay them a visit before he returned to Firenze.

When several days later they arrived at Leighton Hall, Luciana was well pleased. The house was in need of repair, but she knew her father would give her whatever she desired to make her new home habitable and to her taste. The gardens looking out over the gentle hills

needed serious tending, but the servants were delighted
to have a new mistress to guide them. And if sometimes
the Countess Luciana's manner was abrupt, they hoped
it was just because she was young and inexperienced.

Master Pietro d'Angelo arrived two months later,
in Midsummer, prior to his departure back to Firenze.
He was very happy to learn his daughter was already
pregnant with her first child. He was relieved to find her
content with her life, and with her lord. He spent an enjoyable few weeks before traveling back up to London,
and from there across the channel as he made his way
home.

Donna Clara had assured him all was well, and that
she would send one of the homing pigeons he had given
his daughter with word when the child was born. "She
frets only now and again about one thing," the countess's companion told her father.

"His daughter?" The merchant knew how jealous Luciana could be.

Donna Clara nodded. "The earl visits his child daily."

"Have you seen her?" Master Pietro d'Angelo asked
his relation.

Donna Clara nodded. "She is a charming little girl,
Carlo. Bright and mannerly. She would make a wonderful companion for the contessa. But Madonna Luciana
will not share her husband. The servants have been
warned to not even mention the child in the lady's presence, for her jealousy runs wild. Perhaps in time." The
older woman sighed.

Master Pietro d'Angelo shook his head. "Nay, Clara.
If she will not accept the child now, she will never accept her. Especially as she is carrying her own babe. You
know what I say is truth. Pray Luciana births the son the
earl wants. It may ease my daughter's jealousy, but it will
never erase it. Just do not allow her to harm the earl's
little daughter. You know how she can get sometimes."

"I will keep them both safe, Carlo. For the love I bear
your daughter, and for the many kindnesses you have

done for me, especially after my husband died," Donna
Clara said quietly. "I will allow no shame to fall upon
the house of Pietro d'Angelo." Then she bade her rela-
tive farewell, and promised to pray for his safe journey
home to Firenze.

The summer slipped into autumn, and then winter.
On Candlemas, the second day of February in the year
of our Lord 1414, Luciana, the Countess of Leighton,
gave birth to her firstborn, a son, baptized Charles, after
her father. Thirteen months later, on the twenty-third
day of March, the countess birthed a second son, Richard, and ten months later, on a snowy last day of January,
Henry Bowen entered the world.

The earl was more than satisfied with his three sons,
all healthy and thriving to his pleasure. But he feared
for his wife's health, for she was easily impregnated,
and three babes within three years would have killed
a lesser woman than Luciana. He voiced his fears to
Donna Clara. "I will take a mistress so my lusts may be
eased," he told her.

Donna Clara shook her head. "She would kill you
if she finds out, my lord. And she would find out. You
know her jealousy. I know a remedy that I can give her
that will prevent her from getting with child again unless
you wish it."

Robert Bowen raised an eyebrow. "What would the
Church say to such a thing?" he asked her softly.

Donna Clara smiled a small smile at him. "What would
they say to you taking a mistress?" she countered.

The earl chuckled. "Do what you need to do, old
crow," he told her, using the affectionate term that his
wife used for Donna Clara.

The older woman knew Luciana too well to suggest
she refrain from continuing to populate the nursery at
Leighton Hall. Instead she began to serve her lady a
special drink each morning to strengthen her. And when
a few weeks had passed she offered Luciana another
beverage that would keep her skin smooth and blem-

ish free. Being vain, the countess accepted her longtime companion's advice, and sipped from the cup each day. The earl continued to enjoy his wife's favors, but for the interim there were no more children.

On a perfect summer's day when Henry Bowen was barely six months old, he was taken to the house's gardens to be set down upon a small silk blanket, where he enjoyed the sunshine with his two slightly older brothers. The Earl of Leighton's heir, Charles, was two and a half. He chased a ball his nursemaid threw for his amusement. Richard, the earl's middle son, had just learned to walk. He eagerly toddled everywhere, his young nursemaid chasing after him. They suddenly came upon a little girl.

"Orva!" Richard's nursemaid greeted the woman accompanying the girl. Then she looked nervously around. "Should you be here?"

"The gardens aren't forbidden to my mistress, Alice," Orva said. She was a tall, lanky woman with prematurely iron gray hair and sharp, dark gray eyes.

"Who are these little lads?" Cicely Bowen asked, curious.

"They are your half brothers, poppet," Orva answered. She looked to Alice. "Which one is this? The eldest?"

"Nay, this is Lord Richard, the second-born," Alice replied, holding him by her side as he squirmed.

At the sound of his name the child broke free of his nursemaid and, giggling, began to run off on fat little legs. Alice shrieked, but Cicely quickly caught the little boy by his hand, laughing.

"Nay, nay, naughty one," she said. "You must stay with your Alice." She turned to Orva. "How many brothers do I have now?"

"Three," Alice volunteered. "We've been on t'other side of that hedge."

"Ohh, let me see them!" the little girl cried, and she dashed around the tall green hedge, where she observed Charles and the baby, Henry. "Hello," she greeted them.

"I am Lady Cicely Bowen, your big sister." Plunking herself down next to Henry, who was lying upon his back, she tickled his little tummy. Henry chortled with delight, waving his fists at Cicely. The two other nurse-maids stared, horrified. They knew the difficulties where the earl's daughter was concerned, although they did sympathize with the little one's predicament.

Orva came around the hedge and, taking Cicely's hand, pulled the girl to her feet. "Come along, my lady. Your father has carefully explained to you the state of affairs with his wife. If you are found here with her sons there will be merry hell to pay."

And the words were no sooner out of Orva's mouth than the Countess of Leighton stepped into view and, seeing the four children together, shrieked as if the very portals of hell had just opened and demons were coming to take her away. At once the three little boys, fright-ened, began to howl in response to their mother's ap-parent distress.

"She is attempting to bewitch my sons!" Luciana screamed for all to hear. "Kill her! Kill her! Donna Clara! Donna Clara! Come quickly. Do not let her harm my boys!" And the countess ran forward to grasp Cicely by her long hair, and began beating the little girl. *"Bas-tarda!"* she cried. "You will not have anything here! My sons are the true heirs! *Bastarda! Bastarda!"*

Orva had been taken by surprise by the countess's attack upon her charge, but now, without hesitation, she stepped forward and pulled Luciana from Cicely. "You will not touch my lady, madam," she said in her deep voice. Then, quickly gathering Cicely up in her strong arms, Orva strode off, carrying the weeping child.

But Luciana recovered quickly from her shock at being manhandled by the big woman. She whirled to face the three nursemaids, who now stood cowering with their individual charges. "You will all be beaten," she said in a dark and dangerous voice. "There will be no help from my lord for any of you, for you well know the servants are mine to command. Get back to the house now! Leave my sons in more capable hands in their nursery. Then you will come to me for your punishment. How dare you allow that bastard brat near my precious children."

"It were Alice!" cried Henry's nursemaid. "She brought them near us."

"Aye," Charles's nursemaid agreed, hoping like her companion to deflect the worse of their mistress's ire to the unfortunate Alice.

"My little master ran away, and I came upon them chasing him," Alice protested, seeing where the situation was headed. "I told them to go away, my lady. I did!"

"But they didn't, did they?" the countess said. "You will receive the most blows, Alice. You are indeed responsible."

"*She* let the little girl touch Master Henry," Alice responded, pointing at the baby's nursemaid, who had started all of this.

"She touched my precious infant?" The countess fell back, one hand dramatically over her heart. "Sweet Jesu! My son has been cursed by the *bastarda*!" Her brown eyes narrowed as they fixed themselves upon Henry's servant. "*You!*" she accused. "You will feel the blows of my rod harder than the rest. And when I have finished with the three of you, it is back to the village for you all. You will never care for my boys again!"

Alerted by the other servants of some altercation in the gardens, Donna Clara had now arrived. "What has happened?" she wanted to know as she stared at the white-faced trio, the three howling children, and her enraged mistress. They all spoke at once, but from their babble the older woman learned of the incident. She gathered her mistress into the comfort of her arms with soft, soothing words. "There, there, *bambina mia*. No real harm has been done here. It was an unfortunate happenstance; that is all. You must calm yourself, for you have frightened the boys. Alice and the others acted in accordance with your wishes, I am certain. They did their best to send the earl's daughter away. You might have never even known of the incident had you not come upon them."

"The *bastarda*'s servant put her hands on me!" Luciana cried angrily.

"And the earl shall know of it, *bambina mia,*" Donna Clara assured her mistress, stroking her head. "Come now, and let us return to the house. You are distraught and must lie down. I have a lovely soothing draft that will ease your nerves."

"I must beat these women first," Luciana insisted. "They have been disobedient."

"Nay, *bambina mia,* they are good servants, but they were taken unawares. It is no one's fault. They did their best to control the situation, and you must not beat them." She began to draw Luciana away from the others, all the while murmuring to her, half in their native language. "*Andiamo, cara mia.* Everything is all right now."

The earl was apprised of the situation by Donna Clara. Then he interviewed the three nursemaids. Orva was called to the house. "I am told you pulled the countess away from my daughter," Robert Bowen said.

"I did," Orva replied without a moment's hesitation. "She began to beat my lady. The little one has bruises on her arms, her face, her shoulders and back, my lord. Certainly you did not mean for your daughter to be treated in such a dreadful fashion?" Orva's dark gray eyes met those of the earl without flinching.

"Tell me exactly what happened," Robert Bowen said quietly.

Orva related the incident truthfully and without emotion as her master listened. He recognized her version as the truth of the matter. His sons' servants had been terrified out of the few wits they had by Luciana and their fear of her retribution. He knew that the three nursemaids felt their safety lay in lining up on the side of his wife. As for Donna Clara, she had also been truthful with him, admitting she had come upon the chaotic scene after all had been said and done.

"Lady Cicely made no attempt to harm your sons, my lord," Orva repeated. "She caught little Lord Richard by the hand when he tried to run from Alice. She sat by the baby and tickled his tummy. She had no contact whatsoever with Lord Charles."

"The others say she put the evil eye on the two elder, and muttered cabalistic words in Henry's ear," the earl told his daughter's nursemaid.

"What?" Orva's outrage spoke for itself.

Unable to help himself, Robert Bowen laughed aloud. "I know it is nonsense, Orva, but for the sake of peace in my household I must forbid Cicely the gardens from now on. I will tell her myself when I come to see her. I wish I could control my wife's jealousy, for it is unreasonable and unfounded. But, alas, I cannot."

"It is wrong, my lord, just plain wrong that my lady is kept from her brothers and her family," Orva said candidly, "but I will obey, my lord."

Donna Clara came privily to the earl that night as he sat reading alone in his library by the fire. He beckoned her forward and gestured to a small chair opposite his. "My lord," she began, "I hesitate to bring this matter to your attention, but I promised my lady's father, my cousin, that I would keep her safe—and your daughter too. Seeing Lady Cicely today has unleashed a terrible jealousy in my lady. She has spoken to me of poisoning this little girl in order to be rid of her. I cannot let her do such a thing, but neither must she know I have come to you, my lord. If she believes I have betrayed her she will never forgive me. She will find a way to revenge herself. But I cannot allow her to do anything foolish and bring shame upon her father's house. Nor must she have the murder of an innocent upon her conscience."

Robert Bowen was shocked by Donna Clara's revelation. He knew that Luciana's jealousy could run high, but for her to even consider killing a child in her ire horrified him. "I must send my daughter away from Leighton Hall," he said, realizing as the words left his mouth that he had spoken aloud.

"It would probably be best for the little one," Donna Clara agreed. "There is nothing unusual in fostering a daughter out."

The earl nodded. "But to whom?" he wondered.

"Tell my mistress of your plan," Donna Clara said. "It will allow me to defuse her anger temporarily so you may have time to place Lady Cicely with a good family."

The earl nodded. "You are a good woman, Donna Clara," he told her. "Whatever happens, you will always have a home here at Leighton Hall, and a place in my family."

She arose and nodded graciously to him. "Thank you, my lord, but I acted not to betray my lady, but rather to prevent her from blackening her immortal soul."

"Of course," he agreed, nodding in return as she slipped from the library. Then he sank back into his chair to consider what he must do. He should have never married Luciana. But then whom would he have married? When Anne had died giving birth to Cicely he had known he could never really love again. Not like he had loved Anne. They had grown up together. She was his household steward's daughter. They shared family, for his steward had been a distant relation from an even poorer branch of the Bowen family. Then suddenly Anne was gone, but he had Cicely—and an estate with a great house in need of repairs. No coin for it, nor to even pay his servants, who remained with him out of duty, loyalty, the need for a home themselves. There had been no choice but to finally take a wife.

He might have married the younger daughter from another good English family, with a pittance for a dower. He did, after all, have an old and honorable name as well as a title to offer a wife. Or he could have, as he had done, sought out the offspring of a wealthy merchant willing to pay for that title for his child. Luciana's dower was excessively generous, and Master Pietro d'Angelo eager to see his daughter a countess. The earl had quietly investigated the family and learned of the gossip about his prospective wife, but as there was nothing proven and in the end she proved a virgin, he had been content—especially as she had given him three healthy sons in as many years, and her investment advice was excellent. He was fast becoming a very wealthy man.

But Luciana's unreasonable jealousy towards his little daughter was becoming difficult to manage. He could not allow her to harm Cicely, but neither could he expose his wife, the mother of his three sons, to a charge of witchcraft and murder. Robert Bowen drew a deep sigh. Donna Clara was right. Reluctant as he was to do it, he knew he would have to foster out his daughter with another family. But with whose family? And what could he offer such a family in return? He needed to think upon it.

Leaving his library, the earl went to his apartments, entering his wife's bedchamber. Luciana was awaiting him. Her face was tearstained, and when she saw him she began to sob. It was a familiar scene, and he almost laughed aloud. "What is troubling you, my darling?" he asked her as he came to sit upon the edge of her bed, taking her hand up and kissing it.

"I am so frightened, Roberto," she said. "Henry might have been killed today. Your ba . . . daughter wishes them all ill. What will become of our sons?" She sobbed.

"They will, with God's blessing, grow up to be fine men," the earl replied. "As for Cicely, it is time I fostered her out with another noble family so she may take her place in the world. One day, sooner than later, I will have to find a husband for her."

Luciana's brown eyes grew wide. "You are sending the girl away, my lord?" The tears, the looks of fear she had been casting at him had suddenly vanished.

"As soon as I find a suitable family with whom to place her," Robert Bowen said. "It should not take a great deal of time, and until then she is forbidden the gardens, my darling." He stroked her long dark hair, which was loose in her dishabille.

"What of her servant who attacked me?" Luciana's voice was now hard.

"Orva will go with Cicely," the earl replied.

"She should be punished for laying her hands on me!" his wife said angrily. "There is a bruise on my shoulder where the creature's thumb dug into me."

"You beat my daughter with no real provocation, Luciana." Now the earl's voice was cold and hard. "Orva tells me Cicely is black and blue all over."

"She tried to harm my child!" the Countess of Leighton protested.

"*She* is seven years old, Luciana, and her heart is pure. She knows she has half brothers, and was excited to finally see them. We both know she made no attempt to harm the lads. You are jealous of my daughter, Luciana, and I have tried to reassure you in this matter, but you will not be comforted. This unfortunate incident will not be repeated, because I will send my daughter from Leighton Hall for her own safety. Know, however, that I have already settled a large amount on Cicely so that one day I can make a good match for her."

It was not often that the Countess of Leighton heard her husband speak so sternly to her, but when he did she knew that he meant exactly what he said. Still, she would not allow him to cow her completely. "I am satisfied with your decision, my lord," she murmured meekly. "But do not dally in finding a place for the girl," she added sharply. "I cannot have our sons living under the threat of danger."

"There is no danger," the earl said, "but that which you have invented in your imagination, Luciana. Put it aside, and the matter will be quickly settled."

Chapter 2

Henry of Lancaster had died on the twentieth of March, and his heir was crowned on the ninth of April as King Henry V. The young king was eager to go to war with France. The Earl of Leighton consulted with his friend—and blood relation—Sir William Rogers, as to where he might foster his daughter.

" 'Tis a bad time, Robert," Sir William said candidly. "But perhaps there is a chance you can get your lass into an important house if you can offer the king something in return. He's like all the Lancasters, ready to do a favor for a favor."

"He'll need financing for his war," Robert Bowen said. "I can probably aid him there. The Florentine bankers are always looking to make another profit, and I have many friends among them."

"The king will be at Windsor next week," Sir William said. "I'm leaving in another day or two. Ride with me. I can at least get you into his presence."

"You have a new daughter, don't you?" the earl said to his relation.

"Born on the day the old king died," Sir William responded.

"She'll need a husband one day," Robert Bowen said.

"And he'll need a rich wife," Sir William observed. "My lass won't have much, but I thank you for even considering it."

"You don't know what will happen in the next few years," the Earl of Leighton told his kinsman. "Let us wait and see."

When Sir William had departed Leighton Hall, Robert Bowen called for his horse and rode to the cottage where his daughter resided. Hearing his horse approaching, Cicely flew from the little house to greet her father. When he saw her, his heart contracted painfully. She was her mother's image, with her rich auburn hair and her blue-green eyes. When she was grown she would be every bit as beautiful as Anne had been, if not more so. Even her creamy skin tone was Anne's, and the long, dark eyelashes that brushed her rose-hued cheeks. The perfection of her skin, however, was marred by a purplish bruise upon her left cheekbone.

"Papa! You came! I thought you might be angry at me." She looked up at him, concerned.

"Now, why would I be angry with you, poppet?" the earl asked her as he swept her up into his embrace, kissing her right cheek, gently fingering the bruise, disturbed when she winced slightly.

"I didn't mean to anger your lady wife, Papa," Cicely said as he set her down upon her feet. "Why does she hate me so?"

Taking her small hand in his big one, the earl led his daughter to a bench outside of the cottage door and they sat together. "I cannot sugarcoat the truth, poppet," he began. "Your stepmother is a jealous woman, Cicely. She wants no other woman in my life but her. Sadly, I cannot change her, which brings me to why I have come today. Orva," he called. "Please come and join us." And when the serving woman stood by his side he continued. "For your own safety, and for the welfare of your half brothers, I am going to foster you out to a good family. There will be other girls with you from other families.

The lady of the house will teach you all those things you must learn and must know one day when you become the lady of the house. Eventually I shall make a fine marriage for you, Cicely. Orva will go with you and continue to look after you as she has always done, poppet. You could not remain at Leighton Hall forever."

"Where are we to go?" Orva asked the earl quietly.

He looked directly at her. "I do not know yet. I am going with Sir William to Windsor in a few days. The court is very busy now, and if I am fortunate I will speak with the king himself. I will choose wisely, Orva. In the meantime you must keep close to the cottage. There must be no opportunity for the countess to see you, or to see Cicely. Do you understand me?" he asked her softly, meaningfully.

Orva nodded. "I will keep the little lady safe, my lord."

"Will I ever see you again, Papa?" Cicely asked her father, and he heard the fear in her young voice.

"Of course you will see me, poppet!" he assured her. "Sadly, your stepmother will not share her excellent household skills with you, and if you are to wed one day you must have those skills. Most girls your age are sent to other families. You will follow an age-old pattern, Cicely. And while I am at Windsor, Orva will make you some fine new gowns from the materials she takes from the storerooms. You will be the prettiest young lady in whichever household you join." And Robert Bowen bent and kissed his little daughter's cheek, careful to avoid her bruise. He arose from his seat. "I must return now to the house. When I come again, Cicely, I will know where you are to go."

"Go into the cottage, child," Orva said quietly. "I need to speak with your papa."

Cicely obeyed immediately.

"Would you send her away if it had not been for the incident with your sons?" Orva asked her master frankly.

"I don't know," he answered honestly. "She does need to know the things that only a lady of rank can teach her. Donna Clara tells me my wife speaks of harming Cicely, for the jealousy assailing her cannot be quenched. Sending my daughter away will keep the child safe, I believe. Don't let Cicely eat anything you have not prepared yourself while I am gone. Do you understand, Orva?"

Orva nodded, her mouth quirking with her disapproval. "I have heard these foreigners like to use poison," she noted.

The earl sighed and shrugged. "What else can I do but what I'm doing?" he said.

"Find us a good home, my lord," Orva replied. "And find my mistress a good husband when she is old enough."

The earl nodded. "I will," he promised.

At Windsor his cousin managed to introduce him to the king, but the young man was more interested in preparing for war than in the fortunes of the daughter of an unimportant man. But Henry V was not heartless. Seeing the disappointment on the earl's face, he said, "Such a request is not within my purview at this time, my lord, but I shall send you to my most excellent and well-loved mother, Queen Joan, with my request that she aid you in your endeavor."

Relieved, the Earl of Leighton bowed low and thanked the king, who sent him off with a servant, promptly forgetting him.

Queen Joan's antechamber was filled with petitioners. Robert Bowen was forced to wait, but the king's servant waited with him to introduce him and present the king's request of the lady.

Queen Joan had been Henry IV's second wife. The daughter of King Charles the Bad of Navarre, and his wife, a princess of France, she had been married first to the Duke of Brittany, by whom she had had nine children. After her husband died she had acted as regent for her oldest son until he came of age at twelve. She had then married the widowed King of England, a father of six children himself. While both the king and queen were still young enough to have children, none were born to them. But Henry IV's offspring adored their stepmother.

After sitting in the queen's antechamber for several hours, the Earl of Leighton and the king's servant were ushered into Queen Joan's presence. The earl bowed low and kissed the elegant beringed hand held out to him.

"His Highness, the king, would have you aid this gentleman, madam," the servant said, and then he backed from the room, leaving the earl to face the queen, along with her attendants, who sat about the chamber sewing and chattering softly.

"You are?" Queen Joan asked Robert Bowen seated in a high-backed chair, a footstool beneath her feet.

"Robert Bowen, the Earl of Leighton, madam," he told her.

"What is it I may do for you, my lord?" the queen inquired of him softly.

Quietly, as carefully and quickly as he could, the earl explained his situation. He did not wish to heap criticism upon his wife, but he did need Queen Joan to understand the desperate situation that he faced in the matter of his daughter.

The queen nodded slowly, and when he had finished she said, "Aye, I can see the difficulty, my lord, but you are partly to blame for it. When you took your bride you were not firm with her. Your daughter should never have been made to live outside of your house in another dwelling. Like my dear late husband's uncles were, you legitimated your daughter. Your wife was obviously spoiled and allowed to have her own way by her parents." Queen Joan shook her head. "But even if your wife had accepted your little girl, it would be better that she be fostered out. She has a dower portion, I assume."

"With the goldsmith Isaac Kira, in London," the earl said, and then he told the queen the amount he had placed with the goldsmith.

The queen drew in a sharp breath. "Indeed, my lord, 'tis a considerable amount. You will have no trouble finding a worthy husband of impeccable breeding for your child one day. But for now we must find a suitable family for her."

"I would be honored if you could suggest such a family, Your Highness," the earl said. "My family is old. It is honorable. But we have always lived quietly, avoiding entanglements that might bring dishonor to us or those we serve."

Queen Joan nodded. "There is nothing wrong with being prudent, my lord. Now tell me how old your daughter is."

"She is seven, madam," he answered.

"Has she been taught? What languages does she speak?" the queen continued.

"She speaks both English and French, and can understand church Latin, madam," he told her. "She can do sums. She rides well, and her manners are good."

"Then she is fit for the best company," Queen Joan concluded. "Somerset's widow has remarried herself to Thomas Plantagenet, the Duke of Clarence. She has left her children by John Beaufort in the care of others. Henry, the eldest, now holds his father's titles, and remains in his own home. His three brothers are all fostered out, and serve different masters. His sisters are at home. The youngest will remain there for the interim, for she is only four, but I am considering bringing my namesake, Lady Joan Beaufort, who is almost nine, into the royal household. She is a sweet girl. Perhaps your daughter would make a good companion for her. Yes. I shall bring young Joan here, and your daughter will have a place among her maiden companions." Queen Joan looked at the Earl of Leighton. "It is settled. Bring your daughter to me, my lord."

Robert Bowen was astounded. Never had he anticipated such a high place for his wee Cicely! To be fostered within the royal house was an honor belonging to a greater name than his. "M-madam," he stammered, and he flushed at his own awkwardness. "My family is not worthy of such an honor. Forgive me, but are you certain you would have my daughter? I am in your debt to such an extent I doubt I can ever repay you."

"I am told you are clever with your investments, my lord." Queen Joan surprised him again. " 'Tis an interesting pursuit for one with so old and respected a name as yours. Is there truth to the rumor?"

He nodded. "My wife is extremely knowledgeable in such matters, having learned from her father in Firenze. I in turn have learned from her. I will advise you in any way that I can, madam. You have but to ask me."

The queen nodded. "I will send to you now and again, my lord, for your thoughts in certain matters of finance. Now have your child delivered to my favorite home, Havering-atte-Bower, at the beginning of July. You may send a servant with her. When she is older I shall suggest a suitable match for her, with your permission, of course, my lord," Queen Joan said graciously.

"Thank you, madam," the Earl of Leighton said. He bowed again as, with a nod and a languid wave of her hand, the king's stepmother dismissed him. Robert Bowen made his way from the queen's chambers and found his cousin.

"What happened?" Sir William asked, and the earl told him all that had transpired. "What good fortune you have had, Rob!" his cousin exclaimed. "You will never have to worry about your Cicely again if she gets on with the other girls in Queen Joan's household. You must instruct her to make certain that she pleases the queen in particular. If she has that lady's favor her future will be secured."

"I still cannot believe all of this," the earl said. "Of course I cannot tell Luciana exactly what has transpired. She will be jealous that I have obtained such a fine place for my daughter. I think she would have preferred I give Cicely to the Church with a meager dower portion and never see my child again. A cloistered order would have been her choice," Robert Bowen said with a wry smile.

"Does she not realize that if your daughter makes the right friends at court, and marries well, that all of that would be of advantage to your sons?" Sir William said.

"Nay, she does not envision such things," the earl answered. "When she considers Cicely she sees only a rival for my affections."

"I am sorry for you then, Rob," his cousin replied. "Surely then little Lady Cicely is better off leaving Leighton Hall."

Robert Bowen nodded, but his eyes were sad.

He returned home, stopping at the cottage where his daughter lived before seeing his wife. Cicely ran to greet him, welcoming him home. Orva stood in the door to the dwelling, and their eyes met, hers questioning him.

"Let us sit down by the hearth," the earl said. "The air is damp, and the fog not yet lifted from the fields." He took his daughter onto his lap as he lowered himself into a chair by the small fire.

Orva put a small goblet of wine that was kept for his visits by his hand, and then she sat down too. When Robert Bowen visited his child they did not stand on ceremony.

"I have had an extraordinary piece of luck, poppet," the earl began.

"You have found a family to foster me, Papa?" she asked, and to his sorrow he heard the fear in her young voice.

"Not a family, poppet, but Queen Joan herself!" he replied, forcing an enthusiasm into his voice that he did not feel. "And you will have another young lass for company who is coming to Queen Joan as well. Her little namesake, Lady Joan Beaufort. She is a year or two older than you, I am told, but it will be her first time away from her home too. Her father is dead, and her mother remarried. Her older brother is the Earl of Somerset. They are the king's cousins, poppet. This is incredible good fortune for you to be taken into a royal household. And Orva is to come with you."

Cicely began to cry. "But I don't want to leave Leighton Hall, Papa," she told him. "Please don't send me away! I will be good, I promise! I will never leave the cottage, and my stepmother will never see me again. I swear it!" She sobbed into his shoulder. "Please don't make me go, Papa! *Please!*"

His heart was breaking, Robert Bowen thought, but he had no other choice. If Cicely remained Luciana would work herself into a dangerous fury. And he had no doubt that she would attempt to rid herself of the child in any manner possible. Swallowing down his own anguish, he said to his daughter, "Cicely, you are not being punished. This is a great honor you are being given, being allowed admittance into the royal household. Our family is an ancient one but unimportant. Our lack of wealth has not allowed us to marry into the more prestigious families, nor gain any foothold on the rungs of power. Now we are gaining that wealth, but we have no entrée into the court. If you please Queen Joan with your sweetness and your manners you will have an opportunity to meet the most important folk in the land. And that will one day help our family to gain ingress into the court. Queen Joan will see that you make an advantageous marriage. And once you are involved in the court I shall be able to make the best matches for your brothers, thus increasing our family's strength and importance. I need you to take this first step for Leighton."

Cicely's sniffling had stopped. She was an intelligent child. She heard and digested her father's words carefully. She understood them. "What will you tell my stepmother, Papa?" she asked him astutely. "She will not be pleased I am going to court."

"I will say that I have found a place for you in the house of a wealthy widow," he said with a small smile. "In time she will learn the full truth, but knowing then that you can aid our sons one day will help to temper her jealousy towards you, I am certain."

The child nodded. "Perhaps it will," she agreed. "When must Orva and I leave? Where are we to go, Papa?"

"Havering-atte-Bower, which is Queen Joan's favorite residence. It's about fifteen miles from London. She wants you there in early July, so you have several weeks before you must leave Leighton."

Orva had sat silent. Now she said candidly, "My lady will need proper clothing, my lord. She must have some jewelry, and an allowance to be paid quarterly. And her own horse. It won't be easy seeing to these things, for your lady will not want to give Cicely anything. As you can see, the child's gown is shabby and worn, as are all her few gowns. I do my best to keep them in good repair, but the material will go only so far, and Lady Cicely is growing. *And* I have had to loosen the stitching on the toes of her shoes, for her footwear no longer fits."

"How is this possible?" the earl wanted to know. "My storage rooms are full with whatever you need, Orva." His look was one of confusion.

"But the Lady Luciana holds the keys to those storerooms, my lord. She has refused my last two requests for material to make my little lady gowns," Orva said.

"Why did you not come to me?" he asked his daughter's serving woman.

"It would have but caused more difficulty for us, my lord. I hoped that in time you would see the state of my mistress's wardrobe, and correct the situation," Orva said.

"By the rood!" the earl swore softly. "I will not have this! Cicely shall have everything she needs, and more. How dare her stepmother withhold necessities from my daughter." His arm tightened about the little girl. "You shall be denied nothing, my darling," he promised her. Then he tipped her from his lap. "I must now go and speak with my wife. In the morning, Orva, you shall have access to the storerooms. Take all you need, but remember I shall have to return the keys to my lady wife the same day, lest I send her into a greater temper than she will already have." Standing, he bent and kissed his daughter on her forehead, then strode from the cottage to ride home. Entering his house he asked the steward where his wife could be found.

Luciana was in her apartments with Donna Clara, who was brushing her hair. "My head aches," she greeted him languidly, waving him to a chair.

"Give me the keys to the storerooms," he replied, not sitting.

A wary look came into her large brown eyes. "Why do you want them?" she asked him boldly. "Do not stop brushing! It eases my pain," she snapped at Donna Clara. "Must I live in agony always?"

"Give me the keys to the storerooms," he repeated, not answering her. "Am I master of Leighton or not, madam?"

"Have you found a place for your daughter?" she wanted to know.

"I have," he said, "and now I will see that Cicely is properly garbed and equipped for her new home."

"I am the mistress of this household," Luciana said in a hard voice. "It is my duty to see your daughter supplied with what she needs."

"You have laid eyes on Cicely but once, and not by choice, madam," the earl said in an equally hard voice. "You have denied her serving woman the cloth necessary to make the child gowns. Her garments are worn, shabby. Have you no shame, Luciana? Cicely is an earl's daughter, not some stranger I have taken in."

"She is your bastard!" Luciana cried angrily.

"Her mother died before we could wed, but our daughter was legitimated by Rome, Canterbury, and the laws of England," the earl shouted furiously. "Why do you refuse to admit the truth, Luciana? This was all long before I even knew of your existence. You have given me three sons. My respect for you is great. What more do you want of me?"

"You loved *her*!" the Countess of Leighton accused.

Robert Bowen looked surprised. "Loved whom?" he asked her.

"My ladybird," Donna Clara cautioned, "do not pursue this, I beg you."

"Your daughter's mother!" Luciana spat. "And everyone says the brat is her mother's image. The whore who was your servant's daughter!"

The Earl of Leighton slapped his wife across her angry face.

Luciana shrieked, outraged, her hand going to her burning cheek.

Donna Clara gasped in shock. Never had she seen her English master lose his control. He was always calm, always the voice of reason. The look in his eyes now, however, was one of uncontrolled fury. Her mistress stood on the brink of disaster.

The red haze faded slowly from before his eyes as the earl fought to regain some measure of control, struggling with himself not to put his hands about her slim white neck and snap it. Finally he felt calm, but he was very angry. His wife stood glaring at him, totally unaware of how close she had come to death. Donna Clara knew, and her eyes filled with relief as Robert Bowen came to himself again, and spoke.

"Aye, I loved Anne," he told Luciana. "She was everything you are not. She was beautiful, and Cicely is her image. She was kind and generous. She was genuinely devout. We were blood kin, madam, but not so close that a marriage between us was forbidden. Old families like mine frequently parcel out the responsibilities of their estates to kin, because in most instances blood will not betray you. Your interests are their interests, madam. Whether your estate is large or small, such loyalty is important.

"I might have wed the daughter of another noble, but an honorable family like mine was left with little dower. However, I fell in love with Anne, and we planned to wed. The banns had already been posted when her father was killed in an accident. She was his only child, and his own wife, her mother, had died when Anne was ten. The shock of her father's death caused my beloved to go into an early labor. She lived long enough to push our daughter from her body, and then with a great sigh she died.

"I was content to remain unmarried, but Cicely needed a mother to teach her the things a girl of her rank should know, and I needed a legitimate son. And then your father learned I sought a wife. As your behavior in Firenze had made you unmarriageable, he had to seek a husband for you here in England. I was poor, but I could give you a title. You could bring me a fat dower, and give me sons. It was an ideal match, Luciana. I swore to your father that I would honor you and respect you. I have done these things. I have treated you well. You, however, have not kept your part of our bargain."

"I gave you wealth!" she cried. "I have advised you in which trading ventures to invest in, and you have become rich in the process. I have given you three sons! I am faithful to you. What more could you want?"

"I wanted a mother for my daughter," he said.

"I told you before the wedding contracts were even signed that I would not raise that child," Luciana said. "You agreed!"

"I believed that once you felt secure, once you had given me a son, that you would no longer feel the need to reject Cicely," the earl replied. "What kind of woman are you that you could hate an innocent little girl so greatly? What could she have possibly done to you before you even met her that you hate her?"

"You love her! You love her as you loved her mother! But you have never loved me, Robert, have you?" the countess said bitterly.

"How many marriages are made for love, Luciana?" he asked quietly. "Certainly not among our kind, nor even among the poor. Marriages are made to gain cer-

tain advantages. Among the peasantry they are made
for children to help in the fields. And among the nobility
they are made for land, for wealth, for a higher position
on the social scale. You are my wife. I have a fondness
for you. I am grateful to you for the sons you have given
me, for the wealth you brought me, for the knowledge
you have given me that has aided me in acquiring more
riches. You have my respect in all but one matter, and
that is your inability to accept my daughter. For you and
for your peace of mind I have agreed to foster Cicely
out, but I will not send her from this house, from her
home, without all she needs to survive, to succeed in
the world beyond Leighton Hall. But even now, gaining
your own way, you cannot be generous to my daughter,
which is why I will have the keys from my storerooms
from you." He held out his hand to her. "Give them to
me now, madam!"

Luciana stood up. Her look was murderous, but she
unfastened the chatelaine's keys from her satin girdle
and flung them at him. "Here, and be damned to you,
Robert! But why the wench needs a fine wardrobe in
the house of a widow, I do not know."

He knew he was being foolish, but she had angered
him so greatly he needed to strike back at her. He knew
there would be more difficulties with Luciana over it,
but he couldn't help himself. "She does if the widow is
the king's beloved stepmother," the Earl of Leighton
said with a wicked smile.

"Your daughter is going to live in Queen Joan's
household? The queen is fostering her?" The Countess
of Leighton was astounded. "How did you manage to
arrange such a thing, Robert?" There was new respect
for him in her voice, and she was already considering the
possibilities for their sons.

"It was pure luck, Luciana," he told her, "but if Cicely
does well she will be able to ease the way to introduce
our sons into the court one day."

"Yes," his wife replied slowly, "perhaps the brat will

prove useful after all. And I will not have to see her ever again."

"Nay, you will not," Robert Bowen agreed.

"Take whatever you desire from the storerooms," the countess told her husband graciously, although in truth it was all his to take. "The wench should not disgrace Leighton. Has she manners? Is she educated at all or will she be an embarrassment, my lord? She must not be forward in any way."

"My daughter has manners, and enough learning to please the queen," he said, amused by this sudden shift in her attitude.

"Even if she proves of value to us I will always hate her because you love her," Luciana told him bluntly.

"I love our sons too, madam, and I was never aware that you sought my love. Have I not been a good husband to you? A competent lover?" he demanded.

"I thought it would be enough," Luciana answered him slowly, "but I find it is not enough for me now. I suppose it is my warm nature that makes it so."

"I am sorry then that I must disappoint you," the earl told his wife. "But we need not be enemies, madam." Nay, they would not be enemies, yet he could never forgive her for the cruel way she had treated his daughter, would continue to treat Cicely. With a polite bow he turned and left her.

"Does he hate me?" the countess asked Donna Clara.

"Nay," the older woman replied. "But had you made the slightest effort towards little Lady Cicely, had you shown her even a modicum of kindness, my lady, you might have gained his love. The love he had for his daughter's mother was one born of familiarity, longevity, and kinship. They had much in common because they were raised together. Do you not recall your brother Gio's first love was your cousin Theresa?"

"He outgrew her," Luciana said.

Donna Clara shook her head in the negative. "Nay,

he did not. He would have willingly wed her had your father and hers allowed it. But they would not because each family needed a wealthier mate for their child. Your husband was not as practical a man. He was ready to wed his lover. Only her death prevented it, and then he did what he should have done in the first place: He sought an heiress bride. He might have given you his love had you accepted his daughter. I warned you, my lady, after little Carlo was born, to relent and bring Lady Cicely into the house, but you would not. Now the earl's patience is at an end. 'Tis you who have driven him to it."

"I do not care," Luciana said irritably. "I do not need his love. I am his wife. I am the Countess of Leighton." Then a calculating light came into her eyes. "I shall give him a daughter too! When he has another daughter, Donna Clara, he will not think so much on this one. And she will be gone from Leighton."

Donna Clara did not argue with her mistress. She doubted another daughter would change the earl's attitude towards his wife. Oh, he would love the child, for he was a good man, but he would not love her mistress. "You are worn with birthing your three sons in so short a time, *cara,*" the older woman said. "You must rebuild your strength, for if you are to have a daughter you will want her to be strong and healthy, as your sons are."

The countess nodded. "Aye, I do want a healthy daughter. You must continue to give me that strengthening drink you prepare each day for me."

"I will, my lady. You may be sure that I will," Donna Clara promised her mistress. And as long as Luciana drank the potion there would be no more children, but of course the Countess of Leighton did not know it. And if her mistress convinced her husband to have another child Donna Clara would cease adding her special ingredient to the mixture. She was relieved that the earl had taken her advice and was fostering his daughter out, for her mistress, she firmly believed, would not have let the matter go.

On the following morning Orva came early to the hall and sought out Bingham, the steward. Bingham was filled with gossip. "The earl fought so loudly with *her* yesterday that you could have heard them in the next village," the steward informed Orva. "It was about our little lady." He reached into his pocket and drew out a ring of keys. "These are for you. What's going on?"

"Come with me to the storerooms, and I'll tell you," Orva said, and he followed her eagerly. "He has decided it will be safer for Lady Cicely to be fostered by another family," Orva began. "And I'm to go with her!"

"Lady Cicely is being sent from Leighton?" Bingham was surprised. "So the countess has had her way in the matter."

"My lord does it for his daughter, not for the countess," Orva said sharply. "And into whose household are we going? We are being sent to Queen Joan herself!" Orva crowed. "We'll be a part of the royal court!" Her eyes scanned the bolts of material.

"God's boots!" Bingham swore softly. "How did the earl manage that? Leighton isn't an important house."

"He says it was pure good fortune that put him in Queen Joan's eye," Orva said. "I think Saint Anne, to whom I always pray, looks out for her namesake's child." She reached for a bolt of medium blue velvet and, unrolling it to the length she desired, took the scissors on her girdle and cut the piece. Folding it, she then set it on a small table.

"Praise God and his blessed Mother that the child will be safe," Bingham replied. He was Lady Cicely's great-uncle on her mother's side. "The others will be glad to learn your news, Orva. May I tell them?"

"Shout it to the skies if you will," Orva said, taking another bolt down, this one of burnt orange brocade, and cutting the piece she wanted.

"I'll leave you then to your picking and choosing," Bingham answered. "Lock the door from the inside, Orva. That way you'll not be disturbed." And he gave her a broad wink. "The mistress isn't pleased at all this morning, I'm told." Then he left her.

Orva took his advice and turned the big key in the lock before going back to her task. There was much to chose from, and Orva took her time. To the blue velvet and the burnt orange silk brocade she added a dark green, a cream, and a burgundy-colored velvet, along with a violet silk brocade, a medium blue and a grass green silk. She took a length of deep blue wool and another of rich brown to make cloaks for her mistress, as well as a packet of rabbit fur and another of marten to line the cloaks. She took linen and lawn for undergarments and veils, trimmings, buttons, several narrow lengths of satin, and another of leather to make girdles. The shoemaker belonging to Leighton would make Cicely new shoes and boots.

In a dark corner Orva found a small dusty box almost hidden beneath several bolts of heavy wool. Curious, she opened it. Seeing its contents, she smiled. Inside the box was a narrow gold chain with a small jeweled cross, a simple band of red gold, and a tarnished wire caul. The gilt flaked from the caul as she lifted it up. These few small possessions had belonged to Cicely's mother, Anne. The chain and the ring had been Bowen family jewelry. Robert Bowen had given them to Anne in pledge of their love. The little wire gilt caul Orva remembered the earl buying for his love at a Michaelmas fair. She could still picture Anne in her mind's eye, tucking her thick auburn hair into the caul and twirling about happily as she showed it off to Orva and to her father.

"These should belong to Cicely," Orva said aloud to herself. The chain and the ring were hardly impressive pieces, and the little caul needed to be regilded. But the serving woman knew that her little mistress would appreciate that these items had belonged to the mother she had never known. She added the box to her pile. Then, unlocking the door, letting herself out, and relocking it, she hurried off to find some servants to aid her in taking her prizes back to the cottage, where she would begin to fashion the gowns her little mistress needed.

When the earl came to visit his child later that day Orva showed him everything she had taken from his storerooms. The earl nodded, thinking to himself that Cicely could not be in better hands than Orva's. The serving woman had taken enough material to make his daughter a wardrobe fit for a princess. Then Orva showed him the box with the few small pieces of jewelry that had been Anne's.

Robert Bowen's eyes welled up. "I had forgotten these," he said softly, fingering the chain with the crucifix. "Aye, Cicely should have them. You were right to bring them, Orva. But the caul has seen better days, hasn't it?" He smiled at his remembrance of Anne's squeal of delight when he had bought it for her.

"A bit of fresh gilt, my lord," Orva assured him, "and 'twill be fine."

"My daughter should have a real gold caul, and some bits of good jewelry," the earl noted. "I will see to it."

"Remember, my lord, she is still a little girl. Perhaps a strand of pearls, and two or three rings. As she grows older you will gift her," Orva advised.

Several days later Robert Bowen brought his daughter a beautiful long strand of pearls, several gold rings decorated with brightly colored gemstones or pearls, a fine golden caul, and a gold headband with an oval piece of green malachite in its center. And when another week had passed he arrived with a beautiful dappled gray mare with a black mane and tail for Cicely, and a sturdy chestnut gelding for Orva.

The weeks flew by, and then it was Midsummer's eve. There was dancing, and there were games, drinking of sweet honeyed mead, and bonfires on the hillsides. In just a few more days Lady Cicely Bowen would be leaving her childhood home to be fostered by the widowed Queen Joan. The new king, rumor had it, was preparing for war against France. It would be an exciting time to be at court.

On the morning before her departure Cicely slipped from the cottage. Orva was busy finishing the packing, and would not consider where her little mistress had gone; nor would she worry about it, for Cicely was completely safe on Leighton lands. Walking across the fields Cicely made her way to her father's gardens, and secreted herself within a large hedge. And then the three nursemaids came, bringing with them her three little half brothers. She watched them silently, smiling at the antics of the two elder, wishing she might be allowed to play with them. Charles looked like their father, she was happy to see. The other two favored both their parents. Finally she could sit no longer.

"Farewell, little brothers," she whispered softly. "I doubt we will ever meet again. May God and his blessed Mother protect you all. Bring honor to Leighton." Then Lady Cicely Bowen crept quietly from her father's gardens, making her way back across the fields to the cottage where she had spent all of her life.

"Where were you?" Orva asked her when she entered.

"Out walking, and saying my farewells to Leighton," the little girl answered. "I still wish we didn't have to go. Oh, I know the great advantage this is for me, for my family, but I should have been content to remain here forever."

Orva sighed. "I know," she sympathized. "This has been my home for all my life too, and now I wonder if I will ever see it again, my little lady." She sighed again but then said, "Still, it is a great adventure we are about to embark upon. It could be worse. Your father's wife could have convinced him to put you in a convent for the rest of your days."

"I would have made a very bad nun," Cicely said, giggling.

"So would I," Orva agreed with a chuckle.

"Do you think my father will come to say good-bye, Orva?" Cicely wondered.

"Did he not tell you, child? Oh! Perhaps he meant for it to be a surprise," the serving woman said. "Your father is to escort us to Havering-atte-Bower."

Cicely clapped her small hands together with delight. "Ohh, we shall have time together before he leaves me. I am so glad!" She danced about the room.

Orva smiled to see the child happy. This sudden change in Cicely's life was a difficult one to make for a child so young. Orva prayed silently that all would be well, and that her little mistress would be happy in Queen Joan's household. She hoped the earl's daughter would find a friend among the other little maidens certain to be there. She slept restlessly that night—the last night in the cottage she considered her home. The earl had assured her the cottage would be there for her when Cicely was grown and no longer needed her. It was the one comfort she had in all of this great change.

The following day dawned gray and gloomy. Certainly not the most hopeful sign, Orva thought as she directed the loading of the trunks onto the baggage cart. It would take them a week to reach Queen Joan's residence, which was some fifteen miles east of London. The earl had sent word ahead to four convents and three monasteries requesting shelter for his party. Each night they would stop at a religious guesthouse, where they would be given a bed and two meals in the safety of the establishment's sturdy walls. They would travel with a dozen men-at-arms from Leighton to keep them, and Cicely's baggage cart with all her new gowns and other worldly possessions, safe.

They had traveled no more than a few miles when the rain began, and it continued for the next two days. The earl had wisely considered that they would travel slowly, and so, while uncomfortable, they were able to reach the convent in which they would stay the night. The mother superior was impressed that Lady Cicely was to be fostered by the king's stepmother.

"You are aware, though, my lord, of the rumors about Queen Joan, aren't you?" the nun asked the earl.

"What rumors?" Robert Bowen inquired nervously. Were all his plans for his daughter to come to naught?

"Some say the lady practices witchcraft, my lord, although King Henry does not give such chatter credence," the mother superior murmured.

"Why would anyone say that?" the earl wondered aloud.

"Well, my lord, her kingly father in Navarre was called '*the Bad*.' And then she lived in Brittany for many years, and all know that witchcraft is practiced there. And then there is the fact that while she bore her first husband, the Duke of Brittany, nine children, and our own late king had six with Lady Mary before she died and he succeeded to England's throne, together the king and Queen Joan produced no progeny. Both were young enough to do so. So why were there no more children?"

"Perhaps because of their large families their marriage was by choice a celibate one," the earl suggested. "As I recall Queen Joan brought her two younger daughters with her when she came from Brittany, Reverend Mother, and they needed her attention. But as I am not a part of the court circle my opinion on the matter would be worthless."

The nun smiled archly. "Your little girl is very fortunate, my lord," she said.

It rained the next day as well, and the monastery guesthouse they stayed in the second night was very sparse, the supper and meal the following morning scant. But when they awoke the third morning the sky had turned blue and the sun was shining. The weather held for the rest of their journey, and late in the afternoon of the seventh day they reached the village of Havering-atte-Bower, and Queen Joan's residence. The queen, however, was not there. She would be arriving on the morrow, the steward said, with Lady Joan Beaufort. He could not admit the queen's new fosterling until she arrived.

Anticipating that he might need a seventh night of

shelter, the Earl of Leighton had arranged it in the guest-house of a small but prosperous convent just outside of the village. The mother superior herself welcomed them, smiling. She was quite unlike their hostess on that first night on the road.

"So you're to live in the queen's household," the nun said. "You are a very lucky little girl, Lady Cicely. I have known the queen since she came to England over ten years ago. She is very wise and can be a lot of fun. Her daughters Marguerite and Blanche came with her then. Of course, they're married back into France now but I remember them well. Two of the sisters and I used to take them berry picking. And the Decembers we had with all the feasting from Christmas to Twelfth Night. Queen Joan always invited us to her table then, for we are a small order. How lovely to learn there will be two little girls back at the queen's house again to bring it laughter and joy."

"I believe your words are comforting to my daughter," Robert Bowen said. "She has never before been away from Leighton."

"Oh," the mother superior said, and she stooped down so she might speak face-to-face with Cicely. "You must not be afraid, my daughter. You have come to a good place, and within a few short weeks it will be and will feel like home to you. Do you like animals? The queen's house here is always filled with dogs and cats."

"I have a horse," Cicely said. "My lord father gave her to me before we departed our home. Her name is Gris, because she is gray. I've never had a dog or cat."

"Well, you shall probably find you have several once the queen is in residence," the nun said cheerfully, standing up again. "Come now, my lord, my lady. We are about to celebrate vespers. Will you not join us? And then we'll have supper. I know that Sister Margarethe has made a wonderful vegetable-and-rabbit potage for supper. I have smelled it cooking all afternoon." She reached out and took Cicely's hand. "But first we must go into the chapel and thank our dear Lord and his Mother for your safe arrival."

The convent might be small, but the meal they were served after vespers was every bit as good as that served at the earl's table. The rabbit stew was flavorful, the bread warm and crisp, and there was an egg custard flavored with lavender, served last. The beds given them were clean and fresh, free from bedbugs and fleas. And in the morning their second meal of oat stirabout, with newly baked bread and butter was delicious. The earl thanked the sisters as they departed, pressing a generous donation into the hand of the mother superior.

"I hope we will see you again very soon, Lady Cicely," the nun called after them.

"Do you think the queen will like me, Papa?" Cicely asked as they rode towards the village again, and the queen's residence. "What of the other girl who comes with her? Do you know who she is?"

The earl nodded. "You must not fret, poppet," he told his daughter. "Queen Joan is a good woman, and she cannot help but like you. Everyone likes you."

"My stepmother does not like me," Cicely said softly.

"Luciana does not know you, and she is jealous of the love I bear you, and bore your mother. I wish it were otherwise, but it is not. Queen Joan will like you."

"And the girl? Who is she, Papa?" Cicely asked anxiously.

"Lady Joan Beaufort is the daughter of the late Earl of Somerset, John Beaufort," the earl began. "His father was the Duke of Lancaster, a son of King Edward the Third, called John of Gaunt because he was born to Queen Philippa in Ghent. The duke had three wives, and outlived two. John Beaufort, his brothers Henry and Thomas, and his sister, Joan, were the children of the duke's mistress, and later third wife, Katherine Swynford. The Beauforts were born on the other side of the blanket, as were you, Cicely. But like you they were legitimated. They and their descendants are not permitted to be placed in the line of succession, but they are legitimate. You, my daughter, are, however, in my line of succession. When I die you will receive an inheritance along with your brothers."

"So this other little girl is royal," Cicely said. Her stomach stirred nervously.

"Aye," her father admitted, "she is. But she is still an earl's daughter, as are you."

They were now approaching the queen's residence, which, like the village, was known as Havering-atte-Bower. It was a large dwelling that had been built originally by King William, known as the Conqueror, to serve as a hunting lodge. Over the centuries since it had been added onto, and made into a large, livable home. When they had come yesterday it had been quiet. Now, however, the path to and before the house was filled with carts, and horses, and servants of various rank.

One of the earl's men rode forward, shouting, "Make way for my lord, the Earl of Leighton! Make way!"

Carts were drawn to the road's edge, and grumbling people stepped aside until a narrow path was formed, allowing their party through. The queen's steward met them at the door to the house. Grooms hurried forward to take their horses as they dismounted. Robert Bowen took his daughter by the hand and beckoned Orva to follow them as the steward led them into the house and to the hall.

Cicely's little heart hammered with a mixture of both fear and excitement. She had chosen her new burnt orange velvet gown to wear this day. It had a turned-up collar and long, trailing sleeves. She wore the gold chain with the little jeweled crucifix about her neck, and rings on several of her fingers. Her gold coronet was worn about her head, and beneath it was a delicate lawn veil barely hiding the rich russet of her hair. She knew she looked most elegant, because Orva had told her so. Still, she worried that she would not please the queen. She cast a quick glance about the hall.

Queen Joan stood waiting for the child to be put into her care. Seeing Cicely, she smiled. The little girl was absolutely adorable. Leaning to the right, she murmured to the child by her side, "Now, Joan, here is the companion I promised you."

The earl reached the queen's chair. He bowed low with an elegant flourish that his wife had taught him when she'd learned he was speaking with the queen. He looked then to his daughter, and Cicely curtsied prettily.

"So here you are at last, my lord. And this will be your daughter, Lady Cicely Bowen, will it not?" Queen Joan said.

"It is, madam, and again let me express my gratitude for your generosity and kindness in fostering my child," Robert Bowen replied.

Queen Joan nodded graciously, then asked, "This is Lady Cicely's servant, my lord? Come forward." She gestured to Orva.

Startled to be noticed, Orva stepped forward, and then curtsied politely.

"Your name?"

"Orva, madam," was the reply.

"You are welcome to Havering-atte-Bower, Orva," the queen said. Then she looked to Cicely. "Come here, child, and let me see you better."

Cicely stepped forward.

"Your father tells me you speak English and French," the queen said.

"Aye, my lady, I do," Cicely responded.

"And you do sums?"

"Aye, my lady."

"You are a good Christian maid? You make your confession regularly?" the queen continued.

"Oh, yes, my lady!" Cicely said earnestly.

The queen smiled a small smile. "Do you think you will be happy with us?"

"I do not know, my lady," Cicely said honestly. "I have

never before been away from home. But I am told in a few weeks this will be home, and I shall be content."

Again Queen Joan smiled. "Aye, I think you will be. Then you are content to come into my care."

"Oh, my lady, this is a great honor you do me, do my family," Cicely answered her. "My father is not an important man. I am very grateful for your kindness to me."

The child had, of course, been told that the queen understood, but she seemed intelligent. She knew the advantage being given to her. Queen Joan drew the other girl by her side forward. "This is your new companion, Lady Joan Beaufort," she said. "Joan, this is Lady Cicely Bowen. You will share a chamber, and lessons, and learn how to be great ladies in my care. My lord of Leighton, bid your daughter farewell now."

The earl knelt and drew Cicely into his embrace. He kissed her rosy cheeks, and his eyes grew misty as she put her arms about his neck.

Then she whispered, "I will do my best to bring honor to Leighton, my lord father. I swear it on my mother's name."

Robert Bowen's heart contracted. "I know you will," he responded. Then, kissing her smooth forehead, he arose, saying, "Farewell, my daughter. We will meet again, I promise you." Bowing to the queen, he then turned and left her hall.

Cicely stared after her father. She suddenly felt abandoned, as if she would weep.

Then a small hand slipped into hers, and a sweet voice said, "We are going to be such great friends, Cicely. I just know it!"

Turning, she looked into the smiling face of little Lady Joan Beaufort.

Chapter 3

"*H*e's looking at you again, Jo," Lady Cicely Bowen said, giggling. At fourteen she was a slender girl of average height, much admired for her thick and wavy auburn hair and her beautiful, clear blue-green eyes.

"Oh, Ce-ce, please don't tell me that," Lady Joan Beaufort said. "He's been staring at me for weeks now. Why doesn't he just come over and speak to me? If he doesn't stop mooning about, I don't know what I will do! I wish we were back at Havering-atte-Bower instead of here at Windsor with the court." She turned her blond head to look directly at her admirer, and her blue eyes danced mischievously when he flushed, turning away. "There!" She chuckled. "That will teach him to stare so rudely."

"Who is staring rudely?" a deep voice inquired curiously, and the two girls turned to see that Henry Beaufort, the bishop of Winchester, had joined them. The bishop was Lady Joan's uncle, and currently part of the regency council governing for the infant king Henry VI, who had acceded to his throne ten months prior, at the age of eight months.

"James Stewart, my lord," Cicely said. "He keeps looking at Jo, but he will not speak to her. She finds it very annoying."

The bishop chuckled. "The young king of the Scots says he is in love with you, my child. He would speak to your brother about a match between you."

"He would do better to speak with me, Uncle," Lady Joan Beaufort said sharply. "Not one word has the man uttered. He just stares. I'll marry no man I don't know or love. But he is not unattractive, I will allow."

"You could be queen of Scotland," her uncle murmured slyly.

"A queen without a throne," Lady Joan said tartly.

"The regent in the north is dead over a year now, niece. His son is an incompetent fool, as we learned when we held him for ransom with young James years back. A pity the Duke of Albany could not find the wherewithal for his king, although he certainly managed to find ransom enough for his son. Our James will not forget that. Negotiations are already under way to return this king to his throne in Scotland. The Earl of Atholl has arrived, along with the Red Stewart of Dundonald and the bishop of St. Andrew's. They have already discovered to their surprise that James Stewart is neither an easily manipulated weakling or a fool. He has asked them to deal with your brother in the matter of your marriage, Joan," the bishop said. He was a tall, handsome man with piercing light blue eyes and white hair that had once been blond. He was the second of the Beaufort sons, and had been educated for the Church. He had been offered a cardinal's hat by Pope Martin V, but his nephew, Henry V, would not let him accept it. Henry Beaufort was too valuable a politician for England.

"Then you had better discover a way for this exiled king to talk to me," Lady Joan said. "An English queen for Scotland's king would be a valuable asset, considering the age of our current king and the ambition of powerful men, Uncle."

The bishop chuckled. "I wish my father were alive to know you, niece. You have your grandmother's fair face, but you have your grandfather's sharp mind. Oth-

ers might find it disconcerting in a girl such as yourself.
I, however, do not. I shall see that James Stewart makes
himself known to you soon, Joan. I do believe that you
will like him." Then, with a nod of his head, the bishop
strode off across the gardens.

"The bishop is so handsome." Cicely sighed. "What a
waste of a man. The priesthood should be only for ugly
men."

"He fathered a daughter in his youth," Lady Joan
said. "She is named Jane."

"Who was the mother?" Cicely asked, fascinated.

"They say it was Alice FitzAlan, but no one can prove
it for certain," Lady Joan replied. "I saw Jane Beaufort
once. She's a pretty child, and is fostered by one of the
de Bohun family. My uncle will see her well married one
day."

"Do you think His Grace will introduce you to the
Scots king?" Cicely wondered.

"Aye, he will," Lady Joan said. "With little King
Henry still in leading strings, and years ahead of them
to govern, my family will want an ally in the north. The
little brat had a temper tantrum the other day as he
was about to be brought into Parliament, and it had to
be canceled until the next morning, when he was quite
amenable to sitting in Queen Katherine's lap while the
lords nattered on for hours. You know, Ce-ce, I quite
like the idea of being a queen," she said with a smile. "I
mean, if James Stewart is to finally return to Scotland,
whom could he possibly marry there? His mother was
some clansman's daughter, not a girl of high rank. The
Scots earls are a contentious lot, always squabbling, and
each one of them has at least one daughter he would try
to place on the queen's throne. And then the other earls
would fight one another over it. Of course, King James
might seek a princess bride from France, or one of the
northern countries, like the kingdom of the Danes, or
even Spain."

"You're thinking about it!" Cicely accused. "You

haven't even met the man, and you're thinking about it, aren't you, Jo?"

"Of course I'm thinking about it, Ce-ce. He has to marry. I have to marry. It's true we haven't exchanged a single word so far, but don't you think he looks nice?"

"They say he writes poetry," Cicely answered, "and aye, he is handsome."

"Maybe I'll start smiling at him then, instead of frowning at him," Lady Joan said mischievously, and the two girls broke into gales of laughter.

James Stewart was the only surviving son of King Robert III of Scotland and his queen, Annabella Drummond. With his mother deceased, and his older brother, David, dead at his uncle's hands, his father, King Robert, had finally realized that his only surviving son was in danger. The king had trusted his own brother, the Duke of Albany, when he claimed that Prince David, the Duke of Rothesay, was plotting to overthrow his father. Robert Stewart understood his elder son's ambition, and his own health had always been weak. But he was not going to give David Stewart his throne. Not yet. So he had instructed Albany to imprison David, and suddenly his strong, healthy son and heir was dead.

"Unfortunate," Albany had said sanguinely.

But there were rumors that David had been starved to death, and denied liquid of any kind. That the prince had been hurried to his death in a most cruel manner.

"Nonsense!" Albany had declared, but he offered no explanation as to why his nephew had perished in his custody, and so quickly.

Fully aware now of where the real threat to his throne lay, King Robert did the only thing he could do: He sent his younger son, James, to safety in France. But the vessel upon which the young prince traveled, the *Maryenknyct,* which flew the flag of Danzig, was attacked and captured in the North Sea by English pirates. Learning the prince's identity, the pirates had brought the eleven-year-old Prince James to King Henry IV, their own king.

Henry had paid a goodly ransom for the boy and his companions.

Though England and Scotland were at peace, James Stewart remained in England for the next eighteen years. His captors were kind. He was treated with the respect due his station. He was educated in languages and the humanities. The king's elder son, Henry, who would one day be Henry V, supervised his training in the martial arts. James earned his knighthood, and even fought in France with the English prince. Yet he was unable to return home.

His father, King Robert, was not a well man. Upon learning of his surviving son's capture, he had died quietly within the month. King Robert's ambitious brother, the Duke of Albany, ruled as regent for his nephew, but he was unable to find the ransom necessary to return the boy king to Scotland, although he did manage to ransom his own son, whom the king had secretly sent with James in hopes that if the two cousins grew up together, they would become friends. It had not happened.

Albany, a jealous man, had considered his brother a weakling. He had no intention of giving up Scotland's throne to a mere stripling. To return the lad and then see to his death, as he had seen to the death of David Stewart, would have caused a civil war, with the earls and the lairds taking sides. So he had left James Stewart with his English captors. He well knew that the English weren't about to go to war for his nephew. They had their own problems to deal with now. Henry IV had died several years after James had arrived in England. His son and heir, Henry V, had died just last year, leaving the infant, Henry VI, as England's king. The little king's guardians had all they could do to rule England in his name.

So James Stewart had waited to regain his throne. He grew into a tall, handsome man with dark auburn hair and amber eyes. And one day, looking down on the gardens at Windsor Castle, he had spied the loveliest girl he had ever seen. "Who is she?" he asked his companion.

" 'Tis Lady Joan Beaufort, the king's cousin," came the reply. "Why?"

"I am going to marry her and make her my queen!" James Stewart declared passionately, his amber eyes alight.

"You haven't even met her," his friend said, laughing. "Besides, her family adores her. Her grandfather was Gaunt, a king's son. She's royal blood. They'll seek a very brilliant match for her."

"I am king of Scotland," James Stewart said proudly. "Do you think the Beauforts can find a better match for this girl than a king of Scotland?"

And, of course, they couldn't.

Bishop Henry wasted no time in seeing that his niece finally met with James Stewart. The next day in the gardens of Windsor Castle he introduced them formally, and then took Lady Cicely Bowen firmly by the hand, saying, "I am given to understand, young mistress, that you have not made your confession of late. I shall hear it myself now in the royal chapel."

Cicely gasped softly, then said, "But, my lord bishop, I have been good. I swear it."

The bishop of Winchester shook his head sadly. "Ah, the sin of pride," he lamented. "This will take some time, I fear."

But he was near to chuckling, for he knew very well that Cicely Bowen was indeed good. From the moment she had entered the household of Queen Joan she had endeavored to bring honor to her family at Leighton. And five years ago, when Queen Joan was accused of witchcraft, stripped of her possessions, and confined to Havering-atte-Bower, Lady Cicely Bowen had behaved in a most circumspect manner as she and Lady Joan Beaufort were taken away from that lady to be resettled in Queen Katherine's household, where they knew no

one and were virtually ignored. It was that more than
anything else that had cemented the friendship between
the two girls.

Queen Joan had been released just the year before,
and her property returned to her despite the fact that it
was her confessor, Father John Randolph, who had accused her. No charges had ever been filed, and the priest
found himself confined to a monastery for the rest of
his days. Lady Joan and Lady Cicely, however, were not
sent back to Havering-atte-Bower, being considered old
enough to be in polite society. And Cicely Bowen's good
influence on Joan Beaufort was a deciding factor in allowing the two girls to remain together.

"I think perhaps if you remain here in the chapel
meditating for an hour or more," Bishop Henry said as
they reached their destination, "I can absolve you without further ado, my lady."

"Oh, no, my lord bishop, on reflection I believe I do
need to make my confession," Cicely said wickedly. "I
have questioned why God would choose handsome men
for his priesthood instead of ugly ones. Is it not a sin to
question God?" She looked up at him, her blue-green
eyes wide with feigned innocence.

He was startled by the question, and then, realizing
she was teasing him, he said, "My dear child, isn't it nicer
to confess one's sins to a handsome man rather than an
ugly one? God understands the workings of the female
heart, for it is he who created it."

"Oh," she said mischievously, "and I suppose men
making their confessions can feel superior to even a
handsome cleric, for the priest has given up women and
other worldly things, while a normal man may revel in
them, and then say he's sorry. But if a priest envies a
normal man his sin is greater, is it not?"

Now the bishop of Winchester could not refrain from
chuckling. The girl was clever and quick. He understood
why his niece was so fond of Cicely Bowen. "Very well,
then, Lady Minx, you will kneel and, placing your hands

in mine, make your confession now." He led her into the chapel and stood on the steps before the altar.

Cicely did as she was bidden, all mischief gone from her voice as she asked forgiveness for sins she had long since thought she had put behind her. Anger at her stepmother for not loving her, for not being her friend and mentor, for taking her father from her and forcing her from Leighton Hall. Anger that she had not seen Robert Bowen in two years now, and was not even certain he received the letters she wrote to him. And, to her surprise, anger at Queen Joan's confessor for causing that good woman difficulty, and anger at the women of Queen Katherine's household, who did not hold Lady Joan Beaufort in proper esteem. "I am not important, my lord, but Jo is royal, and should be treated with kindness and respected."

Bishop Henry listened. He understood the anger Cicely kept so carefully hidden away from others. He remembered his own childhood, when people had not respected his beautiful mother, and scorned her because of her loyalty and love for John of Gaunt, her lover, and her three sons and little daughter because of the stain of bastardy that touched them. He remembered how their attitudes had changed when his father was finally able to marry Katherine Swynford and legitimate their four children. But his mother had taught them all to be proud of who they were, and allow no one else's opinions to matter to them.

Young Cicely had the same ethic, and he admired her for it, for she was a girl and, but for his niece, without influence. The bishop also appreciated her loyalty to Joan Beaufort. And he was quite interested in what she had to say about the priest who had accused Queen Joan of witchcraft. Though the man had claimed falsely, it was later proved, Queen Joan's malice towards Henry V, it turned out that he had learned from a serving girl that she was teaching her two fosterlings how to prevent conception once they were wives. Outraged but canny, the priest had decided that accusing Queen Joan of treason against Henry V would gain him more than the truth. He had, of course, been wrong, for Joan of Navarre's love for her stepchildren was a well-documented fact. Still, no stone was left unturned in the investigation, which had never learned the real cause of the priest's ire, but had learned there was no threat to the king.

The bishop of Winchester listened to Lady Cicely Bowen's confession, and then gave her a mild penance that would keep her in the chapel for at least another half an hour. Putting his hand on the head of the kneeling girl, he blessed her and left Cicely to her meditations, smiling.

Cicely, however, was not thinking of her alleged sins, or her penance. She was wondering what would happen to her when Joan Beaufort married the young king of Scotland. If James Stewart wanted the king of England's cousin for his wife he would have her. The match was one that would be advantageous to both nations. Where would Lady Cicely Bowen go? Would she be expected to return home to Leighton? If Luciana had disliked the child she had been, she would certainly not appreciate the young woman she was becoming. It was unlikely that Joan could include Cicely among her ladies. A position as one of the queen's ladies would be eagerly sought after by families more powerful than hers. Perhaps, however, Joan Beaufort would not like James Stewart, and would refuse to marry him no matter how advantageous the match to both countries. Just perhaps.

But Lady Joan Beaufort was, to her own surprise, as immediately smitten with James Stewart as he had been with her on first sight. She returned starry-eyed from their meeting and their subsequent meetings filled with chatter about his charm, how wise he was, his beautiful poetry, his plans to bring Scotland into the modern age. Cicely grew more and more depressed. Then one night Lady Joan Beaufort came back to the chamber she shared with Cicely to announce that Scotland's king had asked her to marry him, and that she had accepted.

When her best friend promptly burst into bitter tears, Joan Beaufort was astounded. "Ce-ce! What is the matter? Aren't you happy for me?"

"How can I be happy when I am shortly to lose you?" Cicely sobbed.

"You aren't losing me," Joan protested.

"You're going to be married!"

"So will you one day," Joan replied.

"You're going to Scotland! You're going to be a queen, Jo, and I'll never see you again for the rest of my life!" Cicely wailed.

"You're going to Scotland too," Joan Beaufort said. "You didn't think I was going to leave my best friend in all the world behind, did you? Oh, Ce-ce, I would never leave you. You will be one of the queen's ladies."

Cicely's tears ceased. "But, Jo, there are nobler families who will want a place in your household. My family isn't important at all."

"Your father is a rich man, Ce-ce, but more, he is clever at investing, and his advice is greatly sought by my family, by Queen Joan, by others. Your family has far more to offer me and the king I am to marry than some spoiled get of a duke, or one of my relations. Besides, Scotland is not considered the most fashionable country. Only the families of girls difficult to marry off will be fighting over the places in my retinue." Lady Joan Beaufort chuckled. She hugged Cicely. "I would never leave you behind, Ce-ce!"

Now Cicely began to cry again, but this time they were tears of happiness. "I am so happy!" she sobbed, and then, as Joan's laughter bubbled up, Cicely's tears turned to laughter too. "May I write this news to my father?" she asked her friend.

"Of course! He must, of course, give his permission," Joan replied.

"He will," Cicely said. "Luciana does not want me back, especially now. She was quick to give Papa three sons, but for years she has shown no signs of having another child. Yet she is soon to deliver another baby. She prays, my father writes, for a daughter. I hope she has another boy, Jo!"

Her companion laughed. "We will pray for it," she said wickedly.

But it took many months for the three Scots who had come from the north to settle on a ransom for King James's long sojourn in England, which would be called a remuneration. The price finally agreed upon was sixty thousand marks, to be paid over a period of six years. And the truth was that the English had indeed taken good care of the young king. And before James Stewart left England he would marry the king's cousin, Lady Joan Beaufort.

The Earl of Leighton's wife delivered an infant girl baptized Catherine Marie. Luciana had a daughter of her own, and her husband would soon enough forget his eldest-born, especially as Cicely was leaving England for Scotland. Luciana had considered having the wench assassinated so as to rid herself of the girl forever, but she decided against it, for Cicely's situation at the English court was proving useful to Robert, and would continue to do so as long as the troublesome wench was connected with Lady Joan Beaufort. Her sons would need that alliance, and one day her daughter would too.

Now Cicely was going to another court, and she was in favor with its queen. But Luciana yet resented the very generous dower that her husband had set aside for his elder daughter. Still, if it bought the girl an important husband, so much the better for Luciana's own four children. As long as Robert Bowen lived, Cicely would do anything her father asked of her, and Luciana would see he asked whatever was necessary for their sons and daughter. The girl's dower would be more than worth the favors she would return.

Cicely needed new gowns. She was growing tall, and a queen's lady needed to be more than presentable, for it reflected well on her mistress. She and Orva visited London's cloth merchants, all of whom were eager to supply the queen's lady and the wealthy Earl of Leighton's daughter with the very best. The gowns she had brought to court with her ten years prior had been let out and let down until they could be remade no more. And Orva had made one trip home to Leighton for more fabric, infuriating Luciana, who had insisted her husband have his daughter's future needs taken care of in London.

Joan had been correct in her assessment regarding the ladies accompanying her. Several important families had gotten around the difficult situation by offering their daughters' services for half a year, or a bit more. To please her eldest brother, the Earl of Somerset, and her two uncles, Joan had graciously accepted their services, saying she was certain there would be Scots ladies anxious to be in her service who must not be slighted. James wisely agreed, and everyone was content.

The wedding was celebrated on a cold and sunny February thirteenth in the year 1424. The bridal couple spoke their vows at the riverside church of St. Mary Overy in the village of Southwark, surrounded by her important family: her uncles, Henry Beaufort, the bishop of Winchester, who later feasted the royal couple in his palace; and Thomas Beaufort, the Duke of Exeter, who, like his father, was a great military commander. Two queens stood as witness: Henry IV's widow, Joan of Navarre, and Henry V's widow, Katherine of France. The little king, however, was left at home.

The marriage, unlike many, was a love match. Cicely felt both happy for her best friend and jealous of the time she now spent with James Stewart. However, recognized among the queen's other ladies for her place in Joan's heart, Cicely Bowen was respected and deferred to, although she did not take advantage of her position.

There was just too much to do: packing the queen's possessions, and packing her own for the trip north.

Finally, on the twenty-eighth day of March, the royal progress set out towards Scotland, crossing the border between the two countries on the ninth day of April. Cicely was astounded to see the rough road they traveled lined for miles with the Scots who had come to get a look at their long-absent king. She was thrilled by the cheers that brought smiles to the faces of the young king and queen.

As they traveled along towards Melrose Abbey, where they were to meet up with the king's cousins, the border lairds came forward here and there to kneel before James Stewart and pledge their fealty. He accepted it graciously, asking their names, shaking their hands. Cicely heard the Earl of Atholl, who was riding nearby, murmur to one of his companions when a tall, rough-hewn borderer knelt before the king, "By the rood! 'Tis the Douglas of Glengorm. I wouldn't have expected him. He usually leaves these things to Archie Douglas, the clan chief."

"Aye," Atholl's companion said with a chuckle. "That way he can do as he pleases, and the Earl of Douglas gets the blame."

Atholl laughed. "The Douglases are a difficult clan, I'll agree, but they say Glengorm, while stubborn, is honest and fair."

Cicely looked at the man now rising and shaking James Stewart's hand. He was the tallest man she had ever seen, and big boned to boot. He was dressed in dark breeks, a light shirt, a leather jerkin, and leather boots, and wore on his head a velvet cap with an eagle's feather. There was nothing of the gentleman about him, she thought, and wondered if all the men in Scotland were like him. If they were it did not bode well for a girl who needed a husband, Cicely considered.

They reached Melrose Abbey, where the English would leave James Stewart in the hands of his own nobles. The king's late uncle's son, the Duke of Albany, was there to greet him, along with his own three sons, and a host of noble lords and ladies who had come to welcome their king home. The king was coldly polite to his relations. His cousin's father, the old Duke of Albany, had been responsible for David Stewart's death. He had used one excuse after another in order to delay negotiations for the boy king's release from the court of Henry IV.

Not that that had been a bad thing, James Stewart thought silently to himself. With his uncle regent of Scotland he might have never lived to reach his maturity. James had actually been safer in England, where he was treated with respect, his education continued, and his military training seen to by his captors. He was not the weak and indecisive man his late father had been, bullied by his younger brother and his nobles. Just past his twenty-ninth birthday, this king of the Scots intended ruling, as his cousin the Duke of Albany immediately realized when, upon pledging his loyalty to the king, he was told by James that his fealty came late. In that moment Murdoch Stewart knew he would not find favor with his king.

The king moved on without letting the duke introduce his sons. Others pressed forward to greet James, introducing themselves and their wives. There were a few men whom he knew, for his uncle had sent sons of the nobility to keep him company in his early years in England. The king's eyes lit up at the sight of Angus Gordon, the laird of Loch Brae, a particularly good friend from those days. He walked forward as greater men gave way so he might grasp the laird's hand as they embraced warmly. The laird's beautiful mistress accompanied him, and as chieftain of a branch of the Hay family she pledged her loyalty to James Stewart, as did Angus Gordon.

Cicely thought the nobles crowding Melrose Abbey didn't look a great deal more civilized than the border lairds. "How will I ever find a husband among these wild men?" she asked the young queen.

"They are very different from our English lords, I will agree," Joan said. "But many are very handsome, like my Jamie."

"They are rough-spoken," Cicely said. "The king is not, but he was raised in England. These Scots look like brigands."

"Are you sorry you came?" the queen asked her friend.

"Nay," Cicely said. "I should rather be happy and unwed than unhappily wed."

The young queen laughed at this amusing sally.

On the twentieth of April they reached the capital of Perth and settled into Scone Palace, which was located on the grounds of the abbey. Cicely had to admit that Scotland was a beautiful country. They could see mountains from the palace, and were surrounded by many lakes. In the last few days they had been on the road they had crossed many swift-flowing streams, which were filled with trout and salmon belonging to the king.

The palace of Scone was not grand. The monks from the abbey had originally lived there, but now lived in another building. Cicely and Orva were given a bedchamber with its own fireplace and two lead-paned windows that overlooked the hills behind the palace. There was a comfortable bed with a well-made trundle for Orva, a bedside table, a small settle by the hearth, and more than enough room for the trunks.

"The bed hangings are dusty and have seen better days," Orva noted. "A good thing I brought our own from England." She set to work immediately, pulling down the ancient hangings, giving a screech of surprise when several moths flew from the fabric. "Fold that fabric, dearie, and we'll store it away. If we move, I'm taking our bed curtains with us, and we'll have to rehang these others. Unless, of course, the queen tells us otherwise. Royalty do love to move from place to place, and we have some fine castles in our England. But in this wild land I don't know where they live. This is a pretty place, but it isn't grand, is it?"

"Jo says there is a great castle at Edinburgh, and another at Stirling, but the king remembers this place from his youth. His mother loved Perth. I think it will be his favored residence. I will ask a housekeeper to dispose of these old hangings," Cicely said. "And if it is necessary to take our curtains with us when we move, we will." She walked over to the windows, noting that two of the wooden shutters that could close out the light and the chill were hanging by a thread. "These shutters must be repaired," the young woman noted.

The room had been swept for their arrival. Together Orva and her mistress hung the bed hangings, which were of heavy linen and blue velvet. The straw mattress upon the bed was fresh, for they could smell the fragrance of it. Orva lay the feather bed atop it, dug farther down into the linen chest, and drew out a linen sheet smelling of lavender, several feather pillows, and a down comforter. She quickly made the bed while Cicely carefully lifted her gowns from another chest and hung them in a little stone alcove off the bedchamber. The room had been well aired before their arrival and was chilly on that late April afternoon. Finished with the bed, Orva started a fire in the hearth that was soon blazing merrily, taking the damp from the chamber.

"You had best go to the hall, my lady," she said to Cicely.

"I should change first," the girl replied.

"The lavender gown with the violet surcoat is pretty," Orva suggested. She helped Cicely dress, and brushed out her wavy red-brown hair. Orva then tucked her mistress's long hair into a pretty gold caul dotted with tiny bits of amythyst. "There, my lady. You run along now. The queen will be waiting for you."

The hall was not overly large or impressive. It had several fireplaces; long, high arched windows; and a gray

stone floor. It was the hall of a well-to-do nobleman.
But it was full to overflowing with those who had come
to meet the new king and hopefully get into his good
graces. Everyone already knew that Murdoch Stewart
and his sons were not among the favored. It had been
reported that the Duke of Albany had declared that he
had brought home his own executioner. Enough agreed
that few wanted to be seen speaking with this now
doomed branch of the royal family.

Cicely entered the hall and sought the queen. Seeing
her, she hurried to join her mistress. "Am I late, Your
Highness?" she asked politely.

"Nay, just in time to save me from boredom, Ce-ce,"
Joan Beaufort answered. "The English ladies who came
with us are for the most part terrified of the Scots. There
are more men in the hall than women too. Look at my
ladies, all cowering on their stools, afraid to even lift
their eyes. Jamie is speaking personally with all those
lords who have come to Perth, trying to gauge where
he'll have friends or not. He has little time for his wife.
But when we're alone he makes up for it." Joan chuckled with a wicked wink.

"Look about you, Ce-ce! Isn't it wonderful? And so
different from our English court. The men are so rugged
and fierce, but I think the few women here a bit bolder
than most of our own ladies. Jamie's friend Angus Gordon, the laird of Loch Brae, brought his mistress with
him. Fiona Hay is her name. I think we would like her as
a friend. And Maggie MacLeod, the wife of the laird of
Ben Duff. She is a Highland girl who married the man of
her heart, a border laird, and infuriated her family in the
process. Those two have some backbone, unlike most of
those who accompanied us," the queen said.

"Oh, look!" Cicely said. "There is that borderer who
pledged his loyalty to the king on the road. He's handsome, but too rough-hewn for me."

"We'll find you a good husband," the queen promised.

"Remember, my Jamie promised your father before we left England that he would see you well married."

"Aye, he did," Cicely said softly, remembering the day when her father came to say his good-byes.

"You're even more beautiful than your mother was," Robert Bowen told his daughter. "I am so sorry I could not raise you myself, Cicely." And indeed, he did look quite contrite as he spoke.

"I understand, Papa, and as long as Orva is with me I am content. The Lady Joan treated me like a daughter. She was very kind. By the time Jo and I were sent to court we didn't need mothering any longer. And now I have been given the honor of serving in the household of a queen. Had you not sent me to Lady Joan, Papa, I should have never had such an opportunity."

The Earl of Leighton nodded. "I wish Luciana had felt differently, my daughter, but despite her blindness where you are concerned she has been a good wife to me, and a good mother to my sons."

"She has helped to make you rich, Papa," Cicely said wisely. "And my half brothers have begun to serve in court through my intercession, a fact I hope my stepmother will remember now and again." She smiled mischievously at her father.

The earl laughed. "I have been so fortunate in you," he said. "Your heart is a good one, Cicely, even as your mother's was. I will miss you."

"You have a new baby daughter, Papa, and I know little Catherine will make up to you for my loss," Cicely replied. *Which is precisely what Luciana has intended,* Cicely thought. *She thinks my father will put me from his mind and concentrate on her daughter, but she is wrong.*

"I will never forget you, my child," Robert Bowen said quietly. "You are my firstborn, and will always remain dear to my heart. It is unlikely, however, that we will ever again see each other, Cicely. I have asked King James to find you a good husband in Scotland. You have a large dower portion, which will make you a most eligible bride, and several men are certain to vie for your favor because of it. I have told the king that you are not to be forced to the altar, my daughter. That you are to be allowed the privilege and courtesy of picking your own husband from among your suitors. Choose wisely. I do not know if you will find love. Love among our kind is rare, but make certain that the man you choose will treat you honorably and respect you. Seek out his reputation, Cicely, and listen to what others have to say. You are clever enough to know when another is speaking the truth or lying. Promise me you will take your time choosing a mate, for once you have promised yourself you cannot break your word."

"I will be careful, Papa," Cicely assured her father. "I have lived in court long enough to know the difference between a sincere man and a rogue."

"Isaac Kira is the goldsmith I have entrusted your wealth to, Cicely. He is in Edinburgh, but I think the king may prefer Perth as his residence. Isaac will serve you wherever you reside. You will receive an allowance quarterly for your needs, my child." The Earl of Leighton arose from the settle where he had been sitting with his daughter. "I must leave you now, Cicely," he said, his voice suddenly rough, as if he were choking a little. He drew her up and embraced her, holding the girl close for what seemed like a very long time. Then, taking her face between his two hands, Robert Bowen kissed Cicely on both of her soft cheeks.

Looking up at him she saw the tears in his eyes. "Oh, Papa, do not weep," she said softly, her small hand caressing his face. She gave him a tremulous smile, but her eyes were also moist.

"May God, our Lord Jesu, and his Blessed Mother Mary keep you safe always, Cicely," the Earl of Leighton said to his daughter. "May you always be happy, my darling Anne's baby, child of my heart." He hugged her again.

"I will write to you now and again, Papa, so you will know how my life progresses," Cicely promised him. "But I will send my letters in care of Queen Joan, for I believe that my stepmother, Luciana, would keep them from you."

"Aye, 'tis wise you are, Cicely," he agreed. Then, kissing her on her forehead, he turned to depart. "God bless you, my daughter," he said as he went through the door of the chamber where they had been seated in conversation.

Thinking back on their farewells, Cicely felt tears welling up, and turned away from the queen.

Joan knew intuitively what Cicely had been thinking, and tried to turn the subject. "There's a very handsome man staring at you, Ce-ce," she said. "Turn slowly and look across the room. I think he's a Gordon, for he is with Huntley."

Diverted, Cicely turned around and saw that indeed, across the hall in a group of gentlemen surrounding the king, one tall, dark-haired man was looking directly at her. "Oh, my!" she said, quickly turning away. "He is outrageously handsome, Jo. I don't think I've ever seen hair quite so black. And he is very tall, isn't he? Scotsmen seem to be tall. Do you remember that border lord who paid his respects as we traveled? I don't think I've ever seen a man as tall as that. But he was hardly as elegant as the man standing with Huntley. Still, he's probably as ignorant as the rest of these lords. They are rough, these Scots. Not at all like our English gentlemen."

"Aye," the young queen agreed. "They have been too long without their master, and I am not certain I trust many of them. Still, once I give Scotland an heir it is hoped they will settle down." The queen lowered her voice. "I think I am with child, Ce-ce."

"Ohh!" Cicely's eyes grew wide. "Does the king know?" she whispered. "And when, Jo?"

"Probably by year's end," the queen said.

"So soon?" Cicely didn't know whether to congratulate her friend or be shocked. It was one thing for a woman like her stepmother to birth heirs quickly, but Jo was royal. She should have not had to prove herself to anyone, and yet she seemed happy to do so.

Queen Joan chuckled. "The king is a fine and enthusiastic lover, Ce-ce," she teased her best friend. "I wish you the same good fortune."

Cicely blushed. "Jo!" She giggled. Then, looking up, she saw that the tall, dark-haired man was staring at her again. He smiled, and with another blush she turned away. "He is looking at me again, Jo," she told the queen. "Oh! He is coming over to us!"

Taking several strides, the tall man crossed the hall, and then bowed low to Queen Joan. He took her hand up and kissed it. "I am Andrew Gordon, Highness, laird of Fairlea. I have the king's permission to pay my compliments to you."

"I am pleased to greet you, my lord," the queen said graciously. "I saw you standing with Lord Huntley and the laird of Loch Brae. Are you kin to them?"

"I am, Highness. A portion of my lands border on Brae loch. It is Gordon country, and a fair land it is," the laird of Fairlea replied, his eyes going to Cicely.

Seeing it, the queen said, "I am remiss, my lord. I have not introduced you to my companion. This is Lady Cicely Bowen, daughter to the Earl of Leighton, my childhood friend. We spent several years together in the household of Queen Joan of Navarre."

"My lady." The laird bowed to Cicely.

"My lord." Cicely curtsied prettily in return.

"Ce-ce, do entertain the laird. I see the king is looking about for me," Queen Joan said, and then, before Cicely might protest, she moved away across the hall.

"Do you think the queen is a matchmaker, my lady?" Andrew Gordon asked her.

Cicely blushed, to her dismay. "Why would you say such a thing, my lord?" she asked him, her hands going to smooth an imaginary wrinkle from her surcoat.

"She has left me with undeniably the prettiest girl in the hall," he replied gallantly. "You surely saw that I have been staring at you all evening, my lady."

"I had not noticed," Cicely lied, and then blushed once more, for he surely knew that she was lying. "I thought you looked at the queen," she finished.

"The queen is lovely, but you, my lady, are fairer by far," the laird of Fairlea said. "Will you walk with me?" He offered her his arm.

Cicely hesitated a moment, but then she took Andrew Gordon's arm. He was very handsome, and he did not seem as rough-spoken as so many of the Scottish lords were. And there was no odor or smell of heavy scent about him either, which meant he was clean. His clothing was certainly fresh, and even stylish.

"Look, Jamie! Look! Ce-ce is walking with Huntley's kin," the queen whispered to her husband. "Don't they make a handsome couple, my love?"

James Stewart looked and smiled. "He would be a good match for her, sweetheart. He stands high in Huntley's favor, and has lands of his own. And he spent two years at the university in Aberdeen. He's not crude and strident, like so many of my lords. We must encourage this possible match."

"She has to love him, Jamie. You promised her father that she would have the right to make her own choice. I know Huntley would be beholden to you if Cicely decided to wed his kinsman. And I know you need all the allies you can find, but I will not allow you to sacrifice my best friend if it does not please her."

"I know what I promised her father, sweetheart," the king said, "and I will keep my pledge to him. But it cannot hurt any if we encourage Cicely to consider choosing this young man, can it?"

The queen laughed. "Nay, my lord, it cannot hurt to encourage them."

And in the days leading up to the coronation of King James I and Queen Joan, the young royals did indeed

manage to see that Cicely Bowen and Andrew Gordon
kept each other company more times than not. It would
be a good match. Andrew had lived in France briefly,
studying at the Sorbonne for a few months. He loved
poetry, which of course gave him something in common
with King James. The king loved writing poetry, and had
even written a poem about the day he had seen Joan
Beaufort for the first time, calling her "the fairest or
the freschest young floure that evir I saw." And if the
queen and her husband were encouraging the match, so
too was the Lord Huntley, who better than his besotted
kinsman saw the value in the laird of Fairlea marrying
the queen's close confidante and childhood friend. Any
close tie with the king was all for the good, although
Huntley until now had always thought his kinsman's
education a waste, and poetry for fools.

James Stewart, the Gordon of Huntley had quickly
learned, was no fool. Where his late father, King Robert,
had been a good but weak man; and his late uncle, the
Duke of Albany, a rapacious and ambitious man; James
Stewart was intelligent enough to win friends among the
border lords and the people. The great lords, Huntley
included, were quickly coming to realize that this king
would be a strong king. Now the question remained
whether they could live with him better than without
him.

And while Huntley conferred with his fellow earls,
his kinsman began to court the queen's lovely friend.
One afternoon the two rode to a nearby meadow, where
a picnic had been set up for them. It was early May, and
the hillsides were abloom with yellow and white flowers. Seated upon a white cloth they ate chicken, bread
with butter, and new strawberries while sipping wine
from small silver goblets.

"I have found that Scotland is very beautiful, though
still wild," Cicely said, gazing about her at the green hills
and up at the blue sky. Nearby a small waterfall tumbled
over a rocky streambed.

"Fairlea is wilder yet, but beautiful, my lady. Still, I believe you would like it," Andrew Gordon said. "I have a fine stone house with its own tower at the far and narrower end of Loch Brae. My kinsman Angus Gordon, who is laird of Loch Brae, does not begrudge my wee bit of his loch. I have cattle aplenty, and even some sheep."

"You are a propertied man, my lord," Cicely replied.

"I have almost everything I want in this world," Andrew said, smiling at her. "I lack only one thing."

"And that is?" Cicely asked, smiling back at him. *Blessed Jesu!* He really was handsome. He had blue eyes that seemed to reflect the sky. When he reached out to take her hand Cicely's heart jumped in her chest.

Drawing that small, soft hand to his lips, Andrew Gordon kissed it. "I need a wife," he answered her. "A wife to keep my home, to give me sons."

"And to love?" Cicely asked quietly. "One day I must take a husband, my lord, but I must love him, and he must love me."

"You must respect him," the laird of Fairlea returned.

"Aye, I will respect him, but especially if I love him," Cicely answered. "I was always told how much my father loved my mother, my lord. I did not know her, for she died at my birth. When my father wed again it was for wealth to rebuild Leighton's fortunes. He holds my stepmother in high regard because she has given him three sons. She in return respects him and is a good wife to him. I see how King James loves Queen Joan. That is what I want, my lord. I would love the man I marry, and I would have him love me. It is not, I realize, very practical, but it is how I feel. I am not apt to change."

"What does your father say to such thoughts, my lady?" he asked. "Will he not make the best match for you that he can? You are, I am told, an earl's daughter." He was still holding her hand, and did not seem inclined to release it.

"King James has my father's formal consent to make

a match for me, but there is one condition: I have the right to say nay should it not please me, my lord," Cicely told him. "Perhaps if I find no one in Scotland who pleases me I shall return to England." Now, why had she said that? Cicely wondered. There was no going back for her, but, the words spoken, she could not take them back without making herself the fool.

"Then we shall have to fall in love, my English rose," he told her, giving her hand a little squeeze. "But perhaps there is someone else."

"Oh, no! There is no one else!" Cicely burst out, and then she blushed furiously at her blunder.

"You do realize that I am endeavoring to court you," Andrew Gordon said dryly.

"Aye," Cicely replied nonchalantly, quickly regaining her equilibrium. Oh, she had been flirted with and teased in the past by various young men. But never courted openly. Still, there was no reason for the laird of Fairlea to know that. "Your attempt, my lord, is a bit feeble," she tormented him. Picking several daisies, she began to weave them into a wreath for her hair.

He laughed aloud at her words, and then, taking her small, heart-shaped face between his two big hands, he kissed her a deep, slow kiss upon her strawberry-stained lips. He found the surprise in her blue-green eyes very satisfactory as he broke off the embrace. "Is that perhaps a bit better, my lady Cicely?"

Her heart was thundering in her chest. The firm lips on her lips had been thrilling. Once a boy at court had stolen a kiss from her, but it had been chill and swift. Nothing at all like Andrew Gordon's warm mouth on hers. "Aye, 'tis better, my lord," she agreed pleasantly. "And if you seriously mean to court me then perhaps you will address me by my name, Andrew Gordon."

"*Cicely,*" he crooned to her. "Cicely of the beautiful auburn curls and blue-green eyes. Cicely of the sweet lips that taste like strawberries." And he kissed her again.

Her head spun. Her heart raced. This certainly had to

be the most fascinating thing that had ever happened to her. She couldn't wait to tell Jo! Yet she must not fall like a ripe apple into the laird of Fairlea's big, eager hands. She pulled gently away from him. "You are far too bold, my lord," she scolded him. "I would think one kiss was enough for this day. You are greedy, I fear."

"A thousand kisses would not be enough!" he declared, smiling at her, his hand to his heart. "May I hope you will welcome my attentions, Cicely?"

"First I must speak with the queen," she told him, suddenly prim. He must not think she could be bought so easily for two sweet kisses. And as inexperienced as she was, Cicely knew those two kisses had indeed been delicious. "She is my mistress, and whatever actions I take must have her approval, Andrew."

"Of course," he agreed. He rather liked the fact that she was careful of her reputation. Scotswomen had the tendency to be bolder than most other women. "Should I ask my kinsman Huntley to speak with the king?"

"Nay! 'Tis far too soon, my lord. If you would court me, Andrew Gordon, then you must do it correctly," Cicely told him. "If you would have the prize you will have to win it. There are never any guarantees in life, are there?"

He was just slightly offended by her words. "Are you fickle then, Cicely, that you cannot make up your mind in this matter?" the laird of Fairlea asked her.

"Nay, I am not fickle, my lord. But perhaps upon better acquaintance we shall learn we do not suit each other. Marriage, as we both know, is for eternity," Cicely reminded Andrew Gordon. "Your handsome face, your tempting lips, and other skills not yet known to me may not be enough. We must be friends as well as lovers, even as the king and the queen are. I will settle for no less, Andrew Gordon."

She surprised him, but he was determined to win her over. She was beautiful. She was well-spoken, and to his surprise he could talk with her. And his cousin, Huntley,

had informed him that Lady Cicely Bowen had a considerable fortune. She was a perfect match for him, Andrew Gordon decided. She was fair to the eye, wealthy
with powerful friends, and his clan approved of the
English girl. He could certainly do no better, the laird
of Fairlea considered. He was going to win her over, and
if truth be told, his heart was already a little engaged by
Lady Cicely Bowen.

Chapter 4

A few days before the coronation of James I, the king visited his parliament. It was there that the earls and other lords learned for certain that he was not his father's son. Rather he was like his great-great-grandfather Robert the Bruce. James was fascinated by the workings of his government, and meant for it to run efficiently and honestly. The earls were not pleased to hear him declare in a strong voice, "If any man presumes to make war against another, he shall suffer the full penalties of the law. I will have a firm and fair peace in this land." But as they listened in respectful silence to this king they were realizing he could not be managed or dislodged. A new era was dawning in Scotland.

On the fourteenth day of May, James Stewart, the first of his name, and Joan Beaufort, his wife, were crowned king and queen of Scotland in the abbey of Scone. James stood tall and assured. He was an attractive young man with dark red hair and amber eyes. His face was long, as was his nose. There was an air of dignity about him. The queen, dainty and sweet-faced, stood next to her husband, her dark blond hair and blue eyes a delicate contrast next to her tall husband. Afterwards, in their ermine-trimmed royal purple velvet robes, they had ridden through the city of Perth to the lusty cheers of the people. Above them the sun shone down, and everyone was hopeful of good things.

And behind them their train of attendants and lords followed. Cicely sat sidesaddle upon her horse, although she rarely rode that way. Still, on this day her behavior must reflect well upon her mistress. Next to her the laird of Fairlea rode. He was rarely far from her side now, and it had begun to be noted among those in regular attendance at court. And amid the procession a troop of border lords rode. There were Bruces to whom the king was related. There were Armstrongs, Hepburns, Scotts, and Douglases.

"He seems a good man," Ian Douglas, the laird of Glengorm, said to his younger brother, Fergus. "He was gracious when I pledged my fealty along the road."

"We'll see," Fergus answered.

"What have you heard?" Ian asked his sibling.

"The people are pleased, but 'tis said the northerners are not. He's already shown he's not old feeble Robert, or Albany, who could be easily bought and was quick to buy allies with his nephew's possessions," Fergus said.

"It's different in the borders," Ian answered. "We're not always defying the crown like the MacDonalds, the Gordons, and others to the north."

"We Douglases have had our quarrels with these kings," Fergus noted.

"I'll keep the peace as long as I'm respected by this king," Ian Douglas declared.

"How long do we have to stay here?" Fergus asked. "This town is too close for me. I need the open space of our lands. And besides, 'tis spring and time to go raiding."

"Our queen is kin to England's king. She's here to make peace between our lands," Ian replied. "Unless we are attacked we'll nae attack others, little brother."

"When can we go home?" Fergus inquired again.

"In a day or two," his sibling replied. "What a tale you'll have to tell your bairns one day of how you saw

Scotland's king crowned, and feasted in his hall afterwards."

"I'd as soon find a noisy tavern in which to celebrate," Fergus grumbled. "These high lords chafe me, and besides, the farther north they come from the more difficult it is to understand a word they say. I'm fearful for my life that I might unknowingly insult one of them and end up spitting the fellow on my sword," Fergus complained.

"Then just eat, drink, laugh when those at our board do, and ogle the lovely wenches," his brother suggested.

"You're hoping to see that pretty creature who rode next to the queen that day on the road," Fergus said slyly. "You've spoken of her several times since. She's riding with one of the Gordons. They say he means to have her to wife."

"How the hell do you know all this gossip?" Ian demanded.

"I drink in taverns instead of the palace hall, and I saw him helping her up onto her horse when we came from the abbey," Fergus replied, grinning broadly.

"Who do we know here who would introduce me to her?" Ian wondered aloud.

"Sir William will be among those in the hall today," Fergus reminded his brother. Sir William Douglas was Glengorm's overlord.

"Aye, I'm a dunderhead not to have remembered it! Then I shall this day be presented to that pretty wench. Shall I fall in love with her, Fergus?"

"Why not?" His younger brother chuckled. "Don't you fall in love with them all before you seduce them? I never knew such a lad for the lasses. Our grandfather would be proud of you, Ian. Father lived but long enough to sire us, and I killed our mam with my birth. But our grandfather was a man for the lasses just like you are."

"Aye, I see his face aplenty among those in our glen." Ian laughed. " 'Tis not so fair a face upon the lasses as it is the lads." Then, suddenly finding himself pelted with flowers, he looked up to see a group of women in an upper window watching the procession and waving. Ian Douglas waved and gave them a wink. The maids above squealed delightedly, and he laughed again.

"You had better save yourself if you intend having anything left for the queen's little companion," Fergus said wryly.

Ian Douglas roared with laughter. "Mayhap you're right," he agreed. "But then, I always have more than enough for the lasses," the laird of Glengorm boasted, his hazel eyes twinkling with mischief.

Fergus Douglas shook his head. "Our clan would nae tolerate you were you not such a good laird to them," he said. "Ian, listen to me. It is past time you ceased this constant merriment. You need to find a wife. To sire another generation for Glengorm. I know there are none at home who attract you enough to wed, but perhaps this pretty English girl will please you. She looks biddable enough, and the gossip is that not only is she close to her mistress, but she has a plump dower as well. I've never known you to speak twice of any lass, but you have spoken much of her since we saw her on the road."

"Advice from my little brother," Ian Douglas teased his sibling.

"I'm but eleven months younger, and I already have a wife, a bairn, and another on the way," Fergus Douglas said seriously.

"You're my heir, and your bairns," the laird said carelessly. "Glengorm is safe."

Fergus shook his dark brown head. "You are the laird," he said stubbornly. "It is your duty to wed and breed heirs."

Ian Douglas shrugged. Then he sighed. "I know," he admitted. "But I must be honest with you, little brother. You say I have spoken often of the girl on the road. 'Tis truth, for I have. There was something about her . . . I am not even certain I can put a name to it. But I believe she is the mate for me, Fergus. I must have her to wife!

I want no other. 'Tis madness I speak, and I will never admit it to another."

"Then we had best find Sir William so he may introduce you to this lass," Fergus said in practical tones. "If she's the one then you had best begin your courting quickly, lest the Gordon laird steal her away from you."

The two men returned to the small inn where they had managed to find accommodation, thanks to Sir William, who had wanted a goodly showing of his clansmen at the coronation. Ian Douglas washed his face and his hands. His face bore a skim of reddish stubble, but he had nothing with which to shave. His hair was shaggy, brushing the nape of his neck, not at all the short, fashionable cut worn by the king and many others. He was dressed in dark woolen breeks, a white shirt, and a leather jerkin. His dark velvet cap bore his clan badge and an eagle's feather. His boots were incapable of being polished any more. His brother was dressed no better.

Returning to the palace, they sought out their clan chief, Sir William Douglas, who, seeing the two young men, greeted them warmly. "Well, what think you of this Stewart king?" he asked them candidly.

"He seems a fair man, if hard," Ian answered slowly.

Sir William nodded. "Aye, lad, you have a good eye for men."

"It's women he's interested in." Fergus chortled. "One lassie in particular."

Sir William raised any eyebrow. "Indeed, Glengorm, and who is it?"

"I don't know who she is, my lord," Ian answered. "I was hoping you could tell me, and then perhaps arrange an introduction."

"Is she here in the hall?" Sir William asked. "Can you point her out to me?"

Ian Douglas scanned the hall, and then he saw her. She was dressed in a grass green velvet gown over which she wore a deeper green brocade surcoat. Her auburn tresses were loose this evening, and fell in luxuriant waves about her small face. He couldn't help but contemplate whether that beautiful hair would be as soft as it looked. " 'Tis that lass," he said, pointing. "Near the queen."

"The one with the Gordon standing by her side with a proprietary air," Fergus put in wickedly, grinning.

"Ahh," Sir William said softly. "That is Lady Cicely Bowen, daughter of an English earl. She is the queen's close friend, as they grew up in the same household. The queen invited her to Scotland. You aim high, Glengorm, but my advice would be to forget the lady. The rumor is that Huntley's kinsman plans to offer for her soon."

"He can't have her," Ian Douglas said. "I mean to make her my wife. Introduce me to her, Sir William, I beg you."

"Ah, laddie, do not break your heart. The lass is a lady from the top of her head to the tips of her dainty toes. The truth is that Gordon of Fairlea has more in common with her than you ever could. She was raised in a queen's household, and has lived in the English court. You're a border lord, Ian."

"Does this Gordon have the lands that I do? And the livestock? And a house in which to shelter a wife?" Ian Douglas said. "Or does he live off his lord?"

"He has lands, and cattle, and a house," Sir William said. "And he has traveled abroad, can speak French, and I am told writes poetry, which has put him in good stead with King James. His kinsman is the Lord Huntley, and Fairlea is in his favor. He has much to offer Lady Cicely. Look at the elegance and style of his garb, Ian. The lady appreciates it, and the delicacy of his manners. You cannot compete with such a man, so do not embarrass yourself trying. Accept what you are: a simple border lord. If you are finally ready to settle down and take a wife, I will help you find a good lass with a good dower for Glengorm."

"Introduce me to her, Sir William," Ian Douglas said. "I can do my own courting."

"Very well." His clan chief sighed. "I suppose if you

are determined nothing will do until you have tried to gain the lady's favor and failed. But do not say you were not warned, Glengorm."

"I have everything the Gordon has, and maybe more," Ian Douglas replied stubbornly. "And I will wager I am more man than he."

"Do not go looking for a quarrel," Sir William warned.

"There will be no quarrel as long as the Gordon realizes that the lass is mine," came the assured reply.

"You've said not a word to the lass. You don't know if you will even like each other," Sir William said.

"I'll like her," Ian Douglas said softly.

"There's more to a woman than a pretty face and soft breasts," Sir William replied. "Why this lass, Glengorm?"

"That day upon the road when I pledged my fealty to King James was when I first saw her. She sat upon her horse laughing with the queen. Briefly she looked my way, and in that moment, Sir William, she stole my heart away."

"She wasn't looking at you," Fergus broke in. "She was surveying everything about her. I'll vow she never looked at you, Ian."

"She looked," Ian Douglas said softly.

"God's blood!" Sir William swore low. "The lad is lovesick and heartsore. Come, and let us get this over with, Glengorm. I'll present you." He began to move across the hall, the two younger men in his wake. When he reached the area where the queen was seated he waited politely to be recognized.

Joan Beaufort saw him there with two other men. She thought one of the men looked familiar but she could not place him. "Sir William," she greeted him.

"Madam, I should like to present my kinsmen Ian Douglas, the laird of Glengorm, and his younger brother, Fergus."

"You are welcome to Perth, my lords," the queen said

as the pair bowed low to her. And then she recalled the big, tall border lord who had pledged his fealty to her husband as they traveled. "We have, I believe, met before, my lord of Glengorm," the queen said to him.

"Not formally, madam," Ian Douglas responded.

"You stepped from the crowds along the road to pledge yourself to us, did you not, my lord?" *Gracious,* Joan Beaufort thought, *he is certainly a big, handsome fellow.*

"I did, madam, and I am flattered that you would remember this humble border lord," Ian said, smiling.

"You are not, I suspect, ordinarily very humble, my lord." The queen laughed. "But I could not forget you, for you are surely one of the tallest men I have ever seen. So you came to see us crowned, did you?"

"And to meet, with your permission, a certain lady of your household, madam," the laird said candidly.

"I think I know the lady with whom you wish to become acquainted, my lord, for you stared quite boldly at her that day," the queen replied, laughing again. She turned her head. "Ce-ce, you have another admirer. Come and meet the laird of Glengorm."

Cicely left the small group of young people with whom she had been chatting. She curtsied to the queen, and her eyes grew wide at the sight of Ian Douglas.

"Ce-ce, may I present to you Ian Douglas, the laird of Glengorm," the queen said. "My lord, this is my dearest friend and companion, Lady Cicely Bowen."

Ian Douglas bowed, and then, taking the girl's hand in his big paw, kissed it. "My lady," he said. And then briefly he felt himself tongue-tied, for she was certainly the loveliest girl he had ever seen in all his twenty-seven years.

"You are the big man on the road," Cicely said.

He nodded.

"You've come to court for the coronation?" Cicely inquired politely.

"Aye," he agreed. What the hell was the matter with

him? He had never been so damned speechless in all of his life. She was just a lass. *Ah,* a little voice in his head said, *but she is the lass you mean to wed.*

"I find Perth charming, don't you?" Cicely said to him. He was certainly a handsome man, but one of few words.

"I don't like the city," Ian Douglas said. "I prefer my own lands, and the hills of the border. The air is fresher and the sky wider when it is not hemmed in by buildings."

"You should not like England then," Cicely replied. "We have many more towns than I have seen here in Scotland. London is very big and noisy. More so than here in Perth, my lord. Will you return soon to your home then?"

"In a few days," he told her. His hazel eyes narrowed as Andrew Gordon came to be by Cicely's side. Could the man not leave her alone?

"Then perhaps we shall see each other again, my lord," Cicely said. Then she turned to the queen. "With your permission, Highness, Andrew has suggested a walk in the gardens." And when the queen nodded Cicely curtsied and, putting her small hand upon the laird of Fairlea's arm, moved off, smiling up at him and chattering animatedly.

Seeing the disappointment in his eyes the queen said sympathetically, "I believe your efforts would be better appreciated by another, my lord. The laird of Fairlea seems to have caught Cicely's attentions. They are much alike, I think."

"I will consider your advice, madam," Ian Douglas said. Then he bowed politely to her and, turning, walked away. Fergus hurried after his brother.

"He cannot have been that interested to have given up so easily," the queen said.

"Ian Douglas is not a man used to accepting defeat, madam," Sir William noted. "Nor is he a man to reveal his own thoughts openly or easily. Along both sides of the border he is known as the *canny* Douglas of Glengorm. One cannot predict what he will do. But he is also not a villain." The clan chief looked across the hall. Ian Douglas and his brother were gone. Sir William felt just the slightest unease.

The two brothers had left the palace, riding back to their lodging. Ian's mood was a dark one, and he furrowed his brow in deep thought.

For a time Fergus remained silent, but then he said, "Well, you were warned."

"I behaved like a lad with his first lass," the laird said angrily. "I spoke to her but little. God's blood, Fergus, she is so fair! Her eyes are blue-green. And that hair! It was all I could do not to run my hands through it. Her voice is sweet, and there was the fragrance of violets about her."

"Let it go, brother," Fergus said. "When Andrew Gordon came to her side she dismissed you easily and went off with him. They say Huntley will ask for her for his kinsman before Midsummer. She'll be wedded and bedded by Lammastide."

"*No!*" the laird of Glengorm said furiously. "Fairlea will not have her! Cicely Bowen is mine, and she will be my wife. We need to know each other better, but how can I make her see that I am the husband for her if every time I approach her she is either with that damned Gordon or he is hovering nearby?"

"As long as the Gordons remain in Perth there is little you can do about it, Ian," his younger brother said. "They've set their sights on her. I've already told you that she has a very fat dower portion from her father."

"So the Gordons want her for her wealth! The bastards!" the laird swore. "I wanted her the moment I saw her, and knew nothing of her. I would have her even if she came to me in her chemise and could offer nothing more."

"Jesu!" Now it was Fergus who swore. "Ye're in love!

How the hell can you fall in love with a lass and know so little about her? Or is it lust, Ian?"

"Both," the laird admitted. "Aye, I want to bed her, but it's more than that. There is something about her. I can't even find the right words to explain myself. I just know she is the one I am meant to wed, to have children with, and to grow old together with."

"Then I'm sorry for you," Fergus said, "for it's unlikely you'll gain your heart's desire, Ian. There is naught you can do to change this situation."

"There is always something that can be done, little brother. But I need to go home to Glengorm and consider well what I shall do next. There is nothing more for us here in Perth. We shall leave tomorrow, but I will dream of Cicely Bowen tonight."

Cicely would have been flattered if she had heard his words, but she didn't, of course. She walked in a mid-May garden with the laird of Fairlea. The air was fresh with the scent of early flowers, though still chill. "Does it ever get warmer in Scotland?" she asked her companion.

"Are you cold, sweeting?" he inquired, and put an arm about her.

"A little," Cicely admitted.

"Let us stop and sit," he suggested. "I'll share my cloak with you." He flung it about her shoulders as they sat down, his arm bringing her closer. "Is that better?"

"Ummm, aye, it is," Cicely admitted. "But we shouldn't remain here too long. People will gossip, and I have my reputation to consider, my lord."

"Just long enough for me to steal a kiss, sweeting," the laird of Fairlea said, catching her chin between his thumb and forefinger, tipping her face up to his, and placing his lips upon hers.

Cicely sighed with delight as he kissed her softly, brushing his mouth over hers. She had entertained a stolen kiss now and again. A maiden, even a homely one, didn't get to be seventeen and not be kissed. His mouth was gentle and his breath sweet. But after a moment she drew away. "You are too bold," she said to him.

"You did not resist," he countered with a small smile. "Was my kiss so unwelcome then, my lady Cicely?"

"Nay," she admitted, " 'twas not. Still, we are but newly acquainted, and I am not easy with my favors like some, my lord. It is said Scots girls are quick to kiss, but I am English, not Scots. You would do well to remember it." Her cheeks felt warm.

"If you married into Scotland you would be Scots, but then your kisses would have to be reserved for your husband," the laird of Fairlea said.

"I have not yet wed into Scotland, my lord," Cicely replied. Her heart hammered with excitement. Was he suggesting that they wed? "Anyone suing for my hand," she told him, "must speak with the king, for it is his decision to make. My father gave him the authority, as he himself is too far distant."

"Then you must wed where the king says," Andrew Gordon said.

"Nay. I wed to please myself," Cicely explained. "But 'tis King James who will act for me. My father loved my mother, and she him. He has given me the privilege of following my heart, my lord, and I will do so." She arose from the bench where they had been sitting. "We should return to the hall lest unseemly things are hinted about out absence," Cicely told him.

"Of course," he agreed, standing and escorting her back into the palace. He left her with the queen and went off to find his kinsman the Lord Huntley.

"You are flushed," Queen Joan noted softly.

"He hints at marriage," Cicely said slowly.

"Do you like him?" the queen asked.

"He is charming, aye, and we have much in common, but it is too soon, Jo. We have known each other but a brief time, and he is certainly on his best behavior with me," Cicely said. "But I will not marry in haste, and should he press the issue he will drive me off, for then I shall wonder if he wishes to wed for love, or for love of my fortune. The Earl of Atholl's wife is a bit of a gossip. Few of our secrets are safe once she has ferreted them out. I am no dewy-eyed girl to be gulled by a handsome man's kisses."

"Then he has kissed you!" the queen said excitedly.

"A few kisses, which I most thoroughly enjoyed. But today I put a stop to it in a manner not to offend, but one that allowed us both a wee bit of pleasure," Cicely admitted with a small smile. "He was a gentleman, and his breath did not offend."

"His clan is important, and he stands in favor with Huntley, who has some power," the queen said. "It would be a very good match for you, Ce-ce."

"I want to be in love, Jo. My parents were. You and the king are," Cicely replied.

"Jamie and I, your parents, we are not the rule. You know that," Joan Beaufort said. "Marriage is made for land, for wealth, for alliances. You have wealth and beauty. You are a queen's friend, all of which makes you valuable. Love is elusive. The best you can hope for is a man who will respect you and be kind. And if you are friends it makes it even better. But love is rarely part of marriage, Ce-ce."

Cicely sighed. She knew the queen was right, but she could hope, couldn't she? "We are still too newly met for me to even consider Andrew Gordon as a suitor," she said. "And there are some other handsome men without the encumbrance of a wife here at your court."

"You have been looking about, have you?" The queen laughed. "Who takes your fancy, Ce-ce?"

"I don't know if he takes my fancy, but the MacDonald of Nairn is certainly worth a second glance, and the Douglas of Glengorm, if he were a bit cleaner, is a handsome man. Obviously there is no one to care for him, for his shirt had a ring about the collar."

"The MacDonald of Nairn is too dangerous a man. He's a Highlander, and he eats little English girls like you for breakfast," the queen said. "As for the Douglas of Glengorm, you gave him very short shrift before you traipsed off with your Gordon."

"I thought him bold," Cicely replied.

"You said he barely uttered a word to you," Queen Joan said, surprised.

"He didn't, but he had a look in his eyes I couldn't fathom. Bold, and yet at the same time a bit shy. I felt sorry for him, Jo. Especially when Andrew Gordon came to take me away. Andrew was so perfectly dressed, his hair clipped neatly. The borderer's best had seen better days, and his hair was rough cut. It touched his shoulders. 'Twas not at all fashionable. But he seemed a decent man."

"You minx! You think to test Andrew Gordon with another man," the queen said. "It will not work, Ce-ce. If Fairlea is after you for your fortune he'll never admit to it. And who is to say every man who seeks to court you isn't interested in your wealth?"

"Well," Cicely said, "if that is so I hope I am as fortunate as my stepmother. At least Luciana knew my father respected her and would be kind. But before I shackle myself to any man I would seek love."

May melted away into June. The queen's pregnancy was officially announced. There would be a child before year's end. All of Scotland prayed for an heir. The laird of Fairlea was openly courting Lady Cicely Bowen with the approval of the Lord Huntley. The lady, however, seemed in no hurry to commit herself to him quite yet.

Huntley complained to the king that his kinsman was ready to declare himself and make Lady Cicely his wife, but that she went out of her way to avoid any such talk. "What is the matter wi' the lass? Does she nae understand what a good family we are? Why, Andrew could have any lass he wanted, and the wench would fall at his feet wi' gratitude to be his wife."

"Ce-ce—Lady Cicely—is not ready to leave the queen, my lord," James Stewart said, although he knew exactly what Cicely was thinking, because his wife had told him. "They have been together since girlhood. Wait until my bairn is born, and Lady Cicely feels more settled away from England. I will champion your kinsman's cause with the lady. I think him an excellent match for her, but I promised her father the choice would be hers. I am not a man to break my word. Tell Fairlea if he waits until Twelfth Night he will have my permission to ask the lady, but remind him I cannot compel her."

"He's impatient, my liege, and I can't say I blame the man. The lass is passing fair," Huntley replied.

"The lady has complained of being pressed too hard by your man, my lord. He attempts to stifle other friendships, which is unwise," the king murmured as a soft warning. "Perhaps he should return home, attend to his estate, and return in December."

"Is that a command, my liege?" Lord Huntley asked.

James Stewart shook his head. "Nay, 'tis but a suggestion, but one he should consider well."

It was a dismissal, and Huntley knew it. The conversation was over. He bowed to the king and departed to find Andrew Gordon.

The king watched him go. He was irritated to be bothered with something he considered a trifle. He had a kingdom to rule, and rule it he was, to the dismay of those used to weaker kings and regents. He *suggested* several new laws to the parliament, and they were swiftly enacted. Then James Stewart sent out a decree demanding that every lord of the realm, every lady holding property in her own right, every laird both Highland and from the border bring the patent for their lands, to be examined for authenticity. It was little more than a thinly veiled excuse to test for loyalty, both past and present. Those who could not prove ownership of their lands or titles, and whose fealty was in doubt, lost their lands. The faithful were reestablished in their holdings.

The king then looked about at lands that belonged to the Crown and had been carelessly given away as bribes by his grandfather, father, and uncle. Those lands that were being mismanaged or had simply been usurped by the lords were reclaimed. It was not a popular move, but James Stewart needed to prove he had an iron fist when it came to ruling. He next meant to improve the criminal and civil courts. There was so much to do, and while it was to his advantage that Lady Cicely Bowen marry the Lord Huntley's kinsman, it was the least of his worries.

Joan Beaufort grew fat with her expected child. Andrew Gordon lingered until August. Then he returned home to Fairlea. The summer ended, and the hills about Scone began to grow bright with their autumn colors, and the scent of September heather filled the air. The wind blew more from the north as the days grew shorter and the nights longer. And then came word of a terrible happening.

The king's friend Black Angus Gordon, the laird of Loch Brae, had gone down into England to bring an orphaned cousin of the queen's to Scotland. James knew that eventually Cicely Bowen would marry, and so he brought Elizabeth Williams from York in hopes that when Cicely departed, Joan would have a young friend by her side. The laird's mistress, Fiona Hay, had left Scone in October to travel home to Loch Brae. She had been kidnapped as she traveled, and the court was agog with excitement over the matter. No one knew for certain who had stolen the lady, but suspicion was directed in the direction of the MacDonald of Nairn.

"The Gordons are furious," the queen told Cicely.

"But she was only his mistress," Cicely said. "Did she mean that much to him?"

"He had sent her home to prepare for their marriage," Joan Beaufort replied. "Huntley approved it. The king sent Brae down to York to fetch my cousin Beth."

Cicely shook her head. "Poor Mistress Hay. How unhappy she must be, being stolen away from the man she was to wed."

"The MacDonald of Nairn was very much taken with

her. He'll marry her whether she will or no," the queen confided. "You do not steal someone else's bride unless you mean to wed her yourself. Or kill her. But Nairn had no quarrel with Brae. He simply wanted his woman, and now he has her."

"I should not like to be in Mistress Hay's position," Cicely remarked. "If a man stole me away I should not wed him no matter what he wanted."

"You might have no other choice," the queen said. Then she brightened. "Will you go into town today to the lace-and-ribbon shop for me? I am ready to trim the future prince's christening gown."

"Are you so certain 'tis a prince?" Cicely teased.

"Oh, Ce-ce, it just has to be!" the queen replied. "James is moving so quickly to institute all his reforms and changes. While the people already love him, the lords are not pleased at losing many of their privileges and certainly not some of their lands. We need a strong male heir to help us prevent any rebellion."

"I'll go into town for you," Cicely told her anxious mistress. "But you must not fret yourself, Jo. Not now, when the prince is so near to being born."

"It is another two months." Joan Beaufort sighed. "Although I would wish it sooner. I can no longer see my own feet. All I long to do is eat and pee. It does not add to the dignity of my office," she lamented.

Cicely giggled, but, seeing her friend's aggrieved look, she apologized. "I'm sorry, Jo," she said, standing up. "I think while I am in town I will find some lavender oil for you. It is so soothing. I will rub your feet with it tonight, I promise."

"Aye, that would be lovely," the queen agreed, waving Cicely off.

The girl hurried to her own small chamber, where Orva sat mending the hem of one of her mistress's gowns. "I am going into town for the queen," she said. "Do you want to come with me? I can take a man-at-arms if you prefer to stay."

"Nay, I'll come," Orva said, laying aside her mending and standing up. "I have been indoors all day, and would welcome some fresh air. Where are we going?"

"The lace-and-ribbon shop at the end of the High Street," Cicely answered.

They gathered up their cloaks, and Cicely sent to the stables for their horses. Entering the courtyard they found the beasts saddled and awaiting them. Cicely waved away the man-at-arms. "We are only going to the ribbon shop," she said, and the man nodded his acceptance, for the town was not dangerous. The two women rode the short distance from Scone Palace to Perth's High Street. At its far end on the corner of Tam's Lane was the lace-and-ribbon shop belonging to Mistress Marjory, a widow. Dismounting, Cicely promised a street urchin a penny if he would hold their horses while they were in the shop. Then she and Orva entered the establishment.

Mistress Marjory bustled forward. "My lady, I was not expecting you," she said.

"The queen sent me to seek lace and ribbons for her child's christening gown," Cicely said with a smile.

"Is the bairn born then?" Mistress Marjory asked anxiously. "I had not heard it."

"Nay, 'tis another two months, but the queen is anxious to have everything all ready," Cicely replied.

"Och, then, you've wasted a trip, my lady," Mistress Marjory said. "I sent my apprentice this very day down to the docks to pick up our new shipment. 'Tis fine French lace from a convent near Paris, and beautiful silk ribbons sent overland from the East. It will take me a few days to unpack and check my inventory. Can you come back then?"

"Her Highness will be disappointed," Cicely said, "but happy to know that you will have what she requires here in a few days' time. Will you send to me at the palace when the goods are ready for sale, so I may come and inspect them?"

"Of course, my lady," Mistress Marjory said with a curtsy. "Is there anything else I may help you with today?"

"Oil of lavender," Cicely said. "Where may I find some?"

"The apothecary shop on the far side of the High Street. You passed it on your way here," Mistress Marjory replied.

"Thank you for your time," Cicely responded politely. Then she and Orva left the shop. The street urchin looked to her anxiously as he returned the reins of their horses to the two women. Cicely dug into her purse and drew out a small silver penny. "Here you are, lad," she said, flipping it to him.

He caught it easily and, bobbing his head, dashed off as the two women rode away.

Inside the shop Mistress Marjory watched them go. Then she called to one of her apprentices to come to her. "Watch the shop," she said, gathering up her cloak. "I have an errand to do." And she hurried forth from her establishment. Making her way from the High Street and through a maze of narrower streets, she finally arrived at a small, nondescript tavern. Reluctantly she entered it, clutching her cloak about her so it touched nothing that might soil it. To her relief the tavern room was empty but for a lone man. She shivered when he looked at her, for he had but a single eye. His other eye, having been gouged from his head, was no more than a hollow of scar tissue. "I have a message for the Douglas of Glengorm," Mistress Marjory said.

"I'll see he gets it," the one-eyed man said. "What is it?"

"Tell the laird the item he seeks will be at my shop in three days' time," Mistress Marjory said.

"Best to make it four days," the man said. " 'Tis not a short ride here to there and back, mistress. And this day's half gone already."

Mistress Marjory nodded. "Four days then," she said,

thinking she must send word to the palace. Then, turning abruptly, she quickly left the dark little tavern.

When she had gone, the one-eyed man called out, "Davy, to me, lad!"

"Aye, Da, what is it?" the young boy who answered him asked.

"Take the horse the laird left us and ride to Glengorm. Tell him Mistress Marjory says the item he seeks will be at her shop in four days' time. Go quickly, laddie, for the laird will barely have time to reach Perth if you don't."

The boy dashed from the room and hurried to saddle the horse in the ramshackle shed behind the little inn, then he rode off and out from the town. He rode south for several hours until the moon was high. Then he stopped for two hours to rest the beast and let him graze and drink from a nearby stream while he ate an oatcake from his pouch and drank some water from his flask. Leaning back against a large rock where he had sheltered, the boy closed his eyes and dozed briefly. Then, taking advantage of the bright full moon, he rode on until almost dawn, when he stopped to rest his animal once again. He rode through the next day and night, halting at intervals for the horse's sake.

Dawn was just breaking when, a day and a half later, the innkeeper's son reached Glengorm. Beneath him the horse seemed rejuvenated. His ears perked up. He tossed his head and neighed a loud whinny. His step quickened as he brought his exhausted rider through a treed glen and up a hill to a large stone house, where he finally stopped. The boy half fell, half dismounted and, going to the large oak door, knocked loudly upon it until he finally heard the locks being unfastened and the door swung open.

"What is it you want?" an elderly woman in an apron asked.

"I have a message for the laird from Perth," Davy, the innkeeper's son, said.

"Come in then, lad. Are you hungry? You look like you've ridden all night," the old woman said.

"Two nights, mistress," the boy told her.

"Blessed Mother, you must be fair worn! Is the horse still alive?"

The boy grinned. "Aye, but as tired as I am, I fear. But I know better than to run a good animal into the ground, mistress."

"Come into the hall, lad. The laird is just up, and having a bit of breakfast," the woman said, leading him into a stone-and-timber chamber. "Here's a lad wi' a message for you from Perth, Master Ian."

Ian Douglas waved the boy forward. "You'll be Ranald's son, eh?"

"Aye, my lord," Davy said with a brief bob of his head.

"What message do you have for me then?"

"Mistress Marjory wants you to know that the item you seek will be at her shop in four . . ." He stopped. "Nay, that's not right." Then his brow lightened. "Two days' time!" he said triumphantly. " 'Twas four the day I left Perth, but 'tis two this morning."

"Tell your father you did well, lad. You'll travel back to Perth with me in two hours' time. Go with Mab to the kitchens to get something to eat, and rest yourself by the hearth," Ian Douglas instructed the boy. He turned to a serving man who loitered nearby. "Go and find my brother. Tell him we're going to Perth this day." Then he returned to his breakfast.

Fergus Douglas came into the hall. "Why are we going to Perth?" he demanded to know. "Marion doesn't like my being away when her time is so near."

"We're going bride stealing, little brother," the laird said with a grin. "Glengorm will very shortly have a new mistress."

"What have you done?" Fergus asked his sibling suspiciously.

"Before we left Perth last spring I made the acquaintance of a little lass who serves in Scone Palace. We spent a very pleasant few hours together. She happened to tell me that my lady Cicely goes into town to a certain shop for the queen now and again. I made the acquaintance of the shop's proprietor, one Mistress Marjory. She is a widow, and inherited her husband's lace-and-ribbon establishment when he died. Her daughter was with child and without a husband. I found the young man in question and saw the couple firmly wed. And I've paid for a tutor so her son may learn to read, write, and do his sums in order that he can one day take over the shop.

"In return Mistress Marjory was to send to me when my lady came to visit the shop next. She would claim the items my lady sought were not available for several days, and dispatch word to me. I intend bride-napping my lady Cicely as she browses among the lace and ribbons. Then I will bring her back to Glengorm. Once she comes to know me she will be glad to be my wife. I told you that the Gordons would not have her. She is mine!"

"They'll come after her," Fergus said gloomily.

"First they must learn where she has been taken," Ian said with a wicked grin. "I met her formally but once, and have been gone from Perth for months now. Why would any suspicion fall on me?"

"What of the shopkeeper?" Fergus wanted to know.

"She'll claim we broke into her shop from a rear alley, snatched the lass, and were gone as quickly as we came."

"But why didn't she run screaming into the streets, calling for the watch?" Fergus asked.

"Because she was hit upon the head and rendered unconscious when she began screaming upon our entry," the laird said. "They have to take her word for what happened. And why wouldn't they believe her? Who else is there to say otherwise? I've told her to say she heard the intruders saying that the lass was an heiress. It will be thought at first that she was taken for ransom," Ian Douglas explained to his brother.

"But when no ransom demand is made, and the girl doesn't reappear?" Fergus queried. "What then?"

"By then we'll be safe home and my lady and I will get to know each other better so we may wed," the laird said. "The lass will come around. They all do eventually, Fergus. You know I have a way with the lasses. But I'll not seduce and leave this one. I will make Lady Cicely Bowen my lawful wife."

"What if they find her before then, Ian? What if the king decides to punish us for your temerity? What will happen to Glengorm?"

"By the time they discover where she is, Cicely will be mine, little brother," the laird said assuredly.

"But what if the Gordons come after her?" Fergus wanted to know.

"Do you think Andrew Gordon will want my leavings?" Ian replied harshly. "Once I have her and she is here at Glengorm, no one can take her from me."

"You would risk offending Lord Huntley and his Gordons? Not to mention the king and his wife?" Fergus said.

"I would risk offending God himself to have Cicely Bowen for my wife," the laid said quietly. "From the moment I saw her I knew she was meant to be mine, and she will be, brother. She will be!"

Fergus Douglas shook his head. There was nothing he could say or do but help his brother in this madness. Ian was in love. *Ian!* He found it difficult to believe, but there it was. The laird of Glengorm was in love with a lass who didn't really know that he even existed. "God help us all," he said, crossing himself. "I hope we don't get hanged for this."

Chapter 5

$\mathcal{F}$our days after her initial visit to Mistress Marjory's shop, Lady Cicely Bowen returned to purchase the delicate French lace and the silk ribbon for the expected royal heir's christening gown. Orva had gone off to the apothecary for more lavender oil, for the queen had slept better than in weeks after having her feet rubbed with it. Cicely fingered the beautiful lace with a sigh.

"It's exquisite. Her Highness will be delighted. She sews wonderfully well, you know, and the gown she has fashioned for her baby is beautiful. I will take all of it, for the lace that decorates the gown of Scotland's heir must decorate no other."

"Indeed, my lady," Mistress Marjory said approvingly.

"The ribbon?"

"Did I not bring it out?" the shopkeeper said. "Oh, dear! Let me go into the storage room and fetch it for you, my lady." She arose and disappeared into the back of the shop.

Suddenly Cicely heard a scream, and she jumped up, startled, as two masked men burst into the room. "Where is Mistress Marjory? What have you done with her?" she demanded. She bolted for the door, but one of the men caught her by her arm, swinging her about and hitting her on her jaw. The girl collapsed into his arms.

"Jesu, Ian, did you have to hit her?" Fergus Douglas asked.

"She was about to shout for the watch, damn it," he said. "Come on now, quickly, brother. We need to get her into the cart and out of the gates before she is found missing, and an alarm is raised."

Together the two men returned through the rear of the shop, where Mistress Marjory lay unconscious upon the floor. Ian felt bad about the need to render the shopkeeper helpless, but it would certainly validate her story of what happened, and her outrage would be more convincing. Exiting the building, they carefully put the girl into a sack, its top open so she could breathe, and laid her in the bed of the small wagon. Then they covered the sack with straw to conceal it. Climbing upon the seat of the vehicle, they drove from the back alley and onto the High Street, moving with the local town traffic towards the gates. Fergus Douglas prayed silently as they went that they would not be caught.

Perth had been a town for centuries. Once it was unwalled, but Edward I had attempted to wall it; then Robert the Bruce had torn the half-built walls down. Edward III, however, had forced the Scots clergy to bear the cost of building stout stone walls with towers and fortified gates less than a hundred years before. The gates numbered four. Red Brig Port was at the end of Skinnergate in the district populated by the town's tanning industry. While the artisans of this area made shoes and gloves, hides were also exported, along with timber and fish shipped down the River Tay, for Perth was a busy inland port.

The other gates were Turret Brig Port, at the end of the High Street past St. John's Kirk; Spey Port, at the end of Speygate; and Southgait Port, at the end of South Street. There was also a small minor gate that led to Curfew Row. But it was the Southgait Port that the brothers sought now as their wagon moved along. The wagon turned from the High Street into Horner Lane, where craftsmen worked in shops and open stalls fashioning spoons, combs, and inkwells from cow and goat horns. As they got closer to the River Tay they could smell the wet wool being fulled before being beaten to thicken it, and then pounded with wooden hammers worked by water mills on the river. Finally they turned onto South Street, lumbering through the Southgait and onto the Edinburgh Road. Several miles from the town, out of sight in a grove of thick trees, their horses waited for them.

In the wagon bed Cicely began to shake off the bonds of unconsciousness. She struggled to make some sense of what had happened to her, of where she was. She could feel motion beneath her, hear the muffled drone of voices nearby. Opening her eyes, she tried to look about her, but her vision was blocked by the sack in which she realized she was now confined. She moved her limbs gingerly. With relief she realized she had not been bound. Carefully she began to stretch herself, and her head pushed from the sack.

Wiggling as quietly as she could, she freed herself of the confines of the rough pouch, realizing as she did so that she had been placed beneath a heap of straw. She stifled a sneeze, freezing momentarily to be certain her captors were not aware she was now awake and alert. Then in a flash it came back to her: She had been at Mistress Marjory's shop choosing lace and silk ribbons for the queen when two masked men had burst into the room. One of the men had hit her on her jaw when she sought to flee.

Cicely reached up and winced as her fingers touched her face. Her jaw hurt. She would be bruised, she realized. But what on earth was this all about? And why was she in some conveyance beneath a pile of straw being driven ... where? What could these men want of her? She felt the wagon begin to slow down and, realizing that when it stopped she would have an opportunity to flee these villains, she tensed, waiting. The vehicle had only just ceased its motion when Cicely burst up from beneath the straw covering her and, seeing that the wagon in which she had been transported had no barrier in its rear, leaped from it and began to run. Exiting the little grove of trees, she turned quickly, hiked up her gown, and sped back along the narrow track that the wagon had followed.

"Jesu and Mary!" a male voice roared, and then she heard the sound of boots pounding behind her.

Cicely's legs pumped hard as she ran. Her throat began to burn as her lungs frantically drew in gulps of cold air in her effort to elude her captors. Her caul came loose, and her hair billowed out behind her. She screamed as a hand caught her by her long tresses, yanking her backwards. Spinning about, she flailed at the big man, feeling a small satisfaction as one of her balled fists made hard contact with his cheek, but she cried out as pain shot through her hand.

"Jesu, woman, give over!" Ian Douglas said.

"Let me go, you villain!" Cicely shouted at him as she attempted to hit him again. "I am Lady Cicely Bowen, daughter of the Earl of Leighton, friend to Queen Joan. You will hang for this affront! Take your filthy hands off of me at once!"

The laird of Glengorm ducked her blow and, tucking her beneath his arm, smacked her backside a hard blow. "Be silent, you little harridan," he said in a fierce tone.

Cicely shrieked her outrage, for the blow stung even through her gown. "How dare you strike me! Ohhh, now you are certain to hang, striking your better!"

He set her down and, taking her hand in his, the laird said, "Now, madam, you are going to get on your horse and ride with us. I will have no more of your rebellious behavior." The lass was spirited, Ian thought, pleased. She would give him strong sons.

In response to his words Cicely yanked his hand up

and bit it as hard as she could. "Go to the devil, villain!" she shouted. "I'm going nowhere with you!" Then, as he pulled his hand from hers with a roar of pained surprise, Cicely turned once again and began to run as fast as she could.

Fergus Douglas stood, rooted in amazement at the battle raging between his brother and the lass Ian claimed to love. In spite of himself he found himself admiring the lady. But then his sibling took three long steps, catching up with Cicely, and, picking her up, threw her facedown over the horse he had brought for her. While Cicely struggled and screamed, attempting to escape him once more, the laird tied both her hands and her feet together. Then, taking a piece of silk cloth from his saddlebag, he gagged her, muffling her shrieks.

"Gently, Ian, gently," Fergus cautioned. "She's just a wee lass, after all."

"She's got a fiery spirit and will take a bit of taming," the laird told his brother. "Mount up now, Fergus. We have a long way to go before we get home."

"You can't expect the lass to travel like that," Fergus said.

"For an hour or two until she understands that I'm the master here," Ian Douglas replied. "The vixen has sharp teeth, but at least she didn't break the skin on my hand." He climbed onto his stallion and, reaching down, took the lead rein of Cicely's horse. Then he moved off, Fergus scrambling onto his own mount and following.

Cicely felt sick to her stomach. She suffered a brief bout of the dry heaves before she fainted. When she came to herself again she was being bounced about as she lay across the saddle, for they were traveling at a rapid speed now. She was dizzy, and her eyes would not focus as the horse's hooves pounded and the ground flew by beneath her.

She could not survive traveling in this position. And she certainly couldn't escape flung facedown over a saddle. She would have to beg for mercy, and if she got it she would have time to consider how to escape these two men. What could they want with her anyhow? "Stop! Stop! Please stop!" she called out. The gag had come loose with the motion of the horse.

Ian Douglas heard her but ignored Cicely.

"Ian, for pity's sake, stop and let the lass up. We can tie her to the saddle so she can't escape, but you'll kill her if you don't let her up."

Ian Douglas looked back at his prisoner. Fergus was right. She was only a lass. He brought his horse and hers to a stop. "Help me then," he called to his brother.

Together the two men lifted Cicely from her animal. The laird untied the bonds about her ankles and lifted her onto her mount again, this time tying her legs beneath the beast. Her bound hands he retied to the pommel of the saddle. "There, is that better, Fergus?"

The younger man nodded. "Aye," he agreed.

"Then let us be on our way again," the laird said.

The blood drained from her head, but it took at least half an hour for Cicely's vision to finally clear. The two men were no longer masked, and while one of them was vaguely familiar, she didn't recognize them. Who were they, and why had they taken her?

She looked about her as they rode. The land was simply gorgeous, hills now blazing with their autumn colors. She had never seen any as bright. And once again she marveled at the abundance of lakes, rivers, and streams. Scotland was a beautiful land. But as she had noted on her travels north from England, it was also very desolate. Where was she? And where were they going?

They rode for hours, and Cicely found herself dozing, for she was suddenly exhausted. Her temples were throbbing and her body ached. She was hungry and she was thirsty. She tried to make saliva in her mouth to swallow so she might soothe her parched throat. Finally, as the sun began to sink into the western skies, they stopped in a sheltered hollow near a small stream. The two men dismounted and tethered the three horses. The one who had hit her earlier untied her legs and lifted her from her horse. Cicely couldn't stand and, to her embarrassment, collapsed to the ground. Tears sprang into her eyes.

"Scream if you want," the big man said to her. "But there's no one to hear you. You'll only frighten the horses and probably hurt your throat, my ladyfaire." He untied her hands, wondering if she would try to hit him again.

She glared up at him. "You do understand that you are going to hang for this," she repeated, rubbing her wrists, which had been chafed by her bonds.

He grinned down at her. "Nay," was all he said before he sauntered off.

The other man came over to her. "I think you might be a bit more comfortable with your back to that big boulder over there," he said. "May I help you, my lady? And then I'll bring you something to drink, and an oatcake to eat."

"Thank you," Cicely replied. This man had done her no harm, and his handsome face actually bore a look of genuine concern.

"I am called Fergus Deuce, for I am my father's second-born," the younger Douglas told her. Then he helped Cicely to stand, bracing her while she regained her equilibrium. "Do you think you can walk now if I help to support you?"

"I think so," Cicely replied, leaning against him as she gingerly moved forward.

Fergus led her a few feet across the small clearing. "Do you . . ." His face grew red with his embarrassment. "Do you need to pee, my lady? I can help you into the bushes, and I'll turn my back," he said.

Now it was Cicely whose cheeks grew pink, but she did need to relieve herself. "Thank you," she told him. "Aye. I think I can stand alone now."

Fergus brought her to a thick stand of growth and

then, as he had promised, turned away so she might have a modicum of privacy.

Cicely turned her back on him and, hiking up her skirts, did what needed to be done. She considered attempting another escape, but the skies above were already swiftly darkening into night. She had no idea where she might be, and there was no dwelling nearby where she might seek help. She would be forced to bear the company of these two villains until the morrow. Mistress Marjory would have certainly sounded the alarm when she regained consciousness. One of her two apprentices would have found her by now. And the king would send a troop of his men-at-arms after her.

"My lady?" Fergus's voice sounded anxious.

"I'm done," Cicely said. There was no need to be unkind to this poor fellow who had had compassion upon her. She stepped from the bushes, and he led her back so she might sit down against the large dark boulder that commanded their little clearing. She looked about for the other man, but he was not to be seen, although there was a small fire burning. Fergus helped her to the ground. There was a thick coating of moss on both the earth and the rock, making it surprisingly comfortable.

The other man suddenly appeared from the small wood carrying two dead rabbits. Without a word he skinned the creatures, cleaned them, and set them on a wood spit over the fire to roast. "These two poor coneys had the unfortunate luck to come across my path," he said. "We'll have rabbit for supper with our oatcakes."

"I shall not eat a thing from your hand!" Cicely said haughtily.

He shrugged.

"Who are you? And why have you kidnapped me?" she demanded of him.

"You don't recognize me?" he said, not knowing whether he should feel offended or not.

"Your face is vaguely familiar," Cicely admitted, "but I do not know you, do I?"

"I am Ian Douglas, the laird of Glengorm, madam," he told her. "And I am engaging in what is known here in Scotland as bride stealing."

It took a long moment for Cicely to realize just what he was saying to her. Then she burst out, "You are mad, my lord! Totally, raving mad! I have absolutely no intention of marrying you. Why on earth would I marry *you*? I don't even know you."

Ian Douglas knelt before her. He took her small face between his thumb and his forefinger. "The first moment I saw you on the road to Perth I knew you were the woman for me, Cicely Bowen. I have never given my heart to any, but I am prepared to give it to you." His hazel eyes looked directly into her blue-green ones.

"I don't want it!" she cried, unnerved by both the unexpected declaration and by the passionate look in his eyes. No man had ever looked at her quite like that. Not even Andrew Gordon. That look both intrigued and frightened her.

"Ah, ladyfaire, do not be frightened," he said softly to her. "I will love you."

The gentle tone of his voice frightened Cicely far more than his earlier rough treatment of her had. "You must take me back!" she cried. "We will say it was all a misunderstanding! Though I said it, 'twas in anger—I will not let them hang you. But we must return to Perth, my lord."

"I doubt the poor shopkeeper will consider the bump on her noggin a misunderstanding," the laird said dryly.

"My lord, I cannot wed you!" Cicely told him.

"Why not?" he asked. His eyes were dancing with sudden amusement.

"I am already pledged to marry!" Cicely lied desperately.

"To the Gordon?" Ian said. "Nay, ladyfaire, you lie. The Gordon has not yet asked for you, although I am told he would. What is it, I wonder, that keeps him from it? Is there another he loves, but whose dower portion is not as fat as yours might be? Or perhaps a mistress who needs to be disposed of discreetly before he declares himself?"

"Andrew Gordon is a good man!" Cicely defended her suitor.

"Has he ever kissed you?" the laird wanted to know.

"That is none of your business!" Cicely snapped.

"He hasn't." Ian chuckled.

"He has!" she retorted. "And I liked it! I liked it very much!"

In response Ian Douglas leaned forward and kissed Cicely. It began as a fierce kiss that turned tender and deepened as he felt the petal soft lips beneath his yield.

Cicely's head spun. *Oh, my!* she thought as she felt herself succumbing to the kiss, and kissing him back.

The laird drew away. "Did you like it as much as that?" he asked her wickedly.

"No!" She was practically shouting at him.

Ian Douglas laughed. "Ah, ladyfaire, you are a terrible liar. You kissed me back." Then, standing up, he left her to fume while he went to turn the rabbit on the spit.

She hadn't kissed him back! She hadn't! But she had, Cicely was forced to admit to herself. He was a horrible, horrible man! He had kidnapped her, treated her abominably, and when his mouth had closed over hers she was momentarily lost. It was certainly not going to happen again. Nay, it was not!

When the rabbits were well roasted, the laird brought Cicely a small haunch on a leaf along with an oatcake. "Here," he said.

Cicely turned her head from him. "I'm not hungry," she said. "I will eat nothing from your hand, villain. Take it away!"

"All right," he said pleasantly, his white teeth tearing into the roasted meat as he walked away.

Cicely's belly rumbled. She was hungry. She hadn't

eaten since early morning after the Mass, and she had eaten little, for she was in a hurry to get into the town. She closed her eyes, as if that would block out the delicious smell of the roast.

"My lady." Fergus Douglas knelt by her side. In his hand was another piece of rabbit on a broad, wet leaf. "Please try to eat something. I know all that has happened this day has been upsetting for you, but you need your strength." He held out the meat.

"Why do I need my strength?" Cicely asked him petulantly.

"Because we have a long ride tomorrow, and into the next day. My brother is a wonderful hunter, but he may not be so fortunate finding food tomorrow as he was today. And no one roasts a coney over the fire like Ian. The meat is never tough, and 'tis always moist and sweet." He smiled at her.

Cicely couldn't help herself. There was something so engaging about Fergus Douglas. She smiled back at him. Then, reaching out, she took the meat from him and began to eat. "Where are we going?" she asked.

"To Glengorm. Our home is there. We are the Douglases of Glengorm, a small branch of Clan Douglas. Your new home will be a large stone house with a slate roof that sits on a small hillside overlooking Loch Gorm. Our glen is almost hidden, and can be entered only through a small wood. We're surrounded by the Cheviot hills, which make up the border between Scotland and England," he explained.

Cicely finished the rabbit he had given her, and took the small, flat oatcake he offered. "It won't be my new home," she told him. "It will be my prison until the king arranges for my release. Do you have anything to drink?"

Fergus undid a small leather flask from his belt and, unstoppering it, held it out.

Cicely took the flask and, putting it to her lips, swallowed deeply. A sudden look of surprise crossed her face. She gasped, coughed, and her face turned red. "What in the name of the Blessed Mother was *that*?" she demanded when she could speak again.

"Whiskey," he said, and he grinned. "I should have warned you, madam, but it didn't occur to me until you put it to your lips that perhaps you had never tasted whiskey," he said, looking abashed. "Would you like some water?"

Cicely nodded, and handed him back the flask. "'Tis a potent brew," she noted.

"Aye," he agreed. He helped her up. "We've no drinking vessel, so you will have to cup your hands in the stream," Fergus told her. Then he escorted her to the stream.

Cicely knelt by the water. Her throat was still burning from the swallow of whiskey, and she was suddenly overcome with weariness. Cupping her hands, she drank, and then stood up, swaying.

Suddenly the laird was beside them. He scooped the girl up in his arms to return her to her place by the large, mossy boulder.

"Put me down, you lout," Cicely protested feebly, but the truth was she wasn't certain that she could stand if he did put her down.

Ignoring her, Ian Douglas set her back on the ground. He had spread the gray-white-and-black length of tartan he carried with him over the moss. Cicely was already half-asleep, and did not notice it, nor did she notice that he laid his cloak over her to keep her warm.

"What will you sleep in?" Fergus asked quietly.

"We'll share your cloak when we sleep, but do without when we keep watch," the laird said. "I'll take the first watch."

Fergus nodded and, rolling himself in his cloak, placed his body in front of Cicely's to shield her. Then he quickly fell asleep. When his brother awakened him four hours later he rose obediently, turning the cloak over to his sibling, then adding more wood to the little

fire to help him avoid the damp chill of the late autumn
night. Traveling with the lady, they had another day and
a half's ride to reach Glengorm. Fergus sighed. He hoped
his Marion was all right. The new bairn was due in another few weeks. When the false dawn began to show in
the sky Fergus awoke his older brother.

The laird was immediately on his feet. "Do y'think
we can move out soon?" he asked the younger man. He
picked up Fergus's cloak and handed it to him.

"It will be slow until dawn, but aye, the road is visible,
though the moon be waning. There's still enough light
now to get along," came the answer.

"I'll wake Her Ladyship," Ian said with a wicked
grin.

Fergus shook his head. Ian might believe himself in
love with Cicely Bowen, but she certainly had no use for
him. Given the opportunity, Fergus thought she might
gladly do his brother harm. And he wasn't certain that
taking her by force to Glengorm was going to alter the
situation one bit. The lass was every bit as stubborn as
his elder brother was. He had never known Ian to behave in so reckless a manner.

The laird went over to where the girl lay sleeping
soundly. His instinct was to kiss her awake, but instead
he bent down and shook her by her shoulder. "Wake up,
ladyfaire," he said. "We must be traveling on."

"Go away, Orva! It's too early to get up," Cicely murmured, burrowing back into her bedding.

Ian Douglas reached down, grasped his cloak with
strong fingers, and yanked hard. The material unrolled,
and Cicely awoke with a shriek of outrage. He pulled
her to her feet. "Go into the bushes and do what you
must. We are leaving in a few minutes," he said to her.
Bending, he picked up his plaid.

"Brute!" Cicely said furiously, and hit him on the
shoulder with her fist.

"Madam," the laird said, drawing himself to his full
height to tower over her, "you will have to refrain from

striking me in the future or I will retaliate, I promise you." Then he turned and walked over to where Fergus was gathering their horses.

Knowing she had little choice for now but to go with him, Cicely slipped into the bushes and relieved herself. Then, going to the stream, she put her hands in the icy water, used them to splash some droplets on her face to awaken herself fully, and then drank a few swallows to slake her thirst. When she joined the two men Fergus put an oatcake into her hand. She ate it quickly, knowing it was likely all she would see for many hours.

Cicely mounted her horse, and the laird tied her hands again to the pommel of the saddle, but he did not tie her legs together. She was relieved, for it had been uncomfortable, and also because now she could escape Ian Douglas, given the opportunity. Having her hands tied to the pommel was little impediment. A horse was better controlled with one's knees and heels. She smiled to herself.

But although they rode from before dawn until sunset with just a single brief stop, no opportunity had presented itself for Cicely to make her escape. They had traveled very slowly until the sun came up, and then at a good canter until the sun was at its zenith, when they halted to rest and water the horses, eat another oatcake apiece, and ease their personal needs. Mounting up, they rode again until sunset, when they took shelter in a field by a stone wall. The laird would not light a fire, for they were more in the open this night than the previous one. Fergus had saved a small piece of the previous night's meal, and he gave it to Cicely.

"We'll share it," she said to him.

Fergus gave her a warm smile. "Nay, lass, 'tis for you. I'm used to traveling with an oatcake to sustain me. Ye're a lady, and need your nourishment."

"Would you like to share your meat with me?" the laird taunted her.

"Go to the devil, you villain," Cicely snapped at him.

"There's nothing in this world I would share with you!" She crammed the bit of rabbit into her mouth, chewing.

"We'll share much in the years to come," he said softly.

"I'd sooner take the veil," she told him.

"You're too beautiful to give yourself to the Church," the laird told her. "You're meant for a man's bed, my bed."

"Never! Never! *Never!*" Cicely shot back, and she swallowed the last of her meal.

He knelt by her side, and the knuckles of his hand slipped gently down her cheek. "Your passion will never be wasted in prayers and fasting, ladyfaire." Then he tipped her face up to his and kissed her, his lips playing over hers.

Jesu! Mother Mary! Cicely thought. His kiss was intoxicating. Part of her knew she had to resist him, but another part of her was ready and eager to give herself to him. She moaned softly against his mouth. She couldn't let this happen. *She couldn't!* With the greatest effort she had ever made in all of her life, Cicely pulled away from him. "How dare you touch me!" she demanded coldly of him.

"You have said you would see me hanged, ladyfaire," he told her. "I should just as well be hanged for a sheep as a lamb." He had felt her ambivalence, for he was a man well skilled in the amatory arts. Standing up, he moved away into the darkness.

Cicely pulled her own cloak about her and, her back against the cold wall, she closed her eyes and prayed for sleep. But unlike the previous night, when she had been in shock over her abduction, her stomach filled with hot roasted rabbit, and feeling warmed by whiskey, she could only doze. Several times in the night she had awakened cold, hungry, and just a little frightened. She wanted to weep, but she would show no weakness to this bold man who had stolen her from everything she knew.

Had she not heard the snores of the two men near

her—for tonight both slept, as there was no fire to draw
the attention of strangers to them—she did not think
she could have borne her condition. Even the horses
grazed silently, moving away from the shelter of the
wall now and again. Above them a pale waning moon
shone down, and the still air was icy. She dozed again,
and the next time she awakened the sky was beginning
to lighten, to her great relief. She stretched her limbs out
and then stood up.

Instantly the laird was awake and on his feet.

"I must relieve myself," Cicely said quietly, and moved
off to the other side of the wall. "I have no intention of
running from you until I have peed and you have fed me
one of those flat rocks you call oatcakes. Turn your back,
my lord, and give me some privacy." Then, without waiting to see if he complied with her request, Cicely turned
her own back and raised her skirts.

He had almost laughed, but he did not. Until she was
ready to acknowledge him as her lord and master he
would give her no satisfaction. But he had appreciated
her dry wit. He would not have expected it of so fine a
lady. And then he realized that in his desire to steal her,
to make certain that the Gordons did not take her for
themselves, he hadn't admitted everything Fergus had
been saying to him, that Sir William had said, was true.
He knew absolutely nothing about Lady Cicely Bowen
other than that he loved her and wanted her for his wife.
But how did you love someone you barely knew? He
couldn't answer his own question. His heart had spoken
for him.

It would have been better, he knew, if he had been
able to acquaint himself with his ladyfaire within her
own environment, but the damned Gordons would not
let him. They had hovered and buzzed about her like a
hive of bees surrounding their queen. It had been impossible to get near her long enough to court her. He had
had no choice but to take matters into his own hands.
The Douglases were every bit as good as the Gordons.

And when she came to know him better she would appreciate that.

Ian Douglas bent and shook his brother awake. "If the weather holds we should reach Glengorm before sunset," he remarked as Fergus stood up, stretching.

The horses were caught. Oatcakes were handed out, and they mounted up. Once again Cicely's hands were tied to the pommel of her saddle.

"You have chafed my wrists raw," she complained. "Where can I run to, my lord, that you persist in binding me?"

"I don't know," he admitted, "but we are close enough now to Glengorm that I will take no chances with you, ladyfaire. By sunset we should reach home. I do not wish to waste time chasing you over the hills and moors. Do you not wear gloves when you ride, madam?"

"I do, but I also leave them with my horse, which, the last time I saw him, was tethered outside of Mistress Marjory's shop," Cicely snapped. "You are a monster, and—"

He cut her off. "I will hang. I know. I know!"

The day was gray and lowering as they rode across the hilly countryside. Now and again in the distance a tower house came into view, but they never rode near any dwelling. They saw no one, nor were they seen. There was no one to whom Cicely might appeal for help. Again, as on the day before, they stopped once. But today they did not linger long resting. The laird and his brother were most anxious to reach their home. And at this point so was Cicely.

Traveling to Scotland with the king and queen had been an almost leisurely progression. Each night they had stopped at either the home of some noble or at the guesthouse of an important monastery or convent. When such accommodation had not been available they had been housed within comfortable pavilions set up for them by staff who had ridden ahead. They had been served hot meals. It had been most civilized. This journey had been horrible. The laird's home would certainly be provincial, rustic, but it would be warm and dry. There would be cooked food.

"We are almost home," the laird said, coming up to her side, for he had ridden ahead briefly.

It had begun to rain, and it was an icy rain. There was a north wind at their back now. Ahead of them Cicely saw a wood rising from between the hills. She hunched down into her cloak, her hood pulled up to protect her from the growing storm. They rode into the wood. In summer it would have been thick with growth, but now the branches of its trees were stark and black against the gray sky. The path through the wood began to move upwards, and suddenly she saw the house atop the hill. It was tall and square, and had a single tower that rose from the south corner of the building.

"Why is there only one tower?" she asked, curious, as they rode up the incline.

"Glengorm first began as a tower house," Fergus explained.

"It might be a castle if it had more than one tower," Cicely said.

"We're not a grand enough family for a castle, lady-faire," the laird said. "But our great-grandfather returned from the Crusades with some treasure. He decided to enlarge our home, for he could think of no better use for his small trove."

"Our grandfather told us his father often said if he put his prize in stone and mortar no one could steal it from him," Fergus added.

"Someone might have coveted the house," Cicely said, "and taken it from you."

"Glengorm is too well hidden, and the only bit of it that shows from the surrounding countryside is the tower, which is like so many other tower houses. We are rarely raided," Fergus added. "Only our own people know of our existence. Most of the other branches of the Douglas clans do not. You will be very safe here."

"Where is your loch?" she asked him.

"You'll be able to see it from the house," Fergus told her.

"What does 'Glengorm' mean?" Cicely inquired.

Now it was the laird who spoke up. "*Glen* is our word for a valley. *Gorm* means blue and green. The green trees surrounding us, the blue loch. It is from them that Glengorm takes its name, ladyfaire. I am glad to see you showing such an interest in your new home," he said to her.

"When the king sends his men for me, my lord, I will go with them," Cicely told the laird sharply. "This is not my home, nor will it ever be. I am here under protest, as you are more than well aware." She glared at him.

"You are a strong, proud lass," he said. "It pleases me well to see it. Hold on to your faith, ladyfaire, if it helps you to deal with your situation. But know that I hold tightly to mine. You *will* be my wife. Once you have learned to know me you will love me, madam. All the lasses do, but 'tis you I want."

Cicely burst out laughing. "You think highly of yourself, my lord." Then her face darkened with her anger. "But I do not! You have not stolen just one of the queen's ladies. You have stolen me, and I am the queen's favorite, her friend of long standing. Do you actually believe you will be permitted to retain my person when they come for me, and I say nay to you before witnesses? And I will say nay!"

"We are going to have time to know each other," Ian Douglas told her. "And how, ladyfaire, will they find you unless they learn where you are? And how will they know if they are not aware of who stole you away? And who will tell them? Only my brother and I were involved in your abduction."

"You planned this carefully," Cicely surprised the two men by saying. "You had to know where I would be, and when. It was not by chance that you took me when you did. There is someone else involved, and when the hue and cry is raised, as it already has been, you will be found out, my lord. And then I will be rescued from your clutches. I will not plead for you, but I will ask that mercy be shown to your brother, who has been kind to me. And I will plead for your clansmen and -women, who are innocent of your perfidy."

Now it was the laird who laughed, although again her astuteness surprised him. "If you are found it will be many weeks hence. The Gordons will not want you then, for your virtue will be in question, ladyfaire, after time in my custody. You will end up having to marry me whether you will or no, and the king will consent," Ian Douglas told her boldly.

"The king cannot consent unless I consent, my lord. If you knew anything about me you would know that. 'Tis true the king is my guardian, and 'tis true he may make a match for me. But when my father put me in the care of James Stewart it was with the understanding that I would have the final word on a husband," Cicely told the laird. "My father loved my mother well. He wanted no less for me than a love match. He told the king that I must agree to any match or it could not take place."

"That is ridiculous!" Ian Douglas burst out, very surprised.

"Hah!" Cicely told him. "Now you see your problem, don't you, my lord?"

Listening, Fergus Douglas was astounded by her words. Here was something his brother had not considered when he stole away the lovely girl he called his ladyfaire. His horse came to a sudden stop, and the younger man realized that they had reached the house. He slid from his animal's back and tossed the reins to the boy who had run from the stables.

"We will not discuss this before my servants," the laird said, his voice now hard. He dismounted, and then, going to Cicely's horse, helped her off the beast. "Come into the hall. The rain is getting heavier, and it is almost night." He took her hand in his.

Cicely attempted to pull away from him, but his grip

was firm, his step sure as he led her into the house and down a short passageway into his hall. It was cold, as there was no fire burning. There were two rushlights burning that had been coated with tallow. The fat sputtered and the rushlights smoked, adding to the stink of the hall. There were rushes on the stone floor, and two dogs came forth to greet their master. Then they went back to seeking among the rushes for a bone that had not already been chewed.

"Why is there no fire?" Cicely wanted to know.

"Why would we burn wood when there was no one here?" the laird asked. " 'Tis wasteful."

"It will take hours to warm this drafty hall," Cicely said irritably. "You would have used less wood keeping it comfortable. And have you no beeswax candles? Tallow is dirty when used for light, and it smokes. And rushes on the floor? Blessed Mother, my lord! No one uses rushes anymore. 'Tis old-fashioned. And the stink of the place is not to be borne! Tallow, rotting food, and dog piss! Disgusting! Absolutely disgusting!"

" 'Tis to be your home," he said angrily. Why had the hall not been warm and clean? He had sent a man ahead this morning to alert the house that he would be arriving by dark. "Take charge of the servants, and make it over to please you, madam. Housewifery is not my province. 'Tis yours!"

"I am not the mistress here, my lord, and you should not be giving your servants the wrong impression," Cicely replied stubbornly. "Now, where am I to stay while I am forced to abide your company?"

"Bethia!" the laird roared. "Where the hell are you, woman?"

After a few minutes a woman shuffled into the hall. "You called me, my lord?"

Looking at her, Cicely could see why the hall was as it was. Bethia was of indeterminate age, and from the way she squinted her eyesight was not the best. Cicely shook her head.

"What is it you want of me, laird?" Bethia asked.

"Did you not receive word that I would be arriving before nightfall earlier today?" Ian Douglas asked his serving woman.

"Aye," Bethia answered him.

"Then why is there no fire in the hall?" he said.

"The messenger did not say precisely *when* you were coming, my lord. Why would I waste the wood?" the woman replied. "Look. Here is Pol to light the fire." She pointed at a man who was even now struggling to bend towards the large fireplace. "Will you be wanting a meal, laird?"

Cicely made an exasperated sound that set her suitor into a furious temper.

"Aye, you witch," he exploded. "We'll be wanting a meal that should erstwhile be cooked and be ready to be brought to the high board! And have my mother's old bedchamber made ready for my guest."

"Is she not to share your bed, laird?" Bethia said. "Since you sent no word to have another chamber prepared, and we were not expecting a visitor, how could I know to make ready your late mam's rooms? It will take time. I shall have to send into the village for a lass or two to come, and 'tis already dark."

Cicely now snickered. She couldn't help it. The masterful laird of Glengorm had absolutely no control over his servants. While she knew it didn't bode well for her comfort, she was hard-pressed not to burst out laughing. Seeing the grim look in Ian Douglas's eye, however, she managed to restrain herself.

"I'll be going home now to my wife," Fergus Douglas said as he hastily exited the hall. If his sibling had thought to call after him, Fergus would have pretended not to hear.

"Then send for someone, or do it yourself. This lady with me is to be my wife."

"I am not!" Cicely said firmly.

"Ahh!" A light dawned in Bethia's eye. "You went

bride stealing, laird, did you?" She chuckled. Then she looked Cicely up and down. "She's pretty, and looks sturdy enough to give Glengorm some heirs. Why bother with your mother's chamber if you mean to wed her? Send for the priest, bed her, and be done with it. Her people will certainly be coming after her soon enough. You'll want the deed done, laird, or they'll take her back."

"He will not bed me, and when the priest comes I will tell him so," Cicely said. She turned to the laird. "You have a priest in this hidey-hole of yours, my lord? Ohh, yes, I will certainly want to speak with him."

Old Pol was still struggling to light the fire. Cursing, the laird pushed him aside and did it himself. Then he rounded on Bethia. "Do as you have been told, woman. See to a hot meal and see to the lady's chamber!"

With a shrug Bethia, followed by Pol, shuffled from the hall.

"Come and sit by the fire," the laird invited Cicely. "You'll be warm in a few minutes. Would you like some wine?" He moved towards a sideboard.

"It will take this hall at least a day to warm, provided you keep the fire going," she said as she sat herself in a straight-backed chair that was near the hearth. "And I think if you have it I would prefer some of that whiskey Fergus gave me the other night. It took the chill out of my bones quite nicely."

He poured the requested liquid into a small pewter half-dram cup and handed it to her. "You liked our whiskey?"

"It serves its purpose," Cicely answered him, then gulped it down. She gasped, and tears came to her eyes, but the instant warmth that spread through her was gratifying. Then she looked up at him. "You can't make me marry you," she said quietly. "I don't even know you, my lord. What made you do such a foolish thing as kidnapping me?"

Kneeling before her, he looked up into her eyes. "The

moment I saw you on the Perth road that day I knew you were the woman for me, ladyfaire. I have already told you that. I fell in love with you at first sight, but when I met you at court I could not pay you my addresses, for Andrew Gordon and his kin were always around you. When you come to know me you will see I am a better husband for you than he is."

"He has land, a house, livestock, and powerful kinsmen who would keep me safe," Cicely answered.

"But does he love you? Or does he love your influence with the queen, and your dower portion? My brother tells me you are an heiress."

Cicely smiled. "Nay, no heiress, my lord, but my dower portion is substantial."

"I love you," Ian Douglas said. "I stole you away so you might know and come to love me. I could not do that at court with all the damned Gordons hovering over you."

"How can you love me? You don't know me," Cicely protested. But had not James Stewart fallen in love at first sight with her friend Joan Beaufort? But that had been different, hadn't it? And Joan hadn't fallen in love at first sight with James Stewart. She had gotten to know him, and as she had her love had bloomed. But this was quite different. She and James Stewart had much in common. Both were royal. Both were educated, and could speak with each other on a variety of subjects. The sameness that they shared had bonded them.

But this was unlike the king and Jo, Cicely thought. She was the daughter of an earl. She had been raised with a girl who became a queen. She was a queen's friend and companion. This border lord was an ill-mannered rustic. She had absolutely nothing in common with him at all. Could he even read or write? Speak French? Write poetry?

How could they possibly have anything in common? He had spent his entire life on the border. She knew about the border lords. The Gordons had little use for them. Brigands and battlers, they called them. And Ian Douglas had certainly proved them correct when he had kidnapped her from Mistress Marjory's shop several days ago.

"There is nothing you could possibly do that would make me love you, my lord," Cicely told him. "If you will take me back to Perth I will ask that this entire matter be forgotten, and no punishment will fall upon you or your folk for this ill-advised adventure you have taken upon yourself. Please, my lord. You cannot love me, and love has little to do with a good match, which you certainly must know."

"And yet the king loves the queen, and you have said your own father loved your mother," he reminded her. "Douglases are every bit as good as Gordons, ladyfaire. I have more land than your Gordon. I have livestock aplenty. My house is sound. I can offer you as much as, if not more than, Andrew Gordon."

"Aye, I am certain you speak truth, my lord, but you cannot offer me the one thing that Andrew Gordon can," Cicely told him.

"What is that?" the laird wanted to know. "What can he give you that I cannot?"

"Companionship, my lord. Like me, he has been educated. We have certain likes in common. I think you cannot read, nor even write the letters of your own name, my lord. What could you possibly speak of to me? Would you recite me poetry?"

"Poetry?" He looked surprised. "Why would you want me to spout poetry to you, ladyfaire? I don't want to rhyme with you. I want to make a life with you, share children with you, make love to you."

Cicely blushed at this intimate declaration. Then she said, "But I want to do none of these things with you, my lord. I don't know you."

"You will after we have spent some time together," he told her pleasantly. "And when you know me you will not seek to leave me. You will be happy to spend your life here at Glengorm as my wife. Now, the first thing you need to know about me is that I both read and write, ladyfaire. And I can recite my church Latin at the Mass. As for French, I have no use for it, so why would I waste my time learning it? I do keep my own accounts. A man who cannot keep his own accounts will end up being cheated. Are you warmer now? The fire seems to have caught nicely."

She was frankly surprised. "Oh, I beg your pardon for thinking you totally ignorant," Cicely said.

"Now I have learned something about you, ladyfaire. You are not afraid to admit a fault, and you have pretty manners. I hope you will teach those assets to our bairns."

"Ohhh, you are the most impossibly stubborn man!" Cicely cried.

"Aye, and now you have learned something about me," he replied with a grin.

Chapter 6

"*The watch! Call the watch!*" an apprentice cried, running from the lace-and-ribbon shop. "My mistress has been attacked! Help! Help!"

Orva stepped from Master George's shop, where she had just purchased a supply of lavender oil and balm. People ran past her and, looking down the lane, she saw a crowd beginning to form about Mistress Marjory's place of business. She hurried down the little street, pushing through the curious onlookers. "Get away from our horses!" she said to several men, shooing them with her free hand. "You are startling them, and if they bolt the queen will be most displeased. "*You!* Boy! What are you howling about? Where is my lady? Where is Lady Cicely?" She pushed the apprentice back into the main room of the shop. "What is this all about?"

"My mistress has been attacked!" the boy said, looking terrified.

"And my mistress, lad?"

"She was not here when I returned and found Mistress Marjory lying upon the floor of the storeroom unconscious, a lump quite visible upon her poor head," the apprentice said. He was young, and near tears.

"My mistress was not here?" Orva was astounded.

"Where is she? Our horses are still tethered outside the shop."

The boy shook his head. "I do not know," he wailed. "Will my mistress die?"

"Show me where she is," Orva said in what she hoped was a calm voice. The lad led her back into the storage area of the shop. Orva knelt beside the fallen woman, who half sat, her back against the wall. "Mistress Marjory," she said. "Where is Lady Cicely?"

The fallen woman groaned at the sound of Orva's voice. She opened her eyes briefly, but then closed them. *"Gone,"* she managed to whisper.

"Gone? What do you mean, gone?" Orva demanded to know.

Before Mistress Marjory might answer, a man-at-arms strode into the chamber. "What's going on here?" he asked. "Did you hurt this woman?"

Orva slowly stood up. "I am Mistress Orva, tiring woman to Lady Cicely Bowen, Queen Joan's companion. I left my mistress here earlier to choose some lace and ribbons for the expected heir's christening gown that Her Highness now sews upon. I returned to find a crowd outside the shop, and the apprentice howling about Mistress Marjory being grievously harmed. I entered to find the poor woman as you see her, and my mistress gone. Something wicked has happened here. Where is your captain? I need to return to the palace immediately and inform the queen that my mistress is missing."

"Perhaps your mistress had a disagreement with this lady," the man-at-arms suggested. "Mayhap she hit her, and then fled in a fright."

"Lady Cicely would never have done such a thing," Orva said indignantly. "And if she fled this place for whatever reason she would have taken her horse. It is still tethered outside. Find your captain! I must have an escort to the palace immediately."

The man-at-arms looked at Orva. She was very well

dressed, and he had seen the two horses outside of the shop. They were excellent beasts. He turned and looked at the young apprentice. "Are this woman and her mistress known to Mistress Marjory, lad?"

"Aye, sir. They come for the queen, and have been here before," he answered.

"Kidnapped," Mistress Marjory's voice said weakly. "They kidnapped the lady."

Orva gave a scream of distress.

"Who kidnapped the lady?" the man-at-arms wanted to know. This was becoming complicated. "Go and fetch the captain, lad," he instructed the apprentice.

The boy ran off.

"Who kidnapped my mistress?" Orva demanded of the wounded woman. *"Who?"*

"I do not know," Mistress Marjory replied. Reaching up with one hand, she rubbed her head, wincing. That damned borderer didn't have to hit her so hard, she thought to herself. Her head ached like merry hell. She was suddenly beginning to think better of her part in all of this. Best to claim ignorance. No one could prove anything. She struggled to get to her feet, but her head was swimming.

"Easy now, mistress," the man-at-arms said, and he moved to aid her, guiding her slowly from the storage room.

"Help her into the main chamber of the shop," Orva said. She was suddenly suspicious of Mistress Marjory, and wanted to hear more of what she had to say. Why would two strange bandits enter a lace-and-ribbon shop and kidnap a woman unknown to them who had come to purchase lace? There was more to this than met the eye. She came over to where the shopkeeper now sat and, leaning down, said softly, "I think you know exactly what happened to my mistress. I shall tell the queen what I believe as soon as I return to the palace. You had best tell the truth when you are brought before her, for you will be sent for, and soon."

The captain of the watch strode into the shop. "What has happened here?" he asked.

Orva quickly explained the simple facts of the situation, and then said, "I will need an escort back to the palace, for the queen will want word of this incident immediately, Captain."

"Your mistress is the English lass who traveled with the queen? The one the Gordons are seeking for one of their own?" the captain asked.

"Aye, the same," Orva replied. Gracious, did all of Perth know everything?

"Perhaps her suitor grew impatient and took her off. Bride stealing is an old custom here in Scotland, lady," the captain suggested.

"Nay," Orva said. "Lord Huntley was brokering the match between his kinsman and the king, who speaks for my mistress. They had decided to wait until Twelfth Night before announcing any betrothal that was agreed upon. And nothing had yet been agreed upon."

"Even more reason for the Gordon lad to steal your mistress. Winter will soon be upon us, and there's nothing better than snuggling with a loving woman when the snows fly." He gave Orva a grin and a wink. "Women like a bold man, eh, m'dear?"

She sighed, exasperated. "Nay, that did not happen. Now escort me to the palace. The queen will be most distressed to learn what has happened, and better I tell her than some fool hears of this incident and rushes to inform her first. Her Highness is great with Scotland's heir, man. Would you cause her to miscarry?"

The captain said no more. Going outside, he helped Orva onto her mare and, leading Cicely's horse behind him, he personally escorted the woman to the palace. Once there Orva thanked him for his courtesy, and hurried to the queen's apartments.

Entering, she encountered the queen's old tiring woman, Bess.

"Orva, what is it? You look most distressed," Bess

greeted her. She was a woman older than younger, and had been with Joan Beaufort since her birth.

"There has been an incident in town . . ." Orva began. She paused, and then said, "Och, there is nothing for it but to say it. My mistress has been kidnapped."

"Oh, dear!" Bess's hand went to her heart. She paled and her eyes grew troubled. "The queen! Oh, Orva! The queen will be most distressed by such news."

"Aye," Orva agreed, "but we cannot keep it from her. How could we explain my mistress's absence from her, and especially at this time?"

"And she's been asking if Lady Cicely is back with the lace yet," Bess said. Then she straightened her spine. "We'll send for the king, and while we are waiting we shall tell the queen together of this incident." She spoke to a young page who had been dozing in a nearby chair, shaking him awake gently. "Here, lad, go and find the king. Tell him the queen needs him *now*! Do not dally. The king must come immediately."

The page scrambled up and dashed from the queen's apartments.

"Come along now," Bess said to Orva. "She is in her privy chamber with Lady Stewart of Dundonald and the Countess of Atholl, both of whom bore and irritate her by turns. Only Lady Grey of Ben Duff amuses her, but she will return home soon. Poor Lady Grey is very distressed over the disappearance of Fiona Hay, who was her friend. And now *this*!"

The two tiring women entered the queen's privy chamber, where the women sat sewing on garments for the expected heir.

The young queen looked up and, seeing Orva, said, "Is Ce-ce back then?"

"Now, my dearie," Bess began, "you must not be distressed by what Orva has to say to you, but it seems that Lady Cicely has been taken off."

"*Taken off?*" Joan Beaufort's voice trembled. "What do you mean, taken off?" The queen grew very pale, and

Lady Grey quickly hurried to bring her a small sop of wine as a restorative. The queen gulped it down, and then looked at Orva.

"When we reached the lace shop my mistress instructed me to go down the street to Master George's to purchase the lavender oil and balm that have given you such ease. I did as she bade me, and when I departed Master George's I heard a voice calling for the watch, and, hurrying to find Lady Cicely, I discovered it was an apprentice from Mistress Marjory's shop shouting that his mistress had been injured. I found the woman half-conscious in her storeroom."

There was a murmur of distress from the other women with the queen.

"And my mistress was gone," Orva continued. "The shopkeeper claims she was kidnapped. And certainly there was no sign of my lady, but Mistress Marjory knows more than she is telling, Your Highness. I sense it! She is hiding something."

At that moment the king burst into the queen's privy chamber, startling the women there. "Sweetheart! What is it? Is the child coming?" He knelt by her side.

"Ce-ce has been kidnapped from the lace shop!" the queen cried. "You must find her, Jamie! *You must!*"

The king arose and, seeing Orva, said, "What is this all about?"

Orva repeated herself, concluding with her suspicions about Mistress Marjory.

"Why do you think the shopkeeper is involved?" the king queried Orva.

"My lord, why would two masked bandits break into a lace shop at the exact time that the queen's known favored companion is there? We were at the shop four days ago, and the lace had just come in, for Mistress Marjory said she had sent her nephew to the docks to retrieve it. Why, then, ask us to return four days later instead of the next day? Nay, the woman is duplicitous, and knows more than she is telling," Orva declared.

James Stewart nodded. "You may very well be right," he said.

"The captain of the watch suggested that perhaps the Gordons stole my mistress away to hurry the marriage that they want. He said bride stealing is a custom here in Scotland," Orva added. "Would they do that, my lord?"

"I hope they have not," the king replied, "but Huntley is here, so let us find him and ask him. In the meantime we shall send for Mistress Marjory, and see what she has to say for herself. Bess, remain with your mistress. The rest of you ladies are dismissed, but will remain here in the queen's apartments, for I forbid any gossip in this matter being circulated until the truth of it is known. Orva, you will come with me." The king strode from his wife's rooms, going to his small library, Cicely's tiring woman in his wake. Once there he sent his page to fetch Huntley while ordering two men-at-arms to go into town and return with Mistress Marjory.

Huntley came, greeting the king politely, his eyes going to Orva, who sat silent in a corner of the room.

The king quietly explained that Lady Cicely Bowen had been taken forcibly from the lace shop. He did not mention the possibility that the shopkeeper might be involved. Instead he said, "Has your kinsman in his impatience involved himself in a wee bit of bride stealing? I shall not be pleased if I learn the laird of Fairlea has stolen her away. Especially if the Gordons of Huntley are involved."

"Given what has recently befallen my kinsman of Loch Brae I am surprised that you would ask such a question of me," Huntley replied stiffly.

"Perhaps Andrew Gordon has taken a leaf out of someone else's book," the king suggested.

"If he did," Gordon replied, "I was certainly not involved. 'Tis true the girl is a prize worth having, but her connections are too powerful for Andrew to attempt to force the issue. He is not foolish. Besides, he believes his charm will win the lass over."

James Stewart barked a hard laugh. " 'Tis true. I have noted that Fairlea thinks highly of himself. Where is he at this time, Huntley?"

"On his lands," Lord Gordon said. "I stopped to see him three nights back on my way to Perth. He was over-seeing the refurbishing of his late mother's chambers for his anticipated bride. Besides, his favorite mistress was about to drop her whelp. It's his first child, and he has a soft spot for the mam even now. The wench went into labor the morning I departed. It would have been im-possible for Andrew to keep his promise to her and get into Perth to steal Lady Cicely. I only just arrived myself a short while ago."

"Then," said the king, "I will accept your word he is not involved. But if I find out later to the contrary that he is somehow enmeshed in this situation I will punish him severely, and he will not have Lady Cicely as a bride."

Lord Gordon of Huntley nodded. "I will stand by your side as you mete out your judgment, my lord, but I know Andrew is not so dim-witted as to bride steal."

"It is possible that the shopkeeper may know some-thing," the king said slowly. "Do not send to your kins-man until I have had more time to straighten this out. I do not need an enraged suitor here muddying the wa-ters of my inquiries."

"Of course, my lord," Huntley replied, and then he bowed himself from the king's presence.

"I think he tells the truth," the king said to Orva.

"Aye, but that does not mean the laird of Fairlea isn't involved in this," she noted.

"Let us see what the shopkeeper has to say for her-self," the king remarked. "You will wait here with me until she is brought for questioning."

Orva said nothing more, for who was she to converse casually with a king? They waited. And then a knock upon the door of the king's library came, and it opened to reveal two sturdy men-at-arms. Between them was Mistress Marjory. They half dragged her before James

Stewart. The woman looked terrified out of her mind, and briefly the king felt sorry for her, but then he considered that if she had played any part in Ce-ce's abduction, she should be frightened of him. He was her king, and his pregnant wife was distressed by her best friend's absence and possible fate. He did not invite the woman to sit. Instead he stood, and Mistress Marjory quailed as he towered over her.

"Well, madam, and what have you to say to me? Are you involved in this chicanery? The truth now!"

"I . . . I was attacked," Mistress Marjory said. Her legs began to shake.

"That we know," the king said sternly. "What I have asked you is if you were involved in Lady Cicely's abduction, madam. Orva thinks you were, and I believe her instincts are correct. Tell me the truth! If you do your punishment will be mild. But lie to me, madam—and I will know if you do—then my wrath will be most severe." James Stewart looked the frightened shopkeeper directly in the eye and saw pure terror reflected back at him. It astounded him, for he did not think himself as someone so fearful. And then he realized it was his persona as king of Scotland that awed the woman before him. He would not get the truth if he alarmed her too greatly. He softened his tone. "I suspect you must have had a most excellent reason for doing what you did," he said. "Could no one else have helped you?" he asked a bit more carefully.

She shook her head, and silent tears began to slide down her pale, plump cheeks. "I've done my best since my husband grew ill and died," she began. "I had to take care of the shop, do all he had done if we weren't to starve, and mother my bairns as well."

"How many bairns do you have?" the king asked quietly.

"Two, a lass born less than a year after we were wed. But the lad was slow in coming, my lord. Lucy was eight before he was born."

"Tell me what happened," the king prodded gently.

"Lucy was to watch after her brother while I managed the shop and the apprentices. The shop will be Robbie's one day, and I must tend it well until he can take on the responsibility for himself. I promised my husband on his deathbed that I would do so. But my daughter met a lad, and while my son played they engaged their time in . . ." Mistress Marjory ceased her narrative briefly, and flushed.

"Ahh," said the king. "Aye, madam, you need not say it. I understand. Did he get the lass with child?"

Mistress Marjory nodded silently, hanging her head in shame for her daughter's transgressions.

"And the lad would not accept the responsibility of his actions, eh?" the king said.

The shopkeeper nodded again, now saying, "And then *he* came. He wanted my help in what he said was a small matter. I said until I could help my daughter I could not aid him. He asked me to tell him my woes, and if it were possible he would help us. So I did. He listened, and said to show his good faith he would see done what needed to be done if I swore I would then do what he needed me to do."

"You agreed," the king said.

"I did, my lord. He found Torcull, and had him wed to my daughter. Her child will be born soon, but 'twill not be a bastard. It matters not that Torcull ran off afterwards. My grandchild will be honest-born. But then my deliverer put me further in his debt, for he paid school fees for Robbie so he could learn to read, write, and do his sums. He said the laddie couldn't run the shop one day without certain knowledge." Then Mistress Marjory began to cry again.

Orva had listened to the shopkeeper's entire recitation quietly, but she could no longer remain silent. Jumping up from her seat in the corner, she placed herself directly before Mistress Marjory. "Who is *he*?" she demanded to know. "Who is this savior of yours? And why did he abduct my mistress?"

"Why he did what he did I do not know," the woman answered honestly, "but I do know who he was, for he told me so that I might send to him when your mistress was to visit my shop. He is the Douglas of Glengorm, a border lord."

"A borderer? A rough borderer? Sweet Jesu help my poor innocent mistress!" Orva cried. Then she rounded on the woman before her. "Oh, 'tis a wicked creature you are! My poor child stolen away to God only knows what kind of a fate!"

"I did what I had to do to protect my own family," Mistress Marjory defended herself. "Was I to allow a poor innocent to be born with the stain of bastardy upon it? Besides, he said your mistress would not be harmed. Lovesick he was, I can tell you. Like a green lad with his first lass." She turned to the king. "What else could I have done, my lord, but what I did? My husband's brother would take the shop from me if he could, and give it to his son. And what would happen to my Lucy and her bairn? What would happen to my son and to me? My difficulties did not arise from any mismanagement. They arose from a silly lass who has since learned her lesson, to her regret."

"But you betrayed Lady Cicely, and in doing so you have distressed my queen, who will soon deliver Scotland's heir. For that you must pay a price, Mistress Marjory," the king said quietly. Jailing the poor woman would not help, the king realized.

"I but defended my family, my lord, as any man would have done," she replied.

"You have probably cost my mistress a good marriage!" Orva snapped angrily. "Do you think the proud Gordons will have her now after this misadventure?"

"Your mistress, if the gossip is truth, is a wealthy young woman. And the Gordons of Huntley are not averse to adding to their wealth," the shopkeeper said sharply. "They will wait to be certain she is not with another man's child, and then they will have her happily. Her gold will buy her a husband."

"If your wench had spent less time on her back—" Orva began, but the king raised his hand to silence the two women.

"Mistress Marjory, for the next twelve months, one-quarter of the profit from your shop will be forfeit to the queen," James Stewart said.

"My lord! There is barely any profit to be had at all! How am I to feed my children, my grandchild?" the shopkeeper protested.

"But when it is known that your lace and ribbon is sought by the queen your business will increase," the king said cannily. "If I punish you publicly for what you have done no one will patronize your shop, madam. You betrayed the queen's friend. While my wife would understand your dilemma, she would not forgive you what you have done without some form of punishment. I shall send my man for an accounting monthly. Do not attempt to cheat me, for if you do I will show you no mercy at all." He turned to the two men-at-arms. "Return Mistress Marjory to her establishment, and you will say nothing of what you have heard this day. I will tolerate no gossip in this matter."

The men-at-arms spoke in unison. "Aye, my lord!" They understood that this king was not be trifled with, for he did not make idle threats. They escorted the shopkeeper briskly from the king's library.

"Fetch my secretary to me," James Stewart instructed his page. Then he turned to Orva. "I will send to Sir William Douglas, who is Glengorm's overlord. Your mistress is safe, Orva. If this impetuous young laird is as lovesick as the shopkeeper claims he is, he will not harm your lady. I seem to recall my wife mentioning him briefly. Come, let us go and speak with the queen and reassure her," the king said as he led the way from his library and walked briskly to his wife's chambers.

I wish I felt reassured, Orva thought to herself as she followed him.

The queen's ladies looked up anxiously as he entered,

but the king said nothing, passing them by, Orva behind him, to enter his wife's little privy chamber. Lady Grey was seated by the queen's side on a stool, sorting colored threads. Both women looked up, and James Stewart smiled at them.

"Lady Grey, I will ask for your discretion, but I may need your help," the king said. "And the old cats outside will want to know what was said here."

"I know how to keep secrets, my lord," Lady Grey said with a meaningful look at the king, for she had under duress aided him once before.

"Ce-ce?" the queen asked anxiously.

"Abducted by a lovesick border lord." The king chuckled. "We will get her back. I must send to Sir William Douglas for his help."

"The Douglas of Glengorm?" the queen exclaimed. "Oh, that poor man! To have done such a reckless thing when it is certain Cicely will wed the Gordon laird of Fairlea."

"My mistress had not yet made up her mind," Orva reminded the queen. "She found him handsome and charming, 'tis true, but she disliked his attempting to push her into a marriage she was not certain she wanted. You know my mistress well, my lady. She can be brought to the trough, but not forced to drink."

"Aye, 'tis a truth," the queen said. Then she giggled. "I really do feel sorry for Glengorm, not just because he has been reckless, but because Ce-ce will not be easy to woo." She turned to the king. "That is why he has stolen her, Jamie. He wants a fair chance with her, and the Gordons would let no man near Ce-ce once Andrew Gordon decided that he would have her. Still, he cannot be allowed this behavior."

"I know," the king agreed. "Do I not already have enough difficulty with the northern lords, my love?" He sighed.

"Orva must go with your messenger to Sir William," the queen said suddenly. "Ce-ce will need her, and feel more reassured by her presence. And Lady Grey and her husband must travel with them. Maggie wanted to go home several weeks back, but remained when I asked her to. I was comforted having another woman by my side who is with her first child, but I know Andrew Grey would have his child born at Ben Duff."

Lady Grey threw the queen a grateful look. Helping the king secretly some weeks back had put her in a difficult position. The secret was one she had been unable to share with anyone, even with her husband. Being at court, where everything reminded her of the part she had been forced to play in a betrayal, distressed her mightily. Aye, she had wanted to go home weeks ago, but then the queen had begged her to remain, and she could not deny her royal mistress. "Thank you, Your Highness," Lady Grey said softly. "I very much want to go home to Ben Duff."

"Is it near Glengorm?" the king wondered.

"Aye, they are our nearest neighbors," Lady Grey said. *God's wounds!* What more did he want of her?

A brief smile touched the king's lips, but was quickly gone. He knew exactly what Maggie MacLeod, Lady Grey, was thinking. However, there would be time enough to enlist her aid if he decided he needed it. "I was simply curious," James Stewart said. "There is so much of my country that I do not know yet."

Outside the door of the queen's privy chamber that led directly into the corridor, the Gordon of Huntley heard what he needed to hear. Stepping away from the little portal, he wondered if the king would tell him all he knew. Or if possibly he should send to the laird of Fairlea, and raise a troop of his clansmen to ride into the borders to fetch Lady Cicely back. Of course, by that time the girl's virginity would have certainly been taken, but as long as she was not with Glengorm's bairn, did it really matter? His kinsman was a proud man, but Cicely Bowen's fortune could soothe his pride. Especially if she was a good wife to him both publicly and privately.

Wisdom, however, prevailed. The Gordon of Huntley decided to wait to see what the king would do. To his relief, the king took him aside that evening to tell him what Gordon already knew but dared not admit to, for how could he explain the knowledge he possessed? "My men and I can ride into the borders, my lord, and bring Lady Cicely back," Gordon offered. "The Douglases are no friends of ours."

"I need no clan warfare between you two," the king said. "Keep your men in check, my lord. I will handle this situation."

"I should advise Fairlea of the situation, my lord, for he is to wed the lass, and should know she may be sullied," the Gordon of Huntley said.

"Advise Fairlea if you will, Huntley, but Lady Cicely had not agreed on any match, and I cannot force her to one, for I gave her father my word," the king replied.

"But surely her father would approve the fine match my kinsman can offer," Lord Gordon said. The girl was to be given a choice of whom she would wed? Ridiculous!

"The Earl of Leighton dotes upon his daughter," the king answered. "He gave her his word that she could marry the man she loved, and no other. And I gave my royal word that I would uphold the earl's promise to his child. Tomorrow I will send to Sir William Douglas to aid me in this situation with his cousin. Diplomacy will prevail in this matter." And with those words the Gordon of Huntley was dismissed.

He bowed, and backed from the king's presence.

The king's privy chamber was now quiet. James Stewart sat in one of the two chairs facing each other by the blazing hearth. Rising, he took a few steps and poured himself a goblet of wine from the carafe on the table which was set before the lead-paned windows. Outside those windows the night was black, a sliver of waning moon not yet risen. He turned back to sit again by the fireplace, which was flanked by stone greyhounds. The chamber was small, with paneled walls and a coffered ceiling, but it suited him well and was his refuge from the court. Only invited guests were allowed into the royal privy chamber.

James was irritated by the commotion that the Douglas of Glengorm had caused. And his aggravation extended towards Lady Cicely Bowen as well. The Earl of Leighton was a sentimental fool that he allowed his daughter to choose her own husband. And James had been a bigger fool to agree to see to the girl's marriage under such circumstances. But his Joan had begged him, and he had acquiesced to her plea.

James Stewart had known that Scotland would eventually recall him, and he would need a queen. It had been fortunate that he had fallen in love with the most suitable candidate for his hand. He was not usually a man to be driven by sentiment. The king had to admit to himself that he would have found himself with a difficult choice had another woman been more eligible. Of course he would have done what he had to do in that case. But there had been no other, and what tender emotions he had were reserved for Joan Beaufort.

Marriages among the nobility, however, were not usually love matches. Did his wife's best friend hold out the hope of a love match? Was that why she was so reluctant to commit herself to the laird of Fairlea? Andrew Gordon was a perfectly excellent candidate for the girl's husband. He had lands, cattle, the favor of his overlord. What more could the girl want? James Stewart had thought not to interfere in Cicely Bowen's decision. But he had other, more important considerations, like the impending birth of his heir; like the MacDonald, lord of the isles in the north of Scotland; and a Highlands always on the brink of rebellion. He needed to get these matters under his firm control.

And he was being distracted by a silly girl who could not make up her mind, and a lovesick border lord who was about to cause a feud between himself and the Gordons of Huntley over her. Well, when he got her back he would have Joan speak to her, point out the advantages of marrying into the Gordons. And certainly after her sojourn in a rough border keep, Lady Cicely Bowen could be made to see reason. Aye, the king thought, his eyes narrowing. It would be quite to his advantage to have Ce-ce among the Gordons watching out for the interests of the Stewart queen, and by association Scotland's king.

He called for his page, who he knew was sitting outside of the door to his privy chamber. "Did you find my secretary, Will?" he asked the boy.

"Aye, my lord. He is in the outer chamber awaiting your instructions," the boy answered. "Shall I tell him to come in?"

"Aye, laddie," James Stewart said.

The page departed the privy chamber, and a moment later the king's secretary, in his long black robe, entered with his basket of supplies. He sat at the king's command, setting up his inkstand and taking out a piece of parchment. Then he looked to his master for further instructions.

"Is Sir William Douglas still in Perth?" the king asked the man. He knew that his secretary made it a point to know every- and anything that the king would need to know.

"I believe he left for the borders this morning, my lord."

"Send after him tonight. It is most urgent that I speak with him," the king said.

The secretary nodded. "Will that be all, my lord?"

"For now, aye," came the reply.

The secretary arose, gathered up his supplies, and hurried from the chamber.

When the door had closed the king added another piece of wood to his fire, and then sat back down with his goblet. Autumn was fading fast, and the winter would be upon them soon. He drank his wine down, and called to his page once more. When the page had come James

Stewart said, "Find me Lady Grey of Ben Duff, and bring her here to me privily."

The page went quickly from the king's presence, and returned shortly with Lady Grey. Noticing how heavy she was with child, the king invited her to be seated opposite him before the blazing hearth.

"I have sent after Sir William, who departed for his keep this day. When he returns I will explain the difficulty. I expect him to disabuse his relation of his foolishness, but if winter sets in I will expect you to visit once or twice at Glengorm so you may befriend Lady Cicely, and convince her that her best course lies in marrying Andrew Gordon, the laird of Fairlea," the king said quietly.

"So you would put an unwitting spy among the Gordons of Huntley," Maggie MacLeod said sarcastically. "Even as you put one among the MacDonalds. By the rood, my liege, I wonder if your lords know just how dangerous a man you are!"

"Tread lightly with me, madam," James Stewart warned her softly. "Your usefulness to me will not always protect you from my wrath."

Maggie MacLeod looked directly at the king, and her bright blue eyes were sad. Her hands went to her belly protectively. "Were it not for the love I bear Ben Duff I should have told the laird of Brae what you forced me to do," she said to him. "I betrayed a friend, and I shall never be absolved of that sin. Now you want me to do it again. You are a cruel master, my liege, but I will comply for the sake of my husband, and the child I will soon bear him. And this one final act I will perform for you, but when I leave court this time you will never again see my face."

The king nodded. "I understand, madam," he said quietly. "But I am not the monster you think me. I needed Fiona Hay in the north. As for Lady Cicely Bowen, because her father gave her the privilege of choosing her own husband, she is dillydallying like the foolish lass she is. The laird of Fairlea is an excellent match for her, and he wants her. We might have had a betrothal announced at Twelfth Night had it not been for the rash actions of the Douglas of Glengorm."

"I do not disagree with you, my liege," Maggie Mac-Leod replied. "I just don't like being put in the position of having to cajole her into a decision she is not ready to make. I know her, and I would not consider her foolish at all. But while he is vain and a bit arrogant, the laird of Fairlea is not a bad man. And Lady Cicely is a strong girl. She will have him in hand after a short time."

The king laughed, breaking the tension in the chamber. "Aye," he agreed, chuckling. "Ce-ce will have him well in hand, and quickly. Only after he has put a ring on her finger will he realize she has put one through his nose." Then he grew serious again. "Sir William will return sometime tomorrow, madam. And you will depart for the border the following day. Ce-ce's tiring woman will go with you, and Sir William will bring her to Glengorm himself. I am sure both Orva and her mistress will be happy to be reunited. You might make your first visit with Ce-ce then. I am hoping we can regain custody of her before the winter sets in," the king concluded.

"I will do it," Lady Grey said. Then she rose. "If that is all, my liege, I will return to my husband. He will wonder why I am late from the queen's chamber." She curtsied, and then went from the privy chamber.

Sir William Douglas returned to the palace in late afternoon, and went directly to the king to learn what had made James Stewart send after him. He was brought to the little privy chamber, because while some at the court already knew that Lady Cicely had been abducted, it was not yet public knowledge, nor was the kidnapper known. The king wanted his privacy while he attempted to quickly straighten out the situation.

Sir William was astounded when he was told of his kinsman's rash actions. "My lord, I am astonished that Ian would act in such a manner. He is thought to be a careful man, but then, he was very taken by the lovely Lady Cicely. He will not harm her, for he is an honorable man. I suspect he will attempt to convince her that he would be a better husband for her than the laird of Fairlea. What can I do to aid you in this situation?"

"Leave tomorrow for Glengorm, Sir William. You will not be able to travel as quickly as you would alone, for I would have you take Lady Cicely's tiring woman, Orva, to her mistress. If the lady has been frightened by this adventure Orva's presence will calm her. Grey of Ben Duff and his wife will go with you as well. I understand that they are near neighbors to Glengorm. Lady Grey knows Ce-ce. She will reassure her and help her to convince Ian Douglas to release her. If he does so I will not punish him. A man in love is apt to act in a witless manner."

"And Andrew Gordon will have her to wife then, despite all of this? Does he know she has been abducted by Ian Douglas?" Sir William inquired.

"Huntley will tell him. And if your kinsman is the honorable man you claim he is then there should be no problem. The girl was a virgin when she left the palace yesterday. She should therefore be a virgin on her wedding night. The decision of a husband is hers to make, for her father promised her, but aye, Fairlea is the best choice for her," the king said. "It would please my queen and me greatly if she wed him."

No fool, Sir William understood what the king was telling him. "I shall leave at first light in the morning," he said.

"Excellent!" The king smiled with his approval. "I shall send to the others in your party so they will be ready."

Sir William Douglas bowed himself from the king's privy chamber. *Damn Ian!* he thought irritably. The bloody man was foolhardy, hotheaded, and incautious. Yet until he had laid eyes on Lady Cicely Bowen he had never been any of those things. He had been a sensible man, always watching over his Glengorm clanfolk. Why had he not accepted his overlord's offer of a bride last summer? *I could have found him a good wife.*

But nay! Ian Douglas claimed himself in love. What the hell did love have to do with a good marriage? Love was for silly lasses and old women dreaming of a past that never existed. Love! Bah! The inconsiderate fellow had put all of Clan Douglas at risk over a pretty face. I'll take the wench from Glengorm myself, and return her to the king, Sir William determined angrily.

But when the morning came the Douglas lord had calmed his ire. He had known Ian all his life. His actions had been daring, and, having fought beside him in many a border skirmish, Sir William knew his kinsman could be adventurous. There was a chance that the lass might actually come to like her captor. And as the choice was hers, she might agree to wed Ian. Her dower was not one to be overlooked, and why should the Gordons get such a prize? Had not the Douglases been loyal to Scotland's kings? Certainly far more loyal than the Gordons of Huntley. And if the lass was happy and content, the queen would cajole the king into forgiving the transgressions of Ian Douglas for the sake of her beloved friend.

Entering the courtyard of the small palace, Sir William found his party awaiting him. "Andrew!" he greeted Grey of Ben Duff. Then he looked to Lady Grey. "God's foot, woman!" he exclaimed. "Your bairn appears close to birthing."

Maggie MacLeod nodded. "I want to go home," she said. "Ben Duff's heir should be born in his own home." Two servants aided her into a small padded cart, where an older woman with a dour face sat.

"Aye, aye," Sir William agreed. Then he turned to the other woman. "You'll be Orva then?" he asked her.

"Aye, my lord, I am," Orva said.

"Since we are all here let us be on our way," Sir William said as he and Lord Grey mounted their horses, following the cart as it rumbled over the cobbles of the courtyard.

They were escorted by a large party of both Grey and Douglas clansmen. It was unlikely under these circumstances that anyone would attack them. The trip, which might have taken two to three days riding, was made in seven days. It was at dusk on that seventh day that they approached the entry to the Glen of Gorm.

" 'Tis a lonely land," Orva noted. It had been a gray day, and now rain clouds were gathering overhead. She leaned forward to tuck a lap robe about Lady Grey.

"Aye, but it has its own wild beauty, even as my Highlands," Maggie MacLeod said. "I don't know what I would have done without you, Orva, these past few days. It has been a difficult trip, but you have made it so much easier for me. I thank you."

"Why did we not go straight to Ben Duff?" Orva asked her.

Maggie smiled. "Because the king would have me speak with your mistress," she answered. "He thinks I can influence her to his will."

"Do you think you can?" Orva asked quietly.

Lady Grey shook her head in the negative. "Your mistress is strong-willed. She will make her own decisions in this matter. She will listen politely, and then do precisely what she meant to do in the first place. But my conscience will be clear, for I will have done my best. The king will not be able to fault me. And if your mistress does what the king wants her to do he will credit me for her behavior." She laughed.

Orva chuckled. "You understand my child," she said. "Aye, she will do as she pleases."

"Does she like Fairlea enough to wed him?" Maggie asked, curious.

"She likes him well enough, but finds him a bit overbearing. Still, she knows she must marry, and he is a most suitable candidate," Orva replied.

"The king hopes she will wed him, and then spy among the Gordons for him," Lady Grey said quietly.

"Then Jamie Stewart is doomed to disappointment," Orva told her companion. "My mistress will be totally loyal to her husband. She would never tell tales. It is not in her nature. Now tell me, my lady, for we have spoken on everything else over the course of our journey, what is this wicked laddie who stole my mistress really like?"

Maggie MacLeod smiled warmly. "Ian Douglas is a good man. His clanfolk love and respect him. He is brave in war, honest and generous of heart. He is known here in the borders as *'the canny Douglas,'* for he is quite clever. And he will defend the woman he loves against all comers. Your mistress would not be unhappy with him."

"My mistress is probably still very angry at him," Orva said. "She does like getting her own way, and being dragged off into the wilds of this land will not be pleasing to her, I can promise you. The man will need the patience of a saint to win her over."

"My husband tells me that as a lad Ian tamed a fox kit. He would sit for hours in the heather observing the wee creature. He let it come to him rather than forcing himself on the little fox. I think he has patience enough, Orva."

They entered the glen, the little wagon rumbling down the narrow path. Sir William now rode ahead so that his kinsman could be made aware he was about to have company. He wondered what Ian was going to say to him. He wondered what Lady Cicely would say about her situation. Ian would not be able to refuse them hospitality, and poor Lady Grey needed a warm fire and a soft bed. Had the king not ordered them to Glengorm first, Sir William would have taken the Greys home to Ben Duff. He wasn't certain that Maggie MacLeod would be able to birth her husband's heir in her own bed. Seeing the house ahead he spurred his horse to hurry. The rain was beginning to fall.

Chapter 7

The house that Sir William's party would shortly enter was hardly the house that Ian Douglas had brought Cicely to nine days prior. As she sat by the fire in the hall that night digesting everything he had said to her, Cicely found his gentle words had done nothing to soften her anger. And then Bethia came stumbling down the stone stairs into the hall covered with soot and coughing heavily.

"The chimney in the lady's chamber will not draw, my lord," she told the laird. "It looks as if some bird or beastie has made its nest there."

"I am not surprised, given the condition of this hall," Cicely said dryly. "I suspect your stables are cleaner. It is obvious you have no control over your household."

Ian Douglas gritted his teeth. She was right, of course, but there hadn't been a woman managing his house since his grandmother had died when he was ten years old. Mab was really too old now, and Bethia lazy, but who would replace them? "You can sleep in my chamber, ladyfaire," he said.

"I will not!" she replied angrily. "How dare you even suggest such a thing? Will you destroy my reputation entirely, my lord?"

"I'll sleep in the hall," he told her. "You're my guest."

"Nay, I will sleep in the hall," Cicely said. "And I will remain in this hall until I am rescued from your clutches, my lord!"

"It should be a few days before anyone figures out what has happened to you, and we've already traveled several days," the laird said to her. "There'll be no fighting over you, ladyfaire. They will come to parley with me. And until we have come to know each other better I will not be of any mind to negotiate. I want nothing of you but your time, Cicely Bowen. If after we have come to know each other you decide I am not the man for you, I will reluctantly release you. I have never had to force a woman to my will, ladyfaire. I do not intend starting now. And to show you I am a man of my word who will accept your decisions, you may sleep in the hall tonight, if that is your preference."

"You are used to getting your way with women, aren't you, my lord?" Cicely said.

He gave her a slow, wicked smile. "Aye," he drawled. "I am."

"You will not get your way with me," she told him. Mother of God, he was the most irritating man she had ever met! But in a few days they would come for her, and she would tell him that if he were the last man on the face of the earth, she would sooner die a maiden than marry him. But in the meantime she would occupy her time in seeing that his hall was cleaned properly. She could not bear idle time on her hands.

"Come to the table, my lord." Bethia had shuffled back into the hall with another old lady. "Mab has done her best but 'twas short notice," she complained.

"Your lord sent ahead to you this morning," Cicely said sharply. "You had plenty of time to prepare a decent meal for him." Cicely seated herself at the high board next to the laird. "Where is a man to serve?" she demanded to know.

"Can you not help yourselves?" Bethia asked. "There is not so much upon the table that you need to be aided."

Cicely looked at the table. There was a small, cold joint of some animal, a loaf of bread, and a wedge of cheese. She shook her head despairingly. "I will serve you, my lord," she told him, reaching for the bread. When she began to slice it she discovered it was stale and crumbled beneath the knife. The cheese on closer inspection showed a spot of white mold, and the joint had the distinct unpleasant odor of rot about it. "This will not do," Cicely said angrily, standing up and shoving the food from the high board. The dish holding the joint shattered noisily upon the stone floor of the hall.

"Then you'll go hungry!" Bethia said, equally angry.

"There is no fresh bread baked? No cheese without mold?" Cicely demanded. The dogs in the hall had come to sniff at the joint on the floor. "Look, even the dogs refuse that piece of meat!" Cicely said, pointing as the three hounds walked away from it. She turned to the laird. "There is no excuse for this, my lord! None!"

"I agree," he said quietly. "Now, what will you do about it, ladyfaire?"

Cicely's first instinct was to tell him that he was the master in this place, but instead she stepped down from the high board. Her gaze went past Bethia to Mab. "Take me to the kitchens, woman. What is your name?"

"Mab, my lady," came the reply. "If you will follow me, please." She led the younger woman from the hall and down a flight of stone steps.

The kitchen was of a goodly size. There was a large oak table opposite a big hearth where a fire was burning. A large pot hung over the fire. A delicious fragrance was coming from it.

Cicely looked in and saw a potage with vegetables and chunks of meat bubbling away. "Have you any trenchers, Mab?" she asked.

Mab shook her head in the negative. "With no one here I do not bake daily," she said apologetically. "But I have wooden bowls to put the stew into, my lady."

"Why did you not serve it?" Cicely wanted to know. "It smells wonderful."

"Bethia said bread, a joint, and cheese would do," Mab replied.

"A hot meal after a long ride would have been preferable," Cicely noted. "Is there any other cheese?"

"I have a small wheel in the pantry," Mab answered. "Shall I bring it with the stew, my lady?" And she curtsied.

Cicely smiled slightly, and nodded. Then she turned to Bethia. "Clean up the mess you caused to be made before the high board," she said. Then she walked back upstairs to rejoin the laird. Oh, yes, there was much to be done here to put everything right. Bethia would have to go, and new servants brought in to serve the laird.

"Haughty bitch!" Bethia said angrily.

"You had best watch your tongue," Mab warned. "This is the girl he has talked about for weeks. He means to wed her, and she will be mistress here."

"She says she won't have him," Bethia said smugly.

Mab laughed. "Ha! More fool you if you believe that," she said. "The laird means to make her his wife, and believe me, in the end he will, Bethia. Do not make an enemy of she who will soon be our mistress."

"I'll not serve the English bitch," Bethia said angrily.

"Then you'll end up back in the village, and your husband—who prefers you here so he can live in peace with his old mother—will beat you for losing your place," Mab told the angry woman. "Frankly I'll be happy to see the back of you, Bethia Douglas."

"The laird needs me," Bethia said. "Who else can care for his house?"

"The laird needs a wife more than he needs you," Mab said with a toothless grin. "He'll win over the lass of his heart. I'll wager you'll be back with your man in a day or two." She cackled as she filled two wooden bowls with stew, took the small wheel of cheese from the pantry, and ascended the stairs back to the hall.

The laird thanked her as she set the bowls neatly before him and his guest. His eyebrow rose just slightly as she put the cheese upon the cutting board and curtsied. "Forgive me, my lord, for not serving you the potage, but Bethia said the other was good enough."

Ian Douglas dipped his spoon into the bowl and brought it to his lips. Swallowing it down, he smiled broadly. "You may be an old hag, Mab, but by the rood no one can cook as well as you can. 'Tis delicious!"

"Indeed it is," Cicely agreed. "Thank you, Mab. I hope you will always be here to cook for your master. But from now on you must live by your own rule. No one should tell you how to cook or what to serve but the laird. 'Tis your kitchen, after all."

"And I give you free rein for now to do as you please," the laird told the woman.

"Thank you, my lord!" Mab bobbed another curtsy. Then she said, "Would it be possible for me to have some help in my kitchen, my lord? I have been alone for months now, and I am, as you have observed, not as young as I once was."

"Find those who would suit, and bring them to Lady Cicely for her approval," the laird replied.

"My lord!" Cicely gave him a stern look, but the laird shrugged it off.

"Finding the right servants is a woman's task, ladyfaire. Please do this for me," he said in an almost pleading tone.

"Oh, very well, my lord," she finally agreed. "Having seen the disgraceful state of this house I cannot help but want to put it to rights. And you have asked me nicely. It is a challenge, and I do love a good challenge," Cicely told him.

"As do I," he replied meaningfully with a wicked grin in her direction.

Mab chuckled softly at their sparring. Aye, this lass was the right one for the laird despite being born on the other side of the border. She wouldn't crumble beneath his hand. She knew how to fight and defend herself. "I'll bring some folk in on the morrow for your approval, my lady," Mab said to Cicely.

"What is this?" Bethia demanded to know as she returned to the hall.

"My lady is to bring new servants into the house," Ian Douglas said to Bethia. "As you cannot get along with her you will return home tomorrow to your husband."

"My lord, I have served you faithfully!" Bethia cried.

"Your service was barely passable for a man alone," the laird told her, "but I was too lazy to correct you or make a change. Housewifery is not a man's task. You will have been paid at Michaelmas past for a year's service, and you may keep that coin, though you have rendered barely two months of that service."

Bethia threw aside the broom she had brought into the hall and stormed from their presence, muttering curses beneath her breath as she went.

They would pay! Oh, yes, they would pay. Brought to Glengorm as a captive, she had accepted her lot, married a Douglas, and been faithful. Did it really matter that she stole a wee bit here and there from her master to earn extra coin? All servants stole. Didn't he have more than one man needed? Those in the village were quick enough to purchase her goods. Yet despite her good service, she had been tossed into the road like so much refuse. She would find a way to repay the Douglas laird in kind if it took her years!

Mab picked up the broom and swept the remains of the meat platter, the rancid joint, the crumbling bread, and the moldy cheese into a pile. "I'll be back with a bucket to pick it up," she told them, and hurried from the hall on suddenly spry legs.

"You've made an ally," Ian Douglas said quietly.

"She's old yet hardworking and loyal," Cicely replied. "But Bethia is a bully. I am glad you sent her away. She would continue to cause trouble. Now let us eat before this potage grows any colder, my lord."

After the meal the laird attempted to convince Cicely to take his chamber for her own until the chimney serving his mother's rooms was cleaned and the chamber freshened, but she refused him.

"Tell me about your mother," she said, engaging him in conversation.

"I don't remember her," he said. "She died when I was barely a year, birthing my brother, Fergus. She was a Stewart. Our father died two years later. He was an honorable man, I am told. They were good but unremarkable people. Our grandfather Douglas was still alive, however, and Grandmam too. They raised us. I'm named for him. He taught us how to fight, how to drink, and how to wench. Our grandmam taught us manners. I am called the *canny* Douglas, for I am a careful and thoughtful man, but he was called the *wenching* Douglas." The laird chuckled. "And the women loved him for it, even Grandmam. No man alive could make a woman feel more beautiful or desirable than my grandfather. You'll hear the tale eventually, but he died in the bed of one of our village women. He brought her to total ecstasy, roared with his own pleasure, and then fell over dead. I do not think he ever thought about dying, but I suspect he appreciated the way in which he did."

"Your grandfather sounds like a wicked man, and you obviously take after him," Cicely said. Her cheeks were pink with his story of the *wenching* Douglas. What kind of man—or woman, for that matter—enjoyed coupling? Coupling was for the sole purpose of procreation. Certainly people didn't enjoy it.

"You're blushing," the laird noted.

"Your tale is indelicate. I am not some tavern wench you need to impress," Cicely said in a tight little voice.

He looked closely at her, and then he laughed softly. "Didn't anyone tell you, ladyfaire, that coupling is pleasing?"

Cicely's blush deepened. How had he known what

she was thinking? "My lord, our Holy Mother Church teaches that there is but one reason for coupling."

"And whom will you believe, ladyfaire? A man who has coupled with many women, or a dried-up old husk of a priest whose cock is but a conduit for peeing?"

"You speak blasphemy, my lord!" She stepped down from the high board and made her way across the hall towards the hearth.

He caught up with her in a single moment, spinning her about to face him. "There is no blasphemy in passion. Your friend the queen would tell you that if you asked her." Wrapping an arm about her, he pulled her to him. The knuckles of his other hand gently grazed down her soft cheek as he momentarily lost himself in her blue-green eyes.

Holy Mother! Cicely thought as she realized how hard the body pressed against hers was. And it felt so right, yet how could it be? This brazen laird had no right to handle her in such a way! But while her heart was beating fiercely, she realized that he excited her, and part of her wondered how far he would go. If the truth be told, Andrew Gordon had never excited her like this. But it was wrong! Wrong! Wrong! Wrong! "Unhand me, my lord!" Cicely said in what she hoped was a stern tone.

His arm dropped from her waist, but before she could move his two hands captured her small face between them. His mouth closed over hers, and he kissed her fiercely. The full, soft lips beneath his yielded reluctantly, but they yielded. Finally lifting his head, he stared down into her face. "Was that blasphemous, ladyfaire?" he asked softly. Then, turning away from her, he walked from the hall, leaving her alone.

For a long moment Cicely stood rooted to the spot where she was standing. Then, stumbling to the fireplace, she sank down into a chair. What was the matter with her? She should have slapped his arrogant face for daring to kiss her. She was practically promised to another man. But was she? Did she really want to wed Andrew

Gordon? The king wanted her to wed him, although Cicely knew he would not force her to it. And she was not so much of a fool that she didn't realize the king would want her to spy on the Gordons to make certain they remained loyal. But if she married into Clan Gordon, she would be loyal to her husband's family—unless they attempted to betray James Stewart—but she could not report their daily activities, or who their guests were. And was Andrew Gordon really the man for her?

Oh, yes, he was handsome enough. He could speak French with her, and he wrote passable poetry he liked to recite. But he was also a little haughty, and had been dismissive of her attempts to speak with him on more serious matters. Sometimes Andrew gave her the impression that he was doing her a great favor by considering her for his wife. And he had already attempted to exert control of her by pressing her into this marriage, which was why she had hesitated. He did kiss nicely, however, and while his first kisses had been delightful, for she had never been kissed before, they had not thrilled her from her head to her toes the way that Ian Douglas's kisses had.

But the laird of Glengorm was a barbarian! He had kidnapped her from Perth. Made her ride at breakneck speed for almost three days, trussed up much of the way like a doe ready for butchering. He had made her sleep on the cold ground, and starved her. Had they not reached this house she was certain she would have had chilblains on her hands in another day. His servants were slovenly. His home filthy. And she was tired and cold. Cicely began to cry softly. Never in her life had she been treated so ill.

And what was the cause of all her misery? Men! Andrew Gordon, who behaved as if she were his possession, chasing away any others who would pay her court. And Ian Douglas, who snatched her from Mistress Marjory's shop, and had already commenced his rough wooing of her with his heated kisses. *Well!* She wouldn't have either of them! Cicely wasn't even certain now that she wanted a husband. But she knew she wasn't about to give herself to the Church either. So a husband she would have to have, sooner or later.

The chair in which Cicely sat was sturdy oak with carved armrests. It had a padded back of leather, and a loose cushioned seat with a rough woven cover. The girl seated in it sighed sadly. Her head fell to one side as her eyes closed and an exhausted sleep overcame her, her cheeks still wet with her tears.

Old Mab crept silently into the hall with an armful of wood. She added some to the fire, and stacked the remainder on the hearth. She pulled a large woolen shawl in the black-gray-and-white Douglas plaid from her hunched shoulders, and tucked it about Cicely. Then, sitting down in the smaller chair near the fire, the old woman drew her own worn shawl about her shoulders and settled down for the night. Now and again she would awaken and throw another log on the fire.

When the false dawn touched the sky Mab rose from long habit and, going down into the kitchen, took a bowl of dough from the table where she had left it to rise beneath a damp cloth several hours back. Kneading it with half-crippled fingers, she fashioned several loaves and put them into the oven to bake. Her lady would have fresh bread each day from now on. Her nephew's lad came into the kitchen bearing a basket of newly laid eggs. "Good morrow, Gabhan," Mab greeted the boy.

"Good morrow to you, Auntie," the boy replied. "Bethia returned to the village last night. She has gone from cottage to cottage saying the laird's new whore threw her from the house and threatened to kill her. She showed us the bruises the whore inflicted upon her. She says she fears for the laird, for he has been ensorcelled."

Mab snorted. "Bethia's bruises are probably from the beating her husband gave her when she returned home to tell him the laird sent her away for her slovenly ways, and ill temper towards the lass he means to wed. The

laird went bride stealing, Gabhan, and brought back a
fine lady from King James's court."

"She is not a whore?" The boy sounded almost disappointed. He had never seen a whore, but they did sound
both dangerous and exotic to him.

"Nay, Lady Cicely is a grand lady, laddie. Bethia has
been dismissed because she is lazy and dirty, and was
sullen and rude. It was the laird who sent her from the
house. Go to the cold larder now for me, and get me
both milk and cream," Mab said to the boy. "The bread
is baking, and I am making eggs with cream sauce to go
with the porridge."

"Bethia says no one should come into service here
until the whore is driven out," Gabhan said. He went
into the cold larder and brought out a pitcher of milk
and one of heavy cream, which he set on the large oak
table. "Mmmm, that bread smells good, Auntie. When
will it be done?" He grinned at her.

" 'Twill be done when it's done. Now go back to the
village and tell all the young lasses and lads to whom we
are closest related that the laird needs new servants for
the house. There will be a nice slice of fresh bread and
butter—with jam—for you when you return with our
kin. I'll do the first choosing. Then it's up to the laird and
his bride. Off with you now," Mab said, shooing him from
her kitchen with her apron. *There!* she thought after he
had gone. *Our own kin will fill the places needed. I want
none of Bethia's people here, and neither will the lady.*

Cicely awoke surprised to find a warm fire still burning, and a thick plaid shawl wrapped about her. Where
had they come from? She stood stiffly, and stretched
in an effort to ease the soreness from her limbs. Her
nose twitched at the distinct smell of baking bread. She
needed to pee, but had no idea where to perform such
an act, so she directed her steps to the kitchens, for she
knew Mab could help her.

"Oh, my lady, you're awake," Mab said. "Good morrow to you." She curtsied.

"I need somewhere to freshen myself," Cicely said shyly.

"Of course," the old lady replied. She led the young woman to a tiny room off her kitchen. "In there. I'll bring you some warm water."

She relieved herself in the pot, and was glad for the basin of warm water Mab brought her. She washed herself as best as she could. Her hair was filthy, and filled with dust from their long ride. She wondered if a bath was possible. Removing her caul, Cicely let her hair fall loose about her, then, combing it with her fingers, tucked it back into the bejeweled gold net. Cicely brushed her green velvet gown with her hands, shaking her skirts, pulling the embroidered surcoat straight. She had never worn the same gown for so long. She stepped from the small room back into the kitchens and was surprised to see a dozen young men and women now crowding into the warm gathering place.

"My lady, these young people are from the village. They have come to see if they might fill the positions vacant for so long in our staff," Mab said. "How many of them shall I bid remain?"

"All of them," Cicely responded. "There is a great deal to do to put this house back to rights and keep it well. Please feed them, Mab, and then after the laird has broken his fast send them up to the hall." Then, with a nod of her head and a smile, Cicely ascended the stairs and was gone from their sight.

"She seems a nice enough lass, though she be English," a voice commented.

"She's a good lady," Mab said.

"And she asked you to feed us first," said another voice.

"'Twas well-done," remarked a third approvingly.

"Well, sit you down at the table," Mab said. "I've fresh bread, cheese, and hard-boiled eggs, as well as a nice pot of porridge. Eat up now, and then two of you can serve the hall. The laird is always up with the sun. And you want to get started with your work as soon as he's spoken to you. Gabhan, you're still small enough to sweep a chimney," Mab told the boy as she put the bowl of eggs on the table and began cutting slices of bread. "The one in the room her ladyship will occupy has a nest in it that needs removing. Do you think you can do it?"

The boy nodded agreeably. "Aye," he said. "I'll be the house's sweep, and you'll need a knife boy too, Auntie. I can fill both positions."

"You're a good lad," Mab said as she handed him the promised bread with butter and jam. She looked about the table. "Tam, you and Artair can serve the hall this morning. Sine and Sesi will clean the apartment that once belonged to the laird's poor mam. The lady will live there. The poor lass slept last night in the hall. The rest of you will go before the laird and his lady after they have eaten. Eat up now! There's work to be done here. Who among you will serve in the stables?"

Cicely returned to the hall just as Ian Douglas entered it. "Good morrow, my lord," she greeted him, curtsying. "Thank you for putting the shawl about me last night."

"Good morrow, ladyfaire," he replied, "but I gave you no shawl."

"Then who did?" And then Cicely smiled. "Of course! It had to be Mab, and she will have kept the fire going, bless her! The meal will be served shortly. The fresh bread was just about to come from the ovens, my lord, and the kitchen is full of young people eager to serve you. You will help me choose after we have eaten."

Ian Douglas could not remember the last time he had been greeted so pleasantly in his own hall in early morning. And even from here he could smell the freshly baked bread. He smiled broadly. "You see, ladyfaire," he told her. "A woman's touch is just what has been needed here at Glengorm."

"And you will remember that I will not bide long with you, my lord. The king will send a troop of men-at-arms to rescue me from your clutches, and I will go with them. You cannot hold me here forever."

Before he might reply, however, Mab appeared in the hall carrying bowls, spoons, and two silver cups that had been newly polished. She set the high board, saying, "The meal is coming behind me, my lord, my lady. Please be seated. With your permission I have assigned two young men from the village, Tam and Artair, to serve at table. If they do not suit I will find two others."

Tam and Artair now came into the hall carrying a bowl and two platters. Behind them Gabhan carried a board with fresh bread, a crock of sweet butter, and a small wedge of cheese. He sneaked a long look at Cicely, deciding whether she was a whore, as Bethia said she was. But if, as his old auntie related, she was to be the laird's wife then Ian Douglas was a fortunate man, for the lady was certainly the prettiest lass he had ever seen.

The hot food was set upon the table. One platter held slices of ham, the other eggs poached in cream sauce with dill. The bowl was filled with steaming porridge.

"My lady?" The lad called Tam offered to spoon some porridge into Cicely's bowl. When she nodded he spooned in a small but adequate amount and then looked to her. "'Tis enough, my lady?" he inquired politely.

"Aye, 'tis perfect. Thank you," Cicely responded.

"Cream?" Tam asked, holding a small pitcher, and when she nodded he poured some, again seeking her approval, and smiling when she nodded once more.

Tam then filled the laird's bowl almost full with the hot cereal and heavy cream. Then he stepped back to await further instructions.

They ate in silence, and when the bowls were emptied Tam removed them swiftly, and his companion, Artair, offered the eggs and the meat while Tam sliced bread.

"I'm astounded by this meal," the laird finally said to Cicely.

"Why?" she responded. "Mab is a wonderful cook, but she was being bullied by Bethia, who I will wager was stealing from your larder, so that you ended up being poorly fed while she profited by selling in the village what she stole," Cicely reasoned, and, seeing the quick look pass between the two young servants, she knew she was right.

"You know I love you, for I have said it," Ian murmured to her. "Now do you see how much I need you to care for me, ladyfaire?"

Cicely was forced to laugh at his declaration. "While I am reluctant to admit it, you have charm, my lord," she said. "But Glengorm is not at all the home I envisioned for my married life."

"Then make of it what you want," he said to her. "Have you been to Fairlea's home? Is it any better?"

"I have not been to Andrew Gordon's house," Cicely admitted, "but I am certain it is clean, and his servants well trained. A man who keeps himself neat will surely have a well-ordered domicile, my lord."

"Would you marry into such a house knowing that though you are mistress, its lord would always have the last word?" he inquired of her. "In my house you would have full autonomy over the servants, for as a man I am but interested in a hot meal and a warm bed. Fairlea, I will wager, is concerned with every small detail of *his* life and *his* possessions, ladyfaire."

Cicely was silent. The truth was, he did make a strong point about the laird of Fairlea, and how could he have come to know the man that well in such a short time at court? That was a question she asked Ian Douglas.

"I know men, ladyfaire," he said quietly. "Life here in the borders is not easy, and you need to be able to read other men quickly to know if you deal with friend or foe. The laird of Fairlea is a proud man. Proud of his name and of himself. It is obvious by the way he dresses, by the way he speaks with others that he holds himself in high regard. And he judges others by his own standards. He considers your beauty and wealth worthy of him, but he is not quite as sure of himself as he would have all believe. That is why he kept other suitors from your side, ladyfaire. And that is why it was necessary for me to resort to such reckless measures."

"Andrew is a proud man, but the Gordons are one of the finest families in Scotland," Cicely defended her other suitor. But Ian Douglas was right about his rival. Still, did not a man have a right to be proud of himself and his possessions?

"Fairlea is a fool," Ian Douglas said frankly. "If he were not he would have swept you off to the priest long since, ladyfaire."

"Priest? Who speaks of a priest in such bold tones?"

A tall man in a long black robe tied with a white rope belt strode into the hall. "God's balls! Is that decent food on your table, Ian? I had heard you finally sent Bethia back to her husband, poor fellow. Ahh, and this will be the bride." The tall man grinned and gave her a scant bow. "Father Ambrose, at your service, my lady." He settled himself at the table next to Ian, shoveling the remaining eggs onto the platter that still contained two slices of ham, and then he began to eat.

"I did tell you that we had a priest," Ian Douglas said.

"Bless me," the priest said, "old Mab hasn't lost her touch in the kitchens." He closed his eyes briefly, savoring the sauce on the eggs.

"He looks like you," Cicely finally said.

"I should, my lady," Father Ambrose, said with another grin, "for I am this rascal's uncle. The last of the wenching Douglas's bastards. It was only natural I go into the Church to make up for my old father's sins." He chuckled. "Welcome to Glengorm! I will wager no one has said that to you yet."

"Nay, they haven't, thank you," Cicely replied, warming immediately to the priest. "Now I should be most appreciative if you would tell your nephew to return me to Perth. He probably won't even have to go the entire way, for the king will have sent after me by now, you may be certain."

"Regretfully, my child, Ian does not take direction well, I fear." Then he turned to the laird. "Why in the name of all that is holy have you stolen a bride that King James will want to retrieve, nephew?"

"I love her," Ian Douglas answered his uncle. "It is said our king fell in love with his queen at first sight, and so it is with me. I saw my ladyfaire on the road to Perth the day I pledged my fealty to King James. And in that moment, Uncle, I knew no other woman would do for me. I went to court to woo her, but some damned Gordon had already marked her for himself. No other man could get near her. I had no choice but to abduct her and bring her to Glengorm."

"Are you betrothed, my child?" Father Ambrose asked Cicely.

"Nay, Father, I am not. I made no promise to Andrew Gordon, though he did beseech me to pledge myself to him," Cicely replied honestly.

"Do you love this Andrew Gordon?" the priest inquired.

Cicely hesitated. Then she answered candidly, "Nay, I do not believe that I do. But you know that love is not the point of marriage. Marriage is for procreation. Matches are made for wealth, land, power, good Father."

"More's the pity," the priest answered her, thinking she was a true daughter of privilege and had been well taught. "It is said that the king loves his queen. Is that so?"

"Oh, yes, he loves her deeply, and she him," Cicely said. "And my own father loved my mother, but when he married a second time it was for more practical reasons."

The priest sighed. "So you have two men who would have you to wife. One has declared his love for you. Has the other?"

Cicely shook her head in the negative. "Nay, Andrew has not said he loves me."

"You say you would wed for sensible reasons," Father Ambrose said. "And you claim to love neither of your suitors. Yet you must wed, so why would you not wed the man who claims he loves you as opposed to the one who has not said those three words so dear to a maiden's simple heart?"

His argument gave Cicely pause for thought.

"At last!" Ian gloated. "Someone to take my side in this matter."

"Of course he would take your side," Cicely snapped. "He is your blood kin."

"If Mab is going to continue to cook like this," the priest said, "I shall take my meals with you." He snatched up the last crust of bread, scraped the remaining butter from its stone crock with his thumb, and spread it over the bread before popping it into his mouth, chewing with great relish.

When Tam and Artair had cleared the table, Mab returned to the hall with a group of young men and women. "Good morrow, my lord, my lady, Father Ambrose," she said. "I have brought you this group of men and women eager to enter your service, my lord, my lady. They are hardworking and honest, and will not steal, like some others who shall remain unmentioned." Tam had told Mab of Cicely's intuitive remark. She curtsied to the laird, and waved half a dozen girls forward. "I should like Bessie and Flora to remain in the kitchens with me. Sine, Sesi, Una, and Effie are more than competent to work above stairs, if it please Your Ladyship." She curtsied again.

Cicely turned to Ian. "My lord?"

"'Tis your choice, ladyfaire," he replied.

"They are all Mab's nearest kin, and good choices," Father Ambrose murmured softly.

"The laird is pleased to welcome these girls into his

service. And Tam and Artair have done well this morning. Who are the others, Mab?" Cicely asked the old lady.

"My nephew's lad, Gabhan, who will sweep the chimneys and keep the knives sharp," she said, pulling Gabhan forward. He ducked his head to the high board.

"He looks a fine lad," Cicely responded. "He is welcome."

"The other lads will care for the stables, my lady," Mab told her.

"You have done well, Mab, and the laird thanks you. Thank you all." She stood up from the high board. "Come along, lasses. We have a full day's work ahead of us."

"You will work with them?" The laird was surprised.

"I am nobly born and nobly raised, Ian Douglas," Cicely said. "But I was brought up in the household of Queen Joan of Navarre, who did not tolerate sloth or idleness. She believed that for a woman to direct her household she must know exactly how all that needed to be done was done. I will teach these lasses the proper way to keep your household so that when I return to Perth your home will not fall into slovenliness again."

"Ah, nephew, I see your lass is a stubborn girl," the priest said softly, and he chuckled wickedly. It was a most unpriestly sound.

"When that time comes, ladyfaire, you will not want to return to Perth," the laird said, "for your heart will be mine, as mine is already yours."

Cicely shook her head. "I have never known a man so big or so softhearted as you are, my lord. You are a conundrum." But she gave him a small smile as she turned and, gathering the young maidservants to her, began to direct them in their duties.

"You have discovered a treasure for yourself, Ian," the priest said, low. "Now you must find a way to keep her. Will the king send after her?"

"Undoubtedly," the laird answered his uncle. "My ladyfaire is Queen Joan's best friend. They were raised together."

"Sweet Jesu!" the priest exclaimed. "Could you not have fallen in love with an ordinary lady, nephew? Aye, they'll be coming for her, and for your head as well."

"She's mine," Ian Douglas said, and his eyes went to Cicely, who was now showing the new maidservants the proper way to polish his ancient oak sideboard. "Look at her, Uncle. Does she not belong here in this hall directing her staff? I will give her anything she wants to make this the home to suit her."

"Perhaps if you get lucky we'll have an early winter, and they'll have to leave her until the spring. That will give you time to work your wiles on the lady. Aye, that's your only hope, Ian. And I'm going to pray for it," Ambrose Douglas said.

By day's end the hall was cleaner than it had been in years. But while Cicely had worked side by side with her new maidservants, old Mab had sent for several of her older relations, for she was determined that the lady not spend another uncomfortable night in the hall. Mab meant to see that the bedchamber was ready for an occupant.

Gabhan spent half of his day in the chimney that drew the hearth in the bedchamber. He swept the passage free of soot, and removed several birds' nests, one built on top of another. Then he lit a small torch and, stooping down, held it to see if the chimney would now draw properly. When he saw it did he notified Mab, and immediately a trio of women he recognized as his own kin hurried to the chamber with mops, buckets, and brooms to sweep, wash, and dust its furniture, window, and floor.

By day's end the bedchamber was clean, a bright fire burning merrily in its hearth. The room had a lead-paned double window that could be opened by swinging the twin halves out. The window had a wide

stone sill. There was a large, comfortable oak bed-
stead with a tall linen-fold headboard and two turned
posts at its foot to hold up the plain wood canopy.
The natural-colored linen bed curtains that old Mab
found in a trunk had seen better days, but they were
clean and serviceable. Mab set Gabhan to polishing
the brass curtain rings, and when he was done the bed
curtains were hung.

There was a small round oak table by the bed. It was
now topped by a small brass candlestick that contained
a short beeswax candle. There was a beautiful brass-
bound trunk at the foot of the bed and a single tapestry-
backed oak chair by the hearth. The rope springs on the
bed were tightened, and a newly made mattress placed
upon it, along with a feather bed. Fresh linens, plump
pillows, and a warm comforter completed the bed.

Mab came to inspect her relations' hard work. "Ah,
cousins, you've done well, and I thank you for it. Her
Ladyship will be most comfortable here."

"You like the lass," one of her kin said. "I saw her in
the hall with my daughter and the others scrubbing with
her own hands. For all she is a lady she has no fear of
hard work," the woman noted approvingly.

"She'll make a grand mistress for Glengorm House,"
Mab said.

"If she'll have him," another of the women said. "I
heard the king is sending to fetch her back to her mistress, the queen."

"The laird needs but a bit of time with her," Mab replied. "He'll win her over."

"I hope our laird does," the first woman agreed.

"She looks strong too," the third woman said. "She'll
give Glengorm heirs. I'll not rest easy until we have
them, and know we're safe for another generation."

The others nodded in agreement with her. Then Mab
had them pick up their brooms, buckets, and mops, and
they returned them to the kitchens, departing for their
own cottages in the village. Cicely had sent the maid-

servants home just before dark. The servants' quarters weren't ready for them yet, and after all the hard work they had done that day she felt they deserved a comfortable bed to sleep in this night.

Mab came back up from the kitchens to see Cicely walking slowly about the hall, taking the measure of it, inspecting it all, her hand running over an ancient sideboard as she wore a smile that bespoke her pleasure in a job well-done. "My lady," Mab addressed the girl.

Cicely looked up. "Aye, Mab, what is it?"

"Will you come with me for but a moment, my lady?" And when Cicely nodded Mab led her upstairs and to the chamber that had once been the room of Ian and Fergus Douglas's mother. Opening the door, she ushered the girl inside. "We cleaned and freshened the chamber today. You cannot continue to sleep in the hall, my lady. 'Tis not right that you should. This chamber belonged to the lady before you," she said.

Cicely looked slowly around. The fire had warmed the room. Beyond the windows she saw the blazing horizon, the sun gone. The room had been aired. The floors were spotless. And the bed! Ohh, how comfortable that bed looked. She was startled to feel Mab's hand touch hers. The old lady was handing her a key.

" 'Tis yours, my lady," she said quietly. "The door can be locked from the inside."

"Is there a tub that might be brought to this chamber so I could bathe?" she asked. "I am filthy from my travels, and especially from my exertions today."

"Will you bathe now or after the meal?" Mab asked her.

"After," Cicely quickly said. " 'Twill give everyone more time to prepare it for me. Oh, Mab! How can I thank you for this? And you must thank your helpers too."

Mab smiled, very well pleased. This was the first step in making the lady comfortable, and certainly she would be more amenable if she were content at Glengorm. But instead she said, "It were a mercy you didn't catch an ague in that hall last night."

"You were there too," Cicely replied, knowing who had kept the fire going, and who had covered her with that thick woolen shawl. "It seems I owe you much."

"After the meal I'll take your garments, my lady, wash what I can, and brush what I can't," Mab told her. Then she bustled off, leaving Cicely to examine her chamber more closely.

The meal that evening was a merry one. Suddenly there were men-at-arms coming into the hall to be fed. The word had quickly spread that Bethia had been sent home, and that Mab was cooking again without interference. There was venison stew, bread, and cheese below the high board. There was a capon and trout at the high board, along with a salad of braised lettuces, bread, butter, and cheese. And Mab had found the time to bake apples for the laird, which she knew were his favorite. Ale flowed generously to the men. Cicely drank red wine.

Father Ambrose, true to his word, was the first into the hall, and ready for his meal. He did it full justice, mopping his pewter plate with bread until it seemed as clean as if it had been scoured in the kitchen sink with sand. There were six baked apples, and having devoured two the priest gleefully took the last one from the platter as the laird eyed it for himself. Ian's look of disappointment, and the priest's chortle of triumph, made Cicely laugh. Ambrose Douglas grinned conspiratorially at her.

"Is not greed a sin?" the laird asked dryly.

"I'll give myself a penance," Ambrose replied. He turned to Cicely. "Will you come to Mass in the morning? I have a small church in the village, and I say the Mass daily. If you follow the path from the house down the hill you will find the church at its foot. I will absolve you from daily attendance for now, but do come and satisfy the villagers' curiosity. Bethia is claiming you are a wicked whore, while those who have met you cannot say enough good things about your character," the priest told her.

"I'll have Mab awaken me," Cicely said. Then she arose from the board. "I would go to my chamber, my lord. I am exhausted, and I have a lovely bath waiting."

The laird nodded. "The hall has not looked so well in my entire lifetime," he told her. "Thank you."

Cicely curtsied, and departed their company.

"She has a bath waiting? How did she manage that?" Ian Douglas said to his uncle. "If I want a bath I have to swim in the loch."

"Perhaps you have never asked as nicely as she has for what she wants, nephew. You roar your orders. The lady is courteous. She asks and she says thank you. I am pleased you thanked her for what she did this day. It was well-done, and if you continue to behave in a civilized manner you may have a chance with her."

"She's sleeping in my mother's chamber tonight," the laird said slowly.

"Aye, Mab and her kin spent the day cleaning. The lad Gabhan swept the chimney directly after the morning meal. I am told he removed three rooks' nests," the priest said. "Then the women cleaned and freshened the chamber for the lady. She will be comfortable tonight, and if she begins to become more content and your rough manners improve, you will please her well."

"Ambrose, I have never felt this way before," the younger man admitted. "It isn't just lust, though I will admit to wanting to bed her. I know that compared to Gordon I am roughshod and wild. But if she came to me in nothing but her chemise I would want her to wife. She is beautiful, is she not? That rich auburn hair! Those blue-green eyes! I could lose myself in those eyes forever, Uncle. At the sound of her sweet voice my heart leaps. Even when she is scolding me." He laughed ruefully. "I do not believe that I can live without my ladyfaire."

"God's balls, nephew!" Ambrose Douglas exclaimed.

"You are indeed in love, and may God and his Blessed Mother have mercy upon you. Well, you probably have two or three days in which to win your ladyfaire over. I will pray that you can." He arose. "Well, I am off to my bed, having been so well fed. It probably wouldn't harm your cause to come to Mass on the morrow." Then the priest strode out of the hall.

The laird came down from his high board and sat for a brief few minutes by the fire. Aye, he would go to Mass tomorrow. It would please his ladyfaire, he had not a doubt. He thought of Andrew Gordon. He didn't want to be like him, but certainly he could change enough to win Cicely over. *"Cicely,"* he whispered her name aloud.

"If you need nothing more, my lord, I will go to my kitchens." Mab was by his side. "The lady is settled."

"What are you carrying?" he asked.

"Her clothing. It needs attention, for she had been wearing it for several days. I found a chemise that belonged to your mother, and gave it to her to sleep in. You mother has been gone for years, yet there this garment was, neat and clean, in the trunk." She curtsied and left him after seeing there was nothing more he needed.

The laird stood up. It was time to make his rounds to ascertain that the house was safe for the night. He barred the doors. Snuffed the candles. Banked the fire in the hall and ascended the stairs to his bedchamber. In the upstairs hallway he heard her singing softly, and determined to stop so he might bid her good night. Knocking upon her door, he opened it and stepped into the chamber.

"My lord!" Cicely scrunched down in the small oak tub, clutching the washing cloth to her breasts. *Blessed Mother!* She had never felt so vulnerable in all of her life as she did at this very minute. Would he force her to his will, thereby sealing her fate?

"I came to say good night," Ian said, as if bidding such a sentiment to a lady in her bath were quite normal, and something he did regularly. "Do not worry, ladyfaire.

You are so hunched over there is little but the grace-ful angle of your back that is visible to me." He grinned wickedly. "That and your beautiful, outraged face."

"Go away!" she said, attempting to shrink herself fur-ther from his bold look.

"I can see you will need a larger tub," he said thought-fully. "I will order the cooper in the village to begin building one tomorrow, madam."

"Do not waste his time," Cicely snapped. "I will cer-tainly be returning to Perth shortly, my lord. I'm quite certain the king's men will be here for me tomorrow."

Ian could scarcely take his eyes from her. Her rich, long auburn hair piled atop her head, obviously newly washed. The creaminess of her skin. And those blue-green eyes! He watched those eyes widen as he walked to where she sat in the small tub. She almost cowered from him as he reached out to tip her face to his. She was helpless to resist him else she reveal that which should not be seen. He bent, and his lips touched hers, gently at first, and then more fiercely.

Her heart was beating so rapidly that she could hear the sound of it in her ears, but when his mouth closed over hers Cicely could not resist kissing him back. *Blessed Mother,* she thought to herself. *What am I doing?* But she simply couldn't help herself. There was something so compelling about his kiss, she was unable to withstand him.

He broke off the embrace, smiling down into her face. "Good night, ladyfaire," he said, and then he left her.

Cicely sat in the cooling tub for several minutes. This was madness. It had to stop. His kisses left her weak-ened. And what would happen when he did not stop at one kiss? What would happen if one kiss blended into another and another? The very thought of it made her sigh with longing, and that was terrible. Did their kiss make him feel the same way as she did? Probably not. Men were freer with their kisses than respectable girls were. And again the notion slipped into her thoughts that Andrew Gordon had never made her feel the way Ian Douglas did.

She had to escape the laird of Glengorm before she allowed herself to do something very foolish. Surely her rescuers would be here tomorrow.

But they were not. It wasn't until the tenth day of her captivity that Sir William Douglas and his party rode into Glengorm, even as an icy rain was beginning to fall.

Chapter 8

$\mathcal{M}$aggie MacLeod, wife to Andrew Grey, laird of Ben Duff, was helped into Glengorm's hall, supported by her husband and Orva. The child in her belly was going to be born soon, and there was no denying it. The hall was warm and inviting. Once Maggie was safely seated by the hearth Orva looked about. She and Cicely spotted each other at the same time, and flew into each other's arms.

"Ohh, my baby, have you been harmed?" Orva said, stepping back and looking her young mistress over carefully. "I will kill the brute myself with my bare hands!"

"Only my pride," Cicely said wryly. Taking Orva's hand, she walked across the hall to where her guests were being greeted by Ian Douglas. "Maggie." She signaled to Tam to bring refreshments. "You are as pale as the moon."

"I think my bairn is coming," Maggie said softly. "Perhaps I'm just weary, so make no fuss lest you frighten my poor Andrew." She accepted a small dram of whiskey that Tam offered her and, sipping it, closed her eyes.

"I'll have a chamber made ready for you," Cicely said. "Tam, fetch Sine to me."

"You speak like the mistress here," Maggie noted.

"I have spent my time awaiting my rescue putting the

laird's house in order. It was a pigsty when we arrived ten days ago. I've brought in staff from the village, and the laird sent the housekeeper, a nasty creature named Bethia, packing. The cook, Mab, has been a godsend. Who is that with your husband?"

"Sir William Douglas, clan chief of this branch of the Douglases. He's been sent by the king to reason with your laird," Maggie said.

"There is no reasoning with Ian Douglas," Cicely replied tartly. "The man is impossible! He insists he loves me, and that he will wed me."

"Well," Maggie said, "you must have a husband, and you couldn't seem to make up your mind about the Gordon of Fairlea. Do you like Ian?"

"I don't dislike him," Cicely evaded.

Maggie laughed softly. "I can see his charm is beginning to touch you," she said. "Has he made any overtures towards you?"

"He kisses me," Cicely replied.

"And do you like it?" Maggie probed.

"Aye, I do," Cicely admitted. "I shouldn't! But I do. He doesn't force himself on me. Suddenly he is there, and kissing me. One kiss. No more, but oh, Blessed Mother, how sweet that kiss is. 'Tis nothing at all like Andrew Gordon. His kisses were quite nice, but after the first time I never tingled. With this wretched border lord I tingle from the top of my head to the soles of my feet each time he kisses me. And I shouldn't!"

"Why not?" Maggie asked innocently.

"Because I shouldn't!" Cicely said vehemently. "He's practically no better than a bandit, Maggie."

"I've known Ian Douglas ever since I came into the border from my Highlands and married my Andrew Grey," Maggie said. "He is respected, and well thought of by his fellow border lords, Cicely."

"He isn't a suitable husband for me at all," Cicely said.

"Why not?" Maggie inquired.

"He's a ruffian," Cicely declared.

"Most Scotsmen are." Maggie chuckled.

"His family has no stature," Cicely said.

"The Douglases are very loyal to the king. If they were not he would not have entrusted Sir William to come and reason with his kinsman in this matter," Maggie pointed out. "The Gordons, on the other hand, cannot always be trusted. They live in the eastern Highlands, and their loyalties are often torn between Scotland's kings and the great Highland lords who rule more like kings from their lands."

"The king, I think, wants me to marry Andrew Gordon," Cicely said.

"Do you love him?"

"Nay, I don't, but is not love the exception to the rule when one marries? The queen is the best friend I have ever had. I was sent away when I was barely seven, because even though I did not live in my father's house, I lived on his estates. My stepmother, Luciana, hated me before she even met me. She was very jealous of any attention my father lavished upon me. She accused me of trying to kill my little brothers. My father knew then that if I were to be kept safe I would have to be sent away. I entered Queen Johanna's house at the same time Lady Joan Beaufort did. We became friends immediately.

"Jo did not have to bring me to Scotland with her. I might have been left behind. But my stepmother bore my father a fourth child, this time a girl. My father begged the Beauforts to see that I went with the new Queen Joan, for Luciana began anew to fret about my small presence in their life. Oh, she had been happy enough when I used my tiny influence to get my little half brothers places at court. Fortunately King James agreed I might go with them. While it is my decision whom I marry, my father asked the king to see that I married well. I think, like the king, he would want me to wed where I might be of use to the Stewarts." Cicely sighed. "But I will admit, Maggie, that after these few days Ian Douglas is growing on me. The *canny* Douglas does have his charms."

"If your father gave you the right to choose your husband, then you must choose the man who will make you happiest, Cicely. But if you would be practical, be warned that the Gordons will do what is best for the Gordons, and not necessarily Scotland," Maggie advised the young Englishwoman. "The Douglases stand firmly for King James."

"But one of the king's best friends is a Gordon," Cicely said. "The laird of Loch Brae, who was in England with him for a time when they were boys."

A shadow crossed Maggie's pretty face. "If the laird of Loch Brae knew the secret I keep for the king they would no longer be friends," she said, low. Then, seeing the curiosity in Cicely's eyes, she held up her hand. "Nay, do not ask, for I will never divulge it. Just trust me when I tell you that you are better off with Ian Douglas than you would be with your Gordon suitor." She shifted uncomfortably in her chair. She felt a little better now that she was warm and dry. But she still did not believe she would reach Ben Duff in time to birth her child there. "I believe my bairn will be born here," she told Cicely.

"We can help you and keep you safe," Cicely promised.

"My lady." Sine was by her side.

"See that a bedchamber is made ready for Lady Grey. She believes it is possible her child will be born here shortly. Ask Mab what is needed, and see that it is upstairs for us."

"At once, my lady," Sine said, and she curtsied.

Orva now came to be with them. "How do you feel now, my lady?" she asked Maggie solicitously. "Your color is coming back."

"I'm better, but the child will be born here," Maggie said. "I can go no farther."

Orva nodded understandingly. Then she turned to

her mistress. "I have brought a trunk of garments for you," she said quietly.

"But we shall not be here long," Cicely insisted. "Although I will say I am glad of clean clothing, for I have worn this same gown since I was taken from Perth. Mab has done her best to keep it fresh. Oh, Orva, you will like her! She is the cook, and has been my friend since the day I arrived."

"Well, thank goodness for that, for I have been worried sick about you." She paused. "This laird is a bold man, but as long as he has not harmed you I am content. Sir William Douglas, the older gentleman who brought us to Glengorm, is his clan chief. He will see all is made right, my dearie. The king has sent him to bring you back to Perth. The queen has been so fretful in your absence. She is almost ready to deliver her child."

"I have missed Jo, but we shall shortly be on our way back to Perth. I hope the king will not punish the laird of Glengorm too severely for this. He stole me because, he says, he loves me. It's really very sweet, Orva. He says he couldn't court me in Perth because the Gordons wouldn't let any man but the laird of Fairlea near me."

"Did he now?" Orva replied. "Well, I can't fault him too badly if he says he loves you, for he is not mistaken about the Gordons. There were several young men who sought to catch your eye and might have but for the Gordons." Her tone was disapproving.

"She should not marry Fairlea just to please the king," Maggie MacLeod broke in.

"Do you know this ruffian who stole my mistress?" Orva asked.

Maggie nodded. "He's a good man, respected, and his holding is as big as, if not a wee bit bigger than, Fairlea's. I've known him since I wed Grey and came into the borders. Ian Douglas has said he loves Cicely, Orva. That should count for something. You know her father. Which would he choose for her?"

Orva smiled, nodding her head. "He would choose

the man who loved his daughter, for he has always loved her. He has always wanted my lady's happiness."

At this point they were joined by Sir William Douglas. He bowed to Cicely. "I do not have to ask if you are well, my dear, for I know that Ian would not mistreat you. Ian tells me that you are responsible for this miraculous transformation of Glengorm. I have never seen this hall so clean and welcoming."

"Thank you," Cicely said, smiling. "The king has sent you to bring me back to Perth, I assume. When may we leave?"

"Ahh," Sir William said with a sigh. "While I have indeed been sent for you I am afraid that my kinsman is not quite ready to release you. He tells me that he loves you, and wishes to make you his wife. He says if you are not ready to remain of your own accord then he must continue to keep you here so he may convince you that he is the husband for you, and no other."

"But you speak for the king!" Cicely said, suddenly angry.

"I do, madam, but I am one man with a few men-at-arms accompanying him. I cannot remove you physically from Glengorm, for I could not defend either you or my actions, I fear. I will, however, return to Perth and tell the king of the laird's wishes in this matter. You have but to be patient. We will negotiate this situation and bring it to a successful conclusion shortly." Sir William patted her hand in what he hoped was a comforting gesture. "Glengorm is a pleasant habitat, my dear, and I can see that you are not uncomfortable here."

"Your kinsman promised that when the king's representative came, if I was not content to remain here I might depart," Cicely said furiously. "He has lied to me then!"

"I suspect your sweet company has only made him more determined to win you over, and he has changed his mind. Do not women change their minds?" Sir William asked her with a twinkle in his eye.

Maggie giggled, and even Orva was forced to smile at Sir William's remark.

Cicely stormed across the hall to where Ian and Andrew Grey were now in conversation. "You said you would let me go!" she fumed at him.

"I thought better of it," he replied calmly.

"Liar!" Cicely shouted. "If you really loved me you would let me go!"

"To Fairlea? *Never!*" he shouted back. "The Gordons would crush your spirit and squander your dower. I love you, ladyfaire! I will not allow that to happen. I am the husband for you, and soon you will realize it."

"I would sooner take the veil than marry you, you loutish border ruffian!" Cicely told him.

"Now who is telling lies?" Ian Douglas chuckled. "Look, here is the priest. Ambrose, the lady would enter a convent. Can you arrange it for her?"

Cicely was standing near the sideboard. Reaching out, she grasped a small silver goblet and hurled it at the laird of Glengorm. "Ohhhh, I hate you!" she raged.

The little vessel whizzed past his head, falling to the floor. Ian Douglas leaped forward and, catching hold of Cicely, turned her over his knee, smacking her bottom several times through her gown. "No, you don't," he said. Then, "Were you never taught, ladyfaire, not to hurl objects at people's heads?" He tipped her back onto her feet.

Cicely stamped her foot at him. "How dare you strike me, you monster!" Then she swung at his head with her small, balled-up fist.

He caught the fist in his big hand, and, yanking her into his arms, the laird of Glengorm kissed Lady Cicely Bowen a hard, long kiss. Then, heedless of their guests, he looked down into her face and murmured against her lips, "I love you, you impossible little termagant. *I love you!*" And he kissed her again slowly, passionately, his mouth moving over hers until he felt the anger seeping from her slender form, and her lips worked on his, kissing him back, and she sighed a sweet sound of contentment.

"Oh, my," Maggie MacLeod said.

"There is one maiden who will never be a nun," Father Ambrose said with a grin.

Finally the laird released Cicely. "Now go and see to our guests, ladyfaire," he told her. "We'll need to feed and house them all this day."

Orva had watched the interaction between her mistress and the laird of Glengorm with interest. Ian Douglas wasn't lying when he said he loved her mistress. The poor man did, heaven help him. And Cicely, Orva realized even if her mistress didn't, was falling in love with the big border lord. Her interaction with the Gordon laird of Fairlea was polite and pleasant. There was no fire between Cicely and Andrew Gordon. She hurried over to her bemused mistress's side, putting an arm about her. "Come along, dearie, and take me to this Mab who has been so kind to you." She met the laird's look. "If you would see that my lady's trunk is brought to her chamber, my lord," she said.

He nodded his acquiescence, giving Orva just a small smile before she turned and took his ladyfaire from the hall.

"She's a high-strung mare," Sir William noted. Then he turned to greet the priest. "What think you, Ambrose Douglas, of a match between this lady and your nephew?"

"It would be a good match for them both," the priest replied. "He does love her, my lord, and despite what just took place she has been softening towards him. The Glengorm folk like her too. She has brought order to this house again. I can't recall it ever being this clean, even in my father's time. Ian and Fergus's mam was a frail lass. It was all she could do to birth her two sons."

"Was Fergus involved in this abduction?" Sir William wanted to know. "I do not believe Ian could have carried this out alone, and the shopkeeper did say she was attacked by two men. Of course, she did confess her part in it all. The king has punished her, but gently. He is angrier at Ian for spoiling his plans to see Lady Cicely wed into the Gordon family. He is not certain he trusts them. 'Tis amazing how knowledgeable he is in spite of his many years in English captivity."

"I imagine all courts have a certain amount of intrigue," Father Ambrose remarked dryly. "Aye, Fergus went with Ian. And then the two of them rode like the very devil to get her back safely to Glengorm."

Sir William nodded. "And now I have the task of telling the king he won't give her back." He shook his head. "Is there a chance she will agree to wed him? If you think there is, Ambrose, I will try to prevent the king from sending a troop of men-at-arms to collect the lady and return her to the queen's household, so he may have his chance with her. From what I saw this afternoon they are well matched. He won't get entirely around her, as he's always done with the lasses."

"Is it not true, cousin," the priest said, "that that which you fight for and win is more precious than that which is simply given to you?"

Sir William chuckled. "You are on his side, aren't you, Ambrose?"

"He's been such a rascal, emulating his grandfather his entire life. But now his heart is engaged, not just his cock," the priest said. "And she's a fine young lass, cousin. Why should the Gordons have her and her dower? Are not we Douglases just as good?"

"Some of us, aye," Sir William replied. "But some of our clansmen are not in the king's good favor, as you know. Still, Glengorm's people have always been loyal."

"We are too small a branch of the family to be bothered with," the priest remarked. "We haven't got a great amount of wealth or influence. We're plain border folk, and we want to be naught else."

"The weather is not good," Sir William said. "The rain is icy, and the cold is deepening. I expect an early snow, and certainly that would prevent the lady from traveling in safety and comfort. But I will assure her I will return to the king with the laird's answer to his request so she does not feel entirely deserted. This matter is aggravating the king, for he has greater problems in the north with the MacDonald of the isles. He doesn't want to offend the Gordons, but neither does he want the distraction of this problem when he has more important matters that need attending. Of course, he can always find a suitable bride for the laird of Fairlea from among the queen's ladies. Her distant cousin Elizabeth Williams has just arrived at court at the queen's request. Her dower, of course, is nothing like Lady Cicely's, if the gossip is to be believed, but she is blood kin to Queen Joan, pretty, and most suitable. I believe the Gordons could be placated with such a bride for the laird of Fairlea. I will mention it to the king."

A hot meal of rabbit stew filled with carrots and leeks was served in round bread trenchers. The was also trout broiled in butter with dill and pepper. Fresh bread and cheese was upon the table, and finally Mab herself brought in a bowl of apple and pear halves stewed with sugar and clove. While Cicely preferred wine, the male guests enjoyed their October ale.

Cicely noticed that Lady Grey ate very little, and only sipped at her wine. "Are you all right?" she inquired solicitously.

Maggie stood up. "Can someone help me to my bed?" she asked, suddenly pale again. She swayed slightly, and her voice was tremulous.

Mab and Orva were immediately at Maggie's side, helping her from the high board. Cicely excused herself and followed, turning briefly to tell Lord Grey she would come back shortly to tell him what was happening. Then she hurried after the others.

Ascending the stairs was difficult for Maggie. Her belly was great, and she was having difficulty putting one foot before the other. Halfway up the stairs she stopped, gave a gasp, and a stream of water was suddenly flooding the stone steps.

"What has happened?" Cicely cried to Orva and Mab.

"Her waters have broken, my lady," Mab replied. "The bairn wants to be born."

"I told you," Maggie gasped weakly, then struggled with the two women at her side to reach the hallway above.

Finally they attained the landing and, half dragging the woman between them, arrived at the guest chamber prepared for them. Cicely had pushed ahead of them on the steps and, dashing down the passage, flung open the door to the room, relieved to see a fire blazing merrily in the hearth. Mab and Orva quickly and efficiently stripped Maggie of all her clothing but for her chemise. They helped her to lie down upon the bed, which she did with a groan. Orva propped pillows behind her so she was half seated.

"I can do this meself," Mab said, "but I should far rather have the assistance of the midwife in the village, my lady." She looked anxiously to Cicely.

"I'll send for her at once," Cicely said. "What else is needed now?"

"Hot water, clean clothes, some oil for the baby's skin, swaddling, and there is a cradle in the attics that should come down," Mab said. "If Orva will remain with Lady Grey I can organize those things more quickly, and Lord Grey should be informed that his bairn will be born soon."

"I can do that too," Cicely said. She walked over to Maggie's side. "I'll be back quickly," she promised. "Are you in pain?"

"Just in my back," Maggie replied. She grasped Cicely's hand. "Thank you," she said softly. "Now go and reassure my Andrew that I'm fine." She smiled a weak smile, but behind it was great strength, for Maggie was

Highland born, and Highland women were strong. Her own mother had birthed eight sons and four daughters in safety. She could certainly birth this one child, Maggie thought, but she still prayed a silent prayer to Saint Anne for herself and her child in this travail.

Cicely ran downstairs to the hall, Mab lumbering behind her. She went immediately to Lord Grey. "Your wife is in labor, my lord. Your child has decided to be born here at Glengorm, and we are honored."

The laird of Ben Duff was an older man without children who had been previously widowed. On a trip to the north he had met Maggie MacLeod, and they had fallen in love. Defying her family, Maggie had gone south with Lord Grey, and they had been married. There was no doubt that Andrew Grey adored his young wife. "Is she all right?" he asked anxiously.

"Her labor has just begun, but her waters have broken. Mab is competent to deliver the child, but she has sent for the midwife from the village," Cicely explained.

Lord Grey nodded. "Can I see her?" he asked.

"I don't see why not," Cicely said.

Lord Grey almost ran from the hall.

"I shall go to my church and pray for them," Father Ambrose said. "I'll stop at the midwife's cottage if you want," he offered.

"Thank you," Cicely replied. Then she joined the laird and Sir William. "Maggie is going to have her baby," she told them.

"There hasn't been a bairn born in this house since Fergus," the laird noted. "May this one be the first of many. Will you give me many bairns, ladyfaire?"

"My lord! I have not said I would marry you," Cicely protested.

"You will have to if our bairns are to be legitimate," he teased her.

Cicely stamped her foot at him. "The king wants me to wed Fairlea," she said.

"If the king could give the Gordon of Fairlea another equally suitable bride," Sir William asked, "would you consider my kinsman's suit, Lady Cicely?"

Cicely looked surprised by the question. "All the queen's ladies but for me are Scots," she told him. "And none have my birth or dower, Sir William."

"Do you know the queen's cousin Elizabeth Williams?" he inquired of her.

"Aye, I do," Cicely said slowly. "She was with us for a short time in Queen Joan of Navarre's household. When we were brought to Queen Katherine's court she was sent elsewhere. Why?"

"She is now with our Queen Joan, and while she has not your dower, madam, she is blood kin to the queen, and would be a more than suitable match for the Gordons," Sir William told Cicely quietly. "You will understand that my loyalty to my own kin leads me to suggest such a match to the king so Ian might pursue and win you for his wife."

She was astounded by his words, and wondered if she should not be offended at his suggestion that she might be replaced so easily in the laird of Fairlea's affections. But then Cicely considered that Andrew Gordon had never declared his love for her, and as much as she disliked admitting to it, she suspected he was pursuing her for her dower and her connection to Jo. If the king decided to abandon her—which he might well do, for he did have greater problems to attend to—then he would see that Beth Williams's dower was good enough for the Gordons, and her blood tie to the queen actually made her a better match than Cicely, with her large dower and close friendship with Scotland's queen.

"The queen would never desert me," Cicely said defiantly.

"Of course she will not, for you are her friend," Sir William noted. "But it is not the queen who will decide this matter, Lady Cicely. It is King James. If he can put both the Douglases and the Gordons in his debt he will do it, I assure you."

Aye, he would, and Cicely knew it. James Stewart was a charming man, but he was also a hard man who was determined to bring all of Scotland under his rule. The border lords would be loyal, even those with closer ties to England, because of Joan Beaufort. But James would need to spend all his time and his energies to bring the north to heel before he would be satisfied. And while he loved Jo and would do much for her, he would not endanger his plans for her best friend.

"You don't love Fairlea," Ian said.

She glared at him. "This is not your decision to make, my lord," Cicely snapped. "If the Gordons will have Beth Williams then they will have her, but it does not mean I must have you for my husband. Remember the choice is *mine* to make. Not yours." She hated being hedged in, Cicely thought.

Ian had already realized that, and so now he said to her, "Give me a chance, ladyfaire. Are you not already mistress here, and comfortable?"

"There is much to be done before Glengorm is truly habitable," Cicely said.

"I will share your dower with you," Ian Douglas told her.

"What?" She looked startled.

"You may keep half of your dower for yourself, to do with as you choose. The other half will be mine. Sir William has heard me say it, and Ambrose will make it a condition of our betrothal and marriage," the laird promised her.

Cicely was very surprised by his words. She knew without even thinking about it that Andrew Gordon would not have suggested such a thing to her. She would have been dependent upon her husband for everything for the rest of her life. But if Ian Douglas meant what he was saying, then she would have the freedom within her marriage that she sensed she needed. "You may court me," Cicely told him, "but that does not mean I have agreed to wed you, my lord."

"I understand," he replied, his heart soaring with pleasure. He was winning her over at last, and soon she would be his wife.

Sir William smiled, well pleased. Now all he had to do was convince the king that the queen's cousin would be a better match for the laird of Fairlea, and that Ian Douglas was the right husband for Lady Cicely Bowen.

The village midwife bustled into the hall. "Where is the laboring lass?" she asked. "Good evening to you, my lords." She curtsied.

"Upstairs," Cicely said. "Lady Grey has gone into labor with her first child," she explained. "Her husband and my tiring woman are with her. Mab is gathering supplies."

"My name is Agnes, my lady," the midwife said, and she curtsied to Cicely.

The two women hurried upstairs. Mab had already seen the cradle from the attics brought into the bedchamber. Sesi had cleaned it thoroughly, and Sine had brought fresh straw in from the stables to line the cradle. The straw was covered by a piece of wool, which was topped with a softer cloth. A black iron pot of water was heating over the flames in the hearth. There were clean clothes and a little flask of oil on a table.

Maggie lay upon the bed groaning with her labor, but Agnes the midwife, upon examining her, nodded, pleased. "You'll birth this bairn in no time, my lady, and you're made for birthing, I'll vow."

"Cicely," Maggie called, "take my lord downstairs to the hall and stay with him. Look at his face. He frets, and needs not."

"I'll come back," Cicely said.

"Nay," Maggie told her. "You're still a maid, and have not been raised in a house with birthing women. 'Tis better you remain in the hall. I'll have them call you back when the bairn is born, and you'll carry it to its sire. *Please.*"

"She's perfectly right," Orva agreed. "I'm not needed here, as Mab and Agnes and Sine are perfectly capable. I'll go with you, and when my lord Grey is settled with the laird and Sir William, you and I will come upstairs to unpack your trunk."

"Very well," Cicely agreed.

Lord Grey kissed his wife's damp brow, and murmured something that caused her to smile. Then he departed the bedchamber, assuring Cicely he could find his way downstairs to the hall by himself. "Go and tend to yourself, madam," he said.

Together Cicely and Orva hurried to her chamber. The trunk the tiring woman had brought had been set at the foot of the bed next to the other little trunk.

"You were wise to bring my possessions," Cicely said.

"I brought them all," Orva replied, "including your horses, my lady. I did not think it advisable to leave anything, for you know how some of the younger girls are."

"It seems I will be remaining at Glengorm, at least for the interim," Cicely said, and then she went on to explain the conversation she had had with Sir William and the laird. "It is somewhat disconcerting to know I can be replaced so easily in the laird of Fairlea's heart," she finished wryly.

"He had no care for you, my lady," Orva said. "It was your dower, not just your beautiful face, that attracted him, and frankly I am not certain which came first, but I do know which he valued more: your dower."

"You did not say it before!" Cicely accused her tiring woman.

"You appeared to be seriously considering the man, and I did not want to interfere with that decision, for your father made it plain that the choice was to be yours

alone," Orva defended herself. "And the laird of Fairlea
was a gentleman who would have treated you well had
you wed him."

"And the laird of Glengorm?" Cicely asked.

"I do not know him well enough yet to render you my
opinion should you desire it," Orva responded. "But you
have been in his house for over ten days now, and he has
not attempted to force himself upon you. Indeed, he has
given you free rein over his household and his servants.
That alone speaks well of him."

"The house was a pigsty when I arrived!" Cicely exclaimed. "There was no one in service but Mab and that
wretched creature Bethia, who was stealing from the
laird's stores to profit herself, and bullying poor Mab as
well."

"And the laird gave you permission to do what you
would with his house?" Orva asked, curious. "He might
have left you to languish in the wretched slough, but
he didn't, did he?" Orva pointed out.

"Indeed, he told me that if I didn't like his house
to make it over to suit myself," Cicely admitted. "And
now he says that half my dower portion will remain in
my hands. I will confess to you, Orva, that this reckless
rogue of a border lord is beginning to intrigue me, for I
do not believe I have ever met a man like him."

"And I think your interest in him is far greater than
your interest in your Gordon laird ever was," Orva
replied.

Cicely nodded. "Perhaps you are right," she said.
"But I cannot help but wonder if my father would approve such a match. He is an earl, a noble of high rank.
Ian Douglas is naught but a simple border lord. And
how my stepmother will crow with delight should I wed
a plain border lord. I am certain she is already planning
an important match for my baby half sister."

Orva sighed. "May I speak plainly, my lady?" And
when Cicely nodded she continued, "'Tis true your sire
is an earl who springs from an ancient line, but your

mam, God assoil her good soul, was the daughter of your father's steward. They were blood kin, 'tis true, but your mother's family were not noble. You were fortunate in that your father loved your mother, and sought to wed her. That he saw you were made legitimate when she died, and raised you as his own. That you were placed in a great household and became the dearest friend of a girl who is now a queen. It was unlikely that there was any great match for you here in Scotland. Lady Joan sought to have you with her because she was going into a strange situation and wanted her friend. And in England you would have had to be satisfied with a second or third son. Here at least you can wed a propertied lordling, and be mother to his heirs. And that being said, you should marry the man you love, or at least one who loves you."

"I love no man," Cicely said.

"Mayhap if you gave your laird a chance . . ." Orva began.

"He is not *my* laird!" Cicely responded firmly.

Orva smiled and, opening the trunk, she began taking out the garments she had so carefully packed for her mistress. "Mab tells me there is a small chamber next to this one. With your permission I shall take it so I can be within call."

" 'Tis not my house," Cicely said. "You must ask the laird."

Orva smiled again. Her mistress had always been a stubborn girl, but in the end she would come around. *And I will ask the laird,* she thought to herself.

The two women unpacked the garments and put them away. Cicely had to admit to being relieved to have her own things about her again. It somehow made Glengorm feel more welcoming. When they had finished Orva said she would go to see how Lady Grey's labor was coming. She went first to the hall to request permission to use the small chamber next to her mistress, and the laird gave it to her with a smile.

"I think my ladyfaire is happy to have you with her again," he said.

"You must not beat her again, especially before others," Orva said quietly.

"God forgive me, but I lost my temper when she threw that little goblet," he admitted. "Do you think I hurt her?" He looked genuinely concerned.

Orva gave him a small smile. "Only her pride," she told him. "It is as great as yours, I suspect." Then she gave him a quick curtsy.

Orva did not stop to speak to Lord Grey, who was deep in conversation with Sir William. She hurried back upstairs, stopping first to see how Lady Grey's labors were progressing. She arrived in time to see the infant slip from its mother's body, howling loudly. Not even waiting to learn the child's gender, she ran to fetch Cicely, who came swiftly.

"It's a boy!" Agnes the midwife crowed. "And hear him howl, and look at that bairn's manhood! It's large for a newborn." She looked to Lady Grey. "Does the laddie take after his da then, my lady?"

Maggie laughed weakly. "Aye," she said. "Ohh, give him to me, please!"

"A moment more, my lady, so he may be cleaned and swaddled. And you must be refreshed now that all is done," Agnes said.

"What is that?" Cicely was staring at a bloody mass in a brass basin.

" 'Tis the afterbirth, my lady," Mab told her. "We'll bury it beneath an oak so the bairn may be strong."

The infant was wiped free of blood and rubbed down with oil. Then he was wrapped in swaddling bands and brought to his mother.

Maggie's eyes filled with tears. "He looks just like Andrew," she said, sounding both pleased and happy. She touched the baby's cheek with the tip of her finger. "He's perfect. Take him to his father now, and then bring him back to me."

They handed the child to Cicely, whose face was suddenly filled with panic. "I've never held a baby before," she half whispered. "What if I drop him?"

Maggie smiled. "You won't. Tell my husband to come back with you, and thank you for giving us shelter, and such a good place for our son to be born."

"There, dearie," Mab said. "You're holding him just right."

Cicely walked from the bedchamber cradling the newborn infant in the crook of her arm. Orva moved ahead of her. They descended the staircase into the hall. The child had decided to howl loudly once again, and Cicely was terrified she was doing something wrong, but Orva assured her she was not.

As they entered the hall Lord Grey ran forward. "Is it . . . ? he asked.

"A boy, my lord," Cicely told him.

Andrew Grey looked down into his son's face. Tears sprang to his eyes. "Maggie?" he asked.

"Well, and anxious to see you," Cicely said.

"She said she would give me a son," Lord Grey said wonderingly. Then, pushing past Cicely and the baby, he ran up the stairs to see his wife.

Cicely brought the baby into the hall for the others to see. The Grey heir was suitably admired, and then Orva took him from her mistress.

"I'll take him back upstairs to his cradle," she said.

Cicely suddenly found herself with Ian Douglas. Sir William seemed to have disappeared. "They wouldn't let me see the birth," she said, not knowing what else to say.

"It's a fine strong lad Maggie's given her husband," the laird said quietly.

"You want children," Cicely said.

"Aye, don't you?" he responded.

"Aye, but I don't know how many, and I pray I am not like my own mam. She died after I was born. If I loved you I wouldn't want to birth your son and then die," Cicely said. "It would be far too sad, my lord."

"Could you love me, ladyfaire?" he asked her.

"I don't know," she answered candidly.

"But do you like me more than when I first brought you to Glengorm?" he wondered. His warm hazel eyes searched her face.

"I might," Cicely said, "if you did not smack my bottom publicly."

"Might I do it privately?" he teased, and chuckled when she blushed.

"You are unseemly, my lord," Cicely scolded him, suddenly shy.

He took her hand in his; raising it to his lips, he kissed the back of it, and then, turning the hand about, he kissed both the palm and the wrist.

"Oh!" Cicely exclaimed as a shiver of pleasure traveled down her spine.

He drew her close, still holding that hand, placing it upon his chest over his heart. He smiled gently at her. "You are a prize to be treasured, ladyfaire. I am going to teach you to fall in love with me now that Sir William has solved the problem of the laird of Fairlea for us." Then he took her face between his two hands and began to kiss her slowly, his warm lips traveling over her face first, and then reaching her lips.

Cicely sighed. She was simply helpless to this man's kisses. She kissed him back, feeling his heart beneath her hand begin to race. He released her face, one arm slipping about her waist to bring her even closer to him, the other lightly caressing one of her small round breasts. Cicely stiffened. Not even Fairlea had been so bold with her.

"Nah, nah, ladyfaire," he crooned against her mouth. "Am I the first then?"

She was speechless with the emotions now overcoming her. Jo had never shared with Cicely the intimate details of her courtship, and Cicely had never asked, fearing to intrude upon her friend's privacy. Was he supposed to be touching her? Should the hand cupping her breast feel so good? "Should you be doing this?" she finally managed to gasp. "You are not my husband. Oh, Blessed Mother!"

"It is part of courtship, ladyfaire," he told her gently. God's balls, her breasts were so sweet. Perfectly round and firm, yet soft. Unable to help himself, he pinched her nipple lightly. His cock was already straining against the fabric of his breeks.

"Please," Cicely said, "I did not know, my lord."

His hand fell away from her breast. So Fairlea had not gone as far as caressing her. That was to the good, for then his were the first hands to touch her. And now no others would. She was his alone.

"Why have you stopped?" Cicely asked him.

"Because I would not frighten you," he told her. "No man has ever fondled you, my ladyfaire. But I long for much more. Do not, I beg you, keep me waiting too long."

"How can you know I have not been touched before?" Cicely demanded.

"Did you not tell me *'I did not know'*? Had another touched you as I did you would have known that after the kissing came the caressing, ladyfaire," the laird said.

"I am not easily seduced, my lord," Cicely said.

"Nay, you are not easily seduced," he agreed, his hazel eyes twinkling at her. "If the truth be known you have been extremely difficult to approach."

"You are a rogue," Cicely told him.

"Aye, I am," he replied, close to laughter now. "But I suspect you are discovering that you like a rogue."

"You had no right to kidnap me, my lord," she said sternly.

"My name is Ian, and as I fully intend winning you over, ladyfaire, I should like to hear you say my name."

Cicely looked directly at him with her big blue-green eyes. *"Ian,"* she said.

"How sweetly you say it," he replied. "Soon you will cry out my name in passion, my ladyfaire. We shall bind our bodies together, and you will cry my name." His gaze had suddenly become very intense.

"I am a virgin, you must know," Cicely said nervously, stepping back a pace. "I know nothing but that if you become my husband I must submit my body to you for whatever purposes you devise. I do not know if I am ready to consider such a thing."

Now he laughed at her proper speech, which he suspected she had been taught by some priest. *A woman must submit. Coupling is for the purposes of procreation only.* "As you submit to me so will I submit to you, lady-faire. And there will be pleasure between us, for while the Church wants more souls to baptize, there is no reason we cannot enjoy each other while we give them what they want," the laird told her. "For now, however, I am content to learn all I can about you, and you must learn about me."

Lord Grey returned to the hall. "Maggie is well, and says we must have more bairns," he said, grinning delightedly. "Our son is strong, but I would like Father Ambrose to baptize him before we return to Ben Duff. And if you two will stand as his godparents, both my Maggie and I would be honored."

"I've never had a godchild," Cicely said. "Aye, 'tis I who am honored, my lord."

"And I also, old friend," Ian Douglas said, and he smiled at Cicely, for being godparents to Lord Grey's son was the first act they would perform together.

Sir William left in the morning to return to Perth. He wanted to go home to Drumlanrig, but this duty came first. Lord Grey departed as well so that his Ben Duff folk might know of the new heir, and his home be prepared for his wife and son. But on the following day it began to snow in the borders. As much as Maggie Mac-Leod wanted to go home, now she knew that she would probably have to remain at Glengorm until spring, when her son would be able to make the day-and-a-half journey. Cicely was happy to have her company.

And the laird of Glengorm realized that it was very unlikely Sir William would be able to return from court with whatever decision the king rendered. Cicely would have to spend the winter with him, but she did not seem unhappy about the news. Christmas came. A Yule log was dragged through the snow into the hall. There was greenery hung, and candles that Cicely had made earlier in the month for the holiday. Father Ambrose had decided it was safe to wait to baptize Torquil Grey until his father could be there.

On Christmas Day, Lord Grey managed to ride from Ben Duff to join his wife and son. As he had a responsible bailiff he had decided to remain at Glengorm with his wife and son until spring, when they might journey safely home. Ian could not remember when his home had been so filled with life and laughter. His younger brother, Fergus, came from the village with his wife, Marion, their two-year-old daughter, and their newborn daughter, who had been born on the first day of December, as had Torquil Grey.

And for the first time in all of her life Cicely felt as if she had a real family. Living in a cottage with Orva on her father's estates had not been the same. Neither had her formative years in Queen Joan of Navarre's household, or the brief time she had spent at the court of England's French queen, Katherine, or her even briefer time at the Scots court. Maggie MacLeod and Marion Douglas were like sisters to her. And there were the children, little Mary Douglas, and the two wee bairns. Lady Cicely Bowen suddenly realized that she was happy, truly happy, for the first time in her life. She found the informality of Glengorm more comfortable than court life had been.

If only she could decide what to do regarding Ian Douglas. She already counted Andrew Gordon gone, but had not really sorrowed over the loss. It was the laird of Glengorm who was driving her to distraction. She couldn't make the most important decision of her life just because his kisses drove her wild. Or could she? But she had to admit to herself that she was coming to like him very much. Was he the man for her? Or should she return to court in the spring and seek further for a husband? She had to be sensible, practical. Certainly she wasn't some silly lass who could be easily cajoled.

But in the meantime his caresses were becoming bolder, and Cicely found herself considering that it might be very nice indeed to be seduced by Ian Douglas. Or perhaps she should allow Jo and the king to pick a husband for her. Demonstrate her loyalty to them both for their kindness to her. But then if they chose her man, would he love her? Cicely had found she was becoming quite used to being loved. And she liked it. She wasn't certain what to do. But then Ian Douglas made the decision for them both on a snowy late February day, and her fate was suddenly decided.

Chapter 9

The day had begun like any other winter's day. Outside the skies were gray and lowering, with promise of another snow to come. The ewe sheep were beginning to drop their lambs in the small barn that kept them safe from the predators outside. When Lord Grey had returned from Ben Duff at Christmas he had brought with him two small white terrier pups, a male and a female but half-grown, for Cicely. The active little dogs had bedeviled the larger dogs in the hall until the single big wolfhound among the pack had taken the little male terrier by the scruff of his neck, shaking him gently several times before he set him down with a warning growl. Witness to this act, Cicely had laughed until tears came to her eyes, but from that moment on the terriers had behaved. Now they followed her wherever she went, sleeping at the foot of her bed at night.

The day was quiet. With little work to do the villagers were cooped up in their cottages. The house servants under Cicely's firm hand kept the house in perfect order now while Mab dozed by the hearth in her kitchen, the main meal of the day already in progress as Bessie and Flora sat at the large table working and gossiping. Fergus and his family were back in their house in the village. Lord Grey and his wife were seated by the fireplace in the hall admiring Torquil, who, at two months, was becoming active. The baby had been baptized immediately after Christmas, for winter could be a dangerous time for a newborn infant.

The wolfhound, two greyhounds, and a deerhound sprawled sleeping before the large open hearth, their snores audible. Now and again one would open an eye to view the infant, who waved his arms about as he began to discover what he could do. Cicely sat quietly sewing on some new shirts for the laird. Entering his hall, Ian Douglas looked about and found he was a contented man but for one thing: He was not yet a married man, and he very much wanted to be. But Cicely insisted that she was not ready to make the decision that would bind them together for life. Oh, she encouraged his kisses and caresses, but nay, it could go no further than that, she insisted.

He looked at her now, her deep auburn hair plaited neatly into a single thick braid, her beautiful face set in serious contemplation as her head was bent over her sewing. He longed to take her to his bed, remove her gown, undo that braid, and spread her glorious hair about her shoulders. Then he would kiss her until she submitted willingly to him and admitted her love for him. The cock in his breeks tightened with his thoughts. Winter was half gone. Would she wed him in the spring? Or would she return to Perth? Yet there was nothing for her there now, and everything she could desire here at Glengorm. And then, realizing someone was standing by his side, he looked down to see Orva.

"You love her," Orva said quietly. "I can see it. You want her. I see that too. What is it that holds you back, my lord?"

"She values herself so highly," he said. "I fear what would happen if I forced the issue between us. She would surely hate me."

"Perhaps for a little while, or perhaps not," Orva replied. "I have seen her this way before. When my lady dallies it is best for you to make the decision that you know she wants but cannot quite bring herself to make. Who knows whether your kinsman has been able to convince the king to give the Gordon laird the queen's cousin. And who knows if he will even want this lass. You had best set your mark firmly upon my mistress before the snows melt, if indeed you truly want her for your wife, my lord," Orva advised him, and then she left him to contemplate her words.

The laird of Glengorm stood for several more long moments considering what Orva had said to him. The tiring woman had raised Cicely, and surely knew her better than even his ladyfaire knew herself. And she was encouraging him to do what must be done if Cicely was to be his wife. Winter was half gone, but there was still time. The day ended with a faint smear of color on the western horizon that indicated sunset.

The hall was warm, and filled with laughter as the two trestle tables below the high board were filled with the laird's men-at-arms. The supper was served and eaten. The laird's old piper, Owen, played, and to everyone's delight Lord Grey and the laird of Glengorm danced among the crossed swords laid upon the stone floor of the hall, for entertainment. Finally the hall emptied but for Ian Douglas, who was seeing that the doors of the house leading to the outside were locked and barred for the night, and Cicely, who went about snuffing out the candles, extinguishing the hall torches, and seeing that the fire was set for the night so that it would burn low, but not go out.

She looked about the hall, pleased with what she saw. The stone floors were clean. The furniture was polished. The tapestry hanging over the sideboard had been beaten free of years of dust until the subject of its design was once again visible to the eye. Soon the two chairs of the master and mistress that stood behind the high board would have new tapestried cushions, for she had begun them just after Twelfth Night. Turning, she stared into the low fire. She was not quite content, but she was happy. Feeling his strong arms slip about her waist, she leaned back against him.

He bent down to kiss the side of her neck. The fragrance of white heather assailed his nostrils, and Cicely sighed. She was wearing a loose velvet gown called a houpeland that had a short waist and flowing sleeves with a high collar that had a slashed opening at her neck. It was dull orange in color and went well with her pale skin and auburn hair. One arm still about her waist, Ian slipped his hand into the opening of her gown and past her camisia, cupping her breast in his palm.

He kissed her ear now, murmuring softly into it as he felt her stiffen, " 'Tis time for this now, ladyfaire." Gently, ever so gently, he fondled the soft globe of flesh. His callused thumb stroked the nipple over and over again until she sighed once more. Ian smiled to himself. Cicely might not know it yet, but she was more than ready to be loved. Removing his hand, he turned her about, kissing her hungrily. Her sensuous little mouth yielded, her lips parting to let his tongue forage within her mouth, a skill he had only recently taught her. Their kisses were heated and grew deeper, more passionate.

Cicely moved her hand to caress the nape of his neck, threading her fingers through his unfashionably long hair as he pulled her tighter against him. She could feel his hard body pushing into hers, his muscled legs, his strong torso. She pressed herself against him, the masculine scent of him filling her nostrils, rendering her almost dizzy with a sudden longing she had never before known, but recognized. How long had she wanted him? And why was her body suddenly reacting in so wanton a manner?

Then against her thigh she felt a thick ridge of hard flesh. Never had she been held so closely, or felt a manhood pressing against her. Cicely knew she should thrust him away now. But she didn't want to, for that column of desire he exhibited excited her. For the first time in her life Lady Cicely Bowen was pierced with desire and overcome with lust. His tongue swirled about hers, and she moaned deep in her throat. Together they slid to their knees on the stone floor before the warm hearth. *"Ian!"* she managed to cry before his mouth took hers again in a wild, fierce kiss.

He pushed her back upon the floor, lying half atop her. *"Let me!"* he whispered hotly in her ear. *"Please!"* His hands pushed her gown, her chemise up.

Blessed Mother! Cicely knew she should push him away. If he had her maidenhead of her she was lost! Did she love him? Could she marry him? *Blessed Mother, help me decide,* she cried out silently. But no immediate answer came. His fingers caressed the soft inside flesh of her thigh over and over again until she thought she would scream. It felt so good, and she wanted to know what came next.

A single finger brushed up her slit, then pressed past her nether lips, causing her to gasp with surprise. He explored the wet flesh slowly, and then his finger touched the tiny nub that lay between those nether lips. He began to play with it, his fingertip teasing it until Cicely was squirming. Her eyes were tightly shut, so she did not see Ian watching her face as he brought her to pleasure, but her eyes flew open as she experienced it, and she blushed as he smiled down into her face.

"Was that nice, ladyfaire?" he asked her softly.

Wordlessly she nodded, her eyes closing again as he kissed her once more. And then she felt him probing her carefully, inserting a single long finger into her body. She tensed once more, but he murmured softly against her mouth, reassuring her, and Cicely relaxed. The finger moved within her, and she whimpered as once more he brought her to pleasure. She actually made a distinct sound of satisfaction. Opening her eyes, she looked up into his face and saw the passion there. It was too late now to forbid him. But Cicely also realized she didn't want to enjoin him from what she knew must come next.

She realized to her surprise that she wanted it every bit as much as he did.

Reaching up, she touched his face with her fingertips but said nothing.

He groaned, and briefly buried his head in her shoulder.

"You mustn't stop now, my lord," Cicely heard herself saying.

"You should be my bride, and we should be in our marriage bed," he replied, realizing he meant exactly what he was saying, yet he had begun this sweet madness.

"The moment would be lost, my lord," Cicely told him. "Do not lose it for us." Then she pulled him back down into her arms and kissed him passionately.

He kissed her back, hungrily, again and again. His cock ached and was as hard as iron, and there was only one place to soothe it. Mounting her carefully, he positioned himself, his hand guiding the burgeoning manhood to the narrow opening of her sheath. He rubbed himself against it several times. *Dear Jesu, don't let the pain I give her be too great,* he prayed silently. Then he began to push himself into her virgin's body.

Pulling her head from his, Cicely pressed her lips tightly together as she felt the head of his male member just enter her. As he moved forward she felt as if she were being impaled upon a large pole. She whimpered as he carefully moved himself back and forth several times, helping her to grow used to his invasion, and Cicely did feel her body beginning to ease. "It feels nice," she admitted shyly to him.

"There is more to come, ladyfaire," he warned her softly, and then before she considered his words, Ian thrust deep into the girl beneath him, stifling her cry of amazed pain with his mouth. Then he lay quiet a moment, and felt her tears upon his cheeks. He kissed those tears, and licked them from her face. "I have had your virginity of you now, ladyfaire, and it will not hurt again," he promised her. Then he began to move on her, slowly at first, and then with more rapid, quick strokes of his manhood.

The sharp burning had come as a surprise, but then, no one had ever discussed the intimacies of coupling with her. Perhaps Orva would have had Cicely been a bride. But she had been too eager, and now it was done. But as his cock flashed smoothly back and forth Cicely began to feel intense delight. The pain was quickly forgotten, and without even understanding what she was doing she found herself wrapping her legs about his torso so he might delve deeper into her. It was done with an instinct as old as Eve's. She sighed, and then as the intensity grew she clutched at him, gasping as it burst over her, and she was filled with a satisfaction she had never contemplated. *"Oh, Ian!"* she cried out to him softly. *"Oh, Ian, yes!"*

The sweet sound of her voice caused his creamy tribute to burst forth. With a groan of utter pleasure he rolled away from her, saying, *"Oh, ladyfaire, yes!"*

They lay upon the stone floor beside the hearth for what seemed some length of time until Cicely's terriers awoke, and came to nuzzle and yap at her. Quickly she pushed her gown back down and sat up. She didn't know which way to look, for she was suddenly shy with him. Standing, she said, "I should go to bed, my lord."

The laird jumped to his feet. "I will go with you," he told her, taking her hand.

"We should wed, if you still wish it," Cicely said softly.

"*If* I should still wish it?" He looked astounded by her words.

"I have proved wanton, my lord, and you have had the best of me. Do you still wish to wed such a girl as I've proved to be?" Cicely asked, blushing deeply.

Ian Douglas burst out laughing. "Cicely," he said when he had once again regained control of himself, "I have been trying to get you to the altar for several months now. I finally decided the only way you would agree to

marry me would be to seduce you as thoroughly as I
could. I love you, ladyfaire. I have wanted you for my
wife since the first day I saw you over ten months ago. I
have not changed my mind. With your permission I shall
speak with Ambrose in the morning."

"It does not disturb you that I am wanton?" she asked
him, surprised.

"Cicely, I want you to be wanton, but of course only
with me. Now let us go to bed. I want to see you naked,
and I want to kiss every inch of you before morning,"
the laird told the blushing girl.

"You have twice now called me by my name," she
noted.

"I think now, perhaps, I have the right to do so," he
responded as he led her to the staircase, followed by the
two terriers, who bounded gaily along ahead of them, and
waited expectantly by the door to Cicely's bedchamber.
But the laird decided he would not permit them inside
her room this night. Barred, the two little terriers began
to yap and howl outside of her door.

"Let them in before the whole house knows what
we've been about," Cicely pleaded with him, laughing.

"I'll not share the bed with them," he grumbled.

But the terriers seemed to understand that their residence in their mistress's room now depended upon their
good behavior. Admitted to her chamber, they immediately lay down before the hearth and went to sleep.

Twisting the key in the lock of the bedchamber door,
the laird turned to Cicely. "May I undress you?" he asked
her softly, and she nodded. He turned her about and unlaced her gown, drawing it down so that it puddled about
her ankles. Beneath it she wore a soft linen camisia with
long sleeves that came to just below her knees. He had
earlier undone the ribbon at the camisia's neck, and so he
bent to gain the bottom of the undergarment and lifted it
off of her. For a moment he held the crumpled garment
in his hand, staring down at the blood upon it. He had
had no previous doubts, but this certainly proved with-

out a doubt that Cicely had been a virgin. He dropped the camisia to the floor and stood silent for a moment, admiring the graceful curve of her back as it swept down from her neck to meet the perfectly matched twin halves of her buttocks. Her shapely legs were bare, for she wore no leg coverings in the house.

"Why do you not speak?" Cicely asked him shyly.

"I am admiring how beautiful you are in form," he told her, and, pushing the plait aside, placed a warm kiss at the nape of her neck. He slid his hands about her to take both of her breasts in his hands. Fondling them, he whispered in her ear, "Would you like to undress me now, ladyfaire?" Then he kissed the ear, nipping at the plump lobe.

"I've never seen a naked man," she told him.

"You had brothers, did you not?" he asked.

"My stepmother would not allow me to live in the same house with her," Cicely told him. "I rarely saw them, and usually only from a distance. When I found them places at court I was surprised to see that had I not been told they were my half brothers I should never have recognized them at all."

He was surprised to learn this. They had not spoken of her family but for her father, and girls always admired their fathers. "If you have never seen a naked man then we must remedy this lack in your education," he told her, spinning her about to face him. Then he laughed, for her eyes were closed. "Open your eyes, Cicely. I am not yet naked."

"But I am," she said. "It's easier to be naked with you when I don't have to meet your gaze, Ian." Then she laughed. "I am being a fool, aren't I?"

"Would it ease your natural modesty to be told how beautiful you are both in face and form, my ladyfaire? I have never seen so perfect a woman as you," he responded.

Her blue-green eyes flew open. "I am pleasing to your eye?"

"You are more than pleasing to my eye, ladyfaire," he said softly, kissing her.

Cicely began to undress him. In his home the laird wore a long-sleeved shirt and breeks, beneath which were a chemise and drawers. They were simple country garments. On his feet he had a pair of house slippers, but no hose. Cicely drew each piece of his clothing off slowly, carefully. But as curious as she was, she was still too shy to look too closely at him.

Understanding, he waited until she had him stripped and then, taking her hand, said, "Let us get into bed." Their nakedness would not seem so intimidating within the bed and beneath the covers, he knew. But once there he drew back the coverlet to admire her body. Cicely found herself inspecting his as closely, rising up on one elbow.

Ian was very tall, and his frame matched his height, which was four inches over six feet. He was lean without being thin, and well muscled. His shoulders were broad, as was his hairy chest, which moved into a narrow waist and hips. His legs and arms were long and also furred. Then, for the first time she looked upon his manhood lying supine within a nest of thick, dark fur. Curious, she reached out and touched it gingerly.

"Why isn't it hard?" she asked him. "It felt hard before."

"It does not remain hard all the time. Only when it is eager for coupling does it gain its strength," he explained.

"Your feet are enormous," she noted, and they were. Long and slender, with big toes to match their size. "But all in all I find you most pleasing," she told him.

He chuckled at her remark. "I find you most pleasing as well," Ian replied.

Cicely lay back. "Are you going to kiss me?" she asked him.

He was relieved by her query. She hadn't really been afraid before the hearth in the hall, and if she had been he sensed her uneasiness was now gone. Leaning over, he began kissing her while his hand began roaming across her slender but lush frame. Their kisses grew deeper and more impassioned. He felt his cock stir. "I want you to touch me, ladyfaire," Ian said to her. "Are you not curious to do so?"

"I didn't know if I should," Cicely answered him. Then, leaning up again on her elbow, she began caressing him shyly, trailing her fingers across his chest. A fingertip touched one of his nipples, and then rubbed it. "Is it sensitive like mine are?" she asked.

"Aye," he answered.

Her hand investigated him further, fingers sliding through the curly hair on his chest, down to his navel, and finally to his groin, where she hesitated.

"Touch it," he said softly. He was practically trembling in his anticipation of the feel of her small hand.

Cicely ran a curious finger down the length of his manhood then looked to him.

"Take it in your hand." His voice was almost pleading, which she thought odd.

She carefully wrapped her hand about him. The manhood was soft, yet she felt it pulsing with life as her fingers tightened about it. She squeezed him gently and he groaned. Still holding him, she looked at the laird questioningly. "Am I hurting you?"

"Nay, far from it," he said with a small smile.

Suddenly a startled look came into her eyes. "It is hardening! And it is growing within my hand!" Her eyes widened as, unable to tear her gaze away, she watched with amazement as his manhood grew hard and long while thickening until her fingers could no longer contain him, and she released her hold upon him, looking questioningly at him.

He took the hand that had been holding him and kissed the palm. Then, pressing her back into the pillows upon the bed, he began to kiss her lush mouth, and then his lips trailed down her body, her throat, her shoulders, her chest. He took one of her nipples into his mouth and began to suck upon it.

Cicely moaned with surprise, and her hand began to caress the nape of his neck, moving up to slide into his thick, dark brown hair, digging into his scalp with strong fingers. "That feels good, my lord," she told him as he suckled upon her. "Don't stop!"

Slowly, slowly he stoked her passions. He moved to her other breast and his other hand slid between her thighs. She was very wet, and, pushing past her nether lips, he thrust two fingers into her. "Ohh!" It felt so good, but she wanted to experience his long, thick cock inside her once more. She didn't care if there was pain. "I want you inside me," she whispered hotly into his ear. "I need it!"

His desire for her was too great to deny her. In the nights to come he would take more time, educate her further in the pleasures of bedsport, but now he needed her too. He covered her with his body and drove deep.

Cicely cried out as he filled her, surprised that there was no pain this time and at how eagerly her body received him. She wrapped herself about him, encouraging him, so that they quickly experienced a crescendo of such utter satisfaction that it left them both replete with pure delight. She nestled against him, and shortly fell asleep.

Ian Douglas lay awake. He could hardly believe it. She was *his*! His ladyfaire was his, and no other man would have her. Finally exhausted by his physical efforts and his happiness, he fell asleep briefly. But, unable to sleep for long, he arose from her bed, drew the coverlet over her, put on his clothing again, and went from her chamber. Hurrying downstairs, he snatched up a cloak and let himself out of a small side door in the rear of the house.

While the night was overcast, the winter moon was full; it backlit the clouds and reflected on the snow, mak-

ing it possible for him to find his way down into his village. The laird made his way to the priest's house and
knocked upon the door. His uncle finally came to open
it, looking irritable.

"What is it that you want, nephew?" Father Ambrose
demanded to know.

"I want you up at the house first thing in the morning," the laird said. "You'll marry Cicely and me. I want
no further delays."

"Cicely now, is it?" The priest chuckled. "She's willing?"

"She's willing," Ian answered with a grin.

"Come in, come in!" his uncle said. "We must write
up the marriage agreement before I can bless your
union. And what brought about this change of heart on
the lady's part, nephew? Or perhaps I should not know,
for then I expect I would have to give you both a most
severe penance." He chortled again. "Let me fetch the
parchment. There's whiskey on the table. Pour us both a
dram, and refresh my fire. It's almost out, and 'tis dam-
nably cold in here."

The two men each performed their individual duties,
and then, the fire blazing once more, they sat down at the
priest's table with their dram cups. The parchment was
spread, the quill inked, and Father Ambrose began to
write quickly.

"It's mostly the usual," he said. "If there is anything
special you want written into the contract tell me now."
The quill scratched quickly across the yellow vellum.

"I will return half of her dower portion to her," the
laird said.

"What?" The priest was shocked.

"Her dower is said to be large, Uncle. And by keeping my word to Cicely, I prove to her that I want her not
for her dower but for herself. What can she do with the
monies? She will use them for our home, our children.
In a sense it is the same as having it myself, but that it is
she who will control that small portion. It means a great

deal to my ladyfaire, Uncle. I have promised, and will not break my word."

"Very well, very well," the priest said. "Is there anything more foolish than a man totally in love with his woman? I think not." His quill scratched swiftly across the parchment. Finally he was finished. "There! It is done. It's simple, but legal in both the eyes of the Church and the laws of Scotland. I will bring it up to the house in the morning. You can both sign it, Lord Grey and I will witness it, and I'll marry you. Now, get out! You took me from a warm bed."

"Thank you, Uncle," the laird said, and he departed, walking back through the icy winter's night to his home. He did not rejoin Cicely, but rather went to his own chamber and lay down. The dawn came a bit earlier in February, but he would be ready. He slept for several hours, and when he arose he went down to the kitchens to find Mab busily at work with Flora and Bessie. They were just now taking the fresh loaves from the oven.

"My lord, good morning to you," Mab said, bobbing a curtsy. Her two helpers followed suit.

"There will be a wedding today, Mab!" the laird declared, smiling broadly.

"Lord bless us all!" the old lady cried. "My lady has at last agreed!"

"Last night," he told her. "And I'll not delay a moment longer."

"Delay what?" Orva came into the kitchens.

"They're going to be wed today!" Bessie burst out.

"Blessed Mother!" Orva exclaimed. "My lady said aye?"

"After a wee bit of my persuasion, she did," Ian admitted.

"Tam, Artair!" Orva called. "Hot water for my lady's bath. Quickly now, for she'll not be wed without washing." She looked at the laird, her nostrils flaring almost imperceptibly. "And you had best wash yourself too," she said.

"Aye," he agreed, surprising the others. "I could probably use a good bath. I'll have mine here before the kitchen hearth."

"Get the large cauldron," Mab ordered. "The water will need time to heat, for 'twill be icy from the well."

Orva hurried from the kitchens. How much of her advice had the laird taken? she wondered. Her question was quickly answered when she entered her mistress's bedchamber. Cicely was naked in her bed, sitting up with a dreamy smile upon her face. "Good morning, my child," Orva greeted her.

Cicely's eyes focused. "Good morning," she said.

"The laird says you are to marry this day," Orva responded.

"Aye, we are," Cicely replied. "Oh, Orva, I was so wrong about him. He is the kindest man in the world, and he really does love me. I need not dissemble with you. You surely know what happened last night, but none of it was done without my acquiescence. And when afterwards I offered to allow him his freedom he refused most firmly. Oh, I know he is not sophisticated like Andrew Gordon, or well dressed, or well connected, but I think I am falling in love with him. And I know that because he loves me he will be a good husband to me, and a good father to our children."

"Aye." Orva nodded, her eyes tearing up. "He will be, and your father would be happy for you, my child."

"Orva! What am I to wear? 'Tis my wedding day!"

"First you will bathe, and the laird is bathing too in the kitchens," Orva informed her mistress. "It will take a little time for the water to be heated and brought up."

"Ohh, Orva! He is bathing for me!" Cicely sighed happily. Then she said, "Will you go and tell Maggie and her husband what has transpired?"

"Aye, my lady, I will. Now you stay right there in your bed until your bath is ready," Orva told her young mistress before she hurried off to oversee all the preparations necessary to having this wedding today.

In the kitchen a small oak tub was brought for the laird. Tam was sent to his master's chamber to fetch the clean clothing Ian Douglas would wear today. The laird had never felt it necessary to have a body servant, like other men of his class. Mab sent Bessie and Flora from the kitchen, saying they were too young to be regaled with such splendor as the laird's naked body would present to them.

"But you're not going," Bessie complained.

"I helped his mother birth him," Mab said. "I know what he has." Then she shooed her two giggling helpers into the pantry and locked the door behind them. "Use your time to organize the dry food stores," she called to them through the door. Then going back into the kitchen, she handed her master a sliver of soap and a rough towel.

"Aren't you leaving too?" he asked her mischievously.

"You've nothing I haven't seen, my lord, and if I go who will be left to prepare the wedding breakfast?" she said to him. Then she went about her business.

He laughed. Then, stripping off his garments, he stepped into the small round tub. *Aye,* he thought as he sat down. *We need a much larger tub, and I did promise my ladyfaire to have the cooper build one. He can spend the rest of the winter doing it.* Taking up the small washing cloth, he soaped it, and then scrubbed himself. His knees poking up touched his chin as he leaned forward to wash between his toes.

"Scrub that mop of yours," Mab said. "I'll rinse it for you."

He followed her advice, gasping as she poured first one, and then a second pitcher of lukewarm water over his head. Finally satisfied with his ablutions, he stood up, the water sluicing down his body. Reaching for the toweling, he rubbed himself as dry as he could before stepping from the tub onto the stone floor of the kitchen, wrapping the cloth about his loins.

Tam came back into the kitchen. "I think I have what you want, my lord," he said nervously. He laid the laird's clothing upon a chair by the table.

Ian Douglas nodded, reaching for his clean, soft linen chemise. It had long sleeves, and came to just below his thighs. He put it on, and then drew on one of the new silk shirts Cicely had made for him, lacing the neck up neatly. The shirt had wide sleeves but was fitted at the wrists. Next he picked up a length of gray-black-and-white plaid, and wrapped it about his loins, securing it with a wide black leather belt.

"I'll help you with your stockings, my lord," Tam said, kneeling and rolling them up his master's calves. The laird stepped into a pair of heelless dark leather shoes the serving man placed before him.

"Sit down!" Mab ordered him. Then to his surprise she pulled a wooden comb with large teeth from her pocket, and combed his damp hair out over and over until it was almost dry. Satisfied, she tied the length with the narrow length of leather he used daily. "You're ready," the serving woman said. "Now go up into the hall and await your bride."

Ian Douglas bent and gave the old woman a kiss on her withered cheek. "Let the lasses out of the larder now, old woman," he said with a grin.

Mab swatted at him. "As if I'd forget them," she said, pretending to sound offended. "Get along with you now, my lord!"

He ran up the stairs into the hall to find his uncle had arrived. There was a narrow linen cloth down the center of the high board, and a crucifix between the two silver candlesticks that usually decorated the table. The marriage contract was spread out upon it, along with an inkstand and a quill.

"God's balls!" the priest swore. "You've washed your entire body! This certainly is a special day, nephew. I suppose the bride is still primping. We'll eat after this folderol is all over with, I assume. Mab is doing something wonderful in her kitchens, isn't she? I'm ravenous!" He snatched up a goblet of wine from Artair's tray. "Your lady will have to do something about the villagers. There were but three at the Mass this morning. She's going to have to start setting a good example for them."

Lord Grey and his wife came into the hall.

"Cicely is almost ready," Maggie said excitedly.

Suddenly the laird's face grew panicked. Turning, he dashed back down to the kitchens. "Mab! There are no flowers!" he said to her.

Without so much as a blink Mab handed him a bunch of dried purple and white heather tied with a narrow white ribbon. "I was wondering if you would remember," she said. " 'Twill please her muchly that you did."

"If I weren't in love with my ladyfaire, old woman, I vow I would marry you!" he told her, and, taking the heather, dashed back up the stone stairs to the hall, where Cicely was just entering the room.

Her gown was lavender brocaded velvet with a low V-shaped neckline, a laced bodice, and fur-trimmed sleeves. Its undergown, which showed in the front, was of violet silk. She wore her thick auburn hair loose and unadorned.

"No need to tell the world what you've been up to," Orva had said sharply as she helped her mistress dress.

Cicely came almost shyly into the hall, but, seeing Ian Douglas standing so tall and strong, she managed a small smile.

"Come along, lassie!" Father Ambrose called to her, beckoning her to the high board where the marriage contract lay. "Make your mark there." He pointed.

"I can write, but first I will read what has been written," Cicely told him. She bent over the table, her eyes scanning the parchment. They widened just slightly as she found what she sought, and, raising her head, she looked at the laird. "Thank you for keeping your promise," she said softly.

"I will always keep my promises to you, ladyfaire," he replied.

Cicely took up the quill and signed her name. Ian then signed his, followed by Lord Grey and Father Ambrose as their witnesses. The couple then stood before the priest, Cicely clutching the little bouquet of dried heather Ian had tendered to her, and their union was blessed, the priest declaring them married until death separated them. Then, with the help of the two manservants, the priest removed the cloth and the crucifix from the high board so the breakfast might be served. The household's men-at-arms had eaten earlier, at first light.

Mab herself brought a large platter of eggs that had been poached in marsala wine and cream, setting it before the newly married couple. She was grinning a broad, toothless grin. Small round trenchers of oat stirabout with bits of apple and spice were placed before the guests. There was a platter covered with rashers of both bacon and ham, fresh bread still warm from the oven, a crock of sweet butter and one of plum jam. This morning there were two small wheels of cheese: a hard round yellow, and a soft ripe French cheese.

Cicely raised an eyebrow. "Where did that come from?" she wondered aloud.

"Mab buys things now and again from passing peddlers," the laird answered. "She must have been saving this for a special occasion." He chuckled. He caught her hand up and kissed it as his eyes met hers. "I love you, my lady wife," he told her.

Cicely blushed, and then she heard herself saying, "And I love you, my lord husband." And as the words echoed softly between them she realized that they were true. She had come to love this rough-hewn border lord who had taken a bath for her on their wedding day. Who had loved her enough to steal her away, and incur the wrath of the king by doing so.

"Do you think Sir William will be back soon?" she asked Ian.

"Perhaps, but the deed is done whatever James Stewart may say," he answered.

"The people love him because he has been hard on his lords," Cicely remarked. "But it is not for the benefit of the people; it is for his benefit. He will *rule* Scotland, but he will not be ruled by his lords. Remember he has spent more of his life with the English court than here in Scotland. He fought with King Henry the Fifth in France. From what I have heard said of the king's father, King Robert, James Stewart is his direct opposite. King Robert did not want to be king. He thought himself the most miserable of men, and only Queen Annabella's good influence kept him from fleeing a throne he never wanted. But James Stewart wants his throne. He will be a good king of Scotland, but he will be its only king. I know for a fact that when spring comes he will plan a campaign to force the northern clans and their lairds to his will. He will unite Scotland."

"He will have to overcome the lord of the isles," Ian said.

"He will do exactly that," Maggie MacLeod, who had overheard their conversation, said softly. "James Stewart can be a hard man."

Cicely nodded in agreement, wondering what secret Maggie kept for the king, and why that secret burdened her so greatly.

Mab now returned from the kitchens carrying a large dish with plump baked apples. Bessie followed behind with a big pitcher of golden cream, and Flora brought small, clean pewter plates upon which the treats would be served. Baked apples were the laird's favorite sweet.

"An excellent wedding feast!" the laird complimented his old cook. "I suppose we will have to keep you on, Mab, and not send you off to a cottage," he teased her.

Mab preened with pleasure at his compliment, but swatted him fondly at his final remark. "And who, my lord, would cook as well for you as I can?" she demanded.

"If he ever throws you out, Mab, come and cook for me," Father Ambrose invited.

Mab looked at the priest. "You may have taken holy orders," she said, "but you are more like that old reprobate your da than is realized."

"Your rheumy eyes are too sharp, Mab," he replied with a chuckle.

" 'Tis my ears that are sharp, priest," she said wickedly. Mab curtsied to them all and returned to her kitchen, Bessie and Flora in tow.

"What did Mab mean?" Cicely asked Ian softly.

"My uncle may be a priest, but he has his needs," the laird answered his bride.

She considered a moment, and then said in a shocked tone, "You don't mean ..."

"Many priests keep hearth mates, or have occasional companions to fill their needs. Given my uncle's sire I would have been more surprised if he were celibate."

"*Oh,*" Cicely said, pursuing it no further.

The morning meal over, the laird suggested to Cicely that they ride down into his village and announce their marriage to his Glengorm folk. The priest agreed it was a good idea, as Bethia continued her campaign of slander against the English girl. Cicely hadn't been out of the house but for the gardens since she had come to Glengorm several months prior. There had been no need for her to go anywhere. The horses were brought from the stables to the front of the big house. Orva had brought her mistress her light brown fur-lined and -trimmed cloak. The garment had silver frogs to close it at its neckline. Cicely slid a pair of purple leather gloves upon her hands. She was then boosted into her saddle and her skirts were spread over her horse's flank.

Cicely found the village charming. There were no more than a dozen cottages with turf roofs set about an ancient stone fountain. There was a small smithy, and a little mill on the edge of the fast-moving stream that ran through the wood at the rear of the village. Glengorm's chapel was at the end of the street. The village had been set on the shores of the small loch, and there were several smallish boats drawn up on its rocky shore.

They stopped by the fountain, and Father Ambrose called out in a stentorian voice, "Good folk of Glengorm, come out of your houses this fine morning that God has given us, and hear your laird's happy news."

The doors to the cottages began to open, for the people inside already knew that their laird was among them. There was always someone peeping from the small windows of each dwelling. Tall Douglas clansmen, their women clutching their woolen shawls about them, and curious, bright-eyed children came forth, nodding and bobbing curtsies.

Father Ambrose mentally counted them, and when he was satisfied that the majority of the villagers were there he spoke again in his loud, deep voice. "Kinsmen, this morning our laird has taken to wife this fair maid. The contract is signed, the blessing given. Come now and greet the new lady of Glengorm, and then let us pray that her womb be fertile, and an heir be given to us within the year!"

The Glengorm folk began coming forward to congratulate their laird and Cicely. And then a voice shrieked out, "Glengorm is cursed! He has married the English witch!" Bethia pushed forward, a bony finger pointed at Cicely.

"I am not a witch!" Cicely defended herself.

"Of course ye're a witch!" Bethia retorted. "Did you not ensorcell my master to send me away? I have served in the lord's house for more than ten years. Then you came, and the laird sent me from him. It was surely witchcraft!"

"The only service you gave me was to steal from my stores, and then sell what you stole," the laird said angrily. "You kept a slovenly house, and forced poor Mab to serve me slops unfit for even the pigs. No one is responsible for your fate but you, Bethia. And if you continue this slander of my wife you will find yourself and your man sent away from Glengorm. I will take pity on your mother-in-law, for she is innocent in this matter. But if your man cannot keep you under control, woman, you will both go. Do you understand me, Bethia?"

Bethia shrank back, cowering. Publicly exposed before her kin, she knew nothing she ever said again would be believed. She would take her revenge when she could, but she was wise enough to say nothing further, slinking away from the laird.

Seeing the look in her eye, Father Ambrose imagined her thoughts and called out to the retreating woman, "I can forbid you and your family the sacraments, Bethia Douglas. Remember that when you consider your next actions," he warned her.

"My lady." A tall, ruddy-cheeked woman with dark red hair stepped forward. "I am Mary Douglas, Marion's mother, and you are most welcome to Glengorm!"

"Thank you," Cicely said, relieved to see that, now that she'd been welcomed by this obvious leader of the village women, all the other women now pressed forward to greet her. She slipped down from her mount that she might walk among them, taking their hands in her hands, smiling warmly. Aye! She was home. Home for the first time in her life.

Chapter 10

Cicely was happy. So very happy. A year ago if any-one had told her she would be the wife of a border lord—and content—she would have laughed and called them mad. She could hardly wait for the spring thaw or for Sir William Douglas to return to Glengorm to tell them that the king had accepted her decision to take Ian Douglas as her husband instead of Andrew Gordon. Certainly Sir William's suggestion to solve the problem of offending the Gordons of Huntley would be accepted. It was, after all, most practical.

She and Ian had discussed what they would do with her dower. He meant to add a flock of black-faced sheep to his livestock, and keep the rest of the monies to dower any daughters they had. Cicely had decided she would put some of her dower aside as well, but she also planned on using some of it to enlarge their house. There would be a new space on the main floor for a li-brary, and above it would be a large new apartment for them to share. Right now Ian would either share the bed in her small chamber, or she would share his bed in his chamber, but the rooms did not connect as in other houses, keeps, or castles. Their new rooms would face south, east, and west to guarantee warmth.

"And we'll need a new, bigger bed," Cicely told her husband.

Ian grinned. "I'll still be able to catch you, ladyfaire," he teased her.

And she laughed. "I don't think I'll really flee you, husband," she admitted.

Their passion for each other had grown greater with each passing day. And their love had grown as well. She began to forget what it had been like not to be loved. She must write to her father and share her happiness with him. She knew he would be pleased and only wished he might know Ian. But when she had bidden Robert Bowen farewell Cicely had known that it was unlikely she would ever see him again. Leighton was too far away, and Ian could not leave his lands. So she wrote her letter, and waited for a peddler who was going south to take it with him.

And then one afternoon Sir William Douglas rode into Glengorm. He looked tired as he dismounted and made his way into the hall.

Ian came forth to clasp the hand of his kinsman in greeting. "It's too late to move on to Drumlanrig," he said. "You'll spend the night. What news do you bring?"

Sir William shook his head and asked, "Have you wed her yet?"

The laird nodded. "Aye, in February. Did James Stewart forbid it?"

Cicely hurried into the hall holding her pale blue gown up so she would not trip over it in her haste. "Sir William! Welcome back! I was told you had come. Tam! Wine for Sir William. He looks fair worn. Come, my lord, and sit by our fire. It may be April, but the day is still sharp." She led him to a tapestried chair and gave him a goblet of wine from Tam's tray. Then, sitting opposite him, she said, "Now, my lord, what news do you bring us? Has the queen birthed her prince, and are mother and child safe?"

"Princess Margaret was born in December, and the

queen is again with child," Sir William said. "The queen is strong, and says she will give her husband many bairns."

"If she says she will, she will," Cicely agreed. "Jo . . . the queen always keeps the promises she makes. But what of the king?"

"He is well," Sir William said shortly.

"And?" Cicely probed.

"Duke Murdoch and two of his sons have been executed, as well as some others. It was to be expected, of course. The king holds the old duke, Murdoch's father, responsible for all those years in England. He is showing no mercy to those he deems his enemies." He turned to Ian. "You'll have to go to court to present the patent you hold for your lands, kinsman. Every laird and earl in Scotland is required to do so. Do you have the patent to show? I know Glengorm goes back several hundred years."

"The patent for these lands was given to us by King Robert the Bruce," Ian answered him. "Aye, I have it. Do we have the king's permission to wed?"

"Aye," Sir William said.

"Thank God!" Cicely said, relieved. "When will the king turn over my dower to my husband, Sir William? Ah, but perhaps when we go to court with the patent." She paused a moment. "Did the king give the queen's young cousin to the Gordons?"

"Aye, they were wed before Lent. She's gone from court now to Fairlea," Sir William said. He had bad news for them, but hesitated to speak. If they were going to court they would learn soon enough, the clan chief decided. Why should he be the bearer of unfortunate tidings? "The king will be in Edinburgh next week. You should take that opportunity to make your peace with him, my lady," Sir William suggested. "And you, Ian, will want to get the patent to your lands firmly confirmed. The sooner the better."

"Glengorm has belonged to my family for centuries," Ian said.

"Kinsman, the king is still angry at you for stealing Lady Cicely. And getting the Gordons to accept the queen's cousin, Elizabeth Williams, was not easy. The cost was dear, for her dower was not the size of Lady Cicely's. Andrew Gordon had gathered his Fairlea clansmen together, and was prepared to ride into the borders to retrieve your lady. It took tact and diplomacy to calm the Gordons and get them to see the advantage of having the queen's blood kin married to one of them."

"I doubt it not," Ian replied scornfully, "for they could see nothing but my ladyfaire's wealth."

"Bring your patent to the king, Ian, and let us be done with this. You will have to apologize for your actions as well," Sir William said.

"Apologize? For what?" the laird demanded.

Cicely put a gentle hand on her husband's arm. "For abducting me and spoiling the king's plans, my darling. You are a big enough man to do that, for you have me for a wife now, and I love you. You say you love me. Then make your peace with James Stewart, even if it means you must briefly bow your head in subservience to him."

"Very well," the laird of Glengorm said to his wife. "I will do this for you, but why the king, who claims to have fallen in love with his queen at first sight, cannot understand that the same thing happened to me is beyond comprehension."

"Thank you, Ian," she answered him. *Blessed Mother!* The king was overly proud, and so was her husband. But Ian Douglas had no real idea of how ruthless James Stewart could be. His decisive actions and firm grip on Scotland were not those of an easy man. Everything the king did was done with a purpose, and carefully thought out beforehand. She would have to apologize too, Cicely knew. And not just to the king, but to Jo as well. "Let us leave for Edinburgh in a few days," she said.

The laird nodded. "I'll have Ambrose bring me the patent for our lands. He has them."

Sir William found himself relieved, but he feared for his kinsman when he learned how the king planned to take his revenge on Cicely and Glengorm. He hoped his kinsman had been speaking the truth these many months.

He spent a pleasant evening with Ian and Cicely, departing in the morning after a good night's rest in a comfortable bed and two excellent hot meals. The laird and his wife would survive James Stewart's wrath. He had seen for himself how much they loved each other. Their love would sustain them.

Ian was not pleased at having to ride to Edinburgh to prove his ownership of his lands, but every man and woman holding property in Scotland was required to do it. But spring was a busy season. There was some planting to be done. The cattle and sheep had to be driven to their spring meadows. And spring was the beginning of the raiding season. Hopefully with an English queen the raiding would cease, or at least lessen. It was not safe to leave one's lands.

But then Andrew Grey of Ben Duff sent word that he would be going to Edinburgh also, and suggested that if Ian was going they might travel together, for safety's sake. He would bring six men-at-arms with him. Ian sent the Ben Duff messenger back, saying he intended departing in two days, and that Cicely had to travel with them, as she was going to claim her dower from the king.

Cicely packed for them both, for the only way to get her husband off in a timely manner was to tell him when to get on his horse the morning of their departure. They had no intention of remaining long in Edinburgh. They would do what was necessary and quickly return home. She was certain Andrew Grey would agree, for he was leaving Maggie and their child alone. She packed lightly. They would both wear breeks to ride, for it was easier, and they could make better time. Orva helped her carefully fold her dark green velvet gown to wear when they spoke to the king. It had a wide, low neckline and fur-trimmed sleeves. She would tuck her long hair in her gold caul and set a sheer gold veil atop her head. Her garb would show respect for the king's majesty but would not make her appear proud. For Ian she put in a fine silk shirt. He would wear his breeks with a length of his Douglas plaid slung across his chest and fastened with his clan badge. She folded the wool plaid and tucked it into a saddlebag.

"Will you take any jewelry?" Orva asked.

"A gold chain, three or four rings," Cicely answered her. "I don't want to appear overproud. I am the laird of Glengorm's wife, and no more."

"Nay, you are the Earl of Leighton's daughter too," Orva said. "You have married for love, 'tis true. You must never forget that, or let your children forget it."

Cicely reached out and patted Orva's hand. "I never forget who I am, but I also know I must beg the king's forgiveness meekly so that he will continue to be our friend."

"Lady Joan will protect you," Orva said.

Andrew Grey and his six clansmen arrived just as the spring dawn was breaking. Cicely invited them all into the hall to eat, for the loss of half an hour would not trouble them, as the days were longer now. But as soon as they had eaten they departed. Six Douglas men-at-arms assured their protection. That night they stopped at a small monastery, where they were given shelter and a meal. They departed the following day at sunrise, reaching Edinburgh just after sunset. One of the Douglas men-at-arms traveling with them was married to the daughter of a man who kept a small inn on the edge of the town just off of the High Street. They would be staying there.

As they arrived the innkeeper himself rushed forward to welcome them, and brought Cicely and the two lairds to a small private room, where a hot supper was immediately served, along with a surprisingly good wine. The two men fell into conversation while Cicely slipped into the little bedchamber, washed, and, climbing into the bed, fell asleep. She was half wakened when Ian joined her, but fell back to sleep.

As the inn was small, Andrew Grey had slept before the common room fire on a pallet their host had brought for him when the dishes were cleared away. Ian awakened him early, already dressed to ride up to Edinburgh Castle. Cicely came forth from the bedchamber, inviting the laird of Ben Duff to use the chamber to refresh and relieve himself. He thanked her, and a short while later came forth. Like Ian he was dressed in border garb, the difference being his plaid, which was dark green with a design of stripes in red and deep blue and black.

"I didn't know the Grey family had a plaid," Cicely said.

"The Greys don't," Ben Duff replied. "We are an allied family of the Stewarts, and I am wearing old Stewart, for the clan has several different plaids. The allied families usually wear either this one or the one called dress Stewart."

They left their men-at-arms at the inn. There was no need to take them to the fortress castle on the hill that overlooked the town from a height of three hundred feet. They had no need to make an entrance that would draw attention to themselves. They were simply two border lords coming to obey the king's command. Riding through the town they arrived at the esplanade, which was set before the curtain wall of the castle. The space was always left open so any enemy approaching might be seen and identified. They traversed the open space, their horses clopping across the drawbridge spanning a wide moat, finally arriving at the gatehouse, where they dismounted and identified themselves. Their horses were taken, and a soldier called to bring them to a chamber where they would wait until the king deigned to receive them.

"Where is the queen?" Cicely asked the man-at-arms escorting them.

"She is probably in her apartments, madam," he answered as he brought them into a small paneled room with a single window.

"You will take me to her," Cicely said in an authoritative voice.

The man-at-arms looked confused. He was not certain what to do.

"Ladyfaire," Ian said to his wife.

"I must make my peace with her first," Cicely said. "I am in her service. Besides, the king, when he learns who has come, will keep you waiting for several hours so there is no doubt in your minds that he is in charge."

Andrew Grey snickered. "She's right, Ian," he said.

Cicely turned back to the man-at-arms. "I am Lady Cicely Bowen, the queen's close companion, and you will take me to her *now,*" she said firmly.

"If you will follow me, my lady," the man-at-arms said, and led her away through several narrow corridors until he stopped before a large oak door. He rapped sharply, and shortly the door was opened by an older lady who peered out.

"My lady!" she cried, a smile wreathing her face. "Come in, come in!" She looked at the man-at-arms. "Go about your business now." She waved him away.

"Thank you," Cicely said to the soldier, who bobbed his head to her.

"Oh, the queen will be so happy to see you, dearie," Bess, the queen's old tiring woman since her childhood, said. "And wait until you see the child she birthed. Bless me, the wee princess is sturdy and healthy, praise God!" She crossed herself piously as she led Cicely into the queen's apartments and through the dayroom to the queen's privy chamber. Cicely recognized some of the women, for they had been there before. And they obviously recognized her, for they began to whisper to one another.

Bess threw open the door to the queen's private chamber. "My lady, my lady, look who has come to see you!"

Queen Joan looked up from her sewing. It dropped from her hands, and she jumped up to embrace Cicely. "Oh, Ce-ce! I have missed you so much!" She stepped back. "Are you all right? Was it dreadful in the borders? Did you really wed *him*? Oh, come and sit by my side and tell me everything." She looked to Bess. "Don't let anyone disturb us, and I promise to enlighten you afterwards."

Bess chuckled and exited the chamber.

"In answer to your questions, I am fine. The borders are beautiful. And I love my husband very much, Jo. He is the best of men!"

"But he abducted you!" the queen said.

"Aye, he did," Cicely said with a smile. "He trussed me up like a sheep to market, and rode hell-bent from Perth to Glengorm. I was very angry, I can tell you, Jo. But then Ian told me why he had done it, and my anger lessened. He swore he had fallen in love with me at first sight, even as the king did with you. He said that when he saw me that day on the road to Perth he knew I must be his wife, and he would have no other. But then when he came to court he could scarce get near me for the Gordons."

"I remember," the queen replied. "I felt so sorry for him, for it was obvious then that he had fallen in love with you. I thought his cause doomed."

"Ian isn't a man to give up easily," Cicely said with a small smile. "He was determined to have me to wife, and so he made a plan to kidnap me."

"We were so worried at first when we did not know what had happened. The Gordons were furious, especially Andrew. I thought he would be a good husband for you, but when he came to Scone to learn the details of your abduction I overheard him say to Huntley that even if Glengorm had had his way with you, he would wed you so as not to lose your fine fat dower. From that moment on I disliked him. I didn't want Jamie to give my cousin Beth to him, but she had seen him and had stars in her eyes. She was not only willing; she was eager to be Fairlea's bride. But tell me, why are you here?"

"The king's decree that the lairds come with their patents to prove ownership of our lands," Cicely said. "Ian wanted to do it quickly, for spring is a busy time for Glengorm. We came with Ben Duff. Maggie had her child, a lad, Torquil. He was born in our house when they stopped on their way home. He's healthy, and Ben Duff is more in love than ever before with his Highland wife."

"I wish I had been as fortunate as Maggie," the queen said. "Margaret is a dear little baby, but I would rather have had a lad first. I've another in my belly already."

"I am not yet with child," Cicely said, "but 'tis not from lack of trying." She giggled mischievously.

The queen laughed. "It would seem we are both wed to passionate men," she said. "I am glad you came, Cece. Will you remain long?"

"As soon as the king approves Ian's patent of ownership and turns over my dower portion from my father, we must return to Glengorm," Cicely told her.

The young queen nodded. "I understand," she said, "but it may not be as quickly as you would want it. Jamie has a group of justices from the courts going over each patent with a fine-toothed comb. There are those that have not stood up to scrutiny."

"The patent for Glengorm was given to Ian's ancestors by King Robert the Bruce," Cicely told her friend. "I have seen the parchment. It is very old. Ian says that the Douglas who inhabited Glengorm in those days was one of the Bruce's few supporters. Bruce had met with the Red Comyn at Dumfries in the Greyfriars church there. He hoped to gain his support, reconcile their differences. But they argued, and the Bruce killed the Red Comyn. Before the English king could get to the pope, the Bruce made for Scone, and was crowned that Palm Sunday in 1306.

"The Stone of Destiny was missing, as was the crown,

Ian says, so he sat on a hastily constructed throne and was crowned with a plain gold circlet. It took three years before Bruce could actually hold a parliament at St. Andrews, where the clergy and the nobility finally swore him fealty. And Ian's ancestor, Walter Douglas, loyally remained by that king's side. In 1310 the Bruce rewarded that Douglas and his descendants with the lands at Glengorm in perpetuity," Cicely concluded.

"What a wonderful tale!" the queen said, clapping her hands in delight.

"It is, isn't it?" Cicely responded. "But the family had existed on those lands before then," she explained.

There was a light scratching on the door. The queen looked annoyed, but she said, "Come in," and the door opened to reveal old Bess.

"I apologize, my dearie," she said to the queen, "but a man-at-arms has come to fetch Lady Cicely. The king is calling for her man, and would see her too."

Cicely arose from the stool where she had been sitting. Bending, she kissed her friend upon her rosy cheek. "I will come and see you before I go," she said, and, hurrying from the room, found her escort waiting for her outside the door to the queen's chambers. She followed him quickly as he led her back to the chamber where her husband and Ben Duff were waiting.

"They've taken Andrew's patent to examine," Ian told her.

"I had pledged my fealty to the king when we were last here at court," Ben Duff said. "I promised to return with my patent so it might be approved. The king granted me time, although he said that even if my title was not quite perfect he would approve it in return for a small service Maggie had done for him. Maggie said it was because she had been kind to the queen when the others who hurried to gain places in her household had not."

"Aye," Cicely said, not knowing why she was confirming Maggie MacLeod's story for her husband, but she somehow felt she should. "There were those who were rude to the queen, myself, and the lass who was to wed the Gordon of Loch Brae. Jo would not be intimidated, and Maggie stood by our side. Once that had happened the others grew meek." She smiled at the laird of Ben Duff. "Maggie is a good woman, and has become my good friend, my lord."

The king's page entered the room, saying, "The laird of Glengorm and his lady are to come with me."

"I'll wait," Ben Duff said.

Cicely and Ian followed the boy, surprised to be led to the king's privy chamber. The small paneled room with its little hearth and lead-paned window was cozy, and Cicely felt less intimidated now; the king would be kind to them. But when she saw his face as she entered the room her heart plummeted in her chest. She curtsied low as Ian bowed.

"You have brought your patent, my lord?" the king said. He gave them no greeting at all, which indicated to Cicely, who knew him well, his displeasure.

"I have, my liege," Ian Douglas responded, unaware.

"Give it to my page," the king directed the laird. "He will take it to the justices, and it will be reviewed in due course."

"The parchment is fragile, my liege," the laird said, but he handed the roll to the young boy, who, to his credit, took it carefully and hurried off.

"Consider yourself fortunate, my lord, that I do not have you thrown into the gaol. You abducted an innocent girl and forced her to your will. Because my queen loves Lady Cicely Bowen I will show you mercy."

"Thank you, my lord!" Cicely quickly said. "But would you allow my husband to explain his actions? When you learn them you will understand."

"Will I?" the king said coldly.

"Oh, you will!" Cicely assured him, causing a small smile to touch the king's lips.

"Very well, madam, I will hear what your husband has to say," the king replied.

"I fell in love with her when I first set eyes on her," Ian began.

"And that would be when?" James Stewart demanded to know.

"That day when I stopped your train to pledge you my loyalty, my liege," the laird of Glengorm said. "But when I came to court I could not get near her for the Gordons. If my ladyfaire was to know me, to love me, I had no choice but to carry her off."

"I will accept that you were attracted to her when you saw her that day," the king answered. "But once you got to Perth you certainly heard the rumors of her large dower. I know Glengorm is not a rich holding, my lord. Perhaps you sought a wealthy bride, and carried her off for no other reason than her dower."

"My lord, I would have taken Cicely in her chemise and with nothing more!" Ian Douglas declared passionately. "I love her!"

The king's amber eyes narrowed as he looked at the laird. Then he said, "I hope that is so, my lord. When Orva left to join her mistress at Glengorm she took with her all of your wife's personal possessions. 'Tis all Cicely has now. There is nothing more."

"That is not so!" Cicely burst out. "My father placed a large sum of gold in your keeping, my liege. What has happened to my dower?"

"I have taken it, madam, in forfeit," the king said in a hard voice. "Do you know how insulted the Gordons were by your behavior? I had to placate them by paying them a mulct. Did you think it would come from me? And then I had to convince that fool Fairlea that taking my wife's kinswoman for his bride was far better than having you for a wife. Our children would be blood kin. But Beth's dower was small. I had to supplement it, and so I did. The Gordons never knew how much you actually possessed, and so by adding some of your wealth to Beth's dower I was able to placate them quite nicely."

"You gave Huntley and his kin *all* of my dower?" Cicely demanded angrily.

"Nay, not all of it," the king told her. "Some remains, madam."

"Then I want what is left," she replied. "How can you do this to me, my liege? I did nothing wrong! I was abducted. I did not go willingly. I am not to blame that all your plans to have me marry Fairlea, and spy upon the Gordons went awry."

"I never asked you to spy, madam," the king said in an icy voice.

"Nay, not in so many words, my liege, but am I a fool that I could not read between the lines? You are ruthless, James Stewart, but I have done you no real harm. I want my dower, at least what is left of it. Why do you blame me for what has happened? And in the end has it not all worked out for the better?"

"I might have forgiven you, Ce-ce," the king said, "had not Sir William Douglas come to me with his clever plan for his kinsman to gain you and your wealth while the queen's cousin would be given to the Gordons instead. Am I a fool that I could not see he meant to have his kinsman profit by his lawlessness? The law *must* be upheld!"

"My liege." Ian Douglas spoke. "I did not take Cicely for her wealth. I took her because I loved her. It makes no difference to me that she no longer has her dower. I still love her. I will love her past death. Knowing how I felt, Sir William sought but to aid you in what he knew would be a difficult situation. In the larger scheme of things neither Cicely nor I is important or should be considered. You have problems in the north that need your attention far more." Suddenly Ian Douglas knelt before the king. "I humbly request that you see me confirmed in my lands, my liege. 'Tis all I seek. Nothing more."

James Stewart actually looked uncomfortable. "Get up, man!" he said. He believed this border lord, and honest men were few, he knew. "The justices will look at your patent, then see what other sources may be used to confirm it. You will be notified. For now, Glengorm is yours. Take your wife. Go home." He waved them away.

"I want my dower!" Cicely said angrily.

"Come, ladyfaire, it matters not to me," Ian Douglas said.

"But it does matter to me," Cicely retorted. "Without my dower I am valueless." She turned to the king. "Do not do this to me, my liege. Do not render me valueless, I beg of you!" Tears sprang to her eyes, and she swallowed hard to prevent a sob from escaping her throat. The king couldn't do this to her. *He couldn't!*

"Farewell, madam," James Stewart said coldly.

She wanted to remain, to scream, to protest, but her husband drew her away. "Cicely, I love you. The dower matters not."

"But it does, Ian," she said as he pulled her from the king's little privy chamber. She stopped in the narrow corridor outside as the door behind them closed firmly. The tears she had valiantly tried to stop now began to pour down her face as she looked up at him. "A woman is judged by what she brings to her husband, to the marriage, be it gold, or land, or powerful kin. Without my dower I have brought you nothing, and am not worthy to be your wife. I can be naught but your housekeeper, your whore. For without my dower I am nothing more than that."

"That is ridiculous!" he almost shouted.

"You don't understand, do you? Men seldom do," Cicely said, her face wet with her tears. "You are the laird of Glengorm. You have lands. A house. A village full of people. The wife you take should bring something to you other than her body. Any woman can offer her body. But now I have nothing for you. Go and find Ben Duff," she told him. "I promised Jo I would come and bid her farewell before I left. I do not break my promises." And she hurried off to return to the queen's apartments.

Ian Douglas stood, shocked by what she had said to

him. Did his love mean so little to her that it was not enough? Oh, he was disappointed he would not so easily get the flock of black-faced sheep he wanted, but eventually he would. And Cicely would surely forget this nonsense once they got home. He needed to get her with child. A child would calm her, and she would think more clearly. He found his way back to where Ben Duff waited, and told him what had happened.

Ben Duff sympathized, but he also understood Ian's point of view. "She has jewelry, and brought plate and linens to the marriage," he said. "It's not what you expected, but it will do because you love her. My Maggie brought me little too, because we ran away to wed, and they don't approve of me, for I'm a borderer. Those Highlanders think very highly of themselves"—he chuckled—"and my Maggie is a proud lass too."

Cicely had carefully marked the route in her mind when the man-at-arms had come for her. She now retraced it, entering the queen's apartments and going to old Bess. "We must leave now," she said, "and I would bid Jo a proper farewell."

"Of course, dearie. 'Tis a pity you cannot remain longer." Then, looking closely at Cicely with her sharp eyes, she said, "What is the matter, my lady? What has happened? Do not tell me 'tis nothing, for I can see otherwise." And, realizing that Cicely was about to cry, she hurried her into the queen's privy chamber. "Something has happened to distress Lady Cicely," she said to the queen. This time she did not withdraw from the room, nor did the queen ask her to.

Unable to hold back her tears now, Cicely flung herself down next to the queen, weeping bitterly. "Oh, Jo! You have to help me!"

"What has happened?" the queen asked her friend. She had never in all the years they had known each other seen Ce-ce like this. Reaching out, she stroked Cicely's auburn head.

"The king! He has taken my dower, and will not give

it to Ian!" She sobbed afresh, looking up at the queen with a woebegone face.

"He has taken your dower?" The queen looked genuinely puzzled. "What can you mean, Ce-ce? How could he take your dower?"

"He used some of it to pay off the Gordons, for they claimed they had been injured by what happened. He supplemented your cousin Beth's own dower with mine so Fairlea would take her. And now he will not restore what remains to me!" Cicely wailed. "Without my dower I am worthless, Jo! You understand that, but Ian does not. He says it doesn't matter to him, but it matters to me!"

The queen was stunned by her friend's revelation. She knew Jamie could be hard, for she had seen incidences of it, but he was king of a hard land and often had no other choice if he were to uphold the law, keep the peace. And he could be tightfisted, because his own resources were not unlimited. But taking Cicely's dower was unconscionable.

This was her best friend since their shared childhood, two little girls who had been fostered out by their families so that those families could widen their sphere of influence with England's king. They had shared a bed in Joan of Navarre's household, and again when they were sent together to Queen Katherine. They had shared their girlish dreams and hopes, kept each other's secrets, giggling together in the dark of night. What her husband had done was unfair and it was cruel, the queen thought. Cicely did not deserve to be treated so unkindly. She had done nothing to merit it.

"I will speak with Jamie," the queen told her friend. "It will take time, of course. You know how he can be if you push him. But he was generous to me when our daughter was born. Think how much more grateful he will be when I birth his son and heir. And when I do I shall ask him to restore your dower in full to you. Now stop weeping, Ce-ce. Has your patent been approved, or must you wait for the justices to go about their business in the usual slow and timely manner?"

Cicely felt a little better with the queen's reassurance to her, but she was not certain that the king would return her dower. She saw a James Stewart that Jo did not, but, thanking the queen, she then said, "We were told to return home, and that we would be notified whether the patent was approved or not." Cicely looked up at her friend. "It has to be approved! 'Tis an honest patent."

"Do not fret," the queen said. "Jamie is using the law to regain crown lands that his uncle of Albany and his cousin Murdoch parceled out in their efforts to buy loyalty. But if he just asked for those lands back, and did not review the patents of all landholders, it would appear as if he were singling out some while favoring others. My Jamie would not do that. Establishing the rule of law back into Scotland is important to him. So he has required his justices to go over each patent carefully. And indeed they have found some that were fraudulent. But if the holders of those patents were innocent of the fraud and are good lords to their people, their patents are corrected, then returned to them."

"Glengorm's patent is genuine. My husband and his clansmen are proud of their ancestors' loyalty to Robert the Bruce," Cicely told the queen.

"Then in a few months your husband will have his patent returned to him," the queen said. "Now dry your eyes, Ce-ce, and bid me a proper farewell."

Cicely wiped her tears away with a small handkerchief she had tucked in her sleeve. Then, rising, she curtsied low to the queen. "I wish Your Highness a fine, strong son this time, and many years of happiness."

"Aye!" the queen said, holding out her arms to her friend, and when Cicely flew into them Joan Beaufort kissed her on both cheeks before releasing her. "All will be well," she promised. "You have my word on it." She smiled into her friend's face.

"Thank you! Thank you!" Cicely responded, returning the smile.

"Go home to your Glengorm, Ce-ce. Do your duty as you were taught, and give your husband children. God preserve you until we meet again, for we will."

"God and his Blessed Mother preserve Your Highness," Cicely said, and then she backed from the queen's little privy chamber to depart the royal apartments and return to her husband. The queen had given her a small sliver of hope with regard to her dower, but she would not believe it until her monies were in her hands. She considered writing to her father, but the truth was that Robert Bowen would not be able to help her. Better not to fret him unless she absolutely had to, but Cicely had no intention of being dowerless. Ian deserved more. 'Twas true her birth was better than his, but what did that matter if she had no dower?

She said nothing to him as they returned to the inn, for she did not know how much, if anything, he had told Ben Duff. They changed from their court garments into their riding clothes, preparing to depart. The innkeeper brought Cicely a tied napkin he told her contained a small roasted chicken. He also gave her a loaf of fresh bread and a small wedge of cheese. They tucked the food into a saddlebag. The two lairds paid for the accommodation and, their combined force of men-at-arms mounted, the little party departed the inn and Edinburgh for the borders.

Reaching Glengorm two days later, they sheltered Ben Duff and his men for the night, bidding him farewell the following morning. Cicely had been very quiet since returning home. Her almost silent demeanor worried the laird, and, noticing the change in both of them, Orva finally had to ask what had happened.

The laird explained.

"Shame on the king!" Orva said angrily. "He has no right to retain my lady's dower, or parcel it out to others. I would not have thought it of him."

"He's the king," the laird responded. "He can do what he wants."

"I must go to my lady," the tiring woman said, and hurried to find her mistress.

Faced with the knowledge that Orva knew, Cicely wept afresh in the older woman's arms. "I am worthless," she said despairingly. "How can Glengorm even bear to look at me?"

"Do not be foolish, my child," Orva replied. "The laird loves you, and whether or not you have a dower matters not to him. I'm certain he has told you that. Besides, you brought him plate and linen, for I packed it among your belongings when I came from Perth. I told you then I left nothing behind. Two horses, a dozen silver goblets and spoons, a silver saltcellar that stands on the high board even now, and a chest full of fine linens for your table. You have your own clothing and jewelry. 'Tis a respectable dower you have brought to your husband."

"I had coin, and now it is stolen. The coin was my dower. Every girl brings plate and linen to her marriage, Orva. Well, perhaps not all, but women of my stature do," Cicely said. "The gold my father entrusted to King James was for my husband, not the king. But Jo says she will get the king to return my dower."

"And how does she expect to do that?" Orva wanted to know.

"She says when she births her son he will be so grateful he will give her whatever she wants. She will ask him to return my dower," Cicely said. "Still, I cannot be easy until Ian has my monies."

"Then you should not fret yourself, my child," Orva said soothingly. But she wondered if Joan Beaufort could indeed deliver on her promise to Cicely. In a sense they were both still trusting girls, and men, even husbands, were not necessarily to be trusted. Although Orva would not know it, her instincts were correct.

On the same day that Cicely had visited the queen before departing back to the borders, James Stewart came to visit with his wife. The queen dismissed her ladies, for she wished to spend time alone with the king. She was almost halfway through her second pregnancy, and had begun to feel comfortable once again. Now, sprawled in her husband's arms while he kissed her neck while caressing her belly, she felt deep contentment. "I'm certain 'tis a lad," she told him.

"I saw wee Meg today," he replied. "Praise God she is so healthy. Aye, give me a son like that, sweeting, and I will be satisfied."

The young queen smiled. "And what will you give me in return?" she teased.

"Whatever you desire will be yours," the king vowed passionately.

"I want you to return Ce-ce's dower to her, and then give it to Glengorm," the queen said. "You should not have taken it."

James Stewart's brow darkened. "I need to keep the Gordons allied to me," he told her. "They were insulted by what happened."

"You behaved no better than your father and your uncle," the queen accused, "bribing those you desired as friends. The Gordons were given my blood kin for Fairlea's wife. Was not the queen's cousin enough to assuage their pride?"

"Her dower was small." The king attempted to defend himself.

"Aye, it was," she agreed. "But they knew not how large was Cicely's dower, and you might have lied to them about it. Because of Fairlea's marriage to my cousin the Gordons are now bound to us. That should have been enough for them, my lord. Ce-ce did them no wrong. Their quarrel, although they had no cause to quarrel, should have been with the Douglases. But there were no marriage contracts drawn and awaiting signature. And Ce-ce had given no promise to Fairlea. Even he admitted that. So it was nothing more than a matter of pride between two young men who both wanted the same woman. Yet only one could have her. Fairlea, in the belief that he had run off all comers, simply found himself outwitted by a border fox. My cousin was more than compensation enough, Jamie. You did not have to pay off the Gordons.

"If they brag on it your earls will think you are no better than those who came before you. They will decide that you can be managed. You made a mistake, my lord. Let us hope the Gordons will remain silent. And after our son is born you will return the monies you should not have taken from Ce-ce. Not having her dower for Glengorm has devastated her. She feels worthless. You had not the right to do that to my best friend," the queen scolded her husband. "She has been loyal to me since the day we met."

James Stewart was well chastised by his wife, but he refused to feel any lasting guilt. "And where do you propose I get the monies to repay Cicely's dower?" he asked her glumly. "Do I not have enough expenses of my own?"

Queen Joan smiled, turning her head to look up into her husband's face. "Oh, Jamie, we both know you have a knack for finding gold, especially when there is something that you particularly want. Well, this is something that I particularly want," she said sweetly. "I know that you won't disappoint me, my lord."

He laughed a quick laugh. "Give me a son, my sweeting, and the laird of Glengorm will have his wife's dower in full, I promise you," the king said.

The queen smiled at him again. "You are so good to me," she said.

"May God have mercy on me," James Stewart replied. "I love you."

"I know," the queen told him. "Now leave me so I may write to Cicely of your promise, and put her mind at ease." And when he had gone the queen called old Bess to bring her writing box and, taking up her quill, she wrote to her longtime friend.

> *To Cicely, Lady of Glengorm, from Joan, Queen of Scotland, Greetings!*
> *I have spoken with James about the matter we*

discussed, and he has agreed that when our son is born, he will return to you fully what is yours. I could not ask him to restore it immediately, for his pride's sake, but you may tell your husband that all will be resolved in this matter by year's end. May God and his Blessed Mother grant you the same joys that I have. I will pray for you, as I know you will for me.

    Jo

Finished, the queen carefully folded the piece of parchment into a small square, sealing it and pressing her signet ring into the hot wax, which was already solidifying. She handed the message to old Bess. "Tell my page to have this dispatched with one of my own messengers to Glengorm," the queen said. Then she sat back in her chair as Bess removed her writing box and left her alone in her privy chamber.

She had done what needed to be done, and with a sense of great satisfaction Queen Joan sat back in her chair, pleased. In a few days they would travel to Scone, where they would remain for much of the rest of the year. Her son would be born there, as was fitting. She smiled.

Chapter 11

*C*icely had come to love Ian Douglas, but not as deeply as he loved her. Yet despite his reassurances that what little she had brought him was more than enough, she was not content. She wanted her dower portion like any other woman. She was the Earl of Leighton's daughter, not the daughter of some simple man. For the laird, however, the matter was over and done. He was a man of practical needs. His house was clean and comfortable. He had land, cattle, and sheep. He had a wife he adored, and the border was currently quiet. Glengorm lacked but one thing: an heir.

And so he told his wife one rainy late-autumn afternoon as, bending her over the edge of the table in the small chamber in which he attended to the clerical matters pertaining to his lands, he fucked her lustily. There had been something about her that afternoon that aroused his desires. She had been sitting in the hall weaving on a tapestry when he had passed by. He called Artair to him. "Tell your mistress to come to my privy chamber," he said to the servant, and the man had hurried to do his bidding.

And when Cicely had entered the small room he had boldly turned the key in the door's lock and taken her into his arms. An interlude of kissing and fondling had followed. Her skin was soft and scented, her breasts lush, and his cock hardened. She murmured a slight protest; then he bent her over the table, pushing her skirts up to her waist. The sight of her perfectly rounded bottom sent a jolt of heat throughout his entire body. Bending, he kissed, nibbled, and licked her buttocks, nuzzling the dimple at the base of her spine until his impatience got the better of him. Releasing his manhood from his leather breeks, he grasped the curve of her hips and thrust himself into her wet heat. He drove into her hard and deep, unable to help himself, almost whimpering with his need.

His sudden lust had surprised Cicely, but it was not displeasing to her. Her breasts were mashed against the table, but it didn't prevent her hips from wiggling beneath his thrusts. Then for a moment he ceased moving, and she felt the long, thick peg of flesh piercing her throb within her sheath. She moaned and, unable to help herself, released her pleasure.

He laughed softly, and leaned forward to bite the nape of her neck. "Do you like this?" he whispered in her ear. Then he tickled it with his tongue.

"Aye!" she said. "But I want to kiss you, and I want to see your face when I pleasure you, my lord." Her hips pressed against his belly tauntingly.

"Then do what I tell you without question," he instructed her, withdrawing himself from her and quickly turning her onto her back. "Wrap your legs about me, ladyfaire," he said, and when she did he plugged her with his hard, steaming cock as he pulled her gown open so he might bury his face between her breasts. "Aye, that is better," he said. Then, lifting his head slightly, he clamped his lips about one of her nipples.

Cicely squealed as his tongue encircled the nipple until it was so stiff she thought one more sweep of his tongue would cause it to snap off. His teeth grazed the sensitive flesh, and then he sucked hard on her breast until Cicely was moaning with the excitement she felt.

When he transferred his attentions to her other breast Cicely thought she would expire from the fire he was kindling within her.

But then, having roused the second breast, he began to lick her torso with his tongue. The tongue probed beneath her breasts. It swept slowly, slowly across her warm, smooth flesh, sending tingles of heat down her spine. Raising his head, he leaned forward and began to kiss her mouth with slow, hot kisses that left her breathless. His tongue found hers, fenced with it, sucked it sensuously, subdued it.

Cicely couldn't move, she was so weak with her own desire. Her entire body felt boneless, though her raised legs clutched at his torso. When he began to move again within her she sighed a long sigh. She wanted to cling to him, but he raised her two arms above her head, one hand holding them prisoner as he pumped and pumped and pumped himself within her. It was as if he wanted to subdue her totally, and would not be content until he did.

"Ian!" she whispered to him.

"Say nothing," he growled. "I would hear only the sounds of your pleasure, ladyfaire." Then he fucked her harder and deeper than he ever had before.

Cicely suddenly realized that for the first time she had no control at all over her body. It absorbed his lust and begged for more. Her breath came in short, fierce pants. Her head spun as she found herself climbing, climbing, and then as quickly plunging down into a warm pool of heated desire as stars exploded behind her tightly closed eyes. Whatever was happening, she didn't want it to end. She screamed softly as she peaked, and realized that what had been was even now draining away as his love juices spurted within her body to fill her with his seed.

"I love you so damned much," he groaned into her tousled hair.

"I love you, my bold border lord," she responded. "Do you think we have made a child?" Her legs fell away from him, and, moving away from her, he reached out to pull her to a seated position so she might recover herself. A brief wave of dizziness overcame her. Cicely let it subside, then drew her skirts down modestly and tried to straighten her hair. "We have never before made love of an afternoon, nor have you had your pleasure of me outside of our bedchamber," she remarked.

He chuckled. "I saw you in the hall at your tapestry, and you looked so delicious I found myself wanting you," he told her. "Aye, we have surely made a bairn from this day's work, for I believe you have drained me of all of my seed, my sweet ladyfaire." Then he kissed her mouth again.

But despite his love and all of his reassurances, the lack of her dower kept nagging at Cicely. It wasn't right that the Gordons had been given a portion of it, nor that the king retained the remainder. Oddly, she did not begrudge the queen's cousin Beth Williams whatever James Stewart had taken from Cicely to add to the girl's dower. Beth was a sweet-natured girl who would be a good wife to Fairlea. In truth she was the perfect wife for him, because she had fallen in love with him. And in time that laird would come to realize the treasure he had in Beth Williams. *If a bit more gold had been all that was needed to soothe Andrew Gordon's pride over what had happened and assure the happiness of the queen's cousin,* Cicely thought, *I would have given it to her myself.*

But she hadn't. And seeing the need at Glengorm for her monies, Cicely fretted more and more. True, the king had promised he would return her dower when the queen birthed a son, but Cicely didn't want to wait. She would write to her father and tell him what had happened. Hopefully he would aid her. And she would send her letter by one of the Douglas men-at-arms so her father would receive her message quickly.

Ian was not pleased by her plan at all. "Why can you not wait until the queen has her bairn? It's sure to be a son this time, and the queen will see the king keeps his word to you, ladyfaire."

"The king has four sisters," Cicely reminded her husband. "If Jo births another daughter I will never see my dower again. These are not James Stewart's monies, my lord. He did not promise me a dower. My father, the Earl of Leighton, dowered me. He deposited my dower with a reputable goldsmith. The king took it, and I want it back!"

The laird shrugged. He would not prevent her from corresponding with her father. She was unhappy enough at the lack of her dower, and perhaps a message from her father would calm her. He was certainly not going to replace the monies he had put aside for her. He had other children to consider, especially Cicely's half sister. "I'll send Fergus to carry your letter, and await a reply," he said to his wife. "Will that suit you?"

She flung her arms about his neck. "I knew you would come to understand!" And she kissed him enthusiastically.

He didn't understand, but if it made her happy to think he did, then so much the better, the laird thought to himself. He sent for his younger brother.

"How would you like to take a little ride?" he asked Fergus.

"How far?" his brother demanded, already suspicious.

"England," Ian answered.

"England is just over the border," Fergus said dryly.

"To Leighton, Cicely's family home," the laird responded. "She is sending to her father regarding her dower. Now, I know he's not going to restore what the king took, but if it will make her happy to write to her father about it and receive his counsel in the matter, then I cannot complain."

Fergus nodded. "Actually he might be able to help, although I will agree with you that he'll not replace what James Stewart stole."

"Watch your mouth!" the laird cautioned his younger brother.

"Well, he did," Fergus retorted. "The money wasn't his. It was Cicely's father's until she wed, and then it should have been yours. Aye, I'll take her message to her da."

Cicely wrote to her father explaining how the king had seized her dower and used it for his own purposes. That the queen had gotten him to agree to restore what remained when she birthed her son. *But what if she does not have a son?* Cicely wrote. *What am I to do, Papa? Ian says it does not matter to him, for he loves me, but it matters to me. This lack has made me feel worthless. Please tell me what I should do.* She then went on to tell him of her life at Glengorm, and of how happy she was. When she had finished she folded the parchment and sealed it, pressing the little signet with the Leighton coat of arms into the hot wax. And the next morning Fergus Douglas departed for England.

When he returned to Glengorm just over a month later he had an unhappy tale to tell them as they gathered in the great hall of the house. Cicely's half sister, Catherine, had died the previous winter, just after her second birthday. Cicely's stepmother, Luciana, had lost her reason, although at first no one realized it, given her normally volatile nature. She had attempted to poison her husband, Cicely's father, but fortunately Donna Clara had learned of it before it was too late, and saved Robert Bowen's life with an antidote.

"But your da will never be the same again," Fergus told Cicely. "He is weak, and unable to walk more than a few feet at a time, poor man. And it is difficult for him to reflect for too long. Your eldest half brother has come home from court to help."

Cicely shook her head. "Charles is only twelve," she said. "What has happened to Luciana, my stepmother?"

"They have confined her to her apartment with her servant," Fergus said.

"Donna Clara," Cicely noted.

"She's as mad as a rabid fox," Fergus said. "I saw her being taken for a walk in the gardens. Her hair and garments were in disarray, and she spoke not. But then when she saw the gardener's small child she began to screech and tear at her hair, poor soul."

"She belongs in hell," Cicely responded coldly.

"I spoke briefly with your da," Fergus said. "He sends you his tenderest love, but he cannot aid you financially. He will, however, send to the goldsmith in London who put your dower with his kinsman in Edinburgh. The earl says the goldsmith in Edinburgh had no right to give what was yours to anyone but you. He will press his man in London to see what can be done."

"The goldsmith in Edinburgh will avoid responsibility for fear of the king," Cicely said. "He will claim that as the king was my guardian he believed he might give him my monies. And who will fault him? I should go to Leighton and look after my father."

"You cannot be in the same house with that madwoman who is your stepmother," Ian Douglas protested. "She will know you are there and seek to harm you."

"I can stay in the cottage where Orva and I lived when I was a child," Cicely said.

"I agree with the laird," Orva spoke. She had been in the hall and heard all. "Your father will be well cared for at Leighton. You are no longer a child, my lady. Your duty is here with your husband, and your Glengorm folk."

Ian Douglas felt sorrow for his wife, but at least now she had something else to think about besides her wretched dower. Why wouldn't she understand that he was satisfied with what he had? It was her he had wanted, and nothing more.

And then came word that Queen Joan had given birth to her second child, another princess, Isabella.

Upon hearing the news Cicely burst into tears. "I shall never be able to give you my dower now," she wailed.

"I don't give a damn about the dower," Ian said angrily. "I don't care about it! Can you not understand that, ladyfaire? Give me what I really want. Give me an heir! At least the queen is trying to do her duty."

Her tears suddenly ceased. She was astounded by his words. "Ian," she began.

"Nay, Cicely, not another word!" He looked angry, and she had never before really seen him angry. "I will hear no more about your dower. The king has taken it. He is unlikely to return it to us. Do not tell me again that without your dower you are valueless. All the gold in Scotland would not suffice me if I lost you. You are precious to me, and of great worth to Glengorm. You have fretted and fumed over your monies since the day the king told you he took them; but I swear to you that if I had them in my hand at this very minute I should throw them into the middle of the loch and be done with it!"

It took a moment but his words finally made sense to her. He was right, of course. It was unlikely she would ever see her dower, and to ruin her happiness over a pile of gold was worse than foolish. He loved her for who she was, not for the gold she might have brought him. *Blessed Mother!* She was so fortunate. Little Beth Williams had had to prove her worth with a fat dower. Andrew Gordon wouldn't have had her otherwise. But she, the Earl of Leighton's daughter, was loved for herself and naught else. What a fool she had been! And how fortunate she really was.

"The matter is closed, my lord," she told her husband.

"For good?" he demanded.

"Forever," she said with a small smile. She moved to stand before him. "Now you must kiss me, for your words were harsh, and you frightened me."

Wrapping his strong arms about her, he kissed her a hard kiss and then he laughed. "I have never frightened you, my love. Even when I trussed you up and stole you from Perth you assailed me with your fierce spirit.

You are as braw a lassie as I have ever known. Now, that other matter we earlier discussed ..." he said, smiling into her face.

"We will simply have to try harder, my lord." She giggled.

In early autumn Glengorm found itself assailed by raiders from the English side of the border, and a flock of sheep was driven off, but no one was harmed. Ian was surprised, for like everyone else on the border he had hoped an English queen of Scotland would help keep the peace. Andrew Grey arrived to say Ben Duff had been attacked, and he had lost some cattle but no lives were lost.

"Do you know who it is?" Ben Duff asked Ian. "They came before moonrise, and I couldn't identify anyone or anything."

"I suspect 'twas Hunter Grahame and his ilk. An English queen of Scotland wouldn't make a difference to him," Ian replied. "That family has little respect for anyone or anything. We can't let these two raids go unpunished, Andrew."

"I know," the laird of Ben Duff answered with a sigh. "Maggie's breeding again, and I don't want her upset, but if we don't strike back they'll take it for weakness. God knows what will happen then."

"We should strike at them at dawn," Ian suggested. "They won't be expecting us to do that. They will think of us coming in the night, as they did. We'll take our livestock back and leave them to themselves. I have no real quarrel with the Grahames of Greyhome. How many men did you bring with you, Andrew?"

"Only a dozen," he replied. "I didn't want to leave Maggie unprotected."

" 'Tis enough," Ian said. "Let us get it over and done with before they slaughter any of our beasts to eat."

Cicely had never seen a party of border raiders. They had been sleeping when the Grahames had stolen the Glengorm flock. At least three dozen men filled the hall, crowding the trestles as supper of rabbit stew and ale was served up. One of Ben Duff's men found himself smacked upon his head when he slid a hand beneath Flora's skirts as she served him. There was much good-natured laughter. Cicely's terriers slipped beneath the high board, hoping for fallen tidbits. Finally, with the meal cleared away, the men settled down to catch some sleep before riding out several hours before the dawn.

"We should be back by afternoon," Ian told his wife, giving her a quick kiss. "I've told the men to keep a sharp watch, but 'tis unlikely you'll be bothered. Still, keep the doors barred, ladyfaire."

Cicely went back to bed, for it was nowhere near dawn. She arose at her usual time and went about her day as she always did, telling Mab to prepare a hot meal for when the men returned. Cicely began to worry as the afternoon wore on, but then one of her husband's men rode in to tell her that when they had reached Grey-home the sheep and cattle were not there. Storming the house, they found it virtually empty but for two terrified old women who told them the Grahames had gone to the Michaelmas fair in a nearby village.

"The two lairds decided to travel on to the fair be-cause they realized the English borderers had probably taken their livestock there to sell," the young messen-ger said. "My lord bid you not to fret. They will be back tomorrow."

"Are you returning to join the laird?" Cicely asked.

"Nay, mistress. The laird told me to remain here," came the answer.

"He's totally reckless!" Cicely said to Orva. "He and Ben Duff both. They plan to ride into an English village and take back their livestock? They'll be killed!"

"Nay, lassie," Mab, who had come up from her kitchen, said. "They'll lay waste to the village first to secure a safe retreat before they take the beasties back."

"What? There are innocent women and children in

that village!" Cicely exclaimed. "What is going to happen to them?"

"What always happens in these raids," Mab said with a shrug.

"Blessed Mother!" Cicely swore softly.

"And there is certain to be more raiding now," Mab predicted. "Ah, well, these months of peace have been enjoyable, my lady."

"Will we be safe?" Cicely wanted to know.

"Safe as some, but not as safe as others," Mab said.

Cicely grew pale suddenly, swaying slightly. "Nay! Not now! *Not now!*" She gripped the back of a chair to keep from falling.

"My lady, what is it? What do you mean, not now?" Mab asked nervously.

"She's with child," Orva said bluntly.

"Bless us," Mab said, smiling her toothless grin, "Glengorm is to have an heir!" Then she patted Cicely's small hand. "Don't fret, my lady," she said. "Glengorm is one of the safest houses in the border. This bit of thieving by the Grahames is nothing, and the two lairds will stop it. Nothing more will come of it."

"I hope not," Cicely replied. "The English king is an infant yet, and those ruling for him have enough on their hands with the French. Scotland's English queen was meant to give England peace in the north."

"I had heard that our King Jamie loves his queen," Mab said.

"Oh, he does! Very much!" Cicely told her. "But that was God's blessing on them both, Mab. For if they hadn't fallen in love the marriage still would have been celebrated for the very reason I have previously said. England needs peace with Scotland, and nothing seals a peace between nations like a marriage between its king and the other king's kin. Queen Joan and the king are well matched."

"She had better cease having daughters," Mab said

darkly, "and give Scotland a fair prince. Two princesses in two years! We need a strong lad."

"I know she's doing her best," Cicely replied with a smile.

"Does our laird know he's to be a father?" Mab asked.

Cicely shook her head. "Not yet. I was planning to tell him, but then our sheep were stolen, and Ben Duff came, and off the two of them went. If he comes back I will tell him," she said with a sigh.

"Not *if,* my lady, but *when* he returns," Mab said. "When our men go raiding here in the borders we always say *when* they return."

"Now don't you go upsetting her any more than you have," Orva scolded. "Sit down, my lady, and rest yourself. You have a ways to go till your child is born."

"When?" Mab asked, curious.

"Spring," Orva said. "My lady will have her babe in the spring."

"I'll pray for a son for Glengorm," Mab said.

"It will be what it will be," Orva said sharply, "and the laird will be happy as long as the child is strong, and its mother safe."

"Yes, yes," Mab agreed impatiently, "but first we need an heir for Glengorm. I hope my lady isn't going to be like her friend the queen. A lad or two, and then there is time for the lasses."

The raiding party returned by midafternoon of the following day. They had brought back Glengorm's flock of sheep, and Ben Duff's dozen head of cattle. They had killed several Grahames, but they had spared the English village hosting the Michaelmas fair, for they had arrived before their livestock was to be sold off. And the villagers had very wisely sided with Ian Douglas and Andrew Grey when they learned from where the cattle and sheep had come.

"Mind you," Andrew Grey said, "had the creatures already been sold they would have sided with the buyers. But there we were, and they knew they could save themselves if they were quick. The Grahames were very surprised." He chuckled.

"Were you hurt?" Cicely said anxiously, running her hands over Ian's arms and shoulders, seeking wounds.

"Hurt?" Ian looked surprised. "Nay, ladyfaire, I wasn't harmed at all. This was simply a wee raid. There was no danger."

"No danger?" Cicely looked outraged. "You dare to tell me there was no danger. You ride off with a troop of armed men to accost a group of bandits, and you tell me there was no danger? You send a messenger to say you will be traveling deeper into the English border to retrieve your sheep. Mab tells me you'll burn the village sheltering the Grahames, and you say there was no danger?"

Andrew Grey's face, surprised at first, suddenly took on a knowing look.

"You could have been killed!" Cicely shouted, and then she burst into tears, flinging herself against her husband's broad chest, sobbing piteously.

The laird was astounded. "Ladyfaire, I have been on many such ventures."

Andrew Grey snickered, close to open laughter.

"What if you had been killed?" Cicely wailed. "Who would take care of us?"

"Ladyfaire, I wasn't killed or injured, and I am here to take care of you," the laird comforted his wife. "You have never shown me weakness before. Why are you showing it to me now?" He stroked her hair.

Andrew Grey began to howl with his laughter.

"What the hell is so funny, Ben Duff?" Ian Douglas snarled.

"Don't you know?" Andrew said, doubled over with laughter. "Cicely, you must tell him," he said to her. "It is not my place to tell him."

"Tell me what?" the laird demanded.

"I am going to have a baby!" Cicely sobbed. "And I don't want its da killed."

"A bairn? I'm going to be a father?" Ian Douglas's face lit up with pure joy, and he looked down into her tearstained face. "Ladyfaire, I thank you! And I promise not to get killed, for if I were who would teach my son all he needs to know?"

"It could be a daughter," Cicely said softly.

"Nay, 'twill be a lad, I'm certain," the laird of Glengorm answered her, grinning.

"No more raiding," Cicely told him.

He shook his head. "Nay, I will not promise you that, for if I did not redress any attacks on my lands, my livestock, my people, I would not be a fit laird. And I would be open to attack from all and sundry who believed me a weakling. Raids are a part of life on the border, ladyfaire, but Glengorm has been more fortunate than most. The sheep stolen by the Grahames were still in their summer meadow, which is across the loch. It is the most distant of my lands. There was but a single shepherd and dog, and if he hadn't jumped into the loch and swum across to sound the alarm we probably wouldn't have known who took the sheep. I shall keep that meadow better guarded in the future, and I will build a small stone redoubt on the hill above, to be manned so that we will be able to see who is coming from that direction. But I will never permit an outrage against me to go unpunished, ladyfaire. Weakness leads to far worse things than small wounds."

"Then I will pray the Grahames have learned their lesson, my lord," Cicely told her husband. "May they keep to their own side of the border."

"When is the bairn due to be born?" he asked her.

"Late March or early April," she told him. " 'Twill be a spring child."

He put an arm about her, giving her a small hug. "I shall take him raiding with me as soon as our son can sit a horse," he teased her, and Ben Duff laughed aloud again.

"You will do no such thing!" Cicely said indignantly.

"Ah, Ian, my friend, you are about to see the love of your life change into a mother before your very eyes. It has already begun, as you see, for she is protective of her child against all comers, even its father," Andrew Grey said. "I can't wait to tell my Maggie of this happy event." And on the following morning he departed with his men and his cattle for his home.

Several days later Fergus came to tell his brother that a party of Grahames was on the other side of the loch calling for a parley.

"We've got to get that redoubt built before winter," the laird said. "I don't like it that the Grahames are suddenly coming and going as they please on my lands."

"Don't go!" Cicely begged him.

"Ladyfaire, 'tis a parley, not a battle to the death," he told her gently. " 'Tis better we talk than fight, isn't it?" Giving her a quick kiss, he left the hall with Fergus.

The two brothers walked down the hill through Glengorm village and onto the shore that edged the water. The Douglas clansmen had come out to stand behind their laird in a show of strength. Across the loch upon the other shore was a small party of men. The loch was not particularly wide and so they were able to shout across it.

"What do you want?" Ian Douglas called across the water. "You are trespassing."

"Are you the laird?" a stocky man demanded to know.

"I am," Ian said.

" 'Twas your band of clansmen who killed three of our kin?"

"Your kin stole from me, and when I reclaimed my livestock they attacked me," Ian said. "I was within my rights."

"You owe us a forfeit for those murders," the stocky man retorted.

"You owe me for the three lambs that were missing from my flock, and undoubtedly slaughtered to fill your fat belly," Ian told him. "Consider us even."

"If you will not pay then we shall take our revenge," the stocky man said, and as the words left his mouth a hail of arrows were shot by the mounted men across the narrow loch at the laird and his people.

Fergus Douglas flung himself in front of his brother, taking the arrow meant for the laird directly into his own heart. As Ian bent to catch his sibling he felt himself pierced sharply. Kneeling, his dead brother cradled in his arms, he howled with anguish. Then, dropping Fergus onto the sandy shore, he stood up, shouting to his clansmen not injured, "To horse!" They ran for mounts, and a village lad, anticipating the laird, had already run up the hill to the house, shouting for horses to be saddled.

Cicely, hearing the commotion, came running from the hall. "What has happened?" she asked of no one in particular as she saw their two stablemen leading horses from the stables down the hill, and clansmen racing up to meet them, clambering onto the animals and racing back down the hill again.

Ian Douglas had wisely kept out of his wife's line of vision. He had broken off the shafts of the two arrows that had hit him, so if she managed to catch a glimpse of him he would not from a distance appear wounded. Grasping the bridle of his stallion, he pulled himself up onto its back and marshaled his clansmen about him. "Not one of them lives!" he said grimly. "No mercy! We can catch them fastest if we swim our horses across the loch." Then he led them to the shore and into the water, and urged the beast under him across to the far shore.

The Grahames had already disappeared over the hill. They had not been certain whether it was the laird they had killed or not. But the sound of grief that had pierced the air after their volley satisfied them that they had gained their revenge on the Douglases of Glengorm. They rode swiftly, for they assumed they would be followed, but by the time their pursuers rode around the loch and up the hills the Grahames would have managed to obscure the trail by sending two horses here, and another three there, in different directions. The Grahames considered themselves quite good at making an escape.

They were therefore very surprised to discover the Douglases of Glengorm catching up to them, and not an hour had passed. The sound of their war cry—*"A Douglas! A Douglas!"*—echoed in the clear autumn air. The stocky man leading the Grahames spurred his horse onward, shouting to his companions to scatter, for that would make it more difficult to catch them. But their tactic was countered, for each rider or group of riders breaking off from the main body of Grahames was followed by several Douglases. And each Grahame was caught and killed.

Unhorsed and on his knees, the stocky man looked up at Ian. "How did you come so quickly?" he wanted to know.

"We swam our horses across the loch," the laird answered him. "Do you not know the motto of the Douglas family? 'Tis *Jamais arrière*," and when the Grahame looked up at Ian, confused, he said, "It means 'Never behind.'" He raised his sword.

"Wait! I can see we did not kill you," the stocky Grahame said. "Whom did we kill? At least tell me that before I die."

"You killed my younger brother," the laird told him even as he plunged his sword into his enemy's chest and twisted it hard to ensure the man died. Then, yanking his blade from the stocky man's chest, he wiped it off on the fellow's shirt.

One of his men walked over to the Grahame and, pulling out his dirk, slit his throat. "Just to be certain, my lord," he said.

The laird nodded, and then a wave of both nausea and dizziness assailed him. "Help me to my horse," he said to his clansman. "I am beginning to feel the effects of my wounds." He swayed, and the clansman, putting an arm about him, got Ian to his horse, and then up onto the stallion's broad back.

Mounting his own animal, the clansman said to his companions, who had now rejoined them, "Protect the laird! He is wounded."

With every bit of willpower he had, Ian Douglas managed to remain atop his horse while they returned to Glengorm. Finally, as his mount came to a stop before the house, he was overcome by a wave of weakness, and began to fall. But the clansman who had first come to his aid was there again, half lifting him from his saddle, half walking, half dragging him into the house, where Tam and Artair ran forward to help. One of the serving women saw and ran to fetch Cicely. Another hurried to find old Mab in her kitchens. The two women entered the hall almost simultaneously. Cicely shrieked.

"Get him onto the high board quickly," Mab instructed the men. She turned to Cicely. "He's alive, my lady, and I'll need your help. Go and fetch hot water and clean cloths so I may clean his wounds." She had her basket of healing stores with her.

Cicely ran from the hall to do the old woman's bidding. She prayed Mab knew what she was doing, for Cicely had never seen a wounded man. She didn't know what to do. Neither she nor Jo had been particulary interested in the healing arts when Joan of Navarre had offered to teach them years back. And, of course, their foster mother had later been accused of witchcraft, although she was cleared of all the charges leveled against her. Now, it appeared, it would help her to know what to do with a wounded man. If Mab could teach her she would learn this time.

In the hall Mab saw the two arrows with their broken shafts. One had pierced the laird's shoulder in the front. The other had lodged in his chest just above his heart. She shook her head. These were both serious wounds, and would have to be packed tightly to stop the bleeding once she removed the arrows. "My lord," she said to him.

Ian opened his eyes. "Where is my wife?" he asked weakly.

"Gone to fetch water and cloths for me, dearie," Mab said to him.

"They killed Fergus, but we slew them all, Mab. My brother is avenged," the laird told her. Then he closed his eyes, for it had been a great effort to tell her what he did.

Cicely returned from the kitchens carrying a pile of clean cloths, Bessie behind her with a small cauldron of hot water. "Is he all right, Mab? He has been wounded. Where? What else do you need? Blessed Mother! I don't know what to do." Her voice trembled. "I did not think to see a wounded man."

"Now, my lady, there is naught to it," Mab said soothingly. "Just watch what I do, and do what I bid you. You'll learn."

Cicely nodded nervously. She bent over her husband, and Ian opened his eyes.

"They killed Fergus," he told her. "Go into the village and see if any others were killed, ladyfaire. Comfort Marion. Mab will take good care of me."

Cicely looked to the old lady, and she nodded reassuringly. "I'll teach you the arts of healing another day, my lady," she promised.

Cicely hurried off to do her husband's bidding. She was ashamed to be so useless, and vowed to herself it would not be so again. Being the lady of Glengorm meant more than just being gracious to visitors, managing her servants, and tending her gardens.

"It isn't good, my lord," Mab told him.

"I know," Ian said. "I felt this enormous burst of strength and energy sweep over me after they killed Fergus. But then when it was over . . ."

"You have two arrow wounds, my lord. You broke off most of the shaft from each, but I must draw the arrows from your flesh, and I fear you will bleed heavily from both, less perhaps from your shoulder. Have you pain anywhere else?"

"My right arm is beginning to grow numb," he answered her.

Mab nodded. Then, turning to Artair and Tam, she said, "I will need your help, lads. Removing the arrows will give the laird great pain. You must hold him steady while I pull them so those arrows do not damage him further. I'll take the one in his shoulder out first. When I tell you, I will want you to hold him down by his upper shoulders for me." Stepping down from the high board, she reached for the small decanter of whiskey on the sideboard and brought it back with her.

The two young men had nodded in response to her instruction. Although they looked uncomfortable, nonetheless they did as Mab had bidden them.

Mab carefully studied the placement of the wound. It was at the bottom of his shoulder, almost beneath his upper arm. She placed her hand flat on his chest, the shaft between her thumb and her forefinger. The fingers of her other hand wrapped tightly about the shaft, she nodded imperceptibly to her two helpers, who immediately did as she had bidden them. Pressing down just slightly, she yanked the shaft from his shoulder in one smooth movement.

Ian Douglas screamed, and then, mercifully, fainted. To Mab's relief this wound did not bleed greatly. She poured a bit of the whiskey on it, and then decided that while he lay in a stupor it would be best to remove the other arrow. This time, however, she drew the jagged shaft slowly from the laird's broad chest. The wound spurted blood, but briefly. Again she poured whiskey into the injury.

He moaned and opened his eyes. "Jesu, Mary, that hurts, old woman!"

"I'm sorry, laddie," she told him, "but they're both out now. I'll bind your wounds for you." She set quickly to work, gently patting the ooze from each wound, covering it with a salve made from goose fat and acorn paste, then binding it. When she had finished she said to Tam and Artair, "Help your master to his bed, lads." And to the laird: "I'm going to mix you a soothing draft, my lord. It will ease the pain."

And while Mab had seen to the laird, Cicely hurried into the village to learn whether anyone else besides Fergus Douglas had been killed. She was relieved to learn that no one had, although several of the men had been wounded by the flight of unexpected arrows. Fergus's body had been carried to the large cottage that was his. He was already lying upon the tressle table in the main room of the cottage, which was filled with women.

Cicely went immediately to her sister-in-law. "I am told by women in the village that he put his own body before that of the laird. Fergus Douglas was a hero, Marion. You can be proud of him."

Her two small daughters clinging to her skirts, Marion Douglas said bitterly, "I should rather he be here by my side. Damn the Grahames, and damn all the English!" Then she gasped at what she had said, paled, and looked at Cicely.

"Aye," Cicely said. "Damn the Grahames, but do not damn all the English, for we are not all bad." She took Marion into her embrace and kissed both of her cheeks.

Marion began to weep. "Is Ian safe?" she asked between sobs.

"Mab is tending him now," Cicely answered quietly. "He asked me to come into the village to see who else had been injured or killed. I am relieved that while many were injured, no one else was killed. Fergus's murderers are now dead, and will not bother us again."

"What will become of us without Fergus?" Marion wept.

"You are Douglases," Cicely said. "Ian will take care of his kin."

"Of course he will," Marion's mother said. "You are foolish, daughter."

"I must return to the laird now," Cicely told them, and she left the big cottage.

Mab was waiting for her in the hall. Taking Cicely aside, she said, "I will not lie to you, my lady. The laird's wounds are bad. Especially the one near his heart."

Cicely was overcome with fear. "Will he live?" she asked.

"Perhaps he will, and perhaps he won't. I am no physician, my lady. I got the arrows out, and cleaned and bound his wounds. I brought him a soothing draft into which I had infused some poppy juice. He will sleep for many hours, and sleep is the greatest healer. On the morrow I will teach you how to dress his wounds, for they must be changed regularly if we are to keep ill humors from infecting him."

Cicely nodded wordlessly; then she ran from the hall upstairs to the bedchamber where her husband now lay. He was so pale, she thought as she brushed a lock of his rich chestnut brown hair from his brow. She had never seen an injured man. Never realized a man could look so frail, so helpless. Kneeling by his bedside, she prayed, and then, rising, she lay down on the bed next to him.

But she did not sleep. She dozed in fits and starts for hours, but mostly she lay awake listening for the sound of his breathing. And when he began to snore lightly for a short time, Cicely thought it was the best sound she had ever heard. As the night waned Ian began to moan with his pain, for the poppy was wearing off. Cicely got up and saw that both of his wounds were oozing through the bandages. What should she do? Blessed Mother, why had she not listened and learned from her foster parent?

"Water," Ian croaked.

Cicely stumbled across the chamber and poured some water from the pitcher into a small goblet. Hurrying to her husband's side, she braced him while she put the goblet to his lips. "Is that better?" she asked him as he sipped.

"Aye," he said huskily. "I was parched."

"Do you hurt?" she asked shyly.

"Aye, but 'twill ease with another of Mab's soothing drafts," he said.

"It isn't even dawn yet," Cicely told him.

"Marion and her bairns?"

"She's devastated, but the wee ones don't know what's going on at all. They're so young it's not likely they'll remember their da—more's the pity, for Fergus was a brave man, and a good one," Cicely said quietly.

"Are you all right?" he asked her.

"Of course," she replied.

"This has not disturbed the bairn you carry?"

"Obviously it hasn't," Cicely replied. She had been so worried over Ian she had forgotten entirely that she was with child. "Ian, I am sorry I did not know what to do when you were wounded," she said. "I never thought to be in a place where my husband could be injured. Mab has promised to teach me what I must know."

He laughed weakly. "You'd have been in worse difficulties if you had wed Gordon. The Highlands bubble constantly with clan disputes, more so in the north and west, but also in the eastern regions. Only the Grahames would have been so dishonorable as to send a flight of arrows at a group of unarmed men. You understand why I had to go after them, ladyfaire, don't you? It is important that you comprehend."

Cicely nodded. "It will be some time before the Grahames, or any of their ilk, consider attacking Glengorm. There was no choice but to go after them, Ian. I know it. Even if poor Fergus hadn't been killed you would have had to chase after them and punish them. Had you not we would have been vulnerable to attack from all and sundry. Word of the carrion birds hanging above the moor and hills will travel quickly. The Grahames will regret their boldness, and all in the borders will know of it. Glengorm will be the safer for it. Aye, my lord, I understand now what I did not before."

"Good," he replied. "Should the day ever come that I am gone from Glengorm and it is attacked, I can rest easy knowing you will be able to mount its defense and attack our attackers. Our son will have to depend upon you if I am not here."

"Do not speak such words to me, my lord. You will be here for Glengorm, for me, and for our child." Cicely leaned over and kissed him softly and gently.

"Our son," he said, kissing her back.

"Or our daughter," she returned.

"Or our daughter," he agreed with her, smiling.

Chapter 12

*J*an's chest wound healed quickly, but his right arm was stiff now. Mab taught her lady the use of herbs, like lavender for sleep, and comfrey for healing bruises and knitting bones back together. She showed Cicely how to mix powders and poultices, and how to make pills. Cicely learned how to examine a patient for a broken or dislocated bone. How to bind such injuries.

There was another lack in her education she now had to make up. She began to learn about how to defend the house should they be attacked. The captain of their men-at-arms was a burly, baldheaded Douglas man named Frang. At first he was loath to discuss defense with Cicely. She was, after all, English born.

"I am capable of keeping the house safe," he told her.

"But what if you were away?" Cicely asked him in dulcet tones. "You could come back to find the house burned, and the rest of us dead or carried off. You must teach me what I need to know should you and the laird not be here, Frang. I know I may rely upon you at all times, but if I could not keep my own house and servants safe from attack I should be a poor border wife." She gave him a small smile. "I would make my lord proud of me. You know he has not been well."

Frang looked at the dainty English girl with her swelling belly. And then he looked across the hall to where his laird sat pale and still weak by the hearth, a wool coverlet about his knees like an old woman. He nodded. "I will teach you what you need to know, my lady, though it's unlikely I'll be away anytime soon."

"Thank you," Cicely said softly. She had seen where Frang's eyes had gone as he considered his decision. Ian still wasn't well, and he was as weak as a kitten. The wound in his chest had finally healed, but the one in his lower shoulder was troublesome. Mab was at her wits end, for just when this second wound appeared to finally be cured it would suddenly fill with green matter again, which would sometimes turn yellow and be streaked with blood. And each time Ian Douglas grew weaker. Finally one morning he was unable to get out of bed.

"I'm dying," he told Cicely in a resigned voice.

"Do not say it!" she almost shouted at him, and the child in her belly seemed to jump at the sound of her frightened voice. "You cannot die, Ian Douglas."

"The wound won't heal. I don't know why, and neither does Mab," he said.

"We'll send for a physician!" Cicely cried.

"There isn't one in the near borders, ladyfaire. I'm dying. Send for Ambrose to come and shrive me before it is too late," he instructed her.

"We are having a child," Cicely replied. "You cannot die, Ian. We are having a child! Don't you want to see your child?"

"Aye, I do, but I will not, I fear, ladyfaire. Send word to Sir William, for Glengorm will be without a laird, or the new laird will be a wee bairn. No border keep can be kept by a child or a woman, Cicely. I am sorry to leave you so vulnerable."

This was a dream. A bad dream. *Nay!* A nightmare. Ian wasn't dying. He couldn't be! They had been together such a short time, and she had come to love him.

His child was in her belly. She drew a deep, calming breath. "I'll get the priest," she said. If it would comfort him, so much the better. His uncle would tell him he wasn't dying, and Ian would get better. Leaving him, she found Artair in the hall. "Go and fetch Father Ambrose quickly," she told him.

"Is it time then?" the serving man asked her, but then, seeing the horrified look in his mistress's eye, Artair ran from the hall.

What was the matter with the servants? Cicely asked herself. Why did they all seem to be so fixated with her husband's death? Ian wasn't going to die. He would be here in the spring to hold his firstborn.

Mab came up into the hall and, seeing her mistress just standing there silently, she led the young woman over to her chair by the hearth. "Sit," she said.

"He wants the priest." Cicely spoke low, collapsing into the chair.

"Aye, then he senses his time is near," Mab answered matter-of-factly.

"What are you saying?" Cicely cried. "Do not say it! *Do not!*"

"The wound is infected, my lady. It is poisoning him. I cannot heal it or stop it," Mab said. "I am ashamed my skills have failed him, but if he says he is dying then he is dying. Only a miracle can save him now, and prayers are all we have left."

Cicely did not reply. She sat very still, her face turned to stone.

Father Ambrose found her there as he came into the hall. He saw Mab as she returned to her kitchen. The old woman shook her head sorrowfully at him. Walking over to Cicely, the priest put a gentle hand on her shoulder. "Tell me what is wrong," he said. "And then I will do my best to help."

"Ian says he is dying," Cicely began, not looking at him.

Ambrose nodded. "Let us go to him then, and see

how we may ease what remains of his time, Cicely." His voice was kind and filled with sympathy.

She turned in her chair, looking up at him. "It isn't so," she said, low. "It cannot be! My husband is not dying. Nay! He isn't." Her voice trembled. Her eyes were desperate.

Ambrose put a firm hand beneath Cicely's elbow, gently forcing her to her feet. "Come, my child, your husband needs us both now. We cannot fail him, can we?" He led her from the hall and up the stone stairs to the chamber where Ian lay. Opening the door, the priest ushered Cicely into the room.

"Uncle!" The laird's eyes lit up with relief. "Uncle, I am dying. I feel it. You must confess me before I can no longer do so."

Like the young woman by his side, Ambrose Douglas wanted to deny the evidence of his own eyes. But he was far too practical a man. His nephew was right: He was dying. His skin was paler than pale, with just the faintest hint of gray. His eyes were sunken into his head, and he had lost a great deal of weight. He made the sign of the cross over Ian. "Your sins are forgiven you, nephew. And if it will soothe you to confess to me you may do so, but first I must know what you wish me to do."

Cicely sat upon the bed. A small sound escaped her, but she said nothing.

The laird reached out to take her hand in his as he spoke. "Send to Sir William," he began. "If the bairn Cicely carries is a lad, then Glengorm will have an heir in the direct line. I will depend on Sir William to protect both my wife and my son. If the bairn is female then it is up to Sir William to decide what is to be done. If he means to give Glengorm to another, provision must be made for my wife and daughter. Perhaps he can convince the king to restore Cicely's dower. I do not think the queen would permit her old friend to be left impoverished."

"Why do you say these things?" Cicely whimpered. "You cannot die, Ian!"

"Do you think I would leave you if I did not have to, ladyfaire? Did I not brave the wrath of a king to make you my wife?" He raised the small hand in his to his parched lips and kissed it. "You are a brave lass, Cicely. Do you remember how you came to Glengorm, my love? Oh, how you raged and fought with me in those early days. You must gather that fervor to yourself again—for your sake, and for that of our child. I expect no less of you, ladyfaire. Now, if the bairn is a lad I should like you to name him after me. But if it's a lass, the choice is yours, although I should favor Johanna, after the queen."

There was a heavy, dark rock where her heart had once been. Her chest hurt, but if she wept she would shatter into a thousand pieces. The child in her womb stirred again. It was as if there were a butterfly within her belly, fluttering its wings. She could not allow herself to collapse into self-indulgent hysteria. The child was all she would have left of her husband. The child must be protected at all costs. "I will name our son Ian," she said. "But if I birth a daughter I should like her to be called after Jo. Thank you for that, my lord." Now it was she who kissed his hand, and her eyes met his.

He smiled at her, and she saw a quick flash of the man who had abducted her because he loved her so much.

Cicely felt guilty, for while she had come to love him she had never felt the same deep passion for him that he did for her. And now he was dying. There was no time left for them, and she was suddenly angry at a fate that had thrown her into Ian Douglas's embrace and was now tearing her out of those strong arms. It wasn't fair!

"You will survive, ladyfaire," he told her quietly. "You are strong."

Cicely sighed. "I don't want to be without you. Curse the Grahames! I will take a party of clansmen over the border and slay them all for this. They have taken my husband from me, and my child will have no father because of their dishonorable actions." Her beautiful face was suddenly set in a hard manner.

"Nay, I have avenged Fergus's death, ladyfaire. I want no border warfare disturbing the peace of Glengorm for our folk, or for you and the bairn," he said. "Promise me that you will not attack the Grahames and start a feud."

"You have avenged Fergus's death, my dear lord, but who is to avenge yours if I do not?" she asked him candidly.

"I need to go to God reassured that you and our child will be safe, Cicely," he said seriously. Then he fell back upon the pillows. "I am weary now. Leave me. Ambrose will remain and hear my confession. Give me a kiss now."

Rising, she bent and touched his lips with hers. Did they feel colder? "I promise you I will not feud with the Grahames," she told him. "But they should pay for what they have done, and your revenge for Fergus wasn't enough, my lord." Then she left Ian and his uncle together.

When she had gone Ambrose Douglas said, "I will send to Sir William today, nephew. And I will watch over her, I promise."

"Tell Frang I want no feud," Ian Douglas said. "She has sworn, but when I am gone she may think better of her promise to me, Uncle."

"Sir William will send someone to keep her in check," the priest replied. "Now, Ian, that I have heard your wishes, let me hear your confession, nephew."

The laird gave his priestly uncle a weak grin. "I've been sick for weeks now, Ambrose. What sins could I possibly have?"

The priest chuckled. "I'll stay with you, Ian," he said quietly.

The laird nodded. "Thank you," was all he said, and then he closed his eyes.

Ian Douglas died quietly in the night as his wife and uncle dozed by his bedside, unaware until after the fact. As a male in the direct line of descent, the priest immediately took charge of the situation. Stony faced, Cicely could not cry, fearing that to grieve would harm her unborn child. A messenger was dispatched to Sir William Douglas, who came with all haste to comfort the widow, and to learn how his kinsman had died.

"The Grahames are to blame," Cicely told him bitterly. Her face was pale, her hair unbound, and she could not stop pacing.

Sir William looked to Ambrose Douglas, who quickly explained.

"*Both* brothers gone? Ahh," Sir William said, "this is not good. The lady and her bairn will need to be protected."

"We need no stranger," Cicely spoke up boldly. "Our Glengorm folk are true, Frang, our captain, capable. And we have Ambrose."

"My dear," Sir William responded in as kindly tones as he could muster, "your bairn, be it a lad or a lassie, cannot rule Glengorm from its cradle. I know your folk have good hearts. I know Frang is loyal and able. But this is a border house. I need a strong man to maintain order here. You are the lady of Glengorm, and will remain so, but the welfare of Glengorm will be in a man's hand. But I promise I will send you a good man."

She could feel her resistance to his suggestion rising, but Cicely swallowed back the words she wanted to speak. In her heart she knew he was right. A woman in charge, especially a woman with a large belly, would be considered fair game to any less than honorable border lord. And the border did have its share of dishonorable men. Sir William's protection would keep Glengorm safe. She sighed audibly, and curtsied to him. "I am grateful, my lord, for your care," she said. "Now, if you will excuse me."

"Go and rest, my dear," he replied. "These last weeks

have been difficult, I know." He gave her a courtly bow, thinking how sad her plight was.

Cicely left the hall.

"She goes to the chamber beneath the church where his coffin now rests. The ground was too hard and we could not dig his grave," the priest explained. "She goes several times daily and speaks with him."

"Has she lost her reason?" Sir William asked nervously.

"Nay, she is simply still in shock over his death," the priest replied. "She was raised gently, and is not accustomed to so harsh a life as can occur here in the borders. But she is a strong lass, cousin. She will survive. Tell me now whom you will send us."

"I have a son, one born on the other side of the blanket, but one I have recognized and to whom I have given my name. I'd like to send Kier to look after Glengorm. Your father favored you, Ambrose. You have his name. He educated you, so I now consider you the male who speaks officially for this branch of the Douglases. If Lady Cicely births a daughter I will, with your approval, give Glengorm to Kier."

"What of the bairn?" the priest asked. "If she is not the heiress of Glengorm then what is to become of her? Will you see her properly dowered, cousin?"

"I will," Sir William replied. "You know I cannot let Glengorm out of our hands. But I will provide for Ian's child. If the bairn is a lad then he will inherit the land, and Kier will remain to see he is raised as a Douglas should be raised."

"And the widow?" the priest inquired.

"I will speak to the king on her behalf. I think with Queen Joan's help I can get at least part of the lady's dower portion returned to her. The fact that she has been widowed so tragically while carrying her husband's heir will certainly work in her favor. The king was really angrier with Ian Douglas than he was with Lady Cicely. I am also considering that perhaps Ian's widow might make a good wife for my son. But that is not something I will discuss with her at this point," Sir William said.

"Nay," Ambrose Douglas replied dryly, "'twould be best to wait, I suspect. She should be given time to mourn, and to birth her child. Tell me about your son, cousin."

Sir William paused as if considering his words. "Kier's mother was Lady Sybil Stewart. She was widowed, and we fell in love. Albany forbade us to marry. He feared an alliance between the Stewarts and the Douglases. She died giving birth to Kier. I married shortly afterwards, and my wife raised him with our children. He is a fine warrior, but stubborn. He's never married, although there was a lass once, but it came to naught. Her father wanted a better match for his daughter than the bastard of Sir William Douglas. My son had not until that moment faced the stigma of his birth.

"My wife loves him as she does the bairns she's given me. We never hid the circumstances of his birth from him. He understood his place in the inheritance and line of descent. But Callum Ogilvie sold his lass to wife a fat, elderly Edinburgh merchant. When her husband died the sons born in his first marriage sent her back to her father with nothing but a big belly one of them had given her. She couldn't name the father because it seemed she had had both of her husband's sons to satisfy her when he could not. Her father has died now, and she lives in her brother's house, to his wife's distress. No one knows what happened to the lass's bairn or even when she birthed it.

"Kier thought he loved the girl once, but then he saw her for what she really was. I don't think his heart was broken, and I always thought it was his lust driving him. But he has been cold and guarded where women are concerned ever since. My son does not enjoy being made a fool. He is a proud man. But he is honest, and he is fair. Glengorm will be in excellent hands, Ambrose. You may trust Kier Douglas."

"I am pleased to know that," the priest said. "Cicely must be treated gently and with kindness. Ian loved her deeply, and she has become accustomed to it."

"Did she love him at all?" Sir William asked curiously.

"Aye, she did. Not as he did her, but she did care for him. The tragedy is that they were just really getting to know each other well, becoming more at ease with each other. Cicely never really got over the king's appropriating her dower portion. Only Ian's love took the sting of it away. And now she must continue on without him, with a child, and penniless but for whatever your son will allow her."

"I will see she receives the rents from three cottages annually," Sir William said.

The priest smiled. " 'Tis generous," he approved.

Cicely did not return to the hall that afternoon. She had Orva come to ask Sir William to excuse her, as she was not well. Mab nonetheless saw that a splendid supper was set upon the high board for the priest and their guest. When the morning came and Sir William was preparing to depart Glengorm, Cicely came into the hall to bid him farewell. She was pale, and looked as if she had not slept well at all.

"I could not allow you to leave without a proper farewell," she told him with a small smile. She wore a dark blue gown with a high waist and long, tight sleeves.

Looking at her, he thought how lovely she was. Enceinte with her first child, and mourning a husband she had just lost, she still possessed a beauty that was almost luminous. If Kier were not a total fool she would make him a fine wife. "I was sorry you were not with us at supper," he said. "Mab is a wonderful cook."

"I need to know what you mean to do about the Grahames," Cicely said. "My husband should be avenged, even as he avenged his brother's death at their hands."

"I want no border feuding; nor did Ian, for Ambrose has told me his dying wishes," Sir William said to her.

"But I should not object if you wrote to your friend Queen Joan. Perhaps Scotland's queen can urge her royal relations in England to speak with their warden in the northern marches. Let them punish the Grahames. It will take time, my dear, but other lives will be saved. I want no more widows like you and Marion Douglas weeping for the loss of their men. Nor do I wish to lose any more good men."

He took her small hand in his, tucking it into his arm as they walked from the hall towards the door of the house. "I am sending you my own son to watch over Glengorm. He will come within the next few days, for the ground is already frozen and winter is about to set in. I do not want you and your folk unprotected, for while winter is not usually raiding season, one cannot now be certain, given the dishonorable actions of the Grahames. It is my my duty to see you are protected, Cicely. You need have no fear, for Kier will keep you and Glengorm safe for the Douglases."

They passed through the open door. Sir William's horse and men awaited him. The clan chieftan kissed Cicely upon both of her cheeks, then mounted his animal and, raising his hand, signaled his men to begin their journey home. She waved her hand in a gesture of farewell, watching in the cold morning air until Sir William and his party were out of sight. Then, calling for her fur-lined cloak, Cicely walked down the path leading to the village to see her sister-in-law, Marion Douglas.

Marion's two little daughters tottered towards her as she entered the large, comfortable cottage where they lived. Marion, sewing by the hearth, jumped up to greet Cicely shyly. "Sit down! Sit down!" she invited. "I am honored by your visit."

"I came to tell you that Sir William came last night. He was shocked to learn that both of our men were gone. We were all so intent on Ian's well-being that no one ever sent to him when Fergus was killed. I'm sorry."

Marion Douglas reached out to pat Cicely's cold hand. "I understand," she said.

"Sir William has appointed one of his sons to come to Glengorm to protect us all," Cicely said with a wry smile, and Marion laughed, understanding. "I thought you would want to tell your mother this news."

"I think she would appreciate hearing it from you," Marion said. "She has liked you from the beginning, but you rarely come into the village." Getting up, she went to the cottage door, opened it, and called out, "Fetch my mam. The lady is here."

Within another moment or two Mary Douglas came into the cottage, and with her came most of the women in the village. They crowded into Marion's cottage, looking anxiously to Cicely, and remaining very silent, which was unusual.

"Good morrow," Cicely greeted them when it became apparent that not another of the village women could get into the dwelling.

"Good morrow, my lady!" they chorused back at her.

"I thought to give my news to you first," Cicely said to Mary Douglas, who was acknowledged as a woman of importance among her peers. Cicely understood the importance of respect given within the small community.

Mary smiled, and her eyes twinkled. "This will be easier on me, my lady," she said. "And more will hear it right than get it wrong."

Cicely laughed softly, and nodded. Then she turned her attention to all the women within the chamber. "Sir William came yesterday to pay his respects to the laird, God assoil him, and to bring us his condolences," she began, and there was a low murmur of approval as heads nodded. "He is concerned for the safety of Glengorm," Cicely continued, "and so he is sending us his son Kier Douglas to mount our defense against the Grahames and their ilk." Cicely put her hand on her belly. "My bairn cannot take up the duties his father left him until he is grown. Douglas lands must not fall into the hands of others. Our defender will arrive in a few days' time, and I wanted you to know."

"It is good of you, my lady"—Mary Douglas spoke for them all—"to do us the courtesy of coming to bring this news. I thank you." She turned to the others. "All right, you have heard what you needed to hear. Get you gone back to your own cottages!" And as the others exited, the older woman turned to Cicely. "When it is time for the bairn to come," Mary Douglas said, "I want you to call for me as well as the midwife. I know as much as she does. Now, can you tell me what Sir William said about this son of his?"

"He spoke more with the priest than he did with me," Cicely responded. "I know little other than that the man is his son, and will mount our defense for the heir."

Mary Douglas nodded. "I'll see what Ambrose has to say."

"I swore to Ian before he died that I would not risk Glengorm lives avenging him, but it goes against my grain to allow the Grahames to run free. I have another way of exacting our revenge, however, and when it is complete I will tell you," Cicely told her two companions. Then she arose. "I must get back to the house," she told them.

When she had departed, Mary Douglas turned to her daughter. "If the bairn the lady carries is a lass, then Sir William surely means to give Glengorm to his son," she said. "It is what I would do in this situation if the decision were mine."

"I wonder if the lady realizes it," Marion said.

"If she doesn't know now, she will soon enough," Mary Douglas said. "Well, better another Douglas than a stranger. And Sir William is clever enough to make certain the king will approve what he is doing, lest James Stewart send another to fill our dead laird's place. These be Douglas lands, and have been forever."

Mary Douglas was astute to understand the way of

their world. But before Sir William departed for Perth, where the king was now in residence for the winter, he called his son Kier to him. The two men met privily in Sir William's small library, where father invited son to join him in a comfortable chair by the fire, a dram of whiskey in each of their hands.

Kier Douglas was a tall, slender man with hair as black as a moonless night. He kept it cropped short, for he had no patience to bother with longer locks. His eyes were a startling blue, light, yet rich and deep in color. Those eyes now looked directly at his father curiously. "What happened at Glengorm that they needed you?" he asked his sire.

"Ian Douglas and his younger brother, Fergus, are both dead," Sir William said.

His son raised a questioning thick black eyebrow.

"The Grahames raided earlier in the autumn. Glengorm went over the border and took back what was his, killing several of the English in the process. Ben Duff was with him, for he too had been raided. Several weeks passed and the Grahames returned to demand a parley with Glengorm. They massed themselves across that little loch bordering his village and meadows." Sir William sipped at his whiskey, then continued.

"When Glengorm honored their request, the Grahames launched a flight of arrows across the span separating them. Fergus Douglas was killed when he threw himself in front of his brother to protect him, but Ian nonetheless sustained two wounds. The damned young fool broke the shafts of the arrows piercing him, rallied his men, and rode across the loch after the Grahames, who had now taken flight," Sir William said.

"He rode *across* the water?" Kier Douglas was impressed. "He was wasting no time, was he? He caught up with the Grahames, I assume."

"And put all in the raiding party to the sword. The carrion birds hung above the hills for days, I'm told," his sire replied.

"Why did he die?" The younger man put his booted feet towards the fire.

"One of his wounds wouldn't heal," Sir William said. "He finally succumbed to it, leaving a young wife who is carrying their first child, and no other male heir in the direct line but for the priest, Father Ambrose Douglas. Fergus Douglas had a wife, but he produced only two little daughters. Both Ian's widow and her unborn child stand in danger of being taken over by some other family. But it's Douglas land, and I won't have it fall into the hands of some other clan."

Kier Douglas knew what was coming. He drew his feet back from the hearth.

"I want you to go to Glengorm," his father said. "If the widow births a son you will remain to help raise him. But if she births a daughter I will make you laird of Glengorm, and your male heirs after you."

"And the widow?" Kier inquired casually.

"There's none that I know of who engages your heart," Sir William said, "and 'tis past time you married, Kier."

"Is the widow to have no say in it?" the younger man asked. "Or will she do as she is told, like all women being bartered into wedlock?"

His father smiled. "Ogilvie's daughter was ten years ago, Kier, and you are long past sulking. Her father didn't think you good enough for his lass. I think you were too good for her. Your mother was a Stewart. Glengorm's widow will be practical, for her child's sake if not for her own. Woo her if you will, for your reputation for wooing is formidable, my son. But when the night falls marry her, bed her, and get bairns on her."

"What is she like?" Kier wanted to know.

"Auburn hair. Blue-green eyes. English," Sir William replied.

"*English?* You want me to take an English wife?"

"If an English wife is good enough for the king, an English wife is good enough for you, my son. Lady Ci-

cely was Queen Joan's closest friend. She came with her
from England. It's an excellent match for you. Her father is an earl."

"And she married a border lord?" Kier Douglas was
surprised. "What aren't you telling me, Da? There's
more to it, isn't there?"

"Aye, there's a story there," his father answered,
chuckling. "Get her to tell you how it came about that
she wed Ian Douglas. You'll be amused. Your cousin Ian
was a bold man as well as a brave one, and he loved his
wife deeply."

"When do you want me to go?" Kier asked his sire.

"Immediately," the older man answered. "I don't
want Glengorm unprotected with winter setting in, and
once word of Ian Douglas's death gets about, the avari-
cious will begin to gather. The lady and her folk are very
vulnerable. The captain of the men-at-arms there is one
Frang. Make him your ally. He's loyal to Glengorm."

Kier Douglas drained his dram cup, then stood up.
"I'll be gone before first light. There's a border moon,
and if I leave early I can reach Glengorm by afternoon."
He stood up and held out his hand to Sir William. "Thank
you, my lord, for this opportunity," he told his father. "I
will not disappoint you."

Sir William rose to his feet and shook his son's hand.
"I know you won't," he told him. "I am proud of you as
your mother would have been. You're a fine man." Then
he clapped the younger man on the back and sent him
off.

Kier Douglas walked upstairs to his chamber, calling out for his servant, Quin. "We're leaving Drumlanrig," he said, "and going to Glengorm."

" 'Tis not even civilized at Glengorm," Quin answered
his master.

Kier laughed aloud. "Perhaps not. I've never been
there, but unless you want a new master you'll come
with me, for it's to be our new home."

"Leave you? Never, sir! I've been with you since

you were five, and your da took you away from the old woman in the nursery of the house," Quin responded indignantly.

"Then let's pack, for we're leaving before first light. My father wants us there quickly. Winter is setting in," Kier told his servant.

"Why are we going to Glengorm?" Quin wanted to know.

Kier explained.

"Ah," Quin replied. "Your da is giving you an excellent opportunity. He's always favored you, sir. You'll be the laird of Glengorm soon."

"If the bairn born to the lady is a lad I'll be his governor. He'll be the laird," Kier reminded his serving man.

Quin shook his head. "If the bairn is a lad he will have to be healthy and grow up, sir. Many bairns don't. Some die in their first year. Others by the time they are five or so. Nay, sir, you'll be laird of Glengorm."

"Don't wish bad fortune on the bairn or its mam," Kier Douglas said. "Losing her husband has been tragedy enough for the lady."

"She'll be your wife and give you other bairns," Quin said fatalistically.

"Pack everything," his master said. "We'll take a packhorse."

The two men set about stowing all of Kier Douglas's worldly possessions in a small trunk and several saddlebags. When they were finished Quin bundled his own few belongings into two saddlebags. He didn't have enough to leave behind. The two men then slept briefly, rising as the full border moon spilled into Kier's chamber. They dressed in warm clothing, and Quin woke another serving man who was sleeping in the hall to gather their luggage and bring it out into the courtyard of the house, to be loaded upon the packhorse and the two horses they would ride.

And while the two servants worked, Kier went down into the kitchens of his father's house. He wrapped a small roasted chicken, some bread, and cheese in a napkin. When he had filled both the flasks the two men would carry with watered wine, he hurried back upstairs into the hall. There he stopped a moment, looking about the room where many happy hours of his childhood and youth had been spent. He pictured his stepmother in her chair by the fire, a small embroidery frame and needle in her hands. He saw his younger siblings playing near her. By birth he was bastard-born, but he had been fortunate never to know anything but love from his family. Turning, he left the hall.

In the courtyard the animals were packed and waiting. Quin was already mounted. Kier Douglas vaulted into his saddle and, without a word, turned his horse's head, directing it from the courtyard. Quin, by his side, led the packhorse. The landscape about them had a light dusting of snow from several days past. The full moon reflected off of it, making the track they followed quite clear. They rode for several hours, finally stopping to rest the horses and eat their scant provisions at dawn.

They sheltered by a cairn, sitting with their backs to the stones while their animals browsed, using their hooves to scrape away the thin covering of snow so they might get to the grasses below. Kier opened the napkin, tearing the chicken in half and handing half of it along with half of the bread to Quin. He sliced the cheese into two wedges, and handed one to his servant. They ate silently, sipping from their flasks now and again. All was silence about them, but then as the sun began to peep over the eastern horizon a few birds began twittering and calling. The two men stood up, brushing crumbs from their breeks and cloaks. Then, turning, they simultaneously relieved themselves before fetching the horses and watering them at the little stream that bordered the clearing where they had stopped to eat and rest.

They continued on their way, and then in early afternoon a small party of horsemen came towards them. The man leading them wore a length of gray-black-and-white plaid across his chest and shoulder. He hailed the two riders from Drumlanrig. "Would you be Sir William Douglas's son?" the man asked them.

"Who would know?" Kier asked, watching the man and his companions carefully.

"I'm Frang Douglas from Glengorm, my lord. We've been watching for you, for our mistress said you would probably come today. You're on Glengorm lands now, and I bid you welcome. We're relieved to have had Sir William send you to us."

"I am Kier Douglas, Frang, and no 'my lord.' Just Sir William's by-blow. But my father was concerned for Glengorm, with both my cousins dead and the lady not yet delivered of her bairn. How far do we have to go?"

"An hour, my lord, no more. The lady has instructed that as you are to have charge of Glengorm you will be addressed as 'my lord.' For all she's English she's a good lass, and has pretty manners," Frang noted.

Kier smiled a brief smile. "I will respect the lady, and see to her care," he said.

"Of course you will, my lord," Frang said. "You are Sir William's get. You will know your duty to the family."

Kier was rather amused by this pronouncement but said nothing more, and they rode onwards. The countryside about them was desolate. There wasn't a dwelling in sight. "Where do your folk live?" he asked Frang.

"In the village below the hall," came the reply.

"There is livestock?" Kier questioned the man further.

"Aye, my lord, but in the winter enclosures near the barns. When the snows come we bring them in for safety's sake," Frang explained.

Kier nodded. It was well thought-out. "Cattle? Sheep?" he inquired.

"Both, my lord, but more cattle," Frang answered him.

Kier had no more questions for now. They rode on in silence until at last they came to Glengorm. The house stood dark on its little rise. It wasn't particularly large, but it looked sturdy enough, and had several chimneys from which smoke curled lazily up into the cold afternoon air. There was a stable near the house, and a lad ran out to take the horses as Kier and Quin dismounted.

A servant came up to him. "Welcome, my lord. I am Tam. I will take you to the hall. My lady has been expecting your arrival."

"When you have brought me to her," Kier said, "help my servant, Quin, with my belongings, and see they are taken to my chamber. I do have a chamber, don't I?"

Tam grinned. "Aye, my lord, you have a chamber. There are several for sleeping above the hall. This way, please." He led Kier to the entrance of the hall. "The lady awaits, my lord. I'll return and help your man."

"Thank you," Kier replied. Then he stood a moment, staring into the room. It was not a large hall. His father had a spacious hall. But though it was small, there was a warmth about the chamber, with its big hearth. At one end of the room the high board was situated, and behind it a tapestry hung. The trestles and their benches were set along one wall out of the way, for they would be needed only at mealtimes. There was an old oak sideboard that was black with age against another wall.

Kier stepped across the threshold into the hall. A woman sat quietly in a tapestried chair by the fire, sewing on some small garment. There were several large hounds dozing by the fire. Two small white terriers spotted him, however, and came yapping forward to greet him. Smiling, he bent to pat them, then continued on across the chamber to where Cicely sat, the dogs bouncing along beside him. "Madam," he said, standing before her.

He was here. The man who would take Glengorm. Cicely looked up.

"I am Kier Douglas, Sir William's son, my lady," he said. "I have, as you are aware, been sent to keep you and Glengorm safe."

"You are welcome to Glengorm, Kier Douglas. I am called Cicely," she responded in a quiet voice. "I am your cousin's widow." She motioned him to a chair. "Will you sit, my lord? I am sure there are questions you would have answered." Cicely turned her head. "Artair, some wine for my lord."

"Your servants are well trained," he noted.

"Aye, they are most dutiful," Cicely said.

"For the moment I have no questions, but when I do I hope you will be able to answer them for me." He took the small goblet of wine he was offered, smiled at her, and then sipped at the beverage, for he was thirsty.

"How long have you been riding today?" she asked politely.

"We began when the full moon was at its zenith," he replied. "Perhaps we have ridden for ten or twelve hours."

"Have you eaten?" She seemed concerned.

"At dawn, but not since," he told her.

"I knew you would come today," Cicely said. "I told Mab to make a plentiful meal, for you would be hungry."

"Mab?"

"Glengorm's cook. Ian used to say she has been here as long as Glengorm has been here. She is old, but quite lively," Cicely told him. "She'll want to meet you, my lord. And she is the one who will be able to answer all your questions. I have been here but two years. Mab is Glengorm's heart, and knows everything that is happening here, but you will see." She gave him a small smile.

He returned the smile. "Aye, I shall want to meet her," he agreed.

"I have had a chamber prepared for you. It was my husband's room," Cicely told him. "It has its own hearth, and there is a small chamber adjacent to it for your servant, if you have one or want one."

"Thank you, madam," he responded. "I have a body

servant who has been with me since I was five years old.
I am now thirty-two."

"You are older than my husband was," Cicely said
to him. "Ian was twenty-nine on his last natal day. Oh!"
She had pricked her finger and, putting it to her mouth,
sucked the soreness from it. "I should not attempt to
sew when I am speaking," she said wryly.

"You are sewing for your expected infant?" he asked,
knowing from the size of the garments that it was exactly
what she was doing. But he was trying to keep the conversation, stilted as it was, going with her. If she was to be his
wife eventually, he needed to know her better. And then
he wondered if she knew of the plans his father had made
for her.

"Aye," she answered, holding up a tiny gown for his
inspection. "In the beginning it matters not if it is a lad
or lass—the clothing is still the same." Cicely folded the
little garment back into her lap and said candidly, "I am
trying not to weep, for I fear to harm my child, but it is
difficult, my lord." Her voice trembled.

Kier Douglas was not an easy man, but his heart softened as he looked into Cicely's blue-green eyes. "Perhaps you should weep, madam. Penning up your sorrow
may harm the child more than giving in to it. Why not
ask your Mab? Her age will have certainly given her the
wisdom to know such things."

Cicely pressed her lips together and nodded silently.
"Mayhap you are right, my lord. I feel such responsibility for this child in my belly. He is the heir to Glengorm.
I must bring him forth safely. I must see that he grows to
manhood so that he may wed and sire another generation." Her lovely face was one of complete concern.

"I see you know your duty, madam, but I am here
now to take the burden of Glengorm from your shoulders," Kier Douglas said. "You need fear no longer."

"Thank you," Cicely said softly. A tear slipped down
her face, and she suddenly felt fragile. But she wasn't

some weakling! She had always been strong. Ian had loved her fierce spirit. What was the matter with her?

Kier Douglas didn't know why he did it, but he reached out to touch her clasped hands reassuringly. When he did she looked up at him with startled eyes and burst into tears. He was astounded. He didn't know what to do. "Madam," he said helplessly. Should he take her in his arms and comfort her? But before he could make the decision what to do another woman hurried into the hall.

She gathered Cicely into her embrace, stroking her hair and crooning to her. "There, there, my dearie, my child. Weep now, for it is past time." And as the young woman cried in the comfort of her arms the older woman looked at at Kier Douglas and said, "I am Orva, Lady Cicely's tiring woman, though once I was her nurse."

"I am Sir William's son Kier Douglas, sent to watch over Glengorm," the man said. He arose from his chair. "I will leave you now to comfort your mistress."

"Why did you make her cry?" Orva asked him suspiciously.

Kier almost smiled, thinking Quin was as protective of him as this woman was of her charge. "I didn't. I was just kind, and it was time she gave vent to her grief," he said. Then he turned and walked from the hall to find Quin.

Chapter 13

$\mathscr{S}$eeing a flight of stairs, Kier followed them up to a landing, where he found himself in a hallway. "Quin, where are you?" he called out.

"In here, my lord." His man returned, sticking his head out of a doorway halfway down the hall. "These quarters are not as big as those at your father's house, but they're snug and clean. And there's a wee chamber next door for me."

Kier stepped into the room and looked about. One lead-paned window. A hearth, now burning, a chair angled towards the warmth to one side of it. A large curtained bed, a table on the left side of it with a taperstick set upon it, a chest at its foot. His own trunk had been placed against the wall, and next to it was a slightly larger table with a pitcher, a ewer, and a towel. " 'Twill do nicely," he said, going to the basin and pouring some water into it. "I'll want the dust of our travels off me by the time I sit down to the meal," he said to Quin.

"I saw the lady, my lord. She's a pretty lass, but so sad-looking," Quin noted.

"She's still in shock over her husband's death, I suspect, and just beginning to accept the truth of it. She'll mourn for a time," Kier told his man. "She has a strong sense of duty to my late cousin—and to Glengorm, which is to the good."

Quin nodded. "Aye, a woman with a stalwart character towards her family is one who can be trusted, my lord. She's going to make you a good wife."

"For the love of God, man, keep such thoughts to yourself!" his master admonished him. "Ian Douglas is barely cold in his grave. I understand my father's thinking, and I agree with it, but now is not the time to put forth a marriage proposal. Besides, my father will have to convince the king to permit it."

"Och, he'll do it," Quin said with a grin. "Your da has a clever tongue. Why, he could get the rooster to invite the fox into the henhouse, he could."

The manservant was correct in his assessment of his master's father. Sir William Douglas was a persuasive man. Not certain how his son would approach the matter of the widow of Glengorm, he had ridden from his border home to Perth. The weather was beginning to turn now, and he couldn't be certain that he would be able to return home before the winter hit with a vengence. But it was important that the king know everything that had transpired at Glengorm. That he approve Sir William's decision to send Kier Douglas to Glengorm to defend the land and keep the widow safe. But most important, he needed the king to accept that Glengorm was Douglas land, and to be disposed of by the Douglases, and no one else.

In another time this might not have been difficult, but James Stewart—with his demand that every laird and earl in the land prove ownership of his holding— was not making it easy. Sir William knew that Ian had brought the ancient patents to his lands, and left them with the king for examination of their authenticity by the king's legal council. He also knew the patents were genuine. But the king's pride had been damaged when Ian Douglas had abducted Lady Cicely Bowen. He had taken her dower, but Ian had made it plain he didn't give a damn. It had been Cicely he loved. So the king would take his time restoring the patents to Glengorm's laird, intimating before he did that they might not hold up to scrutiny. James Stewart wanted his revenge.

Of course, now it was a moot point. Ian and his brother were dead. But until the king restored the patents belonging to Glengorm to the Douglases, they could not legally claim the lands. Sir William knew he would have to proceed very carefully in the matter. He debated whether he should go first to the king, or first to the queen. He decided upon the king, lest he offend James Stewart's pride unintentionally.

The court was gathering for the Christmas holiday. In the great hall all was festive with pine boughs, holly, and branches of juniper berries. There were bunches of rosemary tied with red ribbons. There were fine beeswax candles, and the lamps burned rose-scented oil. The hearths were filled with enormous Yule logs, and the flames danced across their length. Sir William moved easily through the crowds, greeting acquaintances now and again, nodding to others, who nodded back.

He was finally able to reach the area where the king stood with his uncle, the Earl of Atholl. Sir William waited to be recognized. James Stewart knew he was there, for the Douglas chieftain had seen a quick flick of the royal eyes in his direction. This was a game the king played to keep his lords in their proper place. Sir William was wise enough to be patient, and finally his patience was rewarded.

"Sir William!" The king greeted him jovially, as if just realizing he was there. "You are welcome back to our court, but I thought not to see you again until the spring."

"I should not have left the borders, my liege, but that I had news I thought you should hear. I will await your convenience, however." *Now,* Sir William thought, *we will see just how piqued his curiosity is by my words and my arrival at his court.*

The king nodded and then turned away, but Atholl murmured something in James Stewart's ear and the king turned back. "Come," he said, leading Sir William into a nearby alcove. "Is the border agitated, my lord? Is it the English? I cannot imagine anything else that would bring you all the way to Perth, and with winter settling in," the king said.

"My kinsman the laird of Glengorm has been killed. His brother too," Sir William began in a low voice. "There are no male heirs unless the bairn that Lady Cicely carries is a son. I have sent one of my sons to Glengorm to defend it, and watch over the lady. Her child is expected in the spring."

"Why is Glengorm dead?" James Stewart asked, surprised and curious.

Sir William told the king the tale of the Grahames.

"He slew them all?" The king sounded impressed.

"All who rode against him that day, my liege. There are plenty of Grahames left. They breed like conies in a summer's field. I think, though, it will be a long time before they steal from us or attack us again," Sir William said.

"You did not just ride to Perth to tell me all this. You might have sent a messenger," the king said astutely. "What do you want of me, my lord?"

"Nothing that is not the Douglases' by right," Sir William said boldly.

"You want the patents to Glengorm back," the king noted.

"Aye, my lord, I do. Glengorm is Douglas land, and should remain so."

"If I give you the patents back—and my legal councilors have declared them legitimate, by the way—whom will you put in charge there? A border house needs a strong man. Can this son of yours manage Glengorm and defend it against attack?"

"Aye, he can," Sir William answered, "but if the lady births a son the bairn is, by direct right of inheritance, the new laird. In that case my son would remain to raise the lad. A daughter, however, can be dowered, but she cannot be Glengorm's heiress, for as Your Highness has so wisely noted, a border house needs a man to defend it."

The king laughed to have his words turned on him. "You won't be like old Gordon, will you?" He chuckled. "His heiress's husband has taken the Gordon name, but the direct line dies with Huntley."

"The direct line at Glengorm rests on the sex of the lady's bairn," he said gravely.

"And the lady?" James Stewart said.

"With Your Highness's permission I should like her to wed my son Kier," Sir William answered. "You should know that his mother was a Stewart."

"I did not know," James Stewart said, surprised again. This was the result of being out of Scotland for so many years. There was much he did not know, but was learning.

"A distant kinswoman of Your Highness's. She was a widow. Albany forbade our marriage, but our son was born nonetheless. He is a good man. You may rely upon him," Sir William told the king. "I hope you will entrust Kier with Glengorm, should it be necessary. He will not disappoint you."

To his surprise the king nodded. "It would be a good solution."

Then Sir William surprised himself. "And her dower?" he asked. "Will you restore it to her? This time she weds with your approval and your permission."

"I will restore the portion remaining," the king agreed. "Perhaps then her father will stop hounding the goldsmith in London who sent it to the goldsmith in Edinburgh from whom I obtained the lady's monies. The goldsmith dares not offend me, but he is frightened because his English counterpart says he should

have given the monies only to Lady Cicely; the Earl of
Leighton is threatening him. I had promised the queen
when she gave me my son that I would restore Cicely's dower portion to her, but while she is with child
a third time, she has birthed only two daughters. Still,
they are healthy, praise God. I mean to match my elder,
Margaret, with the dauphin of France. One day she will
be a queen, Sir William. Aye, you may tell Cicely that
when she weds with your son I will turn over a dower
to him."

"It is too soon, of course, for Kier to even approach
the lady," Sir William said. "She mourns my kinsman,
and Ian is scarce gone two months. May I speak with the
queen, Your Highness? I should like to tell her of these
developments."

"Nay, go back to the borders before the snows become heavy," James Stewart said. "I know that is where
you would rather be. I will inform the queen of what has
happened. And you may carry our affections to Lady
Cicely. But keep in mind that I will expect fighting men
from both Drumlanrig and Glengorm when I am ready
to go into the north against the lord of the isles. You will
be summoned then. Remember my kindness to you this
day. Speak with my secretary, and he will give you the
patents to Glengorm to carry back to your son." Then,
with a nod, he turned and went from the alcove.

Sir William Douglas was relieved that his journey
had been so successful, and that he had accomplished
exactly what he had wanted to so easily. But, of course,
now he and his son would owe the king a favor, payable
upon demand. And kings never asked for little favors.
He would instruct Kier to begin training men for battle,
so that when the call came, Douglas clansmen would
march forth from both Drumlanrig and Glengorm to do
the king's service. He remained the night at Scone Palace, sleeping in the stables with his horse. The following
morning before departing he found the king's secretary,
and was given the patents to Glengorm neatly enclosed

in a thin leather pouch. He rode directly for Glengorm.
It was almost Christmas.

Kier was glad to see his father, as was Cicely. "I have
brought back the patents for Glengorm," Sir William
told her. "They have been approved and authenticated
by the king's men. And I bring you the greetings and the
affections of James Stewart."

Cicely gave a small laugh. "I suspect you would have
brought neither of these things, my lord, had my husband been alive. But I am glad to have my child's inheritance substantiated and approved. And it is comforting
to know my child will have royal favor."

"My son will keep the patents safe," Sir William told
her with a smile as he handed the pouch to Kier.

"Of course," Cicely replied. So that was how it was to
be, she thought. Well, there was little she could do about
it. But one thing concerned her: Would they allow her
unborn son to claim his rightful inheritance? But now
was not the time, she sensed, to broach such an issue.

"There is no Christmas in the hall," Sir William
noted.

"We are in mourning," Cicely reminded him. "Will
you come to the board now and eat, my lords?" she invited.

Later in the evening, when Cicely had left the hall,
Sir William chided his son. "Do not allow her to make
a saint out of her late husband, Kier. Ian was far from
that. You will soon be the master here. Glengorm's people should not have their loyalties divided. Even if she
births a male, you will still be the lord in fact until the
lad reaches his majority. She must put all unnecessary
mourning from her by the time her bairn is born. And
you will need to take her for your wife as soon thereaf-
ter as you can. I want no chance of another courting her,
or misunderstanding the situation here."

"She will wed me, Da. You need have no fear of her
finding another," Kier said.

"I will speak with the priest before I depart tomorrow," his father said.

Ambrose Douglas listened to Sir William's plans for Glengorm the following morning. He didn't disagree with the clan chieftain, and Cicely would indeed have to be married again to protect her, and to protect the child she bore. But he was concerned that, should Kier use too heavy a hand with her, the widow of Glengorm would refuse him. "If she says nay I cannot force her, my lord. Is your son a man who can court a woman and win her over? Or will he do this because he has been told to do it, and because it is the expedient thing to do?" the priest asked candidly.

"We have the king's permission," Sir William said.

"Aye, and therein lies the problem. The lady was given the privilege of choosing her own husband by her father. The king was supposed to relinquish her dower to that man when she did so. You know what happened. She has never really forgiven the king for shaming her that way, despite the fact that it meant naught to Ian, and he told her so. Now, should you attempt to force her to the altar by telling her that the king has approved such a match, well, my lord, I shudder to think what Lady Cicely will do."

"James Stewart will also return the portion of her dower remaining," Sir William said to the priest. "Will that not make a difference to her? And he has returned the patents to Glengorm as legitimate."

"The fact that the king will return her dower now will but anger her," Father Ambrose said. "It is a difficult situation, I know, but if your son can make an attempt to woo the lady you may have an opportunity to make this match a reality. I will speak with him myself. And when the time comes I will encourage her to accept your son as her husband. Lad or lass, Glengorm will need more than one heir."

"I thank you for your help, Ambrose," Sir William

said. "Your father would be proud of you, the way you always put the family first."

"I put God first, my son. Always remember that," the priest told him candidly.

Sir William departed.

Twelfth Night came, and the winter set in. About them the hills were white with snow. The loch was frozen over. Cicely could see it from her bedchamber window now that the leaves were gone from the trees. She worried that the Grahames might use the loch to attack the village and the hall.

"Nay, lady," Kier assured her. "Remember the redoubt Ian ordered built. It was finished before December was half gone, and is manned day and night. If the Grahames are foolish enough to come again we are ready for them. But they will not come, for my cousin beat them badly in their last encounter. Their women will mourn for years."

"As will I," Cicely said.

"Did you love Ian Douglas so much then?" he asked her pointedly.

"I respected my husband, and aye, I had come to love him," Cicely said, a trifle annoyed. She shifted in her chair by the fire, for her belly was large now, and finding a comfortable position sitting or lying was hard.

"It is said when love is tepid and then lost it grows disproportionately," Kier remarked wickedly. He had grown bored with her attempts to be a tortured widow. He had no doubt that she had indeed come to respect his cousin, and had even become genuinely fond of Ian. But she had not been deeply, passionately in love.

"How can you say such a vile thing to me?" Cicely raged at him.

"Because it is true," Kier told her.

"I *loved* Ian!" Cicely insisted.

"And one day you'll love another," he told her.

"I shall *never* love again!" she declared dramatically.

Kier laughed aloud. "Aye, you will, madam," he said.

"I am told my cousin trussed you up like a piglet going to market, and rode you into the borders. Hardly an auspicious beginning for a love match."

"He had to steal me." Cicely found herself defending Ian, although it had been a rather horrible beginning. "The Gordons wouldn't let any man but their own near me."

"If I had wanted to court you, madam, and were being chased away by another who sought to have you, I would have found a way," he said.

"*Indeed?* And how would you have courted me beneath the nose of the Gordons?" she demanded of him.

"I would have crept into your bedchamber at night, madam. And when you protested my boldness I should have wooed you with sweet kisses and ardent caresses until you finally agreed to be my wife. I would have made you fall in love with me, and no Gordon or king could have prevented our marriage," he told her.

"Ian loved me," Cicely said. "He loved me enough to brave the wrath of the king in order to have me. It cost him my dower, but he loved me nonetheless." Kier Douglas's audacious words had enveloped her body in a rush of heat. The child had stirred restlessly within her womb. Had she blushed? She couldn't tell, for she was hot all over, and Cicely didn't dare put her hands to her face lest he realize his words had affected her in any way but with righteous indignation.

"Aye, he did," Kier admitted. "It was the talk of the border, how the Douglas of Glengorm had lost his wits over a pretty English girl." And then to his surprise, Cicely turned the table on him.

"Do you enjoy taunting me, my lord? And to what purpose?" she asked him sweetly. "I am sure there are better things you could be doing now. Are the accounts up-to-date? My father always kept his accounts carefully. Of course, since Ian got rid of a serving woman named Bethia there has been no stealing from our stores. It has made the keeping of our accounts much easier."

"The accounts are up-to-date," he told her stiffly.

"And can you tell me how many lambs have been born so far? Ewes are such silly creatures, dropping their lambs in the dead of winter," Cicely noted. "But, of course, we must still keep a scrupulous accounting, mustn't we?"

"There have been fifteen lambs born so far, two sets of twins among them," Kier said, suddenly amused. This was a new side of Cicely revealed. She was a spirited lass. Would she be as spirited in his bed when he married her? He hoped so, for he enjoyed a passionate partner. It gave a certain piquancy to bedsport.

"Very good, my lord. Then life progresses as it should," Cicely approved.

He sparred with her regularly after that afternoon, and after a few weeks he realized that she was no longer pulling a mournful face all day long. In fact, her lighter attitude reflected itself in the servants' attitudes. Ian Douglas would not be forgotten, but at least he had been put to rest now, and they could all get on with their lives.

March came, and now the anxious waiting for Cicely's child began in earnest. A week passed. Then two and three. The snows were disappearing from the hillsides. The ice was gone from the loch, where but a month ago the men from the village had joined with Kier in games of curling, sweeping a round of granite down the ice to a goal called a house. Now blue water sparkled where those goals had once been. There were already early daffodils blooming in a sunny spot near the kitchen door.

And then one morning Cicely announced that she believed her child was coming. "I have been in pain all night," she told Mab. "Go and fetch Agnes the midwife, and Mary Douglas for me."

Tam heard his mistress's words and immediately ran from the hall. When he returned some minutes later he was accompanied by two women.

Mary Douglas instantly took charge. "Put a clean, heavy cloth upon the high board," she ordered Una.

Agnes went at once to Cicely. "How do you feel, my lady?" she asked the girl anxiously.

"Like I am being torn apart," Cicely told her. "You must help me, for the only child I have ever seen born was Ben Duff's heir."

"There, there, my lady, 'tis a natural event in a woman's life," Agnes said, "and this bairn is so eagerly anticipated." She began to walk with Cicely up and down the hall.

And while she did Mary Douglas saw the flat high board covered with clean cloth, and the Glengorm cradle brought, along with swaddling cloths, a pile of cloths, and a cauldron of water set to boil over the hearth.

The day wore on. Cicely alternated until midafternoon between walking back and forth and sitting by the fire. She was parched, but they would allow her only tiny sips of watered wine to slake her thirst. But finally the manservants were ordered from the hall. Cicely was helped up onto the high board, which would now serve as a birthing table. Mary Douglas stood at her head, propping up her shoulders as Agnes peered between the laboring woman's outspread thighs, nodding. Finally the midwife looked up.

"This child will be born sooner than later," she announced.

"Ohhhhh!" Cicely groaned as another, harder pain suddenly overwhelmed her.

Now both Agnes and Mary began to advise her. They taught her to breathe into her pain. They conferred with each other at one point, announcing that it was time for Cicely to begin to push when the pains began to rack her body again. Kier Douglas came quietly into the hall. Neither Agnes nor Mary suggested he leave, for they knew Sir William would want an eyewitness account from his son as to the sex of the bairn as it was born.

Kier took Mary Douglas's place behind Cicely, his strong arms keeping her propped up firmly. Sensing a different touch, Cicely leaned her head back and her eyes met his. She understood his presence, and did not protest. And had she wanted to protest there would have been no time, for the pains afflicting her now were deep and hard. She just wanted them to stop, and reason told her they would not until the child was safely born. She shrieked with her agony. Her forehead was covered with tiny beads of sweat.

The two women now between her legs called to her. "Push, my lady! Push!"

Cicely bore down with all her strength and did as she had been bidden. The pain subsided. But then it rose up again to assail her. She cried out once more.

"Push harder! Harder!" Mary Douglas said. "And again, lassie! Again!"

"The head is out," Agnes announced.

Another terrible wave of agony swept over her, and without even being asked Cicely bore down, pushing as hard as she could. She was panting with her exertions, her chemise was soaking wet, and, weakness overcoming her, she leaned against Kier heavily.

"Its shoulders are out," Agnes called.

"I don't think I have another push in me," Cicely said, suddenly desperately tired.

"You are doing well, madam," Kier murmured. "Just a wee bit more, and the bairn will be born. You're a braw lassie," he told her.

His breath was warm in her ear. She couldn't help a small shiver and was embarrassed by it. But then another pain overcame her, and she shrieked again.

"Push hard, my lady! Harder! Harder!" Agnes called to her.

"I don't think I can," Cicely moaned.

"The bairn is almost born," Mary Douglas said. "You must do this for Ian!"

Cicely pushed with a strength she didn't think she

had. She actually felt the child slip from her body. There was the crying of a newborn.

" 'Tis a fine little lass," Mary Douglas said, although her tone was disappointed.

Cicely burst into tears. "Blessed Mother! I have failed Ian! I have failed Glengorm!" She sobbed, and the sound was so terribly sad the infant ceased her howling.

"Nay, nay," Mary Douglas said. "We have an heiress. A fine, strong wee lass, my lady. You have not failed us at all. Do you have a name for her?"

"Johanna." Cicely sniffed, and she raised her head to see the child. "After my friend the queen. Ian and I had spoken of it." *Oh, God!* Why couldn't she have birthed a son? She was no fool. She knew the Douglases would not let Glengorm out of their hands. Her son would have been the laird. Her daughter was just her daughter. The baby, cleaned and wrapped, was put in her mother's arms. Cicely looked down at the child.

"She's a pretty bairn," Kier Douglas said softly.

"Do you think she looks like Ian?" Cicely asked him.

"Aye, I do," he agreed, although he actually could see nothing familiar in this child. "You've done well, madam," he told her.

"Not well enough," Cicely said, low.

When Cicely had passed the afterbirth, been cleaned, and put into a clean chemise, Kier Douglas carried her upstairs to her chamber, where Orva awaited her mistress. Cicely's serving woman, who had cared for her since her birth, had not been able to watch *her child* suffer through the agonies of childbirth. Now she hurried forward.

"I have failed," Cicely said.

"A girl?" Orva replied.

"Aye, a little girl. Mary Douglas is bringing the baby up shortly," she told Orva as Sesi and Una struggled into the chamber with the baby's cradle, setting it near the hearth.

" 'Tis God's will," Orva said fatalistically. "Is the wee one healthy?"

"Aye, she is," Mary Douglas answered, coming into the bedchamber with Johanna. "Here!" She handed the infant off to Orva. "See for yourself."

Orva took the swaddled bundle and looked down at the baby. "She has my lady's eyes, but other than that she is pure Douglas," Orva proclaimed. Then she carried the child over to Cicely, who was now in her bed. "Would you like to hold her, my lady?"

"For a moment," Cicely agreed, taking Johanna from Orva. She looked down at the little infant and was surprised to find her daughter looking back at her. Cicely laughed softly. "Ian's daughter is going to be bold like her father, I fear," she said. Then she looked over at Mary Douglas. "Will you be Johanna's godmother?" she asked the clanswoman. "I should be honored if you would."

" 'Tis I who am honored, my lady," Mary replied. "Aye, I will be Johanna's godmother. She'll need another Douglas who understands to teach her how to channel that boldness," the older woman said mischievously.

And when Johanna Douglas was a week old her great-uncle Father Ambrose Douglas baptized her in the village church, with Mary Douglas standing as her godmother, and Kier Douglas standing as her godfather. The day was sunny, and that—along with the infant's obviously good health—was taken as a good omen.

In late April, Sir William Douglas came to Glengorm. Cicely already suspected the reason for his visit. Since Johanna's birth the servants and the clanfolk had been much more deferential to Kier. It didn't take a great intellect to understand that the Douglases had no intention of allowing any of their lands to fall to another family through marriage. And when Sir William had come and was settled in the house's hall, he said just that. He was relieved when Cicely did not cry out, protesting his decision.

"Of course, my lord," she said quietly. "But what of my daughter? Johanna is Ian Douglas's legitimate heiress. If you are giving Glengorm to another, what is to become of her? Will you make a fair settlement on her in exchange for Glengorm?"

"I will," Sir William promised. "I shall provide a generous dower for her in both coin and goods. And in token of my good faith, there shall be brought to you in the next few weeks a fine dower chest with my first contribution towards her future value as a bride. I shall also place with a goldsmith of your choosing five full-weight gold pieces and twenty of silver for Johanna's future. She is my kinswoman by both birth and blood."

"Ten gold pieces," Cicely said in an even voice. "She is a laird's daughter, and Glengorm is worth far more than five pieces of gold and twenty of silver. I want ten pieces of gold and one hundred of silver."

"Madam! You will beggar me. Eight pieces of gold, and fifty of silver."

"Ten gold," Cicely said in a suddenly hard voice. "And seventy-five of silver. I will accept no less, my lord. If you will not dower my daughter as she should be dowered I will go to the king. Remember, he did send me his affections, and Queen Joan—with two daughters of her own—will uphold my child's rights with the king."

Sir William Douglas laughed. "I have heard it said that your father can be a hard man of business when need be, madam. Obviously you have learned from him. Ten pieces of gold, and seventy-five of silver. Agreed!"

Cicely smiled. "I thank you for your generosity, my lord," she replied sweetly. "Now I have one other query to make of you. Are Johanna and I to come to Drumlanrig to live? The new laird and whatever family he has will certainly not want the widow and child of the previous lord of Glengorm living here. And, of course, the house is small." Cicely fully expected Sir William to name his son Kier the new laird, but she thought it was better if she appeared uninformed and surprised by his decision. That was something her foster mother, Joan of Navarre, had taught both her and Jo when they were girls growing up in her household.

Never allow a man to believe you are cleverer than he is, or that you can anticipate what he will do. If you do he will not like you for it, and will be careful of his speech when you are near. Women learn much by feigning ignorance, and men are inclined to ignore them when in serious conversation with another man.

"Why, my dear," Sir William said, smiling broadly, as if he were about to give her a wonderful treat, "my son Kier is to be the new lord here. You and your child will remain in your home."

"Glengorm needs an heir," Cicely said, suddenly nervous.

"Indeed it does!" Sir William replied jovially. "The king has given his permission for you to marry my son, madam. Where you failed with Ian you will succeed with Kier." He smiled broadly at her. "It is really the perfect solution to the problem. Kier must wed, and you have no other choices open to you."

Jesu! Mary! Kier Douglas thought. The same man who had warned him to proceed slowly with the widow of Glengorm was now about to set her into a towering fury, and frankly, Kier decided, he could not blame Cicely for being angry.

She was ominously silent. Her mind raced, attempting to sort out the possibilities. At first Cicely could find none. She was a widow with no wealth of her own in a foreign country with a child. "Have I no choice in the matter, my lord?" she asked him in icy tones. "I could go back to my mistress at court." *Aye!* That was her solution. Johanna would be raised in the royal nursery with the princesses Margaret and Isabella. And Cicely would serve Jo once again. She didn't need a husband at all.

"The king will not permit it, madam. He wants you remarried, as a respectable woman of your birth should be," Sir William said. Then he added, "And King James has agreed to restore to your new husband the remaining portion of your dower."

Kier Douglas caught his breath, waiting. It came quickly.

"*What?* The king will return the portion of my dower that he hasn't already stolen, will he? How dare he? How dare he!" Cicely raged. "He would not give what was rightfully mine to Ian, but he will give it to *your son*? Ohh! I cannot believe this. It is too much to be borne. You would take Glengorm from Johanna and give it to your son. The king would take my dower to bribe the Gordons. Is there no honor in Scotland at all?" Turning, she dashed from the hall, and they heard her footsteps as she ran up the stairs.

"Why in the name of all that is holy did you tell her all of that?" Kier demanded of his father. "She was willing to accept my becoming laird. Why did you feel it incumbent upon yourself to say more, Da? Could you not let me court her gently and win her over?"

"You're laird of Glengorm now, Kier," his father answered him. "And you're past thirty. It's time you were wed. And the sooner you wed, the sooner you can get your wife with child. Glengorm needs heirs. Win her over after the wedding."

"Father Ambrose will not marry us if she is not willing," Kier said. "And do you think Cicely will be of a mind to be willing now?"

"Get her to the altar by whatever means you must, Kier. Glengorm needs sons, and James Stewart is planning a northern expedition sooner than later. The Douglases will be expected to play their part in bringing down the lord of the isles," Sir William told his son. "And woe unto those clans who do not march with the king."

"Christ's balls!" Kier Douglas swore softly.

"Aye," his father agreed. "All most of us want to do is live peaceably, but kings are ambitious, and the men closest to them are ambitious as well. 'Tis all we can do to remain loyal and keep our own lands safe. But we owe

James Stewart this service, Kier. You are laird of Glengorm by his sufferance, when he might have given it to
another."

Sir William returned to his own home the following
day. He did not see Cicely again, for she would not come
forth from her chamber. But he cradled little Johanna in
his arms before he departed, smiling down at the baby,
pleased by her prettiness and obvious good health.
"She's bonny," he said to his son. "Take good care of
Ian's lass, though 'tis you she'll call her da." Then, returning the baby to Orva, he departed.

Kier Douglas watched his father go. Then he returned
to the hall, where, to his surprise, Cicely was now sitting at her loom, weaving on a tapestry she had recently
begun. "He's gone," Kier said to her.

"I am not marrying you, my lord," was her answer to
him.

"Aye, you are marrying me," he responded. "We both
have a duty to Glengorm. But I'm a reasonable man. I
will give you the month of May to accustom yourself to
the idea of a new husband. Speak to Mary Douglas and
find a good wet nurse for Johanna. I am not of a mind to
be denied my marital rights. We need a son and heir."

Cicely jumped up from her chair. "How dare you
order me about! I am not your wife, and never will be.
And my daughter will take her nourishment from my
breasts, not from a stranger's teat. I have nothing else
to give her."

"You have your love," he said. "If you will not speak to
Mary Douglas then I will, Cicely. This is not a negotiation
we are having. I would have taken my time and courted
you properly had my father not spoken yesterday as he
did. But it would seem neither of us has any time. The
king is preparing to march north. The Douglases will be
expected to march with him, which means I will have to
go. This means we must be wed, and you must be bedded.
Glengorm will have its heir!"

"You expect much of me, my lord," Cicely said angrily, "and I do not recall giving you permission to use my name!"

"What would you have me call you then?" he snapped back at her.

"My lady," she told him loftily. "You may address me as 'my lady.'"

"Since you vow you will not be my lady, I will continue to call you Cicely," he taunted her. He stepped forward to stand directly in front of her, and tipped her face up. "You have beautiful eyes, *Cicely.* Did Ian ever tell you what Glengorm means?" He didn't wait for her answer. "It means blue-green. Glengorm is the blue-green glen. Blue-green like your eyes, Cicely." Then he brushed her lips with his.

She slapped him angrily. "Do not dare attempt to seduce me," she hissed.

He slapped her back immediately. "And do not raise your hand to me, madam," Kier said in a tight voice. "We will wed, and I should prefer that we at least be friends. But if you wish an adversarial relationship I will be content to accommodate you, Cicely. *But in June we will be wed.* You had best accustom yourself to the idea." Then he left her, striding determined from the hall.

She was astounded. He had struck her. Kier Douglas was no gentleman; he was a barbarian. She would send to Jo for help. Aye, she would write her this very day and dispatch a messenger. She ran to her room. Orva was not there. She spent most of her time now with Johanna, and Cicely was grateful that she did. Orva had raised her. Together they would raise Johanna.

Opening up her writing box, she chose a small piece of vellum. Then, dipping her quill in the tiny inkwell, she wrote:

> *To Her Highness, Queen Joan of Scotland, from her most faithful servant, Cicely, lady of Glengorm: Beloved friend,*
> *I am writing in the hopes that you can aid me. Sir*

*William Douglas has told me that I am to wed his
son, the new laird of Glengorm. He has also said the
king approves of this match and will return what
remains of the dower my father provided for me
to the new laird. I do not wish to remarry. But I
do wish the return of my monies. Dearest Jo, if you
could but convince the king of my desire to remain
unwed, I should like nothing better than to return to
your service. Please come to my aid!*

> *Your most faithful Ce-ce*

Cicely blotted the words on the paper, folded the
document into a small square, and sealed it shut with red
wax, pressing the signet ring her father had given her
before she left England into the heated softness. Then,
taking the message, she left the house, walking into the
village to find Father Ambrose.

The priest was working in his small garden. Looking
up, he smiled at her, beckoning her forward. "Good morrow to you, my lady. How may I be of service to you?"

"I want someone to take this message to the queen,"
Cicely said, holding out the square of vellum. "Will you
ask Frang for me?"

"Why?" Father Ambrose asked quietly.

Cicely sighed. "Because he will run to the new laird before he sends a man off," she said. "I don't want Kier Douglas knowing that I have sent to the queen for her aid. If you
ask Frang he will do it without question."

"What have you written to Queen Joan?" the priest
asked.

"I have told her I do not wish to be coerced into marriage with this man, and that I would return to her service," Cicely answered the cleric honestly. "If I do then
Johanna will be raised in the queen's household, which
is much to her advantage."

The priest hid the smile that threatened to turn his
mouth up. "I will send your message," he told her. "But
it is unlikely the queen will help you."

"Of course Jo will help me," Cicely said with assurance.

But the queen would not help her old friend. Pregnant with her third child, she was doing everything she could to ensure it was a son this time. She found that Cicely's request irritated her, and said so to her husband. "What is the matter with her, Jamie? She is a widow with a child. Ce-ce must have a new husband, and by marrying this man she does not lose her status as lady of Glengorm. Her daughter will grow up in her own home. I do not understand this childish behavior. Cicely was never like this before. Is the man such a beast then?" She looked to her husband. "Tell me, Jamie, would Sir William give her to a wicked man just to retain Douglas lands?"

"Of course not, sweetheart," the king said reassuringly. "I have not met Sir William's son, but he is certainly like his good father." And he would do whatever he had to do to retain Douglas lands, the king thought, although he would not say it to his wife, who—please God and the Blessed Mother—was carrying a son this time. Nothing must upset his Joan. And especially not her old friend. "Write her back, my darling," James Stewart said. "Remind her she has a duty to me, to you, and to the Douglases. She is to meekly accept this husband chosen for her, and give Glengorm a son."

"I will, Jamie!" the queen said, smiling adoringly at him. "I know Ce-ce will listen to me. She is newly widowed, and undoubtedly skittish about taking a new husband to her bed. She will get over it, I am certain. I shall write her this day!"

And I shall write our new laird, the king considered silently.

The royal messenger arrived at Glengorm several days later. The new laird was surprised to find he carried messages for both himself and for Cicely. He called a serving maid to him, and handed her the folded and sealed parchment. "Take this to your lady," he said. Then he opened the message embossed with the king's seal, which he recognized.

> *My lord,* [the brief message began] *I shall be going north soon, and while I expect you to send me some of your good Glengorm men with Sir William, you will be excused from this expedition. It is more important that you wed and produce an heir for your posterity. To this end you will remain on your lands until this result is achieved.*

It was signed quite clearly,

James R.

Kier Douglas was astounded. What had brought him such a royal command?

In her chamber Cicely read with equal astonishment a brief message from her best friend. Her eyes filled with tears as she scanned the parchment.

> *To Cicely, lady of Glengorm, from Joan, Scotland's annointed queen,*
> *You will wed with Sir William's son and do what is expected of you, Ce-ce. Do not try the king's patience with this childish petulance. You are widowed; you must remarry for your own sake as well as that of my namesake, who is better off in her own home. Your dower is being returned in full. That I have convinced James to do for you without further ado. Pray that we both have sons soon. I send you my most tender affections, and hope to one day receive you again at court.*

> *Joan, Queen of Scotland*

Cicely laid the parchment aside. Her last hope of escaping this marriage was gone. She could hardly run away. There was Johanna to consider first and foremost. And to where could she run? Her father, if indeed he still lived, was frail, with a mad wife. And the queen would not have her back. Yet one good thing had come of it all. Her dower was being returned. Not just a portion of it, but all of it!

Kier Douglas took that moment to step into her bedchamber. "What did you do?" he asked her in a hard voice. "What did you do that has brought us each a message from the king? I want the truth, Cicely, and I want it now!" He stood towering over her, his blue eyes blazing. "What have you done, madam?"

Chapter 14

"*I* but wrote to the queen," Cicely told him. "We are friends of long standing. She wrote me back. Why are you angry, my lord? I understand from Orva, who brought me my letter, that you also received a message from the king. What did he want?" she asked innocently. "Are you being called to war, my lord?"

"I have been ordered to wed you without further ado, and to remain on my lands until you have given me an heir," he said through gritted teeth. "And what did the queen say to you, Cicely?" Kier was furious. Of course he intended wedding the woman before him. He knew what was involved, but he had hoped to make some sort of peace between them first. Now he didn't know how he could manage that.

It was all her doting father's fault. Putting silly ideas in the girl's head. Telling Cicely that she would be able to choose her own husband. It was ridiculous. Fathers or guardians were supposed to make the right matches for their female kin. And the women were supposed to obey. Of course, Cicely didn't really get to choose with Ian. And now again she was being directed into a marriage not of her own choosing. And he was being forced to deal with it. "Well, madam, what did the queen say?" he repeated himself.

"I am directed to wed you," Cicely replied slowly, debating how much to tell him.

"And?" The blue eyes bored into her.

"Jo . . . the queen has convinced the king to restore my entire dower," Cicely said. "Ian and I were going to split it, for he said he didn't need it all."

"Ian loved you unconditionally," Kier replied. "I do not even know if I like you. Your dower is mine as your husband."

"The house needs to be enlarged," Cicely said. "I meant to use my half to do so. The bedchambers are small. We need a large master's apartment, and below it a library."

"The house is big enough," he responded stubbornly.

"If we are to have these heirs that are expected of us, we need a larger bedchamber to share. Neither your chamber nor mine is big enough to contain a bed suitable for two people," Cicely told him. "Of course, we could just couple in the stable!"

"An intriguing idea, madam," he said as he reached out and pulled her close. "I should enjoy putting you on your back in a darkened stall." A single finger moved slowly across her lips. "Would you enjoy being taken on a pile of sweet-smelling hay, Cicely?" The blue eyes locked onto her own blue-green eyes. "Tell me what you want, for I am said to be proficient in the amatory arts."

For the life of her Cicely could not break his gaze or look away. Ian had never spoken to her like this. Nor had she felt such an intense aura of masculinity from him as she did from Kier. Ian had simply loved her. Now, faced with this cold, fierce man, Cicely was not quite certain what to do. He made the decision for them.

One hand reached up to cup her head. Then his mouth came down on hers hard. His lips demanded everything from her, forcing her lips to part, his tongue driving between those soft lips to do battle with her tongue. At first Cicely attempted to elude that ravaging tongue, but at last, unable to, she let him stroke her tongue with his. Heat suffused her whole body, and she actually felt dizzy. Finally she managed to pull her head away from his. *"Please,"* she managed to grind out. *"Please!"*

He nibbled at her lip and her face. "Please what?" He groaned. *Christ's wounds!* His cock was hard and his balls hurt with his need for a woman. He either had to let her go now, or put her on her back. "We're going to be wed June first," he said, "and if you are carrying my bairn then, so much the better, Cicely." He began to unlace her gown.

Shocked by his words, she didn't actually divine his intent until a moment later, when he yanked her gown down. *"No!"* she said as he lifted her from the pile of green fabric that now lay on the floor about her ankles. "We are not yet wed, my lord!" *Blessed Mother!* The bulge in his breeks was . . . was formidable. Ian's cock had been large, but this was certainly larger. Did manhoods come in different sizes?

"Aye!" he growled at her, and, turning, twisted the key in the lock of the chamber door. "The king says we must wed. The queen says we must wed. Yet you demur and consider the ways you may escape this obligation. I intend to be in your bed every night from now on, Cicely. And on the first day of the new month we will marry."

"Why now?" she demanded of him, trying to edge away, but to where?

"Because kissing you has filled me with lustful thoughts," he said wickedly. "And I mean to act on those thoughts. I might seek out one of our pretty serving girls, or some willing lass in the village, but I will not. You are to be my wife, and you shall be the only woman I couple with from this moment on. Now take off your chemise or I will rip it from you. Have you so many that you can afford to have one destroyed?" He began pulling his own garments off of his tall, lean body, and when he was naked he turned to face her once again.

"You have not removed your chemise," he said in a low, dark tone.

"Get out of my chamber!" Cicely cried, her eyes going everywhere in the room but to him. *"Get out!"* She attempted to edge away from him.

Reaching out, Kier Douglas's big hand fastened itself in the round neck of her chemise and ripped. "If you wish, madam, I'll have Father Ambrose marry us on the morrow, for I am certain he has the marriage contract all drawn up and ready." He flung the two halves of the destroyed garment from him.

Cicely shrieked, her hand frantically reaching for something, anything, to throw at him. But there was absolutely nothing.

He backed her into a corner, reaching out to draw her into his arms. Their naked bodies touched. He smiled wolfishly at her gasp, taking her face between his two hands, looking down into her eyes. Her round breasts were soft against his smooth chest. Her belly and her firm thighs pressed against him. His cock pushed back against her. "In time," he told her, kissing her mouth softly, "we may actually come to like each other, Cicely. For now, however, we have a duty, and we will do that duty."

"You are vile!" she spat at him. "Ian treated me with kindness."

"My cousin loved you. To him you were a prize worth having," Kier told her. "But you and I have been matched by cruel circumstance, Cicely. We have been raised to do what must be done, and so we shall do it. Stop quarreling with me, and I will make love to you. Have you not missed a lover's touch?"

She hid her face in his shoulder, and he felt her tears on his skin. "I never thought to know another," she said to him.

"I expect you did not," he replied. "But these are the borders, and women are widowed more times than not here. That is why it is so important that we produce a son for Glengorm. These are Douglas lands, and must remain so."

"Then I am nothing more than breeding stock to the Douglases," Cicely said bitterly. She looked up at him now with bleak eyes.

"For now, aye, you are," Kier told her candidly. "But that could change one day." He stroked her face with the back of his knuckles.

"Is your speech always so direct?" she asked him softly.

"Always," he replied. "I will never lie to you, Cicely." He tipped her face up and kissed her mouth softly, and as her lips parted willingly this time for him, he found her tongue again and stroked it slowly, sensuously, until he felt her begin to relax against him. He released her mouth and, taking her by the hand, led her to the bed.

Had she lost what few wits she had remaining? Cicely asked herself. He was a vile, wicked man! But he was also to be her husband, and the truth was, she found to her confusion that he excited her. It had been months since she had been made love to, for Ian had not wanted to touch her once he knew she was with child. Oh, she had coaxed him now and again, but he had been so fearful of harming her or the child.

The cousins were similar in physical form. Both Ian and Kier were very tall. Ian had been bigger boned. Kier was slender, but well made, and a quick glance at his male part told Cicely that his was longer and, she suspected, would be thicker than her husband's manhood had been. She attempted to put her thoughts from her, but then Kier was pulling her close again, their bodies were touching, their mouths were fused in a kiss that grew deeper and more intense as the seconds slid by.

They fell together upon the bed. Propping himself up against her pillows, Kier pulled Cicely up between his outstretched legs. His hands reached around to fasten upon her breasts as he kissed her creamy shoulder.

Cicely jumped. The touch was so intimate. Ian's touch had never felt so suggestive, so sensual. She distinctly felt the rounds of her breasts resting upon his hot palms. He fondled the warm flesh, and she shivered. The balls of his thumbs stroked her nipples, and a small whimper escaped Cicely.

Behind her Kier smiled. He was hot to have her, but he fully intended taking his time with her. She was still angry. Still resisting. But within a short time she would lie beneath him, and while afterwards she would convince herself he had forced her, she would yield herself willingly if he did not rush her. They would be bound until death. He hoped that eventually they would be friends.

Cicely remained silent. He had entrapped her. Was forcing her to his will. But what choice did she have? She wondered if her father had known in the end that the choice would not be hers at all. He gently pinched her nipples, and another whimper escaped her as the sensation raced between her breasts and to the hidden place between her thighs. She was like a young mare being brought to the bridle, Cicely thought.

Kier shifted himself so he might lay her down. He began to kiss her fair body. What was the seductive fragrance that enveloped her? It intoxicated his senses, and a groan escaped him. His mouth closed over each breast in its turn, sucking upon the tender nipples, nibbling them, licking them. He tasted breast milk briefly before quickly moving away. She had not yet obtained a wet nurse for Johanna, and he would not rob the child of her nourishment.

Cicely felt herself beginning to tremble just a little. He was kissing every inch of her body. Ian had never done such a thing. He turned her this way and that, his lips brushing over her skin. And then he began to lick her. Cicely almost fainted then and there. The sweep of his tongue across her flesh sent chills up her spine, and hot flashes down the backbone. She squirmed to get away from the sensuousness of that tongue.

"You taste delicious," he told her.

"I don't think I want you to do this," she protested faintly. "Ian never did this."

"Then you can hardly compare us as lovers, Cicely," he said. "Being older than my cousin I have had a bit more experience. Ian never left the borders. I have." Reaching for her foot, he kissed it, and began to suck upon her toes.

She would have pulled away from him but that he held her calf tightly in one hand. Her head was spinning. She had never imagined such . . . such . . . "Ohh!"

He had relinquished her foot and was now licking up her legs. His hand pushed her thighs apart, and he licked the insides of the sensitive flesh. His fingers began to play with her folds, running up and down her slit, pressing past it. The tip of one finger touched her love bud. She shuddered. He stroked it slowly, slowly, until Cicely was aching with a need she could not deny. He pushed a finger into her sheath, moving it about, and she moaned. "More?" he queried her, and added a second finger, the two digits imitating what his manhood would soon do. Her love juices were already beginning to flow, creamy and warm over his hand. He leaned forward and kissed her slowly.

The kiss deepened and grew more passionate as the minutes slipped by. Withdrawing his fingers, he sucked on them while she watched him with big eyes. He smiled into those eyes, and Cicely blushed at the knowing look he gave her. "You are ready to be fucked, aren't you?" he whispered against her lips.

"Never!" she lied. "Never by you!"

He laughed softly, covering her body with his, positioning his hard cock at the entry to her love sheath. "There is much I am going to teach you, Cicely, for I can see my cousin did little to tutor you in the arts of love. But tonight I am simply going to fuck you and fuck you and fuck you until you admit your need for me, as I am willing to admit my need for you. And when you have spoken truthfully to me I will give you more pleasure than you have ever received. You are passionate, I suspect. And we will have that much in common on our wedding day: our lust for each other."

And then, pinioning her arms above her head, he drove himself deep into her hot sheath, his eyes blazing as he carried out his threat. He was tireless in his desire, thrusting again and again and again into her heat. "Wrap your legs about me," he growled into her ear after some minutes had passed. He pressed deeper into her. Still dissatisfied, he withdrew his steaming cock from her and pulled her legs over his shoulders before driving himself deep into her body. "Ahhh," he groaned as he plunged deeper. "Ahh, Christ's balls, yes!" But he would not take his release. Not yet.

Cicely's head was spinning. His first entry after so many months of her enforced abstinence was, though she hated to admit it, delicious. She had not realized how much she had missed this. When he ordered her to enfold him with her legs and pushed deeper she wanted to scream with delight. But when he forced her legs back and over his shoulders he drove himself deeper into her than she had ever known a man could. His cock was longer than Ian's, and certainly thicker, but she seemed able to contain it.

Her head was spinning. Her nails clawed at his broad back in her passion. When he laughed she sank her teeth into his meaty shoulder, trying to keep from screaming. Then he touched something within her, and pleasure such as she had never known engulfed Cicely. She could not hold herself back. "Blessed Mother! You are surely the devil, Kier Douglas, and I want you!" And Cicely screamed softly as he brought her to a place she had never before been. "Damn you! Damn you!" she sobbed as he continued to piston her until she was overcome with a fiery gratification such as she had never before known. Then, as her love juices bathed his eager cock, Cicely fell into a swoon. But as she floated away she heard his roar of triumph, and felt his lust filling her.

When she awoke Cicely found herself alone. A bright fire burned in her hearth. She had been carefully tucked beneath the coverlet, and her two white terriers were sleeping in their usual spot by the fireplace. Had she had some wicked erotic dream? she wondered. Or had Kier Douglas forced her to his will? Aye, it was a dream! But she knew it wasn't so. Her body ached with a delicious soreness that only a bout of fierce lovemaking could produce. Her thighs were sticky with their combined juices. And to her shame she had enjoyed every minute of their passionate encounter.

Well, why not? They would be wed. And if she did not love him, at least if she was expected to bear him a son she should enjoy his attentions. But she would make him wait longer before she would say her vows. That much control over her life would be hers. She would speak to the priest. She knew now how she would revenge herself on Kier for the night past. Cicely turned over and fell into a satisfied sleep.

But Kier Douglas had no intention of waiting until June first to marry Cicely. At first light he arose, dressed himself, and went to Mass in the village church, that he might speak with the priest afterwards. "Come up to the hall with me and break your fast," Kier invited Ambrose Douglas after the Mass was concluded. "We'll talk along the way."

The priest looked closely at his companion. "The rumor is that a messenger came from the king yesterday," he said as they left the church.

Kier nodded. "Aye, James has ordered me to wed Cicely without delay, and according to her the queen's message promised that her entire dower would be restored."

"Your da will be pleased," Ambrose Douglas said.

"You've drawn up the contracts, I assume?" Kier asked him.

"Aye," the priest replied. "When Sir William told me

what he wanted I did it. Has Cicely become more reasonable, then?"

"Cicely will do as she is bidden," Kier Douglas told his companion.

The priest barked his laughter. "Ha! Ha, ha! You are a fool if you believe that, my lord of Glengorm."

"I bedded her last night," Kier announced. "She'll wed me now without any ado."

"I will not countenance any rape!" the priest said in a hard voice.

"There was no rape, Ambrose. Just gentle persuasion," Kier assured him. "I am ordered to remain on my lands until she has delivered me a son. There is going to be war in the north, and those doing the king good service will be rewarded for that loyalty. And where will I be? Nay, I want her with child as quickly as possible. I want that son born so I may share in some of the glory."

"Even if you got her with child last night, it will still be months before a child is born, and it could be another daughter, Kier," the priest said. "You had best make peace with your ambitions. You're a border lord. Nothing more."

Kier was silent; then he said, "I know you're right, Ambrose, but I want more. I always have. Perhaps it is the circumstances of my birth. I have a blood tie with this king through my mother, God assoil her good soul."

"Listen to me, Kier. I do not deny what you are saying, but kings are the most fickle of men, and this Stewart in particular. How much of his own family's blood has he spilled since his return? Like me, you're bastard-born, but you've been fortunate in life. Your father's wife loved and raised you as if you were her own natural bairn. Your father has loved you, and has given you a lordship you would not otherwise have had were it not for the death of your cousin Ian, and Sir William's intercession with this king. You are being given an heiress wife who has already proved fertile. With God's blessing she will give you bairns of your own blood. Be satisfied, man. Do not tempt fortune," the priest warned the new laird. "What you have now is more than most men ever get."

The new laird of Glengorm sighed. "I suppose there is time for my ambition. It isn't as if this will be the only battle King James fights," he reasoned.

Ambrose Douglas smiled. "Aye, your ambition can wait. Now you must come to some kind of an accommodation with Cicely. She is a proud woman, if not just a little spoiled. If you cannot love her then you must at least try to become friends with her."

"What was her father thinking that he made her such a ridiculous promise?" Kier wondered aloud. "Women don't choose their husbands."

"Most don't, 'tis true," the priest agreed. "Men are wiser and have clearer heads when it comes to picking a husband for their daughters. But this Earl of Leighton was letting his daughter go off to an unknown land. He was not a man of the English court, and did not know James Stewart. He trusted his daughter to choose her husband before he would trust a stranger to do it, since he could not."

"I wonder if he would have approved of Ian, or of me," Kier said.

The priest laughed. "You just need Cicely to approve of you, my son. And if I might make a suggestion, I would propose you not use so heavy a hand with the lady. Women have subtle ways of taking their revenge, and when they do you will find it is not to your liking." He chuckled darkly.

They reached the house and, entering the hall, found Cicely there directing the servants to bring the morning meal. Seeing the priest she ran to him. "Father Ambrose! Father Ambrose! You must convince the new laird that if we are to wed I need time first to mourn my beloved Ian. He is dead but six months. My husband is entitled to more respect than his cousin is willing to give him. Ian's love for me was more deserving. My lord Kier says we must marry on the first day of June." And Cicely sobbed a small sob, turning her head from them in feigned distress.

Both the priest and the laird knew she was lying. Ambrose Douglas almost laughed aloud. Had he not just warned Kier? The servants in the hall were pretending not to listen, but they were. And they would gossip of what happened here this day. If the new lord of Glengorm did not agree, or at least compromise, it would take years for him to regain the respect of the village folk. If indeed he ever could.

But Kier was not thinking about that. *"Madam!"* he thundered at her.

Cicely pretended to cringe away from him, giving a little cry of distress as her hand flew to her mouth.

Again the priest was forced to restrain his laughter. He was going to have to do something quickly, before Sir William's normally prudent son did something foolish. "My children," he said in his quiet yet strong voice. "Let us break our fast first, and then we will discuss this matter, for it is important not only to you, but to all of Glengorm. Come, come to the table." He led them to the high board. "My child," he said to Cicely as he drew out her chair for her, "we missed you at the Mass this morning."

"Forgive me, good Father, but before I can set foot in our wee church again I must make my confession to you," Cicely said softly, but quite distinctly.

"You vixen," Kier hissed at her. His blue eyes were hard.

"My lord, do not shame me publicly," Cicely murmured, "lest I be forced to stronger measures." She gave him a wicked little smile.

"Ahh, ham!" Father Ambrose said enthusiastically as the dishes were placed upon the table. "I always enjoy ham." He dug his spoon into his bread trencher. "Umm, Mab has flavored the oat stirabout with spices and honey."

" 'Twas Ian's favorite," Cicely said sweetly.

Kier glowered darkly.

"Give over, my daughter," the priest said, low. "You have won this battle."

"But not the war," Kier Douglas snarled.

They ate the hot oats, the ham, and the hard-boiled eggs, along with a crusty loaf of newly baked bread with butter and a berry jam. Their cups were filled with cider. The silence filling the hall now was almost ominous. When they had finished eating Cicely arose, preparing to depart the hall.

"I must see to Johanna," she said.

"Not quite yet, my daughter," Father Ambrose replied in a voice that even Cicely realized was not to be challenged. He stood. "Come, let the three of us sit by the hearth and discuss what needs discussing so there may be no more confusion about this matter."

They followed him from the high board and settled themselves as he had suggested near the fireplace. Cicely was looking particularly pretty this morning in a simple gown of spring green, her auburn hair plaited neatly into a single braid. She spread her skirts about her and looked to the priest. Kier, however, did not sit. He stood, looking fierce and determined.

"Now, my lord," the priest addressed the new laird, "my lady, the widow of Glengorm, has made a salient point in this matter. Your cousin the late laird, may God and his sainted Mother bless him, was both loved and esteemed by his folk. To rush his widow, but a few months after childbirth, into a marriage with you lacks the respect that needs to be shown to Ian Douglas's memory, no matter what the king and Sir William want."

Cicely smiled sweetly at Kier, who glowered back.

"Your father," the priest continued, "can give you Glengorm. King James can approve his decision. But only you can earn the good regard of your folk, Kier. And in times to come you will need that loyalty not once, but often." Now Ambrose Douglas turned to Cicely. "As for you, my daughter, the marriage contract is drawn and ready for your signatures. You *will* marry this man three days after the first anniversary of Ian's death in October. You will not seek to delay your marriage in any way. I don't care if the Grahames are banging on the door to the hall. You will wed Kier Douglas on the eighteenth of October, and we will be done with it! Now, I shall expect you at the church today to make your confession to me." The priest stood and walked from the hall.

"Well, madam, you have gotten your way and had your revenge on me, haven't you?" Kier said darkly.

"And you have gotten your way, my lord, haven't you?" Cicely countered, not denying his accusation of revenge. That was what it had been.

"Do not think this delay will keep me from your bed," he told her. "I will have you with child by our wedding day."

"If you persist in treating me roughly, my lord, I will fight you," Cicely told him plainly. "Are you so lustful that you cannot deny yourself for a few more months?"

Stepping before her chair, he yanked Cicely up, pulling her against him, a hard arm about her waist. He tipped her face up and kissed her not cruelly, but softly, seductively. "Had *I* been in Eden we should still be there," he boasted. "My willpower is strong." The hand on her face slid down into the neckline of her gown to cup a breast. His thumb encircled the soft nipple, which hardened almost instantly. "Eve was the weak one, madam," he taunted her. His lips brushed hers again.

Dizzy though she was, Cicely managed to kick him in the shins. "I am not Eve!" she said furiously. "If men are so strong, why did not God make them carry and bear the babies, my lord? I will obey you all: the king, Sir William, the Church. I will wed you in October, and I will be a good wife to you. But until then, my lord, it is war between us. Now release me! I must attend to my daughter."

He let her go, but as she stamped away, he said,

"What is this need you seem to have to constantly score me, madam? You have surely bruised my shin in your temper, my back is raw with your scratches, and I have the marks of your teeth in my shoulder yet." But he was smiling, although she did not see it. He was going to get strong sons on this fiery woman, he decided.

Cicely blushed at the words he flung after her, but she never turned. *Blessed Mother!* Were Artair and Tam grinning? Were Effie and Sine, their two heads together, giggling? Of course they had overheard, and soon it would be all about the kitchen, and next the village. Then Cicely laughed softly to herself, seeing the humor in the situation. The gossip her servants told would, oddly enough, comfort their clanfolk. The new laird was settling in. He would wed the lady in the autumn, and there would be sons for Glengorm sooner than later.

Cicely was relieved, however, when her female courses came upon her a week later. She was not ready to be with child quite yet. The summer came. The hillsides about Glengorm were green and dotted with the laird's sheep and cattle. The Grahames were nowhere in evidence. The rumor was that that Ian's unforgiving assault upon them had decimated their ranks to the point of weakness. They could not raid without allies, and right now the other English border families considered the Grahames unlucky.

Each day but for the Sabbath, Kier trained the men-at-arms in the art of warfare. Eventually they would be called upon to accompany the king into the Highlands. But for now the king satisfied himself with strengthening his hold on the lower half of Scotland. Most of the Highland chieftains had not sworn their fealty to James Stewart yet. If they did not within another year, James would have to call for a gathering of the clans in Inverness to accomplish that goal. Kier was relieved. No matter what Father Ambrose said, Kier needed to be with the king when he went north. Every border lord with an eye to his family's future would want to go—*would* go. A man's loyalty was judged by things like that. And with luck, by next summer he would have a son.

Cicely both intrigued and fascinated him. He had never known such a strong and independent woman. Yet she could hardly be called forward or bold. Still, her dedication to her duty to Glengorm was to be commended. When he went to war, Kier thought to himself, he would have no difficulty leaving Glengorm in her capable hands. He was fortunate in this wife he was soon to take.

But Cicely also tempted him. After boasting so loudly about his self-control, he was finding it difficult to be near her. He had not since that fateful night entered her bed, and she was quick to tell him shortly afterwards that she was not with child. He knew how very passionate she could be. Yet their celibacy did not seem to disturb her in the least. Had he not known her so well now, he would have wondered if she was sneaking off to meet with a lover.

Cicely would have laughed if she had been aware of his thoughts. She didn't dare get too near Kier Douglas, for she truly lusted after him. She wasn't in love with him. She might never be in love with him, but she wanted very much to be in his arms again. Ian had been tender, and he had certainly shown her a modicum of passion. But he had loved her so desperately that he had not allowed his emotions to overcome him but once or twice. And then his passion had never been as wild and fierce as Kier's had been that night that they had shared.

And Cicely had been amazed by the passions he had unleashed in her. He had plumbed depths she had not known existed. He had touched her heart with fire and scorched her soul with the heat of her desire. She hadn't realized that one could experience such emotions, and yet have no love for one's lover. Cicely was realizing that there was a lot she didn't know. She might have put him out of his misery but that he suddenly took to taunting her. But, realizing that his need was boiling as hotly as her own, she vowed to herself not to give in to his teasing.

It was Midsummer's eve. The light would not fade entirely this day, just go to a lengthy dusk that would last the night through until tomorrow's dawn. In the village by the shore of the loch a large fire was built, and its flames burned bright and high. There was food. There was ale, and as the evening wore on there was whiskey from someone's still. Dancing about the fire began with everyone joining hands encircling the flames while Owen the piper played his pipes for them, the sweetly mournful music echoing about the hillsides. And eventually men and women, hand in hand, began disappearing from the festivities.

Cicely and Kier had come to join their clanfolk, Orva and old Mab remaining in the house watching over Johanna. Both women had declared themselves past such things as the frivolity of a Midsummer's eve. The laird and his intended wife had briefly been civil to each other, to their mutual surprise. It would not last, of course.

"For a lass raised among the mighty," Kier remarked, "you are comfortable among the clanfolk." He thought she looked beautiful tonight dressed as simply as any village woman in a dark gray skirt of light wool, and a white blouse. About her waist was a sash of the gray-black-and-white Douglas tartan. Her legs were bare and her hair in its plait, although bits of her auburn locks had come loose as she danced.

"I would make a poor lady of Glengorm if I held myself apart from my clan's folk, my lord," Cicely told him. "My early years were spent on my father's estates in a setting as rural as this one. Orva can tell you I played with the village children, ate in their cottages, and lifted my skirts to pee in the dirt like any other little girl there. Of course, once I entered the house of Queen Joan of Navarre I was taught to be a lady, as it was expected I would live at court one day when I was older. But I have never forgotten that earlier part of my life. Coming to live in the borders has brought those years back to me, and recalling them, I quite remember how happy I was in a simpler time."

"Then you are happy now?" he asked her.

"I am content," she answered him.

"I was raised in my father's house," he told her. "My stepmother was a gentle and kind woman who loved me as if I had sprung from her womb."

"My stepmother was the spoiled daughter of a Florentine merchant who hated me before she even laid eyes on me," Cicely remarked. "Orva and I were sent to live in our own cottage on my father's estates. In fact, until I was almost seven Luciana never laid eyes on me, even though my father had been wed with her for several years. We met one afternoon quite unexpectedly." Then Cicely related the incident to him, concluding, "And that is how I came to be raised with Joan Beaufort."

He had known none of this, but now he understood why she was such a strong woman. She would not have survived those early years had she not been. "Your own mother died then," he said.

"Aye, at my birth. I never knew her," Cicely replied. "My father loved her very much. They grew up together. She was the daughter of Leighton's steward."

Now, here was another surprise. "Your father married his steward's daughter?"

"Nay, they were to be married, but I came too soon, and she died," Cicely said.

Kier was astounded. "Then you are bastard-born too!"

"Not really," Cicely told him sharply. "My birth was declared legitimate by both Church and state." She drew herself up proudly as she spoke the words. "And do not think my birth lower than yours, for I know your mother was a Stewart. My parents were distantly related. It has always been a custom with the older families in England to put their trust in their relations first. That is why my grandfather, and after him my uncle, and before them other male members of that branch of the Bowens, have held the position of steward and the trust of the earls of Leighton. You obviously do the same thing in Scotland, for has not Sir William seen that your rights to Glengorm were upheld when its legitimate male heirs were gone? Family is all-important, my lord."

Again she amazed him. He had thought her flighty and spoiled, but she really was neither. "I am pleased to hear you say it," he told her. He reached for her hand as they walked the path to the house.

"My lord?" Cicely said questioningly, but she did not pull away.

"Madam?" he queried her.

"Do you weaken in your resolve?" Cicely taunted him cruelly.

In response he pulled her into his arms so that their bodies were not quite touching. One hand tilted her face up, and his lips hovered dangerously near her. "Nay, madam," he said, his breath brushing her mouth. "I have no weakness in me." He smiled a wicked smile. "Can it be that you are weakening in *your* resolve?"

The distance between their two bodies was no more than a whisper. The lips not quite touching hers almost caused her to moan with her need to be kissed by him. But the mocking tone in his voice as he hinted that she was the weakling caused her to shove him away with an angry hiss as she stamped upon his booted foot. "*My lord!*" she said indignantly. "You presume far too much! You are arrogant beyond all bearing." Then, turning from him, she continued towards the house.

Kier laughed, following after her. "You are a little liar," he accused her as he caught up to her. "Your lustful nature matches mine, although I believe it surprises you as much as it surprised me that night a few weeks ago."

Cicely whirled, her hand raised to slap him. Kier caught her hand and yanked her close. "Let me go!" she said angrily.

His mouth brushed hers. "You cannot tell me you are not tempted," he said, low.

"Yet 'tis you who are the aggressor, not I," Cicely countered. *Blessed Mother!* What was the matter with her? She wanted his kisses! And she wanted them now! But she would not be the first to yield. Not even after they were married. This was a man used to getting his way with women. And he didn't love her. "Let me go!" she repeated.

"You are mine," he said through gritted teeth. His cock was preparing to burst through his breeks in his lust.

"I am not yours quite yet, my lord," Cicely told him. "And forcing yourself upon me as you once did cannot make it so. We will be wed in a few months. Until then, leave me be!" She was starting to tremble with her need for him. She did want him. *She did!*

He released her suddenly and, turning, Cicely pushed past him, running into the house and up the stairs to her chamber. Closing the door behind her, she turned the key in the lock and stood gasping for air. She heard him stomp up the stairs. He stopped outside of her door. Cicely held her breath, but then he moved down the hallway. The door to his bedchamber opened and shut.

She didn't know if she was unhappy or not. That one night they had shared had been like no other she had ever known. She had been astounded by the depth and the height of her own passions. It had been both exhilarating and frightening. But worse, it had tapped a vein of pure lust within her that Cicely had not known she possessed. And now all she thought of was lying naked in his arms again, feeling his weight on her as he impaled her with his great cock. She had not touched him that night, but, oh, she wanted to feel the weight of his twin stones in her hand, caress his length until he was groaning with his need for her.

But this was not love. And having known love, how

could she settle for anything less? It was impossible. Unrealistic. Yet her father had loved her mother. And the king loved Jo. And Ian Douglas had loved her, even if she had not completely returned his feelings. What she felt for Kier, however, was not love. It was pure, unadulterated lust, and he felt it for her. Was that so wrong? *Blessed Mother!* Why could life not be simple?

Cicely climbed into bed. And why did she want to couple again so desperately with Kier Douglas, and he with her? They didn't like each other. He was wedding her for expediency's sake. He had told her most bluntly that she was nothing more than breeding stock for the Douglases. Why would any woman with all her wits desire a man like that? But she did, and the knowledge itself caused her a particularly sleepless night.

She did not see Kier for almost a week after that. He left word that he would be inspecting the far pastures. It was actually a relief, for the tension between them had been blazing hot on Midsummer's eve. His absence, however, gave her time to cool her own ardor and begin to consider the wedding they would celebrate come autumn. And if she was to do her duty by Glengorm, it was time to seek a wet nurse for Johanna. Cicely walked down into the village to speak with Mary Douglas.

"Ah, Kate will be the lass for little lady Johanna," Mary Douglas said. "Her two-year-old is about to be weaned, and her man gets her with child every time he takes his breeks off. She'll be glad for the respite, and the coin."

"How many children does she have?" Cicely asked.

"Four in six years," Mary said. "Thank God she's a good strong lass. Healthy. And her milk will be fresh. Bring your wee bairn down to the village tomorrow, and we'll see how she takes to Kate's teat. If you would like I will speak to her for you."

Cicely nodded. "Aye, I should appreciate it if you would."

"There's to be a wedding then," Mary probed gently.

" 'Twas decided months ago by Sir William, and then approved by the king," Cicely admitted. "But I would not agree until I had mourned Ian a full year, and Father Ambrose spoke for me as well."

Mary nodded. "You were right," she said. "Of course, I see the men's side in this too. They are anxious for a male heir for Glengorm. Well, we all are, and one will come in God's good time. But the date has been set?"

"October eighteenth," Cicely told her.

"May I tell the village?" Mary asked.

Cicely nodded. "Aye, for 'tis certain Kier will declare a holiday."

"You don't love him," Mary said candidly.

Cicely shook her head. "But I will respect him as my husband, and as the laird."

"It's as good a beginning as any, and better than some," Mary replied. "And he knows his duty as laird. He will have learned that at Sir William's knee. We are fortunate he was sent to us, and not one of the other Douglases. Some are very wild."

July passed, and then August. Cicely and Kier were careful about each other, making certain that they never touched even by accident. For touching had been what had set off their lust on Midsummer's eve. Johanna had taken happily to Kate's breast, and Cicely's milk had dried up—to her sorrow, for she had enjoyed nursing her daughter. Sir William arrived unexpectedly one September afternoon bringing news.

"The king has decided to come into the borders to hunt grouse at the end of the month," he announced. "The queen will be with him, and she would like to visit her old friend, the lady of Glengorm."

Cicely jumped up. "Oh, there is much to do if we are to receive a royal visit. How will we house them? We have no bedchamber large enough." She turned to Kier. "Now do you see the advantage to enlarging this house, my lord?" She looked to Sir William. "How long will they remain with us, my lord?"

"At least three days," he said.

"If," Cicely said, "you could convince the king to join us the second week in October, we could manage to build a bedchamber to house them. It would be a temporary structure, of course, but it could be done and would be far more suitable than the small chambers upstairs. Have you ever seen them, my lord?" she asked Sir William.

"I have, my dear, and you are right. They are too small for the king and his wife."

"Can they not stay somewhere else?" Kier inquired of his father.

Cicely shrieked. "Have you no idea the honor being done Glengorm?" she demanded. "You are such a d—" She stopped. "You have not considered how fortunate we are to have the king and queen visit us, my lord."

"Cicely is right," Sir William said.

"But the expense!" Kier complained.

"You are gaining a large dower from me," she snapped irritably. "And Ian had promised me half of whatever he gained so I might enlarge the house. You, however, have said you mean to hoard my father's gold all to yourself. Well, now you must spend some of it."

"Do you realize the shrew I am being burdened with?" Kier appealed to his father.

"I am certain that you and Cicely will manage somehow, my son. I am just sorry you are not already wed. The king will want to know why."

"Let Cicely and Ambrose explain that matter to James Stewart," Kier said. "I would have wed her the morning after I first bedded her," he told his father with a wicked grin. "But my lady insists upon the proprieties being observed."

"Are you with child then?" Sir William asked anxiously.

"Your son took a sip of the cream, my lord, but the cow has not been his since, nor will it be until we are wed," Cicely told the older man.

Sir William burst out laughing, and when his mirth had ceased he asked, "You have chosen a day, haven't you?"

"October eighteenth, three days after the first anniversary of Ian's death, my lord," Cicely told him.

"I'll be here." Sir William chuckled. "Now you must begin your preparations to receive the king and his queen in just a month's time."

"We will be ready," Cicely promised the man who was to become her father-in-law. "The Douglases of Glengorm will not be found wanting."

Chapter 15

*W*ith Kier at her side Cicely went to the village.
Father Ambrose rang the church bell to assemble the clanfolk, who came from their cottages and from the fields around the village.

"We are to have a visit from the king and the queen," Kier informed his clanfolk. "The lady will now explain what needs to be done before they arrive in October."

"We have no bedchamber large enough to house King James and Queen Joan," Cicely began. "We must build one before they come. It will have to be of wood, for there is no time to quarry stone."

"There is enough stone in the nearby quarry already cut for a foundation and for floors," said Mary Douglas's husband, Duncan. "The priest's da had intended to enlarge the house one day, but it came to naught. We can do this, my lady. Glengorm will not be found wanting when King Jamie comes calling with his queen."

The clanfolk began immediately that same day. And in the days that followed they worked from first light until dark. The cut stones were dragged from their quarry, fitted together neatly, and secured with a mixture of clay and limestone. Trees in the nearby wood were felled, cut, and trimmed into boards. And while one group of men laid the stone for the floors, another began to raise the walls of the large chamber. The sound of hammering became so common that when it stopped the silence was deafening.

It had been decided that the roof of the new chamber would be flat, with a faux crenellated battlement decor. Cicely had convinced Kier that if they began enlarging the house so they could entertain the king properly, then afterwards they should finish by adding a room above the new room, which would be their bedchamber, while the room below would be converted into a fine library. A practical man, Kier decided she was right. The chamber would need a hearth. One was built with a separate chimney. The new chamber backed up onto the hall behind the high board. An aperture from the hall into the chamber was opened up. A fine paneled door was constructed, and matching paneling fitted to the walls. There was no time to go to Edinburgh and have glass made for the chamber's one large window. Wooden shutters would have to suffice.

A large old bed, some tables, two chests, and some chairs were found in the attics of the house. The bed was given new rope springs. Cicely and Orva made a new mattress cover, which the women of the village stuffed with clean sweet hay and straw mixed with sprigs of lavender from Cicely's herb garden. A new feather bed had been made to lay over the mattress, along with fresh pillows.

But it was in the attics that Cicely found a treasure that would make the chamber truly royal. Opening a trunk she saw a large packet wrapped in linen. Carefully lifting the bundle from the trunk, Cicely laid it upon an old table and began to unwrap it. The wrappings were protecting a set of burgundy velvet bed hangings for the refurbished bed now set up in the new chamber. And in the very bottom of the trunk were the brass rings from which these curtains could be hung. And everything was almost as if new.

"It's a miracle," she said to Ambrose Douglas as they sat eating the evening meal.

The priest smiled at her. "Of a sort, perhaps," he said. "Actually those bed hangings were a gift to my father's wife. The bed you have now set up in the new chamber was hers, as were the hangings. She died shortly after receiving them. My father thought them too fine for a border house. He had them put away. I do not think they hung more than a year or two. They are very suitable for a royal chamber."

The velvet bed hangings were hung out in the fresh air, and beaten to make certain there was no dust left in them. Then they were brushed before hanging. The brass rings were polished, fitted to the bed, and hung. The new bedchamber suddenly had a look of elegance about it. As the day for the royal visit grew near, a basket of peat and wood was brought into the room to be put by the fireplace. The empty chests had sachets of lavender dropped into them so they would smell fresh when used. The bed was made with the linens that had been made for it. Mab and her staff of serving girls had washed the old linens, ironed them, perfumed them with lavender, and then made the royal bed up. On the day of the visit late roses were cut from the garden, placed in an earthenware pitcher, and brought into the chamber.

Cicely was more excited than she had been in a long while. Jo was coming! Her beloved friend was coming, and tonight they would sit by the hearth in the hall and catch up on all that had transpired since they were parted more than two years ago. She dressed carefully. Jo must not think that being the lady of a border house was any less than being in the queen's household. Orva brought forth a gown of blue-green velvet, and Cicely nodded her approval to Orva.

"Aye, 'tis lovely," she said as she brushed her long auburn hair. She would not plait it today, but rather contain it in a golden caul. She had bathed earlier and, now in a fresh chemise, she let Orva lace the gown, with its rounded neckline and graceful long, wide sleeves. Looking at herself in the small glass, she was pleased.

"The queen will undoubtedly be happy to see you," Orva said. "And you have made a lovely chamber for her to rest in."

"I've done little," Cicely said. " 'Twas our clanfolk who have made this happen. They are such good people, and we are fortunate to live among them."

"Are you reconciled to this new marriage?" Orva asked.

"Once again the choice has been taken from me," Cicely said. "But there are worse men in this world than Kier Douglas. I will manage."

"He does not love you as Lord Ian did," Orva noted.

"Kier does not even like me." Cicely laughed. "But he will do what he has to do, even as I will, and we will make a success of this match."

"Yet you liked the bedsport with him," Orva said slyly.

"That much we have in common," Cicely remarked. "Now I must go down to the hall. 'Twill not do for James Stewart and our Jo to arrive and I not be there to greet them. You must be there too, Orva."

Kier watched her enter the hall and thought her beautiful. She was far too good to be a border wife, and yet 'twas exactly what she was. "Madam," he said, bowing to her. He was dressed in his leather breeks, but today over his shirt he wore a long blue-and-gold brocade tunic that made his eyes seem even brighter. He held out his hand to her. "They should be riding up to the house as we speak. Come, madam!"

Together they walked from their hall and exited through the front door. King James and Queen Joan were just now arriving. The king rode a big black stallion. The queen, however, was being transported in a padded-leather cart being drawn by a white gelding. She looked tired, and not particularly happy, but when Cicely pulled her hand from Kier's and rushed forward, a smile came to Joan Beaufort's pretty face.

"Ce-ce!" she greeted Cicely. The queen's cart came to

a halt. The driver jumped from his bench and hurried to open the back of his vehicle, handing the queen out. The two women embraced warmly.

"You are with child!" Cicely said, excited.

"You are not, and that will make Jamie angry," the queen answered her friend. "When were you wed to him? He's a handsome brute. Better-looking, I think, than the other, Ce-ce. I like his black hair. Are his eyes dark?"

"They are blue. An outrageous shade of blue. We are not yet wed, but will be this month. It was necessary to mourn Ian for a full year. His clanfolk would not have been happy otherwise. Come into the house. We have built a brand-new chamber to shelter you, Jo. When our clanfolk heard you were coming they worked to make this new chamber so you and the king would be comfortable. Our bedchambers are too small." Walking arm in arm with Queen Joan, she brought her into the house. "Jo," she said, "thank you for regaining my dower for me. It allows me to be on an equal footing with Kier. He is not an easy man to live with, I fear. I was so used to Ian's adoration and unwavering love, to find myself wedding a man who says he does not like me is hard."

"He does not like you?" The young queen was astounded. "Why not?"

Cicely shrugged. "I don't particularly like him either," she said. "But we do respect each other, and I will be a good wife, Jo. I did not appreciate Ian's true love for me when I had it. Now I am condemned to live out my life with a man who has quite frankly told me he considers me naught but breeding stock."

They were in the warm hall now, and the queen had seated herself by the hearth. "I will speak to Jamie. You shall not marry this monster," she said.

"Jo, how sweet you are, but I shall marry him. I have no other place to go, and my daughter belongs at Glengorm," Cicely said. "You know this is the usual way of our world. How many marriages are made for love? You are fortunate."

"But I want you to be happy!" the queen exclaimed.

"I am not unhappy, and I am content," Cicely assured her.

The queen's eyes sought Kier. "My lord of Glengorm," she called to him.

Kier Douglas came immediately to her and bowed. "Madam, I welcome you to my home." Taking up her hand, he kissed it.

"My lord of Glengorm," Queen Joan said, "you must be good to my friend Cicely. You must give me your word you will be good to her."

"Why, madam, I shall be every bit as good to her as she is to me," the laird swore.

Cicely burst out laughing. "As you see, he is not an easy man," she told her friend.

The king now joined them. "I am told you are not yet married, madam," he said.

Cicely curtsied to the king. "It was decided that a year of mourning for Glengorm's former laird was a right and proper course to take, my liege."

"You have set the date?" he demanded.

"The eighteenth of this month, three days after the first anniversary of Ian's death, my liege," Cicely said tightly.

"We'll come," James Stewart said. "Today is the third day of the month. We had intended to stay with you until the eighth. We shall instead move on tomorrow to Ben Duff, and return here on the eighteenth to celebrate your marriage."

"Will you allow the queen to remain here with me, my liege?" Cicely asked him. "We have not seen each other in over two years now. We can visit. Ben Duff and his wife will return with you, for they have been invited to our wedding. Her Highness can visit with Maggie then." She gave him a smile.

Before the king might speak the queen quickly said,

"Ohh, I should like to remain here with Ce-ce, Jamie." She placed her hands on her belly. "I have missed her."

"If it pleases you, sweetheart, then of course you may remain with Cicely," the king told his wife. It would be easier traveling without her, but he would never say it.

"Remain today and tomorrow, my liege, so we may send to Ben Duff to alert them that you will come early. Maggie would never forgive me if I allowed you to take her unawares," Cicely said to James Stewart. "And our folk would greet you too."

The king agreed, and a messenger was dispatched immediately to Ben Duff so that the Greys might be warned of the king's early arrival, and without the queen. And James Stewart found to his surprise that Glengorm was not quite the rough place he had believed it to be when Cicely was carried off by its former laird.

Mab set forth a fine supper that night, with several more dishes than she usually served up. Two extra trestles were brought into the hall so the king's men might be seated. At the high board there was a platter with thinly sliced broiled salmon set upon a bed of fresh green cress. There was a leg of lamb, and a fat roasted capon stuffed with bread, onions, and apples. There was rabbit stew in a tasty brown gravy with bits of carrot, parsley, and shallots. A bowl of peas was passed about, along with a salad of lettuces. There was the usual bread, butter, and cheese. And when they thought they could eat no more, Mab herself appeared with a great big dish of baked apples, Gabhan coming behind her with a large pitcher filled with golden cream, followed by Bessie and Flora, who each brought a small plate of sugared wafers they set upon the high board.

Cicely presented her kitchen staff to the king and the queen.

James Stewart delighted Mab by complimenting her on the fine meal. "I don't suppose I could convince you to come to Scone?" he said with a serious face.

Bessie and Flora tittered as Mab's face lit up with a smile. "I thank Yer Highness for the invitation, but alas,

I am too old to travel farther than from my hearth to the table." Then she curtsied as much as her stiff knees would allow.

"I shall look forward to my return to Glengorm, Mistress Mab," he told her.

When the cook and her helpers had departed back to their own realm, Cicely said, "That was most kind, my liege. Mab is the heart of Glengorm. Your welcome in the village on the morrow will be twice as warm for your goodness tonight to an old woman."

Owen the piper came to play for them, and when the queen began to nod in her chair Cicely suggested that perhaps it was time to escort their guests to the new chamber that had been built for them. James Stewart was most complimentary when he saw what had been done to accommodate them. A large fire burned in the new hearth. The shutters on the window had been closed. There was water for bathing, and Essie was even now warming the bed with her pan of hot coals. She scurried out when the others entered.

"How lovely!" the queen exclaimed. "And those bed hangings are beautiful."

Satisfied that the royal couple would be comfortable, Cicely and Kier bade them good night. Returning to the hall they began their nightly routine. Kier saw that all the doors to the house were firmly locked and barred. The king's men were sleeping about the hall, and so after adding more wood to the fire, Cicely went upstairs. Hearing footsteps behind her she turned to see Kier. She continued on until she was at her chamber door.

"It went well," he told her approvingly. "The training you received from your royal foster mother serves you well, madam."

"I am glad you are pleased, my lord," Cicely told him quietly.

"There is no escape now that the king and queen will be here for our marriage," he teased her. "I look forward to our wedding night."

"As do I," Cicely surprised him by saying.

"Indeed, madam?" He looked at her quizzically.

"Should I not enjoy our bedsport then?" she asked him. "You say you do not like me, my lord. That I am naught but breeding stock for Glengorm. I do not like you, but I will admit that night we spent together was wonderful. I will respect your position as laird of Glengorm, and you will respect mine as lady. It is enough, and we do not have to like each other to enjoy our bedsport together, do we?"

Never in his thirty-plus years had a woman ever spoken so candidly, so frankly to him. He had enjoyed their bedsport too, but it occurred to him that if he had and if she had, there had to be something more than just pleasure between them. And if there was, what was it? She was confusing him, Kier decided. "Respect and a mutual enjoyment of bedsport," he said to her. "It is more than most couples begin with, madam." Reaching out, he cupped her face with a hand, and to his surprise she did not pull away or scold him. Bending, he touched her lips with his, and to his surprise she willingly kissed him back. His arm went about her waist as the kiss deepened, continued, as their tongues entwined and stroked. He considered other uses for their tongues, and his cock hardened.

Cicely was enjoying the never-ending kiss. Her nipples had hardened, and she was already wet, tingling, ready to be taken. But no! She was going to make him wait, because while she enjoyed this sensual play, she would never allow Kier to think he was totally in charge of the passion they would share. She gently pushed him away.

He looked down at her, surprised, puzzled.

"Forgive me for teasing," she said, as if she had entrapped him in some manner. "I know we are both experienced, but I should prefer to wait until our wedding night." Standing on her tiptoes, she kissed his cheek. "Good night, my lord." And then, turning quickly, she slipped into her bedchamber with a last regretful smile at him.

Hearing the key turn in the door's lock, he was suddenly furious. He would kick down the damned barrier between them and take her then and there. But then he remembered their royal guests. Would they hear the uproar from the comfort of their beautiful chamber behind the hall? Or would they hear nothing at all? He couldn't take the chance of offending James Stewart, but then and there he decided that Cicely would pay for her flirtatious behavior. His cock and his balls ached with his need. Angry, he retired to his own chamber, undressed, and flung himself into a cold bed.

The next day the king delighted the Douglas clansmen and -women by visiting the village. He told them himself that he would leave on the morrow, but return in time for the wedding of their laird and Cicely. "But my queen shall remain behind, visiting with the beloved companion of her childhood and youth, your own lady. Guard her well, my good friends. Keep Glengorm safe for my return." He drank a cup of whiskey with them, praised their past loyalty, and then left them. The next morning James Stewart rode out with his men for Ben Duff.

The laird of Glengorm accompanied the king, for Kier Douglas did not believe, to his annoyance, that he would be able to resist Cicely until their wedding day. If he forced the issue he knew he would be furious with himself for his weakness, and that Cicely would find a way to make him pay for coercing her, even though her own lust obviously burned as hot as his. His bride, he was learning, was a woman with whom to be reckoned.

Watching him go, the former servant Bethia walked from the village. No one paid her any particular attention, for she carried a small basket, and it was assumed she was gathering something. Walking about the loch, she trudged across the small meadow and up the wooded hillside, avoiding the line of sight from the sturdy stone redoubt as she came. The other side of the hill had been cleared almost completely of trees to avoid a surprise attack. Bethia hurried down the hillside using what trees remained to shield her flight. Several hours later she reached her destination, an isolated cottage on the edge of a wood. Walking up to the door of the cottage, she knocked, and the door was opened almost immediately. Bethia stepped into the dwelling's single room.

"Sister, what brings you here?" The man beckoned her forward to join him on a rough-hewn settle by the fire.

"The queen is at Glengorm, Durwin," Bethia said. "Gather your men, and plan your attack. Slay them all and the Douglases will never regain prominence."

Durwin Grahame looked his sister in the eye. "Nay," he told her. "It is not yet time, Bethia. Besides, we should be hunted down on both sides of the border if we attacked Glengorm when Queen Joan was in residence, and did her any harm. She is the English king's kin, married to Scotland's king, woman. Where is your good sense?"

"But what better time to destroy the Douglases, brother?" Bethia demanded.

"We have not yet the men to overcome Glengorm," he answered her.

"But this new laird has gone off with the king," she persisted. "Without him the Douglases would fall."

"Is Frang no longer captain of the guard then?" Durwin asked.

"Frang is a good fighter, but he is no leader," Bethia said.

"I understand your desire to take your revenge on the lady of Glengorm, but this is not the time, sister. Ian Douglas is dead and buried. Was not that enough for you?"

"I want *her* to suffer as I have suffered," Bethia snarled.

Durwin laughed. "Your man has been beating you regularly then, has he?"

"When you come to Glengorm," his sister answered venomously, "I will slay him myself, and his old mother, then blame the deaths upon the *English* raiders," Bethia said. "And I will quit Glengorm, then, for the clanfolk have never really liked me. I will come home and keep house for you, brother."

God forbid! Durwin Grahame thought to himself. *I suppose I shall have to see you slain in that raid as well or live out my old age shackled to you. Nay! I intend bringing back some nubile young lass from Glengorm to warm my bed and keep my cottage. The little bitch might even give me a bairn or two. 'Tis past time I got myself a legitimate heir. Aye, I'll not tolerate my sister any longer than I must.* "The Scots king will go into the north eventually, Bethia. And all the good border lords will go with him and take the bulk of their own men, who defend their houses and keeps. By that time I will have rebuilt my own forces, and it is then, but not before then, that we shall attack Glengorm. You will have your revenge, sister. I told you not to wed with your Douglas, but you would not listen, Bethia. You thought he loved you, when all he sought was someone to care for his mam. You were fortunate to be able to insinuate yourself into the laird's household, sister, else you would have been dead long since."

"If I must wait, then I must wait," Bethia said, irritated, but finally resigned. "I'll cook your supper and stay the night. I don't have time to return."

"Won't your man miss you?" Durwin asked.

"I told him Mab needed extra help at the house because of the queen's visit, and had called on me because of my experience," Bethia said.

"He believed you?" Durwin laughed.

"All he could think of was the coin I would receive for my services," she answered her brother scornfully.

"And when you have no coin to give him?" he queried her.

"I will simply tell him the lady refused to pay me,"

Bethia said. "He will not question me further, for I shall feign outrage. Nor will he go to the lady," she said with a shrug. "I'll be extra gentle and kind to his old mother, and cook his favorite supper. It's unlikely he'll beat me then. Especially if I see that he has enough drink to put him to sleep."

"You're just like our mam," Durwin said. "A nasty piece of work, Bethia."

Bethia cackled with appreciation, and then began to make preparations for her brother's supper. Their mother *had* been a nasty piece of work. "Thank you," she said to him. "You could not have given me a better compliment."

The next morning, as soon as it was light, Bethia set out on her return journey to Glengorm. When her husband held out his hand for the coin she was supposed to have earned, she broke into a tirade. Her explanation had Callum Douglas satisfied, if irritated. He cuffed her once to show his displeasure with her, with the lady, and with the world in general.

The queen came into the village that afternoon, and charmed all of the clanfolk. One of the clansmen took her and Cicely out rowing upon Loch Beag, *beag* being the Scots word for *little*. The trees about the water were turning their autumn colors. Cicely's two white terriers had accompanied them and, paws on the gunwales of the boat, they barked at anything that moved upon the shoreline.

"They be good watchdogs, for all their wee size," the clansman rowing the boat noted dryly. Then he chuckled, for a fish leaped from the waters of the loch, sending the terriers into a frenzy of yapping. Cicely and the queen had to hold on to the dogs to keep them from leaping from their little vessel.

It was almost like old times for the two young women. Happy to be together, they hardly left each other's side. The queen had put many a nose out of joint by leaving her women behind. Only her beloved elderly tiring woman, Bess, had accompanied her. Bess was spending her days either dozing in the hall by the fire or gossiping with Orva, while Cicely and the young queen amused themselves walking, playing cards, and talking for hours on end. The queen was concerned that she had birthed two daughters. While healthy and strong, neither was the desired prince and heir. And now, pregnant again, she feared another daughter would be born.

"They say it is my fault," Joan Beaufort told Cicely. "But Jamie's mother birthed four sisters and three sons, of which only he and his brother David reached adulthood. David was murdered by his uncle, the Duke of Albany. That is why Jamie was to be sent to France, for safety's sake. His poor father realized too late the duplicity of his brother."

"There is nothing for it but that you must keep having children until you give Scotland its prince," Cicely replied. "That is your duty."

"Your little Johanna is a beautiful baby," the queen remarked. "Thank you for naming her after me, but why was I not her godmother?"

"I didn't think the king would allow it, as he still felt anger towards Ian for abducting me when he planned to see me married into the Gordons," Cicely answered. "Will you be godmother to the first child I bear Kier?"

"Are you enceinte?" the queen inquired, curious.

"Nay, we are not yet wed," Cicely replied primly.

"But he's certainly bedded you, hasn't he? He doesn't look like a man to take nay for an answer."

"Once, but I have held him at bay ever since," Cicely said with a smile. "He has the most amazing effect upon me, Jo. He kisses me, and I become absolutely wanton. It was not that way with Ian. I cared for Ian. I don't even particularly like Kier Douglas."

The queen laughed. "It is said that strong dislike often leads to love," she told Cicely. "Perhaps without realizing it you are falling in love with him."

"Never!" Cicely said vehemently. "I lust after him. Nothing more." But Cicely was beginning to wonder if that was true. Could she love a man like Kier? A man who professed distain for her, who thought of her only as a means to his own immortality?

She considered the two Douglas men with whom she was or had been involved. Ian had loved her enough to risk offending James Stewart. For all his reckless behavior he had been honorable, a good man and a good laird. The Glengorm folk had adored him, and his own brother had been willing to die for him. And she had come to care for him. Not with the deep passion he held for her, she admitted to herself. But she had felt affection and respect for Ian Douglas. She knew now that she could have been happy spending her life with him. Why was it one always realized these things too late?

Kier, on the other hand, was an entirely different matter. He was a hard man with a strong sense of duty to Clan Douglas. Perhaps it was his nature, or perhaps because of the circumstances of his birth he felt a need to excel, to please his father, to prove that he was as worthy as any. And yet his mother had been a Stewart, a lady. And his father's wife had loved him as her own. Yet Sir William had not bothered to legitimate his eldest son. And whether he said it or not, that must have stung this proud man.

Especially considering that the wife he was about to take had been born under similar circumstances. While Cicely's mother had not been noble, as Kier's mother had been, her father had cared enough for her and the child she bore him to make Cicely's birth a legitimate one. Could that fact alone cause Kier Douglas to despise her? Or would it not matter to him as long as she gave him the sons he required? Might they come to care for each other one day? But it didn't matter if they did or they didn't. In a few days' time they would be wed to each other. Cicely sighed so deeply that the queen looked at her to see if all was well, but then, realizing her friend had obviously been in deep thought, Joan Beaufort said nothing.

Glengorm prepared for the wedding of its new laird to the widow of the previous laird. As the day that would mark the first anniversary of Ian Douglas's death approached, Cicely found herself growing sadder. Once again the fact that this big, full-of-life man was gone reached out to touch her. How could such a thing have happened? But she knew the answer. The Grahames. The bloody Grahames. But she had sworn to her dying husband not to begin a feud. Ian had understood the futility of it. Still, given the opportunity to have her revenge upon them, she would have taken it.

Kier Douglas returned to Glengorm the day before the first-year commemoration would be celebrated. He would go to the Mass with Cicely, to be held at Glengorm Church on the morrow. The king would come on the sixteenth. That he had not returned with Kier to honor Ian Douglas told Cicely that James Stewart still held a grudge against the man who had boldly abducted her. It saddened her, but then, she knew the king was a hard man who would brook no disobedience to his will.

"Welcome home, my lord," Cicely greeted Kier as he dismounted his horse.

The genuine warmth in her voice pleased him. "Thank you, madam," he said with a smile. "All has been well while I have been gone?"

"Aye, my lord, all has been well." She did not ask about the king. "Was all well at Ben Duff?" she inquired. "Will Maggie come with Lord Grey to our wedding?"

"Ben Duff's lady told me to tell you she is looking forward to seeing both you and the queen," Kier answered, surprised when she slipped her hand upon his arm while walking with him into the hall. He could not resist teasing her, saying, "You have missed me then, madam?" The blue eyes were twinkling as she looked up at him, startled by the query.

She paused, and then said, "Glengorm was quieter with your absence, my lord."

He laughed aloud. "Indeed, madam, indeed." He

suddenly felt happier and more relaxed than he had in months. And she seemed less tense. His getting away with the king had obviously been good for both of them.

The following morning they walked together to Glengorm's little church, where the clanfolk were already gathered. The queen came with them. Her presence would make up for the lack of the king this day. Father Ambrose said the Mass, and the homily he preached was as much an instruction to Kier and Cicely as it was a tribute to his two deceased nephews, for it dealt with the subject of duty to one's king, clan, and self. Afterwards the queen praised Ambrose for his words, and the priest flushed with pride.

The king and his party arrived on the sixteenth. Cicely and the queen shrieked with surprise to see the big belly Maggie MacLeod was sporting. Maggie just grinned.

"Are you planning on having another bairn at Glengorm then?" Cicely teased her.

"Nay, nay." Maggie laughed. "I'm not due until we are halfway through December, I promise. It's another lad! I just know it!" Then she saw the look on Joan Beaufort's pretty face. "Ohh, Highness, forgive me! I spoke thoughtlessly," Maggie said, contrite. How could she have been so thoughtless? she asked herself.

"Nay, nay," the queen reassured her. "It is all God's will." But as Maggie just *knew* the child she carried was a boy, so Joan Beaufort *knew* she was going to birth another girl. She had even decided to name this princess Mary. But she kept these thoughts to herself. Eventually she was certain she would birth a son for Scotland.

The men hunted grouse the next day, bringing home several braces of the birds, which were plucked, roasted, and served that very night. The mood in the hall that evening was very jovial, but they all retired early, for the wedding would be celebrated in the morning. The servants would be up early to sweep the hall and prepare for the day of festivities, when all the village would be invited into the house.

Cicely had asked to have her tub filled after the evening meal. Now she soaked contentedly in the warm water, washing her long auburn hair with soap she had made this past summer. It was scented with white heather. She rubbed the sliver of soap up and down a thick rope of hair, considering what she would wear on the morrow. It wasn't that her wardrobe was so large, but she didn't want to look completely out of fashion. Jo had told her little had changed in the years since she had been gone, which was a relief.

"Have you decided?" Orva asked her as she bustled about the bedchamber. "I need to know, if I am to see the gown is wrinkle free and brushed properly."

Cicely sighed. She had worn lavender brocade when she had married Ian. She had not worn that gown since Ian's death. Somehow the burnt orange didn't seem right, nor the yellow, nor the green. Then she remembered a gown she had worn but once at court. It was cream-colored velvet with sleeves that were fitted to the elbow, then flared out wide. The edges of the gown were trimmed in dark brown marten. "The cream velvet," she said to Orva. "Is it fit to wear?"

"I'll have to alter the waist a wee bit," Orva said. "You've thickened a bit in the waist since Johanna's birth."

"Blessed Mother, have I grown too plump for the gown? 'Tis barely worn, Orva."

"It will need an extra inch if you are to feast and dance on the morrow," Cicely's tiring woman said. "You are almost nineteen, my lady, and have had one child."

Cicely finished bathing, wrapping her long hair in a piece of toweling, stepping from her tub to dry herself with another length of towel. Orva handed her a clean chemise to sleep in, and Cicely went to sit by the fire with her hairbrush. She sat by the warm hearth, brushing out her long tresses until they were soft and dry.

Orva, having fetched the chosen garment from the trunk, now sat opposite Cicely, pulling out stitches at the waistline, resetting the fabric so that the gown's midsection was a little bit larger. "Are you happy, my child?" Orva asked as she sewed with neat little stitches. "He is not Lord Ian, but he seems a good man."

"I must put the past behind me," Cicely told the older woman, "but I chide myself that I did not fully appreciate Ian's love for me."

Orva nodded in understanding. "Sometimes, my lady, we do not see clearly just what is before our eyes. Your first husband lies in the cold ground. Try to appreciate Lord Kier for who he is, and do not scorn him for who he is not."

"But just who is he?" Cicely said. "One minute he is cold and hard. But the next he is passionate. I do not understand him at all, Orva. I knew exactly where I stood with Ian, though I did not appreciate it at the time. I do not understand my lord Kier."

"You will." Orva chuckled. "In the end women always unravel the puzzle of their men. Now, my lady, you had best get into bed and get some sleep. You will not sleep a great deal tomorrow night, I'm thinking. That man of yours looks like a fierce one." She bent her head again to the gown upon which she sewed.

Cicely blushed at Orva's words, but she followed her advice, climbing into her bed. Sleep, however, did not come to her easily, even after Orva had finished the gown and left her chamber. She thought of that passionate encounter with Kier several weeks back, and grew restless with the memory of the heated hours they had spent together. *Fierce,* Orva had said. 'Twas a good word for the man she would take as her husband on the morrow. She had been fortunate that that encounter had not resulted in her being impregnated. She had not wanted to be with child so soon after Johanna's birth. But after tomorrow it would be expected that she have a child as quickly as possible. And not just any child: a son for Glengorm. Cicely finally drifted to sleep.

When she awoke she could just glimpse the gray light

of predawn through a crack in her shutters. Her chamber was cold, as the fire in her hearth had been reduced to a bed of hot coals. Slipping from her bed, Cicely made her way across the icy floor and carefully added some wood to the coals. Within a few minutes the fire blazed up again. Relieving herself in the night jar, Cicely took the pitcher of lukewarm water from the coals, poured some into her ewer, and bathed her hands and face. Then, sitting down, she began to brush the tangles from her long hair.

Orva entered the bedchamber carrying a garment. "I am so sorry, my lady, but I overslept," she apologized. "And on this day of all days, but the gown is ready." She held it up. "You cannot tell I've altered it, and I've brushed it so that the velvet looks thick and luxuriant. The fur on the sleeves has kept well. Are you ready to be dressed?"

"Aye," Cicely said. "Ambrose will oversee the signing of the marriage agreement in the hall, and then do the Mass, as he did before. He'll bless our union at the last."

"I heard an arrival a few moments ago. I imagine it is Sir William," Orva said. She slipped the gown over Cicely's head.

"Aye, he'll have left Drumlanrig and ridden with the border moon to light his way," Cicely said as the fabric of the garment fell to the floor. She shook her hips to settle it. "Where is my gold girdle?"

"Here, my lady," Orva said, holding up the wide band before slipping it about her mistress to rest on Cicely's hips, where she fastened it. "Now," Orva said, "let me get your mother's gold chain and her rings for you to wear." She sought for the pouch in which these valuables were stored and, finding it, gave the sack to Cicely.

The bride removed a few pieces of jewelry from the small bag: a gold chain and five rings, with which she now adorned herself. When she had wed Ian she had worn no jewelry, for the ceremony had been sudden and swift. There had been no true guests. But today Scotland's king and queen would witness this new marriage. Cicely garbed herself not just for her bridegroom, but for their royal guests as well.

Sitting down, she gave her hair a final brush, then gathered it into her gold caul. No maiden now, she did not have to leave her hair unbound today. Then she slipped her feet into a pair of soft leather sollerets. Standing, she said to Orva, "I'm going to take the dogs out, for it is too early for the wedding, and no one will be in the hall but the servants and the men. I shan't be long."

"You'll get your gown dirty," Orva protested.

"No, I won't," Cicely promised, and then she was gone, the terriers at her heels. The hall was still quiet, although the servants bustled about. It would be another half an hour before the wedding began. Her last marriage had been in the winter—February, she thought as she went through the front door, the dogs racing ahead.

The day was beautiful. The sky was clear. Not a cloud marred its perfect color. The sun was just up, and it sparkled on the deep blue waters of the loch. The air was crisp, and the hillsides were bright with patches of color here and there. On the edge of the woodlands across the meadow was a small, fast-flowing stream. Cicely decided to walk to it. Ahead of her the dogs bounded along, yapping at anything that moved: a last butterfly, a fat bumblebee gathering what was left of a daisy's pollen.

Reaching the wood, Cicely couldn't resist taking her slippers off, lifting her skirts, and wading in the water. She squealed, for it was icy, and quickly withdrew herself, slipping her footwear back on. It was so beautiful. So peaceful. Her two terriers sat in a blaze of golden sunshine. With a reluctant sigh Cicely turned from the stream and the wood, calling to the dogs, and together they returned across the meadow to the house.

Orva was already in the hall. She looked her mistress over critically, noting a faint damp spot on the skirt's hem. She shook her head at Cicely, but she was smiling.

"It will dry," Cicely said. "I couldn't resist the meadow or the stream. It's the most perfect day, Orva. Do you think that bodes well for this marriage?"

"I think it does, my lady," Orva answered her mistress.

Descending the stairs into the hall, Kier Douglas heard Cicely. For some reason he found her words encouraging. Was it possible she might just be learning to like him? He hoped it was so, for while he might say he didn't like her, the truth was that he had come to like her very much. But as she always responded in kind to him, he would not tell her of this change of heart he was having. At least, not until she admitted to liking him. His father had always warned of giving a woman the upper hand. He walked into the hall where the king, the queen, and Lord and Lady Grey were now waiting.

"Good morrow, my liege, Your Highness." He greeted the royal couple with a bow. Then he turned, and his breath caught in his throat for a moment. He had never seen Cicely look so beautiful. "Good morrow, madam. Are you ready to wed me without further ado?" He bowed to her.

He was handsome. There was simply no denying it. That coal black hair. The bright blue eyes. They would have beautiful children, she thought. "Good morrow, my lord," she greeted him. "Aye, I am ready to wed you." He was wearing dark wool breeks and a white shirt, and his gray-black-and-white Douglas plaid was slung across his chest, held by his silver clan badge—the family motto, *Jamais arrière*, meaning "Never behind," engraved about its circular shape. On his head was a black velvet cap with an eagle's feather, which denoted his position as laird in this place.

Father Ambrose hurried in, carrying the marriage contracts. He bowed to them all, and then spread the parchments on the high board, where an inkstand and quill had already been set. "This family will be honored if you and the queen will witness these documents, my liege," the priest said. He looked about the hall. "Where is Sir William?"

"I am here, Ambrose," the bridegroom's father said, stepping from among his men.

The priest handed the inked quill to Kier Douglas. The laird signed and handed the quill back to Ambrose Douglas. Re-inking the quill, he handed it to Cicely. She signed with a delicate flourish. Then came the witnesses. King James. Queen Joan. Sir William and Lord Grey. " 'Tis done," the cleric said, sanding the signatures. "Now let us get to the Mass, and I will give this couple the Church's blessing."

The wedding party walked from the hall and out into the bright October day. The entire village had turned out to see them. As they reached Glengorm Church, Mary Douglas stepped forward to press a small bouquet of late pink roses mixed with white heather into Cicely's hand. The bride smiled and thanked her clanswoman.

Everyone who could crowded into the church. Mab's great-nephew Gabhan acted as Father Ambrose's acolyte. The sun shone through the narrow windows of the church. They had no glass, and in the winter, even with the shutters closed tightly, the church was cold and drafty. Today, however, the last of midautumn's warmth made the building habitable. The air was filled with incense today. Beeswax candles, not tallow, flickered on the small altar. Only the wedding party had rough seats. The rest of the congregation stood until the Mass was concluded. Then Father Ambrose blessed the newly married couple, who departed Glengorm Church, their clansmen and -women following behind them.

In the hall trestles and benches now covered the floor. The entire village crowded in, joining the king's men at the tables. Casks of October ale were broached. Everyone had brought some sort of drinking vessel to use. There were fresh-baked cottage loaves on all the tables, with crocks of sweet butter and small wheels of hard yellow cheese. Platters filled with rashers of bacon and slices of ham were brought for the guests, along with hard-boiled eggs. At the high board Mab had prepared a special breakfast of poached eggs in a cream sauce that was flavored with marsala wine. The was a platter of sliced salmon, another of ham, and trenchers filled with a vegetable potage, along with warm cottage loaves, butter, cheese, and plum jam. The wine cups were never allowed to be less than half-full.

The final course served below the salt were platters of plump baked apples sweetened with both sugar and cinnamon. This was a very rare treat, for both sugar and spices were not available as a rule to the clanfolk. But at the high board Mab herself brought in a platter of pears poached in white wine and honey, to be served with delicate sugared wafers. The meal finished, Duncan Douglas, Mary's husband, stood up.

"God rest Laird Ian, and God bless Laird Kier and Lady Cicely!"

There was the scraping of benches as all in the great hall arose to raise their mugs, shouting with one voice, "God bless Laird Kier and Lady Cicely!"

The king leaned over, murmuring to Kier, "You have won their hearts. I am glad to know that Glengorm is in safe hands. Now sire a son on your good lady so these lands are secure unto the next generation."

Cicely heard the king's words. Her eyes met those of her husband, and she blushed as he said, "Now that, my liege, is a command I fully intend obeying with all my heart."

James Stewart chuckled, leaning back in his chair and reaching for his queen's small hand as Owen the piper began to play for their entertainment. "And when that son is born, Kier Douglas, I will stand as his godfather. That is my gift to you both this day."

Chapter 16

*T*heir wedding day had been declared a holiday. There were games both rough and gentle. The men played one in a meadow, kicking a sheep's bladder that had been stuffed with straw towards goals set up at either end of the field. Even the king joined in, and was very adept at getting this ball to its goal. In another field archery butts had been set up, and shooting contests were held. Both Cicely and the queen were excellent archers. Kier was amazed, for he had not considered that his bride might be adept at such a sport. Footraces were run. There was one contest in which the men heaved large round stones as far as they could, the stone reaching the greatest distance being declared the winner. And there was even a caber toss, but few were adept at it, and Mary Douglas's husband, Duncan, battled with Father Ambrose until the priest beat him. Both men were gasping with their efforts, and dripping with perspiration as they filled their mugs with ale and toasted each other's sportsmanship.

"The priest is most familiar with the people, isn't he?" the queen remarked. She almost blushed, admiring Ambrose Douglas's muscled, hairy chest.

"He is related to almost everyone in the village," Cicely explained. "He is one of them, and that is good. He was Ian's uncle."

"Ah, so that is why he could not take the lairdship for himself," Joan Beaufort said, and Maggie nodded, agreeing. "He's certainly a fine figure of a man, Ce-ce."

"He couldn't have had it anyway, Jo. He was born on the other side of the blanket, the last of his father's bastards, but most favored," Cicely explained.

And throughout the day there was music. Several men in the village played the pipes; there were two with small reedlike instruments, and a man with drums. They joined with Owen, Glengorm's official piper, in playing for the bride and groom. And there was dancing. Holding hands, the wedding guests danced in circles to the music. Kier, Lord Grey, the king, and several other men danced the traditional sword dance, their booted feet moving gracefully between the crossed swords as they nimbly leaped and cavorted. The Glengorm folk were impressed that their king, who had spent most of his life in England, was so adept at this particular dance native to Scotland.

The trestles had been brought from the hall to be set up in front of the house. All day long those tables were filled with food that was eagerly eaten. Casks of October ale were set up and available to everyone. And then finally the day began to wane, the sun setting in a blaze of crimson and gold splendor behind the hills. The air grew cooler; the darkening sky above them was dotted with bright stars.

When night fell the hall was empty but for the king, the queen, the Greys—who would leave in the morning with Sir William—and the bridal couple. The king played a game of chess with the Douglas chieftain. The queen sat, her feet upon a stool, little Johanna in her lap. Finally there was nothing for it but to bid their guests good night.

Cicely bent and kissed the queen's cheek. "Good

night, Jo. I will send the baby's nursemaid to take her. It has been a very long day for us all." Turning, she curtsied to the king and Sir William. "Good night, my lords," she said. Then Cicely looked to Kier. "You will see to the house, my lord?" she asked him politely.

"I will, madam, and join you when all is secure," he told her.

Cicely departed the hall. Shortly afterwards a nursemaid came to gather up the baby. The queen arose at that point. "Good night, my lords," she said. Then, putting her hand on her husband's shoulder, she murmured, "Do not linger, my lord."

The king nodded, but Sir William knew what Queen Joan was attempting to tell them all, and smiled to himself. Then he made a rather foolish move upon the chessboard, almost chuckling as the king's eyes lit up and he crowed, "Checkmate!"

Then it dawned upon James Stewart what Sir William Douglas had done. He looked at the chessboard, and then a further enlightened grin split his face. He nodded at his opponent. "Cleverly done, my lord," he said, standing up. "I will therefore bid you good night." He crossed the hall and entered the new chamber at its end.

Maggie MacLeod was already pushing her husband up the stairs to the small chamber where they slept.

The Douglas clan chieftain stood as well and, with an answering smile, bowed. "Good night, my liege," he called. Then, turning to his son, he said, "I believe Tam has prepared a bedspace for me here in the hall. 'Tis been a long day, and I am not as young as I once was, but I am content to have seen you wed this day. The match is a good one for you, Kier. And she will do her duty in all things, I know, for she has been bred to it. Now lock up your house. Then go plow your mare well and deep. I will expect a grandson from you within the next year."

The laird of Glengorm's eyes danced with amusement at his sire's directive. "I live to obey you, my lord," he told him. Then he went off to make certain all was secure as, chuckling, his father pulled off his boots and climbed into his bedspace to sleep.

Cicely had ordered that her bedchamber be prepared for her wedding night. It was slightly larger than Kier's chamber down the hall, and the bed was bigger. The fresh sheets were scented with lavender. Orva helped her mistress remove her gown and shoes. After brushing the gown, she folded it away into a trunk, placing the shoes in a smaller trunk. Cicely handed Orva the gold caul she had removed, leaving her long hair falling loose, along with her few small pieces of jewelry but for the narrow red-gold wedding band Kier had slipped on her finger when Ambrose had blessed them this morning. Then she washed her face and hands in the basin of scented water, scrubbing her teeth with the cloth she used for washing.

"Go along now, Orva," she told her tiring woman. "The fire is set for the night. My lord cannot come until the other guests have departed the hall."

"Good night then, my lady," Orva said, and hurried out.

Cicely climbed into bed. It smelled wonderfully fresh as she leaned against the pillows. It had been a long day, but it had been a good one. She was not unhappy any longer, but she could not help but wonder if Kier would ever come to care for her. Oh, she knew she would never be loved again as Ian Douglas had loved her. His love had been a rare thing, but Cicely knew now that she wanted Kier to at least like her. She fell asleep, not awakening even when he entered the chamber.

Kier Douglas looked at Cicely as she lay in their bed. When she was asleep, all the wariness in her face was gone. She was truly beautiful with her delicate coloring. The cheeks of her pale skin held the hint of peach, quite in keeping with her auburn hair. Her eyebrows arched elegantly above her closed eyes, and the auburn eyelashes brushing her cheeks were tipped in gold. He pulled his clothing off until he stood naked by the side of the bed, debating whether to wake her or not. Deciding to allow her to awaken on her own, he climbed into the bed, noting with just the faintest irritation that she was wearing her chemise. He would remind her that in the future he wanted her naked in their bed.

Kier lay upon his back with his eyes closed. Beside him Cicely slept peacefully, her breathing rhythmic. He felt himself relaxing next to her calm warmth. It had been a long day for him as well, and he easily drifted off into sleep after a few minutes. She was his now, and Glengorm was his. Kier Douglas felt true contentment for the first time in his life. It was a good feeling, he thought just as he fell asleep.

Cicely awakened to see the gray light of predawn coming through the wooden shutters of her chamber. And then she was suddenly aware of the body beside her. Giving a little gasp, she turned to look at him, realizing that he was naked. *Blessed Mother!* It had been their wedding night, and she had fallen asleep! Yet he might have awakened her when he came in, but he hadn't. Did he find her so unattractive, dislike her so much, that he hadn't cared to wake her?

And then she realized with shock that his blue eyes were staring up at her. "So, madam, you have finally awoken," he said. "It is past time we did what is expected of us. Will you remove your chemise, or shall I rip this one from you too?" His eyes were laughing at her, although his demeanor was deadly serious.

"It's almost light," Cicely answered him.

Kier chuckled. "Not quite," he replied.

Cicely unlaced the chemise, and then drew it over her head, discarding it on the floor by the bed. She made to lie back.

"Nay, stay as you are," Kier said. "I would admire you, madam. Your breasts are quite beautiful. Why do you blush? 'Tis truth."

"You did not wake me when you came in," Cicely said softly.

"I was tired, and you were tired too," he said. Then, reaching out, he cupped her face in his big hand. "You looked very pretty as you slept, madam. I will admit to being tempted." The hand caressed her face. "You are more than passing fair, Cicely."

Her heart raced madly. He was the most irritating man, and yet she felt strongly drawn to him. Far more than she had been to Ian. Why was it so? she wondered. Why was she more fascinated by this man who professed to dislike her than she had been by the man who had given her his unconditional love? It was irrational.

"You are pondering something," Kier said, "and you should not be."

"Then what should I be doing, my lord?" Cicely asked him.

"This!" he said, pulling her into his arms and kissing her. "I have not had the pleasure yet of kissing my wife, and I briefly recall her kisses are sweet." His lips returned to hers, feeling her mouth willingly yield to his, parting just enough to allow his tongue to find hers and begin to stroke it.

He had wrapped his arms about her, and Cicely now lay almost beneath him. She was breathless with the pleasure his kisses gave her. But then she stiffened. She remembered how Ian's kisses had left her weak with delight. Kier's kisses were very different, yet they seemed to have a similar, if not the same effect on her. She felt brief guilt at enjoying Kier's kisses.

He lifted his dark head, his lips breaking away from hers. "What is the matter?"

Tears sprang into her eyes. "I thought of Ian," she said softly. "How his kisses and your kisses are the same, and yet they are not."

"Did you really love him then?" Kier was curious. He had not considered that she might have actually cared for his cousin. Ian hadn't really courted Cicely. He had abducted her, and she had had no real choice but to wed him.

"He loved me," Cicely said, low, and she blinked away her tears.

Looking into those blue-green eyes of hers so filled with sadness, Kier was overcome with a wave of jealousy. "Did you love him?" he repeated in a hard voice.

"Aye, but not as he loved me," Cicely whispered.

"My cousin, God assoil him, is dead, madam. You are *my* wife now, and you owe me, my family, a duty," Kier said coldly.

She was startled by his words. Why was he so angry at her? "My lord," she replied as formally, "I know my duty, and will do it."

In response he kissed her again, but this time his kiss was fierce, demanding. But what did he want of her? he wondered. And then with startling clarity he knew. He wanted her to love him. Their kiss deepened, and then she yielded again beneath him, her mouth growing pliant and warm, returning his kisses kiss for kiss until they were both dizzy and breathless. His lips moved from hers down the graceful line of her throat. He buried his face between her breasts, his tongue plunging into the deep valley separating the twin orbs of perfumed flesh to lick slowly at her soft skin.

Cicely gasped softly as he began to cover one of her breasts with his kisses. When his mouth began to play with the nipple of that breast, tongue stroking, teeth grazing lightly, mouth sucking, she gave a little cry. When he moved to her other breast Cicely thought she would expire from the pleasure he was giving her. Her hands clutched at him, fingers digging into his shoulders. And then his mouth left her breasts and began moving down her torso, kissing every inch of flesh that he could reach, his warm lips, his hot, wet tongue branding her. She felt him claiming her as Ian had once claimed her, but with Kier she was afraid. He was stronger. He didn't love her.

His head was spinning. The white-heather scent surrounding her filled his senses. He remembered their first encounter. It had been fierce and rough with the need he felt to conquer her. But he hadn't conquered her at all. He had awakened her passions, as she had awakened his. They had feasted together that day on their mutual lust. But he would not lose his control in this hour before the dawn broke. He would be gentle, because he wanted to put Ian from her mind, and he knew that each touch, each kiss he gave to Cicely caused her to compare him with his cousin. But she was his now!

He worked his way down her torso, kissing, licking, nuzzling. He could feel her trembling ever so slightly beneath his lips. Her thick auburn bush was before him. He cupped her with a hand, pressing down upon her mons, and Cicely shuddered. Kier smiled wolfishly, and then, removing his hand, he buried his face in those tight curls, inhaling the female scent of her. Raising his dark head, he gently pushed her thighs apart. He stared down, debating what he would do next; then, deciding, he licked the soft inside of one thigh and then the other with slow, leisurely strokes of his tongue.

Cicely purred. This was something Ian had never done. The tongue continued to move across first one thigh, then the other, and then it was pushing between her folds. *"Oh!"* She gasped as the pointed tip of his tongue found her love button. Her eyes widened as he shifted his position so that his dark head now lay between her milky white thighs. The skillful tongue taunted her until Cicely was whimpering with her need, which seemed to grow and grow with every touch, every stroke of his tongue. She dug her fingers into his thick, dark hair, kneading his head.

And then he stopped, leaning back to press a finger into her sheath. The finger moved back and forth slowly, slowly, teasing her. Cicely bit her lip until it bled, but then, unable to contain herself, she whispered one word: *"More!"* He said nothing, instead withdrawing the single finger and pressing into her again with two fingers, which again moved slowly, slowly, finally gaining speed. She rode his fingers eagerly, and then cried out as she released her juices to him.

Withdrawing the two fingers, he cuddled her in his arms, one hand caressing her head. She squirmed within his embrace, but not to escape him. He had stoked her lust, and now she was more than ready to take him into her body. *"More?"* he whispered into her ear, and his tongue licked the whorl of it.

"Aye!" she said. "More!"

He pulled her to the edge of the bed so that her legs fell over the side. Rolling her onto her belly, he elevated her bottom with a pillow beneath her. Then, standing behind her, Kier levered her legs apart, grasped her hips, and thrust himself deep into her.

Cicely gasped. *Blessed Mother!*

Her gasp told him what he wanted to know. There would be no comparisons made within her mind between himself and his deceased cousin. A sojourn in France and Italy had taught Kier Douglas much. He began to pump himself within her now, slowly at first, then with increasing rapidity, and when he felt her near to peaking he slowed his pace. His fingers should have drawn the edge off of her lust, and he was of a mind to take his time.

Cicely's head was spinning. *Blessed Mother!* He was so big, and yet she easily absorbed him. And never had she been probed so deeply. The tip of his cock touched an extraordinarily sensitive spot within her, and she felt her juices flowing again. Her sheath clasped and unclasped him, sending ripples of sensation throughout her body. He groaned, and his teeth sank into the sensitive nape of her neck briefly. Her back seemed to be arching instinctively, allowing him even deeper access.

Kier was having a difficult time controlling himself. She was an unknowing seductress, a witch! Her sheath wrapped itself around his cock, embracing it, clasping it tightly, as if to force his juices from him. His fingers dug into the soft flesh of her hips as he attempted to control their situation. He forced himself deeper, and she retaliated, the muscles of her sweet, hot maw enfolding his manhood, exhorting his boiling juices to come forth. He was lost! His seed ejected in a fiery explosion of pleasure.

And it swept over them both. Cicely could feel the staccato bursts of his lust filling her. She cried out his name. "*Kier!* Oh, Kier!" She had been well and thoroughly fucked in a manner she had never imagined.

He somehow managed to keep from collapsing on her. His legs weak, he flung himself down upon the bed and, turning his head, looked over at her. Cicely lay as he had put her, head turned to one side, eyes closed. Kier heaved a gusty sigh.

Cicely opened her blue-green eyes to meet his gaze. Then, to his great surprise, she smiled at him. "That was wonderful," she said, dumbfounding him further. "Did you enjoy it as well? I hope you did, my lord."

"Aye," was about all he could manage to say as he lay breathing heavily next to her. He couldn't think of what he might respond to her astonishing frankness.

She still lay on her belly, and she sighed gustily as she finally rolled over onto her back. "My experience is not great, but I think even a woman with a great familiarity with passion would consider you expert, my lord." Then she sat up briefly before rising to her feet. "I see the sun is rising. I must hurry and get down to the hall, and so must you. The king will expect to hunt again today." She walked across the floor and, fetching the pitcher of water from the hot coals of the fire, she poured some into her basin and began to wash herself quickly.

For a long few minutes he lay watching her. She seemed to evince no shyness this morning at her nakedness, although the chamber was growing light with beams of bright sun starting to push through the cracks in the wood shutters. Finally satisfied with her ablutions, she moved back to the bed and picked up her chemise from the floor, drawing it over her head, lacing it neatly. Then, flinging open the window's shutters, she tossed the contents of her basin out the window before refilling it with warm water. "Come, my lord, you must not lay abed," she said, and then she continued dressing herself, opening the trunk at the foot of the bed to pull out a bright yellow houpeland, which she quickly donned. "Kier, get up!" she scolded.

"I think we would be forgiven if we did not go into the hall this morning," he said.

Cicely laughed, pleased. "Then I have pleased you too, my lord. I am glad. Hurry now, and get dressed." Then Cicely hurried from her bedchamber.

Kier Douglas continued to lie abed, contemplating what had just happened. His bride being a widow, he had taken her roughly for his own pleasure. There was no maidenhead to have a care of, and he had fucked her once previously. Still, she had praised him. Was Cicely mocking him? Or had she really enjoyed the lustful play between them? He was totally bemused by her. What game did the bitch play with him? At least she hadn't compared him again to his cousin Ian. That was some improvement, for the mere mention of the previous laird's name seemed to anger him.

God's balls! Was he jealous? *Jesu!* Why would he be jealous of a dead man? Unless, of course, he was falling in love with Cicely. *Never!* A man in love was a weakling, and he would not allow her to weaken him, for a border lord needed his strength to keep his clanfolk, his lands safe. Ian had not been able to do either, because his love for Cicely took precedence over everything else in his life. *"I will not make that mistake!"* Kier Douglas swore aloud to himself as he finally arose from her bed.

Having reached the hall, Cicely was directing her servants. "Tam, make certain Mab serves a generous breakfast. The laird and the king will hunt today." She had looked through one of the windows in the hall and saw that the day was fair.

"I'll tell her, my lady," Tam said, and ran off to the kitchens.

Cicely went and sat before her loom while she waited for her guests and her husband to join her. She looked at the piece she had woven so far. Its subject was Glengorm. She had finished the house on the hillside, the path leading to the village below, and some of the village cottages. She would complete it by spring. It would be hung behind the high board. And then she would begin a companion piece for it. The subject would show an antlered stag on a hillside above the loch, several does by the water drinking. She imagined herself with child as she wove the next tapestry. Aye, she would give Johanna a brother, for even if Kier didn't like her, he liked fucking her.

The king and queen came into the hall from the new chamber behind it.

"You are up, madam," the king said, seeming surprised.

"I would be a poor example if I did not care for my guests," Cicely said.

"Good morrow, my liege," Kier said as he entered the chamber. " 'Tis a good day for grouse, I think. Will you join us, madam?" he asked his bride.

"I think I shall remain with Her Highness," Cicely said. "We still have much catching up to do, my lord. And I shall see a fine meal awaits your return."

"I have no doubt of that," Kier replied somewhat dryly.

Mab had indeed supplied the high board with a very generous breakfast. And afterwards the king and the laird departed to hunt grouse.

They had no sooner left the hall than the queen dragged Cicely to the chairs by the fire. "What happened?" she asked her friend. "Tell me all! Leave nothing out!" She sat down, putting her feet upon a stool. "Is he a good lover?"

"You know my knowledge is not great," Cicely said, "but I believe him to be a magnificent lover," she told her friend.

The queen's blue eyes widened. "What did he do?" she demanded to know.

"I think the question would be, What didn't he do?" Cicely said, smiling.

"Blessed Mother!" Joan Beaufort responded, and she leaned forward in spite of her big belly. "Tell me, Cece!"

Cicely giggled, and then she began to speak in hushed tones so no one else might hear her recitation. She left no detail of their late wedding night out, and the queen was fascinated by it all.

"Has he been in your ass yet?" she asked her friend.

"Nay," Cicely said. "Is such a thing possible?"

"Aye. I'm not particularly fond of it, but sometimes Jamie wants to do it, and so I allow it," the queen explained. "Your husband, if he is as adventurous as he seems, will want that pleasure eventually."

"I hope not," Cicely said, looking dubious.

"How long did he fuck you?" the queen inquired.

"Forever, it seemed. I thought he would go on until Twelfth Night. He seems to have reasonable stamina, Jo. And he went so deep."

"He's long then."

"Aye, and big too," Cicely responded.

"There is nothing like a stiff, manly cock," the queen agreed.

"I complimented him," Cicely said.

Joan Beaufort giggled. "Blessed Mother! I'm sure you quite startled him."

"Are you not supposed to tell a man when he pleases you?" Cicely wanted to know. "Ian always seemed so happy when I told him."

"It cannot hurt a man to know he is appreciated," the

queen replied. "But I am certain it does embarrass him, for men are like that. Do what pleases you, Ce-ce."

"Indeed I shall, Jo. Since he doesn't like me, it doesn't really matter," Cicely answered the queen. "I'll be a good chatelaine and a good wife to him. I will bear his children and give him the respect he is due. He'll have no complaints in me."

"Doesn't like you? Oh, no, Ce-ce, you are quite mistaken," Joan Beaufort told her friend. "Kier likes you very much, I suspect. But like most men he thinks he must be strong, and being strong means showing no weakness. Men think love a weakness."

"Then why does he tell me he doesn't like me?" Cicely wanted to know. "I don't understand such a thing. Ian always said he loved me. He showed no hesitation in doing so, Jo. But Kier is most blunt in his dislike of me."

"Have you said you don't like him?" the queen asked.

"Of course I have. I do not want him to think me so weak and simpering a little fool that I cannot manage without being assured of his love. I don't need his love to do my duty to Glengorm," Cicely said stubbornly.

"In other words, he hurt your feelings when he said he didn't like you, so you retaliated by telling him you didn't like him," Joan Beaufort replied.

"Aye," Cicely agreed, and then she laughed. "I was a little fool, wasn't I, Jo?"

"But you do like him, don't you?" the queen pressed her friend.

"Aye, I do," Cicely admitted. "He is very different from Ian."

"Blessed Mother, leave your former husband, God assoil him, in the grave, Ce-ce! No man wants to hear the virtues of his predecessor," the queen advised her friend.

"But they are similar, at least where Glengorm is concerned," Cicely said.

"And in bed?" the queen queried softly.

"Different," Cicely admitted. "Ian took a special care of me. Kier is almost demanding. I'm not quite certain what he desires, Jo."

Joan Beaufort laughed softly. "I think he probably wants you to love him," she said. "Jamie learned from Sir William that when Kier was a very young man he fell in love. But the girl's father didn't consider him worthy of her. I believe it hurt him, and I think he was ashamed because of the circumstances of his birth. He never again professed tender thoughts for any female. But I can see it in his eyes when he looks at you, Ce-ce. He wants more than a respectful and dutiful wife. Can you give that to him?"

Cicely sighed. "I loved Ian, but never in the way he loved me. And after his death I felt so guilty about it. Ian offered me everything he had to give. His heart. His name. His child. And while I cared for him, my passion was not great. Now I am brought to the altar again with another man. He is fierce, and he is passionate. He excites me. I believe I could fall in love with him, Jo. But he scorns me. How can I offer my heart to such a man as that?"

"Then you have come to an impasse, Ce-ce. Ian was a special man, but most men are more like Kier. And all men are babies. They will dash into battle without fear of death, but they are terrified to tell a woman that they love her. And heaven forfend that a woman hurts their feelings. Then it becomes impossible for them to speak up. Unless, of course, the woman speaks up first," Joan Beaufort said. "If you come to love Kier one day then you must tell him so, Ce-ce. Only then will he admit what is in his heart for you. And believe me, it isn't dislike."

Cicely sighed. "We are of an age, Jo. How did you become so wise? James Stewart loved you from the moment he laid eyes on you. And you had no trouble loving him back. My father always claimed to love my mother, and those who knew them attested to the fact that he did indeed love her. Ian loved me, offered me that same love, but I demurred until it was really too late. Why, I wonder, did I do such a thing?"

"When your father sent you to our foster mother, perhaps you felt he was rejecting your love," the queen suggested.

"Nay!" Cicely denied. "I understood why it was necessary for him to do it. He was saving my life, Jo. My stepmother, Luciana, truly hated me."

"Your stepmother made him choose between you, Ce-ce. And your father chose *her*," Joan Beaufort said. "Your practical nature excused the Earl of Leighton's choice because you loved your father, and would not think badly of him. But at that moment your perceptions of love changed. How could they not? Love between a man and a woman, however, is a totally different thing. To love you must trust. Both you and Kier have lost faith in love because neither of you can trust in it. That, I suspect, is why you found it so difficult to love Ian, to accept his love. Mayhap you feared to lose Ian's love one day. But now either you or Kier must take the first step if you are to discover the joys of love again. And you will also learn when you can love once more that passion with love is far more wonderful than just passion."

Cicely looked at the queen curiously. "I don't know how it could be," she said.

"What did you do after you shared your passions?" the queen asked.

"I complimented him on his skill; then I got up, washed myself, dressed, and came down to the hall to see to my guests," Cicely replied.

The queen laughed. "Oh, dear," she said.

"Jo, it was dawn! I would not be a good chatelaine had I not come down to see to my guests," Cicely defended herself.

"Was Kier of the same mind?" the queen inquired.

"Nay, he was not," Cicely told her friend. "He wanted us to stay abed. He said no one would think the worse of us for it, since we were just wed yesterday."

"Aha!" Joan Beaufort said. "There is certain proof that he is falling in love with you, Ce-ce. If you would but encourage him just the tiniest bit, you could be as happy and my Jamie and I are."

"You want me to be the first to say 'I love you'?" Cicely said. "But I don't love him, Jo. And the only care he has for me is as the mother of his sons."

"He's falling in love with you," the queen insisted. "I know a man in love. Stop being so damned dutiful, Ce-ce, and let yourself fall in love with him. And when you do, tell him, and put the poor man out of his misery. Ian Douglas loved you, to be sure, but this Douglas will love you as well if you will just allow him to, dearest. Did our foster mother not love her King Henry? And he was her second husband. She wanted him, and she made no secret of it. That is the example you need to follow. Now, promise me that you will at least try, Ce-ce."

Cicely laughed. "I promise," she said. Reaching out, she took the queen's hand and kissed it. "I am so glad we remain friends," she told Joan Beaufort. "Are you making friends among the Scots ladies at your court?"

"Some are pleasant, but the truth is, I find they serve me best by what they have overheard. Some come to me, but with the others I just listen. I prefer to make my friends among the men. They are the allies the king and I might need one day. James is very outspoken, and offends without meaning to do so. Sometimes I can soften what he says, and soothe the ruffled feathers of his nobles."

"The king always said he meant to rule Scotland as it had not been ruled in many years," Cicely remarked.

"And he is, although several in his family have suffered for their past behaviors, or those of our near relations. He has instilled fear in his nobles by executing the Duke of Albany and his two sons, his own kinsmen. He has sent the Earl of Strathearn and the master of Atholl to England to stand hostage until his ransom is paid. He holds his nobles responsible for his long sojourn in England, and now he punishes them for it."

"But if he hadn't been so long in England, or had returned to Scotland as a lad, he probably would have been killed by his uncle, who was not loath to kill his elder brother, David," Cicely responded.

Joan Beaufort laughed. "I know. But James's logic is his own. And he has begun to restore the courts, make new laws that aid the common folk, punish those who would break those laws, and strengthen the coinage of the land. And by taking back royal lands from those who ill-used them, he helps to increase the treasury. Government cannot function without hard coin. Sometimes when you are doing good things you must also do unpleasant things as well. And it does not always rest easy on his conscience, I know. That is why it is so important that I have a son, Ce-ce. The Stewarts will not be safe until I give Scotland some heirs. Jamie's grandfather had a second wife, Euphemia Ross, and she gave him sons too. There are those who would supplant my husband with one of those young men, if they dared."

"I did not know," Cicely exclaimed.

"For now James is safe, for he is the male heir in the direct line of descent. We are young, and I am fertile," the queen said. "You must not worry, Ce-ce."

"Will there be a war with the lords in the north?" Cicely asked her friend.

"I think, and 'tis only my thoughts, that if by next summer the MacDonald, lord of the isles, and the other northern clans haven't come to Scone to pledge their fealty, that James may go north to impel them to do just that. He has not been to Inverness yet."

Cicely nodded. If she gave Kier a son by then he would have to lead his men, and she could lose a second husband. She sighed. Perhaps Scotland had not been such a good place for her to come. And yet she'd had no way to remain in England without a husband. Certainly one could have been found for her, but that Luciana was so jealous.

Jealous enough to have even attempted to murder Cicely's father. "I hope there is no war," Cicely said softly. "I am not of a mind to wed another husband. I was barely used to the first one, and now I have a second." She smiled wryly, and her companion smiled.

For the next few days the two friends sat in the hall for most of the day while the king and the laird hunted game birds and deer. Finally the king announced one morning that they would be departing for Edinburgh, and from there to Scone. "We have very much enjoyed your hospitality, Ce-ce," James Stewart said. "Make your farewells, my love," he told the queen.

"Why didn't you tell me you would be leaving today?" Cicely asked Joan Beaufort. "I must have Mab prepare something for you to eat along the road. You will probably be staying at a religious house tonight."

"James is like this," the queen explained softly. "He makes up his mind on the spur of the moment. He didn't tell me until we were abed last night. Oh, Ce-ce, please pray for me that this child is a son." The two young women hugged.

"My liege, you must allow Mab the time to prepare some food for your journey today," Cicely said. "The queen should not travel in her condition without sustenance. It will not take long. Please!"

"Very well," the king replied, "but I would go within the hour."

Cicely ran to the kitchens and explained to Mab their problem.

The old woman grinned. "Men!" she said with a cackle of laughter. "Well, we're in luck, my lady. I've a fat roasted capon in the larder that I did not serve last night. There is fresh bread, cheese, apples, and pears. Quick, Bessie and Flora! Let us get a basket prepared for our king and his bonny wife."

The two kitchen maids swiftly gathered together

the supplies, and wrapped and packed them carefully in a woven willow basket. They covered the basket with a fine linen cloth, handing it to Mab.

"I shall bid the king farewell myself," the old woman said. "Come, my lady. We do not want to keep Himself waiting. He's an impatient laddie, and does not easily tolerate foolishness or delay." Clutching the basket, Mab hobbled up the stone stairs, Cicely coming behind her. Crossing the floor, Mab curtsied, the basket pulling her slightly off balance.

James Stewart caught Glengorm's cook by the arm, aiding her to regain her equilibrium. "Now, Mistress Mab, have you come to bid me farewell? I'll not go without a kiss from you," he teased her gently.

Mab chortled. "Ye're a wicked laddie, King Jamie Stewart," she teased back, shaking a finger at him. "I've brought our good queen a basket to sustain her today."

"What?" the king cried. "Is there nothing for me?"

"Hee, hee!" Mab cackled. "If Queen Joan will share the basket with you I would be pleased. There's a chicken, some fruit, bread, and cheese."

"Thank you, Mab," the king responded, and, bending, he kissed her withered cheek. "Your lady has said you are the heart of Glengorm. I have seen over my visit here that it is truth. I am honored to have met you and eaten your fine cooking." Then, stepping back a pace, the king bowed a most courtly bow to the old woman.

Mab's eyes filled with tears. "God bless you, King Jamie Stewart," she said to him. "Our Scotland is the better for your coming home. And God and his Blessed Mother bless your good queen with many sons," Mab concluded, curtsying to the royal pair.

Joan Beaufort took Mab's hands in her own. "Thank you," she said. "Watch over my beloved friend, Mab." Then, releasing the hands in hers, the queen turned and left the hall, her husband and her hosts walking with her. Her padded cart was before the house. Kier helped the queen into it, then set the basket of food next to her.

Reaching out, Joan Beaufort caught the laird's sleeve. "Treat her well," she said quietly. "She will love you in time, I believe." And the queen smiled at him.

The laird's face was grave, but his voice was gentle when he replied, "How is it that one so young and fair understands so well?" Kier asked her.

The queen laughed. "You are not really too difficult to comprehend, my lord. You and Ce-ce are very alike in many ways. And remember, she and I grew up together. Be patient. I can see that you are beginning to love her."

Kier Douglas flushed. "I don't even like her," he said stubbornly.

The queen laughed again. "My lord, you are a poor liar. I will pray that both you and Ce-ce gain some sense where your marriage is concerned." She held out her hand to him and he dutifully kissed it.

Cicely had bidden the king farewell, remembering to thank him for returning her dower to her husband. Then she hurried to the cart where the queen was now settled. "I will miss you," she said. "It has been so good being with you again. I will write, I promise, Jo. And perhaps you will come into the borders again to visit us."

"Be good to your man, Ce-ce," the queen advised her. "Love him, and tell him so. Men need such reassurance more than we do. I never let a day go by that I do not tell Jamie that I care for him."

"We shall see, Jo," Cicely said candidly.

Then the royal party rode off from Glengorm, the queen waving from her cart.

The laird and his wife watched them go. Kier Douglas then told his wife that he was going hunting, for their larder needed more game if they were to get through the winter. He walked away, feeling her eyes upon his back as he went. Was it possible, truly possible, that she might love him one day? And was the queen right? Was he coming to love her? He shook his dark head. Love was a weakness. He had to remember that. The only time he had given his heart he had been cruelly rejected. The shock of it had sapped him of his strength, of his very will to live. He had been horrified by how he had felt for so many weeks afterwards.

Kier Douglas had thought he would never recover from the blow to his heart delivered by a small girl with honey gold hair. He could not believe that the bitch had almost destroyed him. And he had vowed never to allow his emotions to get away from him again. But now here was Cicely. Cicely, his wife, who had lain in his arms and praised his prowess in their bed. An English girl. His cousin's widow. He didn't like her. *He didn't!* She was outspoken, beautiful, brave. All the things she shouldn't be. But he had to admit to himself that she was a perfect border wife, and he had a grudging respect for her. And her passions certainly matched his. What more did he want? He wanted her to love him, God help him! *He wanted her to love him!* And if she did, then perhaps he could allow himself to love her.

Chapter 17

$\mathcal{W}$hile he had come to her bed, Kier had not taken her since their wedding night. She had been puzzled at first, but then she realized he was considering all that had happened between them. They had coupled twice, and both times their passions had exploded wildly. Cicely began to wonder if it would always be that way between them. Nay. It was their pent-up abstinence that had brought about such near violence between them. Surely that was it.

Cicely requested a bath that first evening they were finally without guests. She was soaking peacefully when her husband entered the small bedchamber. Both Cicely and Orva looked startled, for he had not bothered to knock.

"Good night, Orva," the laird said in a tone that brooked no refusal.

Orva curtsied, casting a quick glance at her mistress. "Good night, my lord, my lady," she said, reluctantly departing when Cicely said nothing. The chamber door closed.

"You bathe muchly," Kier remarked as he began pulling his clothes off.

"You should bathe more," Cicely replied. "I don't

know why it is men avoid bathing except in the summer, when they swim in the loch and count it a bath."

"I don't want to smell like some damned flower," he said.

"But you like it when I do," Cicely noted mischievously.

"Aye." He grinned. "I do."

"You stink of horses and sweat," she told him.

"If you can swear to me honestly that you got my cousin to bathe more, then I will bathe more, too," he promised her.

Cicely laughed a wicked laugh. "Of course he learned to bathe more. He wanted to please me. Come!" She held out her hand to him over the top of the tub. "You are naked now, and I will bathe you myself. When you learn how to do it properly I will make you a soap that is scented with sandlewood and clove, a more manly fragrance. The quicker you learn how to wash yourself, the less you will smell like a stable."

He had never bathed with a woman. It was an intriguing invitation. Of course, he could haul her from her tub and have his way with her without bathing. He was the laird of Glengorm, her husband, and he was to be obeyed. But he realized she was making an attempt to reach out to him, to offer more than just public respect and private lust. He remembered how it had been between his stepmother and father. They actually seemed to enjoy each other's company, smiled secret smiles at each other, laughed at things he did not consider amusing but they did. They were more than content. They were happy in each other's company.

He climbed the small steps up to the edge of the tub, then lowered himself into the warm water, facing her. It occurred to him that she was fully naked herself, and he began to consider the many possibilities of bathing that had little to do with cleanliness. Kier Douglas began to smile. When Cicely stepped before him, a washrag in her hand, the tips of her breasts touched his chest, and his cock began to stir.

Cicely began to wash his face. The cloth scrubbed his forehead, his cheeks, and his chin. It followed the outline of his nose, and then his mouth. The smell of the soap was actually very pleasant and delicate.

"Your face is even handsomer when it is clean, despite its roughness," she noted, her fingers running over the dark stubble. She next moved to wash his neck. "When I was a child, before I was old enough to bathe myself, Orva did it for me," Cicely told him. "If she saw a neck as dirty as yours is, my lord, she would have asked you if you were growing onions in it." Cicely washed the dirt from his neck, and then rinsed the soap away.

She next tackled his shoulders, chest, and back, her cloth working up a lather, then rinsing it away. Then she moved on to his long arms and his hands. "Your nails need paring," she said. "I shall do it when we remove ourselves from the tub, my lord." She moved with care so as not to splash water from the tub onto the floor. The addition of another person to the tub had brought the water dangerously high, to the tub's edge. When she had finished his arms she handed him the cloth. "You will have to do the rest now," she told him, easing herself up from the water onto the tub's ledge, and swinging her legs about, her feet reaching for the stairs. Finding them, she stood and stepped down.

"But I don't know how," he said in a futile attempt to sound helpless. He was staring at her now, and his cock had hardened as his eyes swept over her nakedness.

"Don't be silly," she scolded him. "Of course you know how to wash your legs, feet, and other parts. If I tried to help you we would have water all over the chamber." Then she quickly picked up her warm towel and began to dry herself, aware of his eyes on her nudity. He had never really seen her quite so fully bared. Cicely reached out for her chemise and made to draw it on.

"*Don't!*" he told her sharply.

"Oh. Very well, my lord, but if you do not mind I will

await you in bed. The night air is chill, and the heat of the fire is somewhat blocked by the tub," Cicely said, climbing into her bed and drawing the covers up.

"Will you not dry me?" he teased, and climbed from the tub down the steps to the floor. His aroused state was so obvious she blushed.

"Dry yourself," she told him. "You are a big lad."

"You noticed." He chuckled, rubbing the water briskly from his body.

Cicely giggled. She couldn't help it. "Aye, I've noticed," she admitted, thinking that something was different tonight between them. What was it? And why? Was there some kind of relief in the fact that their marriage was now a fact, or that their guests were gone, and they were alone in the house but for the staff and wee Johanna? She felt the bed shift as he climbed in, sitting next to her, his back against the pillows.

"Well, madam," he said softly, "here we are once again. Are you satisfied now that I smell like a field of posies?" He took her hand in his.

"I must wash your hair on the morrow to be content with you," Cicely said to him. The big hand wrapped about her fingers was warm.

"I intend that you be content long before the morrow," he replied, bringing her hand to his lips to kiss it. Then he nibbled lightly upon her knuckles for a brief moment.

She was silent, for if the truth be known, she was not certain what to say to him.

"What, madam, I have finally stilled that sharp tongue of yours? How is this possible?" Kier inquired of her.

"There is something different between us suddenly," Cicely said candidly. "Do you not feel it, my lord?"

He did feel it, but he wasn't certain whether he should admit to it until he knew exactly what it was. Now he was silent.

She saw the play of emotions across his face, for Cicely had turned her head to look at him. He was uncertain what to do or say, and it surprised her. Then she remembered that Jo had said men needed more assurance than women did when it came to matters of the heart. The words came out before she could think further. "Perhaps now that you are clean, my lord, I am coming to like you better," she told him.

"Are you?" he answered her, looking wary.

"Aye!" Cicely told him. "I do believe that I like you, *husband*."

She liked him! But wait. Why this sudden change of heart? What mischief was the woman up to? From the moment that they had been matched they had disliked each other intensely. When they came together in conjugal union it was rough and wild. Nay, it was he who had been cruel, not Cicely. Still, he was suspicious. "What has caused this change of heart, madam?" he demanded of her in a hard voice. Then he pulled her into his arms so he might look down into her face when she spoke to see if she lied.

Cicely almost quailed at his tone, but instead she decided she would face him with the truth. Truth was a powerful weapon. Looking up into his handsome face, she said, "I believe that you like me despite what you have said in the past. And I told you I didn't like you only because you spoke the words to me first. They were hurtful, Kier. I had to wonder if your anger was only because you couldn't have Glengorm without me. So when you expressed your dislike of me I responded in kind."

He nodded. "But you like me now," he said.

"I never disliked you, my lord. First I came to love Glengorm. And I loved Ian in my own way. And then he was gone, but Johanna was born to bind me even closer to Glengorm. I was frightened that I would have to hold these lands for my daughter. I am not, for all my fine upbringing, a weakling, but I never expected to find myself in a border house alone with my child. Frang will tell you that I asked him to teach me the art of defending this house, and he did.

"But then Sir William sent you to me as soon as he learned of Ian's death. I cannot tell you the relief I felt when you took charge. I should have done whatever I had to do to keep Glengorm and its folk safe, but I was glad for your coming. And when I went into labor with Johanna, you were there in Ian's place helping me. You were kind, and I thought then that perhaps you were not so terrible. But why did you tell me you did not like me, Kier? What had I done that made you say those words? Though I do not believe for a moment that you ever meant them, even as I did not mean them."

She had indeed surprised him. Finally he said, "I have not had good fortune where women are concerned."

"There are no tales about you, as there were about 'the wenching Douglas,' " Cicely said thoughtfully. "And you are past thirty, but have had no wife. And certainly not because you are unable to please a woman."

"I loved a lass once, but her father would not have me because of the situation of my birth," Kier admitted to Cicely. "Love weakens a man. I would not have believed it until it happened to me. I vowed never to be weakened by a woman again, madam."

Cicely reached up and caressed his jaw. "You don't have to love me, Kier," she told him. "But could you at least admit to liking me?"

God's balls! There she lay, naked in his lap, her soft hand upon his face, speaking sweetly to him. Not love her? Of course he loved her, even if he could admit it only to himself. If she knew how he felt now she would have power over him, and no woman would ever have that power again. "I don't dislike you, lass," he told her.

"That will do for now," Cicely replied with a small smile.

"Madam, I will never love you!" he exclaimed suddenly, sensing he was losing the argument between them over this.

"I am content that you can like me," Cicely said. "Our children should come not just from our lustful pleasures, but from our mutual affections." He said he would never love her, and suddenly Cicely knew that she wanted him to love her, for she was falling in love with him. But he would not know. He could not know! It would only give him an advantage over her. Cicely wanted to cry, but she didn't. Her gaze never wavered.

She was confusing him. Those beautiful blue-green eyes looked up at him. They were incredible eyes, and he felt briefly weakened by them. "Enough, madam," he said, and he pulled her up so he might kiss her. Their lips met, and Cicely sighed. For some reason that soft little sound made him feel as if he were in complete control of their destiny. Her mouth was sweet beneath his, and he devoured her with his lips.

If he truly liked her, Cicely thought muzzily, the love would come eventually. She wrapped her arms about Kier and kissed him back kiss for kiss until her lips were swollen and burning. When his hand moved to cup her breast she arched into him as his thumb stroked and encircled her nipple. Then her hands began a daring exploration of his body as he explored hers.

Her fingers lightly caressed his shoulders, feeling the hard muscles beneath the skin. She reached up to catch his head between her two hands, tangling her fingers into his thick raven black hair. Cicely shifted her body so that it pressed against the length of his, and he groaned. Breast to chest. Belly to belly. She felt the thick ridge of his manhood against her thigh. The hard flesh against her soft flesh was warm, and she could have sworn it throbbed.

Kier moved her beneath him, and his dark head bent to her breasts. He kissed them and suckled hungrily upon each breast, his lips, his teeth, his tongue causing tremors to overtake her. The dark head followed a path of worship down her torso, kissing, licking. He positioned himself between her thighs, and then to her surprise he pulled her up so that her legs rested on his shoulders, her ankles fastening themselves about his neck. Burying his face in her mons, he kissed her there.

Then, using his thumbs, he opened her to his vision, staring at the moist pink flesh already pearling with its cream, the tiny jewel in its center luring him forward. His tongue began to stroke the nubbin of sensitive flesh, flicking lightly over it, slowly, slowly, then faster and faster until Cicely was writhing beneath his mouth.

"Kier! Kier!" she cried his name, then shuddered as she experienced a strong burst of tingling delight that exploded like a shower of heat over her.

He groaned again, his tongue licking and licking and licking her juices until she begged for mercy. He raised his head and asked her in a rough voice, "What do you want, madam? Tell me what you want, and you shall have it!" His manhood was hard with his need for her, but he wanted, he needed to hear her ask, because if she asked then she was not just coupling with him out of a sense of duty. He wanted more than duty.

"I want you inside of me, my lord," she cried out to him. "I need you inside of me!" Her legs fell away from him as she spread herself wide. "Take me now! *Please!*"

"You like me," he said softly, taunting her as his fingers stroked the wet flesh.

"You like me," she countered, reaching out to caress his length with her fingers, which closed about him, squeezing gently before releasing him. Again her eyes met his in a melting gaze. "And, aye, I like you, Kier Douglas!"

He said nothing; instead he swung himself over her and, with a sure hand, guided himself to the gates of paradise. She cried out as he thrust himself into her. He stopped, enjoying the delicious sensation of her silken wet heat as the walls of her sheath closed tightly around him. Then he began to move with strong, rhythmic strokes of his cock as it flashed back and forth, back and forth until Cicely was almost weeping with her delight.

He was so fierce, and yet he was gentle as well tonight. Cicely clung to him, loving the sensation of their bodies linked in passionate union. Her fingers dug into his shoulders. She lifted her head to nip at his earlobe, and he laughed aloud, calling her his wee vixen. The sensations were building and building now. She wrapped her legs about his torso so he might delve deeper, and he did. "Kier!" she cried his name again.

And then the pleasure began to mount. His face above her was set in rapt concentration as he worked to bring them to a fiery completion. Cicely closed her eyes and let herself be swept away on a tidal flow of lustful wonderment. She felt as if she were flying higher, higher, higher yet. Then the tremors began racking her body as they shook the core of her very being. It was too sweet! Too sweet! And then she felt him stiffen within her, his juices bursting forth to fill her full with his seed.

"*Cicely!*" he cried out her name, but she barely heard it, for she was lost in a dazzle of sweetness that reached up to claim them both, enfolding them in warmth and darkness as they collapsed in each other's arms. Exhausted from their labors, husband and wife fell asleep without speaking.

Kier awoke first as the night ended and the dawn was breaking. He felt relaxed, and certainly less irritable than he had been in recent days. Cicely lay next to him, snoring softly. He smiled down at her and, unable to help himself, drew her into his arms, spooning himself around her. Her fragrance rose up to assail him with its subtle scent. He stroked her tangled hair. He could never have imagined a wife like Cicely Bowen, he thought, smiling to himself as one hand closed over a plump breast to fondle it gently.

"Ummm," Cicely murmured, feeling warm and safe. What a wonderful dream she was having. She pressed her buttocks against him.

Kier's manhood responded instantly. He was suddenly as randy as a stag in rut. Pushing her legs apart as she lay on her side, he carefully found his way into her sheath and, satisfied, lay quietly.

She was being filled by a large cock. What a wonderful dream! Cicely smiled to herself. It was buried up to its hilt. She wanted it to fuck her, and not lay silent. She pressed her hips back into his groin to encourage the cock within to dance for her. And as she slowly wakened it did just that, probing deep and hard. *"Oh!"* Cicely exclaimed as her eyes flew open. This was no dream! *"Oh! Oh! Oh, Kier!"* she cried out, but she was not angry. She had simply been taken by surprise. She fell into a rhythm with him. The big hand on her breast squeezed her soft flesh in perfect time with his cock. And once again they reached nirvana together, crying out as the pleasure reached up to claim them.

Afterwards he turned her about to face him and, taking her face in his hands, kissed her tenderly. "I like you too, madam," he told her softly, nuzzling her tangled hair.

Suddenly Cicely wanted to weep. The passion he had shared with her over the last few hours was so different from their earlier couplings. What had changed between them, other than that they had admitted that they actually liked each other? She wasn't certain, but Cicely decided that she wasn't about to question this turnabout of fortune.

"I may wake you like this every morning," Kier whispered in her ear, kissing it.

"I think I hope that you do," Cicely whispered back. "I quite liked it."

He turned and rose from their bed, going to the window to push open the shutters. "There was frost last night," he said, "and a cold mist is still hanging on the hills, though the sun is coming up now. I'll hunt again today, madam. The larder is but half-filled, and winter will be upon us soon enough."

"I'll go out with Orva and gather what plants I can then," she said. "Mab is teaching me some fine remedies, and winter does favor sickness," Cicely answered. "You are proving an excellent provider, my lord. You and the king brought in a goodly bevy of game birds, and a deer too."

"One of the men spotted a boar in the nearby wood," Kier answered her. "'Twill soon be time for slaughtering, smoking, and salting. I'd like to get that boar."

They chatted back and forth as they washed and dressed for the day before going down to the hall. And suddenly in the days that followed it seemed that they had always been together like they were now. Kier and his clansmen hunted game in the daytime, the new laird sharing the spoils with his companions. The great lords did not do this as a rule, granting hunting and fishing rights as rewards to their clanfolk, and then for only a brief, specified time. But the small border lords and their clanspeople depended upon one another for their very survival. If they took two deer in a day, one went to the village to be hung and butchered, then shared among all those on the hunt, as well as any widows.

They fished in the fast-flowing streams. Fishing rights were granted by the king, and all the waterways in Scotland were considered his. But the Stewart kings were wise enough to share with those who were loyal to them. And so the Douglases fished, and salted away their catch for the lean, cold months.

As the days grew colder and shorter, the livestock was brought in from the outlying fields and meadows. Unless a predator was on the loose, and as long as the snows held off, they would be driven out to near meadows in the morning, and driven back to their barns in the late-afternoon hours, before the sun set. The meadows across the loch were no longer used except in high summer. Kier wanted no more incidents such as had killed the previous laird of Glengorm.

November came. A few animals were slaughtered for food, the meat hung, some of it salted, some salted and smoked. The clanswomen and their children spent their days now bringing in firewood for the laird's house, and for their own cottages. There would be some turf, and some coal for the lord, but mostly it was wood that heated their dwellings. In the orchard every apple and pear had been gathered from the trees. The people of the village had been invited to glean what remained and had fallen to the ground. With Orva's and Mab's aid, Cicely had found, dug, and cut every medicinal plant that she could identify. Then she set about drying the roots and leaves, making salves, ointments, and pills so she could care for the sick come winter, as was her duty.

December came, and Johanna was now nine months old. She was crawling, had four little teeth, and babbled a stream of baby nonsense constantly. Her eyes lit up with delight every time she saw Kier. Her first word, spoken on St. Thomas's Eve, was *Da,* which she squealed at the top of her baby voice when Kier entered the hall. He grinned and picked the baby up, telling her what a beautiful little lass she was.

"Just like your mam," Kier said, looking at Cicely, and her heart jumped.

"Da! Da! Da!" Johanna said, patting his face, and giggling with delight when he tickled her, chuckling. "Da! Da! Da! Da!" she singsonged happily.

The laird grinned again, and kissed the soft cheek. "Aye, Johanna, I'm your da, and happy to be," he told her. "And your mam and I are working hard to see that you have a baby brother in the near future."

"Da!" Johanna replied, drooling all over his shirt.

"Orva, take her," Cicely called, "before the little minx soaks him." She was pleased that Kier so obviously loved her daughter. As to his remark about a brother or sister, she might have a happy Twelfth Night surprise for him. It would be a surprise to her if she were not with child now. Kier came to her bed almost every night now. She wondered how ardent he would be once she had given him a son.

They had moved into the new bedchamber behind the hall. In the spring a new chamber would be build above it, and the upstairs hall extended to lead to it. But for now they were content to have removed from Cicely's small bedchamber. There was more room for the tub when it was needed. The hearth was larger, and they had found fabric that matched the bed hangings stored in the attics that Orva and Cicely sewed into draperies for the window. The new bedchamber was therefore warmer.

They had a Yule log in the hall hearth, and a feast on Christ's Mass. The clanfolk had come into the hall that day to celebrate with them. Cicely had distributed gifts to all. There had been packets of fabric, threads, and small lengths of lace for the women. The men had received quivers of new arrows and leather for new boots. The children had not been forgotten. The boys in the village had each been given a small wooden sword. They spent much of their time that day in mock battles with one another. The girls had been gifted with new chemises and bright ribbons.

Cicely had meant to keep her news from him until Twelfth Night. But when Mary Douglas asked loudly what the lady of Glengorm was gifting her lord with this day, Cicely had looked at her husband, saying, "I fear he will have to wait until late June for his gift, Mary." And then she laughed at the look upon Kier's face as the hall erupted in cheers.

"You're with bairn?" he said, almost disbelieving, though, considering their almost nightly bedsport, he didn't know why he was surprised. He was virile, and she had proven fertile when she had given Ian wee Johanna.

"I will give you a child after Midsummer Day," Cicely told him, smiling. "Does that please you, my lord of Glengorm?"

He pulled her into his arms, kissing her heartily, and their clanfolk cheered even louder. "A son!" he said to them. "I shall have a son!"

"A baby," Cicely corrected him. "Only God knows if we are to be blessed with a son, my lord."

"It will be a lad," Kier told her firmly. "God will surely not deny the Douglases." Then, bending down, he whispered to her, "Thank you, madam."

"It seems I can deny you little these days," Cicely teased him, silently reminding him of the passion they shared daily. "Remember that I like you, my lord."

And Kier Douglas laughed. "Nay, madam, you *love* me!" he told her boldly.

"Aye," she surprised them both by saying, "I do love you, though why, I do not know. You are arrogant and difficult, yet you have charm, Kier Douglas. But you love me as well, my lord, though you will not say it."

He flushed. "I *like* you," he told her. She would not weaken him. No woman would ever weaken him again. And to admit to loving a woman was a dangerous weakness no man could afford.

Cicely laughed up into his eyes, but her heart hurt. She had admitted her love for him, but he could not admit his for her. *But you will one day,* she thought silently.

January came. The snows piled up on the hillsides and around the house. The livestock spent some of the time in outdoor pens, but mostly remained safe in the barns. Kier Douglas was not of a mind to lose any of his animals. On St. Agnes' Eve all the young women of the house looked deep into a small mirror belonging to their mistress, and then walked backwards to their pallets, for legend said if they did that they would dream of their true love that night.

February came and the ewes began lactating almost immediately in preparation for the birth of their lambs. Cicely distributed a goodly supply of fine beeswax candles on the second day of the month to Father Ambrose, walking down to the village church with Orva, each woman carrying a basket containing the tapers and larger lights. Cicely now had a belly, and Ambrose blessed her belly, which brought tears to her eyes.

"He wants a son so desperately," Cicely told the priest. "I hope I do not disappoint him. Ian, God assoil him, did not care, but Kier does care."

"He wants a son for Glengorm," Ambrose responded. "It is a natural desire with all men, no matter their status.

A son carries on your name and gives you immortality of a kind. You will not repeat that, however, for it does not hold with Church doctrine," the priest said with a small smile upon his lips.

Cicely returned his smile. "I will not repeat it, Ambrose. You are very learned for a cleric in a border village."

"I had the good fortune to study in France for a time. 'Twas where I took my holy orders, Cicely," the priest told her. "Then I came home shriven and shorn, to my sire's outrage." He chuckled. "I disappointed him greatly, for in my youth I showed a predilection for wenching even as he did. Still, he loved me well, built me this wee church, and saw that I had a living. I should not want to be anyplace but Glengorm."

"Neither do I now, though if you had asked me three years ago I should have made mock of anyone who would have told me I would come to love a little Scots border village, and be content to be the lady of the manor," Cicely said.

"You feel well?" he asked her gently.

"Aye, I do," she answered him.

"And you have truly come to love him, as you declared on Christ's Mass?"

Cicely nodded. " 'Tis odd, but aye, I do, and I know he loves me, though he will not admit to it."

Ambrose Douglas smiled and nodded. "He's a stubborn man, my daughter."

Cicely laughed aloud. "Aye, he is stubborn," she agreed.

March came, and it seemed the spring would come earlier than later this year. The snows began to fade from the hillsides. The puddles were no longer freezing over at night, and snowdrops bloomed by the kitchen door. Cicely and Orva removed the dressing of hay they had put on the little herb garden last October. They loosened the soil gently, and left it to the open air. And after several days the plants began to show signs of life again, small nubs of green beginning to peek through woody stems and through the soil itself at the base of the plants. The winds blew daily, but they were not so sharp as they had been in January. At the end of the month they celebrated little Johanna Douglas's first year of life. She had been born a healthy infant, and she remained one. She now tottered about the hall on surer legs, and spoke several words, *Da* being her favorite, and when she addressed Cicely, Johanna would say, "Ma." Orva was "O" and Mab had been christened Abby. The old cook's face lit up each time Johanna addressed her.

April arrived. Two of the house cats dropped litters of kittens in the dim recesses of the cattle barn. One of the deerhounds birthed three puppies—all male, to Kier's delight, for when the pups were grown he would have a strong pack of dogs to hunt with him. By midmonth the snows were entirely gone. The hillsides were green again, with bursts of color here and there indicating groups of spring flowers. The sheep were once more in their near meadow, the lambs born in February now gamboling through the grass as the shepherds and their dogs watched over the flocks.

It was May now. The few fields that could be tilled had been, and were planted with barley, oats, and hay. The cattle and sheep had been driven to their summer pastures. And word came that the king was considering an expedition into the north, for the MacDonald and the Highland chieftains had still not rendered the king their fealty. Kier trained his men daily but for Sunday. When the time came Glengorm would be ready to march north with James. Whether their laird came with them would depend upon the lady. If she birthed a son he would be free to go. If not he would have to remain while his clansmen rode with Sir William. The fields were green and high as the month ended.

Cicely could never, ever recall being as uncomfortable as she was now. Her belly was enormous, and she could scarce waddle about as June began. Her temper was volatile at best. But each day she walked from the house down the hill into the village, and strolled along the loch. The waters seemed to soothe her. One day, however, as Cicely returned from the little shale beach, she saw a large sow rooting along the edge of the lane. She stopped and stared at the great creature. Then she burst into fulsome tears. Her sobs brought several of the women from their cottages to gather about Cicely protectively.

"My lady!" Mary Douglas exclaimed. "Are you in pain? Should we call for Agnes to come?"

Cicely shook her head as she continued weeping.

"What is the matter?" Marion Douglas asked her sister-in-law.

"Perhaps the demon inside of the witch is hurting her." Bethia cackled.

"Be silent!" Mary Douglas thundered in her deep voice. "'Tis you who are the witch in this village. Your mother-in-law is dead this winter past, and your man run off as soon as the snows were gone. You should go back from whence you came, wherever it was. We never have known where Callum Douglas found you."

"Wouldn't you be surprised if you knew." Bethia chortled. "Perhaps one day you will, Mary Douglas, and 'twill be to your disadvantage, I promise you."

Mary Douglas gave the woman a hard look, but then she turned back to Cicely. "My lady, what has made you weep so? Please tell us, so we may help you."

Still sobbing, Cicely pointed to the grunting sow.

The women looked at the pig, confused, and then Mary Douglas began to chuckle. And when she did all the other women who had borne young understood, and began to giggle too. Soon they were all howling with laughter, and Cicely, her tears vanished, was laughing too at the absurdity of the situation. The clanswoman put an arm about her lady.

"The bairn is near to being born, my lady," she said in a comforting voice. "And we have all felt as you do at some point or another in the months before," Mary Douglas said with a kindly smile.

"He kicks all the time," Cicely said wearily, yet feeling better for her laughter.

"*He,* is it now?" Mary said with a grin.

"Did I say *he*?" Cicely looked confused for a brief moment.

"Aye, you did," Mary replied.

Cicely laughed weakly. "That is the first time I have referred to this child as *he,*" she told Mary Douglas. "Kier insists that it is a lad, and certainly no lass of good breeding would kick so hard and so often. Johanna never kicked me like this." Then a panicked look came into her eyes. "Oh, Mary! What if I am like the poor queen, and produce only lasses? She has had three now, God help her. Glengorm needs an heir every bit as much as Scotland does."

Mary Douglas tucked her hand into Cicely's arm and began walking her back to the house as the other women returned to their own cottages. "If our Lord means for it to be a lad, it will be a lad," she said. "You will give Glengorm an heir. If not this time, my sweet lady, then next. And so will the queen give Scotland a son. She comes from a family of more lads than lasses, I have heard."

"She does! She does!" Cicely agreed. "But my poor mam died when I was born, and so we will never know if she would have given my father any sons. My stepmother, however, birthed three strong boys."

"You are not to fret," Mary said. "Not with the birthing being so close. Midsummer is only a few days away, and there will be a full moon too this year. Is everything in readiness for the birth?"

"Aye," Cicely replied. "And, Mary, you will come with Agnes, won't you?" They had now reached the house.

"If you want me, my lady, I will be by your side," the clanswoman promised.

And the morning of Midsummer's eve, Mary Douglas was awakened as the sky was growing light by a pounding on her cottage door. Her husband, Duncan, grunted and turned over in their bed, but Mary suspected she was being summoned. Getting up, she went to the door, peeping out the window near it, and saw Gabhan Douglas. Mary opened the door. "Am I needed at the house?" she asked him.

"Aye, and hurry!" he said.

"Have you wakened Agnes?"

"Went to her first," Gabhan replied, and, turning ran off.

"What is it?" Duncan asked sleepily from the bed.

"The lady is having her child," Mary said as she pulled on her skirt and blouse, slipping her feet into her boots and drawing her plaid shawl about her. "I'm needed." Then she hurried out the door and up the hill, Agnes Douglas, the village midwife, coming to her side as she walked.

"She births easily, and this should be no different from when the wee lady Johanna was born," Agnes remarked as they walked quickly along.

Mary crossed herself. "I pray you are right, Agnes."

Reaching the house, they were greeted by Orva. "She's in the new bedchamber," Orva said. "She's been having pains since just after midnight."

"Where's the laird?" Mary asked.

"By her side, although I think if it were me I should not like my man there," Orva noted tartly.

"Some do, some don't," Agnes said sanguinely.

The three women entered the large bedchamber. Neither Agnes nor Mary had seen it since it had been built.

"Thank God you are here!" Kier Douglas said nervously.

"I'm having a baby, Kier, not dying," Cicely said rather sharply.

"Go down into the village, my lord, to the Mass. Ambrose will want to know. Then the two of you return and break your fast. You'll be here for the bairn's birth, I promise you," Agnes told him. "But it cannot hurt to pray that the lady's labor is quick, and a man's nerves are always better for a good meal," the midwife said, with a reassuring smile at the laird and a pat on his arm.

"Go!" Cicely told him.

Kier Douglas left quickly. When she had birthed Johanna he hadn't felt so nervous. What the hell was the matter with him? *You love her now,* the little voice in his head said. *You love her.* "Aye, I do," the laird muttered to himself. *May God have mercy on me, I love her, and I can feel my strength draining away even now because of my weakness,* he thought. "God's balls!" he swore softly to himself as, taking the midwife's advice, he left the house, heading for the church and his cousin Ambrose.

In the bedchamber Cicely let herself be examined by Agnes, who nodded and said, "You are just where you should be, my lady. A few more hours and you'll have the bairn in your arms, I promise. Do you want to walk now?"

"Aye," Cicely said. "And I'll use the birthing chair we found in the attics. I'll not bloody the bed with my bairn, nor birth it on the high board as I did Johanna." She looked to Orva, and beckoned her to her side. "Stay with Johanna today, and tell her that if she is very good she will have a baby brother by nightfall."

Orva nodded, her lips pressed together. "Forgive me, my lady, for being such a coward," she said, low. "I cannot bear to see you in pain. I was with your mother when you were born. You went from your mother's womb into my arms," Orva said, as she recalled how Cicely's beautiful young mother had not even had the opportunity to hold her child, but had bled to death before their eyes. From that moment on Orva had not been able to watch any woman give birth.

"I understand," Cicely said softly, "but I am not my mam. However, I need you to be with Johanna, dear one."

Orva nodded again and then, kissing Cicely's hand, hurried from the chamber.

"Why?" Mary Douglas asked.

Cicely explained.

The clanswoman nodded her head, understanding. "Poor woman," she said.

Through the beautiful summer's day Cicely labored to bring her child into the world. Kier returned with Father Ambrose. When the two men had broken their fast they asked permission to come into the chamber. The priest prayed with the women, but Kier held his wife's hand, and, his courage returned now, he encouraged her in her travail. Finally, in late afternoon, the sun still high in the heavens, Cicely pushed the baby forth from her womb with a mighty shriek of more effort than pain as she squatted on the birthing chair, her hands gripping its arms.

Agnes caught the child easily, handing it up to Mary Douglas so she might attend to her mistress and the afterbirth to follow. The child was howling at the top of its lungs. One look and Mary Douglas grinned broadly. Holding the naked, squalling infant in her two big hands, she showed it to his father. One look and Kier shouted with triumph.

"A lad, Cicely! You have given me a fine, big lad!" he told her, and he bent to kiss her mouth.

"Let me see him! Let me see him!" Cicely cried, holding out her hands. They put the bloody, crying baby in her arms, and she looked down at him. "Oh, my," she said softly. "He does take after his da, doesn't he?" But her eyes were not on the baby's face. Then she looked at Kier. "What would you call him, my lord?" she asked.

"Ian Robert," Kier answered her without any hesitation. "Ian for my late cousin, and Robert for your father."

Cicely smiled warmly at him. "It pleases me very well, my lord," she told him.

The baby ceased his howling and, opening his eyes, looked at his parents hovering over him. His eyes were light blue.

"Take him back now," Cicely said, handing her son

to Mary Douglas so she might clean the baby up and swaddle him in warm cloth.

"I'll fetch Johanna," Kier said.

Cicely nodded.

When he quickly returned carrying her daughter, Orva behind him, Kier took Johanna to the cradle where her baby brother now lay. "Look, sweeting, your mam has given us a wee lad for Glengorm. 'Tis your brother."

Johanna looked down at the infant, her thumb in her mouth as she studied him. "Nay," she finally said. "Jana is Mam's bairn."

"Indeed you are, my little love," Cicely assured her. "But now you have a brother, and he will be Mam's bairn too."

"Nay," Johanna replied. "Don't want!"

"Oh, dear," Orva said nervously. "She is jealous, my lady."

"She will get past it," Mary Douglas told them sensibly. "The first bairn is always jealous of the next one to come. After a time she will see she still has your love, my lady, and in another year the lad will be old enough for her to play with, and everything will change. Do not fret yourselves over it."

Orva removed the little girl from the bedchamber, promising to take her to see the Midsummer fires that evening and give her a sugar cake. Satisfied, Johanna kissed her mother and stepfather good night. Agnes and Mary had seen to the afterbirth, which would be taken out to be planted beneath a large oak tree. Cicely was bathed and, in a clean chemise, settled in the bed. The two women bade the laird and his wife good night.

Kier came and lay on the bed next to Cicely, taking her hand in his. He kissed it. "Thank you for the lad," he said to her.

"Do you love me?" she asked him wickedly.

"Aye," he answered, surprising her, for she had not thought to gain her victory over him this easily. "I love you, wife."

"If I had birthed a daughter would you still love me?" she pressed him.

"Aye." He sighed. "I would love you no matter, Cicely, and my love for you weakens me, I fear."

"Nay, Kier," Cicely said wisely. "Love does not weaken a person. Love makes you stronger. The love we have for each other will but strengthen us, my lord. Wait and see. We are one now, and nothing—no one—can stand against us."

And as she spoke the words he realized that she spoke the truth, and he was amazed. All of his adult life he had believed that loving a woman would make him weak. But perhaps it had been loving the wrong woman. Cicely was obviously the right woman. She stood proudly by his side, and was loyal to him. He sensed she would always stand by him and give him that same fealty. Leaning over her, he touched her lips with his, kissing her deeply. "I love you," he told her when he broke off the kiss. "I will always love you, Cicely, my fair wife."

"I know," she responded to his declaration, maddeningly certain. "And I will always love you. We must send to the queen with our news tomorrow."

"Aye," Kier agreed, and then he recalled the king's command to him. He was to remain at Glengorm until his wife had birthed a son. But once she had given him an heir he would be liable to heed the king's call to arms whenever it was time. Part of him was excited that he could answer that call now. But another part of him prayed that the Highland chiefs would yield without further ado, so he might remain at Glengorm with his wonderful wife and their children.

Chapter 18

$\mathscr{A}$ full year passed and Kier's wish was almost granted. It wasn't until the following summer that James Stewart planned his trip north into the Highlands. He had been king of Scotland for over four years. He had instilled just the proper amount of fear in his lords and earls with his swift and impartial justice. They knew now that this king would not be ruled by them, but rather would rule them. And while the Highlands remained relatively peaceful, the lord of the isles and his allies had had more than enough time to come to terms with James Stewart. The rest of Scotland was at peace, and beginning to show signs of true prosperity.

So the king sent his emissaries out to Alexander MacDonald, the lord of the isles, and to all the clan chieftains in the north, many of whom had not yet sworn loyalty to the Stewart king, inviting them to meet with him at Inverness in mid-July. To his irritation James Stewart learned that the MacDonald, upon receiving the king's messenger, had sent out his own messengers ordering the clans to obey and join him at Inverness.

"This lord is overproud," he complained to the Earl of Atholl.

"He is dangerous, which is worse," the earl replied.

There were certain lords among the borderers that

James Stewart wished to accompany him. He sent to Sir William, and Sir William sent to his son at Glengorm to meet him with his borderers at a designated spot. Kier had been expecting to be called eventually, but Cicely was not pleased.

"The Highlands have nothing to do with us," she said to her husband.

"The king is my liege lord, and he has requested a show of my fealty," Kier told his wife. "You are no cotter's daughter, unfamiliar with this duty. I have been called. I must and I will answer unhesitatingly."

"Oh, I know," Cicely grumbled, "but I don't want anything to happen to you."

"A gathering of the clans at Inverness is not likely to be particularly dangerous, sweetheart," Kier assured his wife. "The king will come with a great show of force. The MacDonald will come with a great show of force. Then they will make peace. Alexander MacDonald is no fool, I am told. Having kept James Stewart waiting for four and a half years, he will finally bend his knee, and then the rest of the northern clan chieftains will fall into line and follow suit. Everyone's feelings will be soothed. We will eat and get drunk, and then go our separate ways when it is over. I'll be home quickly enough, but you shall have to see to the haying and probably begin with the harvest before I am back."

"I will," Cicely promised him with a kiss. She found her current situation very different from what she had been taught to expect of life. She was the daughter of an earl, and had been raised by a dowager queen. Yet here she was, the wife of a simple border lord, concerned with her own children, haying, harvesting, and the well-being of a village full of good folk. She didn't envy the mighty among whom she had once walked. She didn't envy the queen who had yet to give her husband a son. And she was happier than she had ever been in all of her life.

"Will you miss me?" he teased her lovingly. Cicely

had been right, he realized, when she had told him that loving each other would make them stronger. It had.

"Mayhap," she teased back as she brushed her long auburn hair in preparation for bed. He would be leaving on the morrow, and she was so used to his presence in her life now that she knew she would miss him dreadfully.

He took the brush from her hand and began to slick it down her tresses. "I am leaving Frang behind with a dozen men. The border has been quiet. England is at peace with us and busy with its own affairs. You should be safe." Setting the brush aside, he wrapped an arm about her waist while his other hand moved to fondle her breast.

Cicely leaned back against him with a small sigh. The passion between them had not died, nor even mellowed after their son's birth. It had grown deeper. "I'm safer with you by my side," she murmured. Then, pulling away from him, she slipped her chemise off and lay back upon their bed, holding out her arms to him with a smile.

Perfect, he thought. Her body was simply perfect, even after the birth of two children. He straddled her and, leaning forward, licked a nipple. Then he kissed it before gathering her into his arms and kissing her as their bodies melted into each other. He ran his tongue along her lips, and she met the touch with her own tongue, which teased at his, playing a game of hide-and-seek within the warmth of his mouth. And all the while his big hand worked its way all over her body, caressing the length of her back, her rounded buttocks.

Cicely loved the hard body against hers. She clung to him, fingers digging into his shoulders as he touched her. But then, as she had come into the habit of doing, she pushed him back and, leaning over him, began to lick his body. Her tongue encircled his nipples. She grazed them lightly with her teeth. Kier lay back, content to be pleasured by his wife. Cicely worked her way across his chest, his torso, his belly with her tongue and lips, kissing, stroking, blowing lightly on the moistened skin. "You are delicious," she told him, and then, reaching his manhood, she took him into her mouth and sucked upon him.

Kier groaned with delight. He had taught her to love him as he loved her several months after their marriage, when she had become more comfortable sharing her bed with him. To his surprise Cicely had taken easily to sucking his cock. She had shown no reluctance to licking the length of him, or playing with the ruby head of his manhood when she had pushed his foreskin back. Her teeth would graze over the sensitive flesh very lightly until he was actually shivering with his own excitement. Then she would open her lips and take him into her mouth, suckling strongly until he would beg her to stop. He far preferred releasing his juices into her tight sheath. "Enough, sweetheart!" he ground out in a rough voice.

Cicely released him, lying back so that he might pleasure her as she had just done for him. He had explained that it was better for them to both attain the same pinnacle of excitement before coupling, and if the truth were known, she loved having his wicked tongue stroking her love bud until it burst, and then licking it again until she was trembling with her excitement. Tonight he pushed his tongue into her and she sighed. He then pressed two fingers into the wet warmth, moving them back and forth until her juices flowed for him. Finally he mounted her, driving hard and deep while she met his every thrust, arching her body up to meet his. And then she could no longer control herself, for she wanted him so greatly. Her juices flowed copiously again, drenching his cock, while her sheath contracted and spasmed about him.

He was not satisfied. He would be without her for weeks, and he was not such a weakling or a fool that he would use one of the whores who would travel with the king's army. "I want your ass," he growled into her ear as he lay atop her. "Did Ian have it?"

"Nay," Cicely answered him nervously. Jo had said he might want her that way one day. But why now?

"Good! 'Tis one virginity I shall have of you, sweetheart. I want you to do as I tell you, and do it when I tell you," Kier said. "Roll over onto your belly." And when she had he pushed several pillows beneath her so that her bottom was elevated for him, and her knees were beneath her. Kier ran his hands over the smooth, plump flesh. Just looking at it tightened his cock more, and it hurt.

"Please," Cicely said softly, "be gentle, my lord."

He didn't answer her. Instead, wetting his first two fingers, he pushed them between the half-moons of her buttocks, inserting them carefully into her forbidden passage.

Cicely wasn't sure she was breathing.

"Don't stiffen your body," he said quietly. "Be easy. I won't hurt you." His fingers remained still. "I'm just trying to prepare you, sweetheart."

Cicely tried to relax.

"That's it," he murmured softly in her ear. He withdrew his fingers and, reaching beneath with them, he began to play with her love bud once more. It did not take long for her to react, squirming on his hand, her juices flowing again. He wet his cock with those slick juices, and then, spreading her open, he pressed against her rose hole, applying more and more gentle pressure until it gave way, allowing him entry into her forbidden passage. Slowly, carefully, he inserted himself until he was sheathed.

Beneath him Cicely whimpered. It felt as if she were being impaled, yet he was so gentle that, other than the momentary pinch of his entry, she felt no pain. But she felt the touch of his male pouch against her bottom.

God's balls! He couldn't ever remember being enclosed so tightly. He was near to exploding, but he restrained himself, because the sensation was so incredible he wanted to retain it for just a moment or two more.

He allowed himself to fuck her three slow and careful strokes, and she squealed a trio of little *Ohs!* Then, with no instruction being given, her passage seemed to clasp him even more tightly. "*Jesu!*" Kier gasped, involuntarily releasing his juices, which exploded in tight bursts until he was finally able to pull himself from her. "Madam," he was finally able to say, "you well and truly unmanned me." Then, turning her over, he kissed her with slow, hot kisses.

Cicely wasn't certain that what he had just done was something she wanted to share with him again. But Jo had said husbands sometimes wanted to use their wives in that manner. And he had been gentle, giving her no real pain. And he was going away to war on the morrow, so she had wanted him happy.

"I love you, wife," he told her, "and so I sense you were not comfortable with what we just did, were you?"

"Nay," Cicely answered, "but if it made you happy then I am content."

Kier kissed her on her forehead. "Go to sleep now, and before I leave you I will show you what really makes me happy, sweetheart." And several hours later he woke her and made tender, passionate love to her that left Cicely breathless, and they were both happy then.

She was up, dressed, and ready to see him off, however. They had gone to Mass together, and then broken their fast with Father Ambrose. And afterwards, with all the men a-horse before the house, almost the entire village gathered, the priest had blessed them, praying aloud for their well-being and a safe return home.

Cicely stood with Johanna by her side, holding Ian in her arms. "Conduct yourself with honor, my lord, and return home to us in one piece, if you please," she told him.

Orva lifted Johanna up so her stepfather might kiss the child. Then Cicely held Ian out to his father for a kiss and a blessing. They had only just celebrated the child's first year the week before. She gave her son to his wet nurse, Ella, and, standing on her tiptoes, raised her face up to him, smiling.

Kier bent, lifted her up, and kissed her mouth most thoroughly. "Be a good lass," he told her with a wicked grin. Then he set her back upon her feet.

"I will try, my lord husband," she promised him.

The laird of Glengorm raised his hand and, turning his stallion about, signaled his men forward. The lady and her Glengorm folk stood waving and watching until the men disappeared down the road that ran through the glen.

They met Sir William a day and a half later, and the Douglases then rode for Scone to meet up with the king. They were joined along the way by many of the other border lords with their troops, Lord Grey of Ben Duff among them, who came with a small party of his clansmen.

Arriving at Scone, they met up with the king and over a thousand clansmen from the west and the east who had answered the royal summons. Then they headed north to the Highland town of Inverness. Created a royal burgh by King William the Lion in the year 1214, the town sat on the banks of the River Ness just where it flowed into Beauly Firth, and from there into Moray Firth. Inverness, considered the capital of the Highlands, had been in existence as long as anyone could remember. It was said that those who came before the Scots, people known as Picts, had lived there. It was a busy market town with many shops, several churches, and even a Dominican friary that had been founded two hundred years prior by King Alexander III.

The townspeople were loyal to the king, and delighted that he had finally come north to visit them. They had worked from the moment he had returned to Scotland to repair for his habitation the one part of Inverness Castle that had not been destroyed by Malcolm III, Duncan's son, after the usurper, Macbeth, had resided there. They knew that eventually James Stewart would come to them, and they wanted a place worthy of him.

The king reached Inverness before the day appointed for the lord of the isles and his clan allies to arrive. He settled himself within the rebuilt Inverness Tower. The majority of those accompanying him set up a tent encampment around the tower house. He invited into the tower's great hall for a meal those earls and clan chiefs who had accompanied him north, and he made it a point to greet each man there, be he high or low, by name, shaking their hands and thanking them for their support.

"He's clever," Sir William said, low, to the laird of Glengorm. "But he is still making enemies. He's taken several more earldoms, and sent Strathearn down into England, along with others to stand as collateral for his ransom."

"The land has been lawless," Kier replied as softly. "He must be hard in order to gain their attention and obedience."

"One day someone will kill him," Sir William answered sanguinely. "I hope his English queen has managed to spawn a healthy son by then."

The next day the MacDonald arrived, setting up a huge encampment with the several thousand clansmen who had accompanied him. His great pavilion was set directly in the center of the camp. The MacDonald had brought with him his three sons, who were accompanied by their retainers. The elder, and his heir, was Ian MacDonald. His brothers were Celestine of Lochalsh and Hugh of Sleate. The four men possessed over four thousand men among them. And they had brought all of their forces with them.

Kier wondered if this great show of magnificence and men was meant to do honor to James Stewart, or to intimidate him. If it was the latter, the lord of the isles had wasted his time, for the king, while admiring, was not in the least cowed, even when all the clans, pipes playing, plaids blowing in the summer breeze, marched down from the hills to Inverness Tower. James stood atop the tower and listened as his kinsman the Earl of Atholl identified the colors worn by the clansmen below.

"The dark green-and-blue plaid with the narrow red and white stripes, that's the MacDonalds. The red with the broad and narrow green stripes is his son, Hugh of Sleate. The Camerons are the red with the broad green and narrow yellow stripes. The Campbells wear the dark blue and green with the narrow yellow stripe. The Mac-Leods of MacLeod wear the green with the red and yellow stripes, or the yellow and black with the red stripe. The MacArthurs are the green with the yellow stripe."

"Enough," the king said. "I'll not remember in any event. It's the men among them I'm interested in, not their garments. They have brought their women and bairns with them, I'm told. Good! Let them see my justice for themselves, so they may report it afterwards," James Stewart said with a grim smile. "Allow the Mac-Donald, his mother, the Countess of Ross, the clan chieftains, and their women into the hall. The rest are to remain outside. I am ready for them, Atholl, although I doubt they are ready for me."

The gray stone hall in which the king received the lord of the isles had no windows. At one end of the hall was a raised wooden dais with a gilded wooden canopy, beneath which the king sat upon a throne with carved arms and lion's-paw feet. He sat unmoving, his face showing no emotion whatsoever as his guests entered the hall.

Escorting his mother, the MacDonald led his chieftains and the other invited members of the Highland contingent into the hall. Alexander MacDonald stopped at the foot of the dais. He offered the king a slow, elegant bow. Next to him the old Countess of Ross curtsied. Her wobble was barely noticeable, and the king could tell her knees hurt her as she rose, but the smile on her face was genuine. He briefly felt regret at what was about to transpire.

"My lord," the MacDonald said, "I welcome ye to the

Highlands. May yer stay be a pleasant one, and may ye return often."

The king's reply was a terse one, and Alexander Mac-Donald, not to be shamed before his clansmen and allies, answered sharply. He was not used to being spoken to in such a manner. He was the king of the north, and resented this Stewart upstart who would attempt to pull him down from his high place.

But James Stewart was not the kind of Stewart he had been used to dealing with in days past. This king was a hard man. Looking first directly at the lord of the isles, and then at the others in the hall, he said, "I am told there are some among you who would have my life." Signaling his guard, who had been notified in advance of what they would do, he watched as Alexander MacRurie and Ian MacArthur were hauled forth from among the other clan chieftains and dragged before him. "You two spoke of my murder. I cannot trust you. Your deaths will provide an example to your companions."

Raising his hand, the king signaled his executioners, who stepped forward and swiftly beheaded MacRurie and MacArthur. Neither man had the chance to cry out. Their heads fell from their bodies, rolling a short distance. The women in the hall screamed and began to weep in their fright as blood gushed from the severed necks of the two clan chieftains.

"Seize them all!" the king roared angrily. "They shall be imprisoned in the dungeons prepared for their arrival." Rising from his throne, he stepped down from the dais, stepping over the river of blood, and offered his hand to the Countess of Ross. "You, madam, will be my guest," he said, "while your son and his friends contemplate their disobedience to me, to Scotland."

"Are you not Scotland?" the Countess of Ross replied, taking the hand offered.

James Stewart smiled grimly. "I am, madam," he agreed. "I am."

This was the tale Kier Douglas told Cicely when he

returned home in early August. "No one, or at least only a very few, knew what he intended," Kier said.

"What happened afterwards?" Cicely asked.

"The MacDonald's sister-in-law stepped forward and upbraided the king for his behavior. She asked if this was the king's justice."

"Did the king throw her in the dungeon too?" Cicely asked, fascinated.

"Nay. He called her a cattle thief and a whore, and ordered her from his hall," Kier told his wife. "But she had the last word and she left the king speechless. She told him, 'Better an honest whore, my liege, than a dishonorable king.'"

"The woman must be mad to have spoken to James Stewart like that," Cicely said. "And he let her go unscathed?"

"A priest stood near his side, his kinsman, I think. He murmured something to the king, and oddly the king refrained from taking any action against her. He said nothing more. The woman left the hall, followed by all the other women."

"What happened then?" Cicely asked.

"Well," Kier continued, "a couplet had been making its way about the encampments. 'To donjon tower let this rude troop be driven, For death they merit, by the cross of Heaven.' The Highlanders were on edge, as were the rest of us. The king, however, did not keep us waiting long. A week after his first meeting with the MacDonald and his allies, he invited all who had come to gather at Inverness to attend his parliament. He announced he would then render his judgment upon them all. The MacArthurs and the MacRuries had already left to take home their dead chieftains. The Highlanders were very fearful, for the couplet was said to have been written by the king himself." Kier chuckled.

Cicely was fascinated by his recitation. Kier had kept a very close account of what had happened in Inverness so he might share it with her.

"In an effort to demonstrate to the Highland chieftains that he was showing no favor to any in particular, the king had hanged that same week James Campbell, who had murdered Alexander MacDonald's cousin Ian MacDonald. His execution got those in the dungeons talking among themselves. But then, to their great relief, the king fined them and released them back to their clanspeople," Kier said.

"And the lord of the isles?" Cicely asked.

"A large fine to fatten James Stewart's treasury, and a lengthy lecture. The king said there could be but one king in Scotland, and that king was James Stewart, by the grace of God, and anointed with the holy oil of the Holy Mother Church. He told the MacDonald that he had to stop taking up arms for every offense, real or imagined. He threatened MacDonald that if he did not cease his rude ways, James would come north again, and stop them for good and all. If Alexander MacDonald would keep the peace in the north he would find favor with James Stewart. Then he instructed the lord of the isles to kneel and pledge his fealty. You could tell the MacDonald was angry at being held up to public censure, but he did indeed kneel, and pledged his fealty to the king. After that we were free to go home, and so our Glengorm men and I hurried south again."

"What an amazing time," Cicely said. "I wish I had been there to see it. My life hasn't been as interesting at all, my lord." Then she went on to tell her husband that the haying had been completed, and the harvest just begun. Summer was coming to an end, and they would need to prepare for the winter ahead.

But Alexander MacDonald had been embarrassed by what had transpired at Inverness. He had lost control of the situation, and on his own ground. He would need to make a public gesture so as not to appear weakened among his own. The king would certainly understand, and then the peace would hold for however long it would hold. Inverness would pay the price for their outspoken loyalty to James Stewart. The MacDonald gathered his clansmen and his allies. Marching upon Inverness, they burned it to the ground. Then, satisfied, Alexander Mac-Donald returned home to his island kingdom of Islay, and his army of ten thousand men dispersed.

However, James Stewart did not understand. A royal burgh had been burned to the ground, its inhabitants slaughtered, the town looted, the few survivors scattered, desperate to survive the coming winter. Autumn was already in the Highlands. The nights were cold, the days little better. But a party of Inverness's survivors trekked south to Scone to tell the king what had happened. Reaching him after several weeks, they begged for his justice, and James promised to give it to them.

The king sent to all of his liege men, the border lords among them. He told them what had happened at Inverness. It was too late now to go north to wreak his revenge upon the MacDonald. They would go closer to spring. Kier Douglas was ordered to be ready at a moment's notice, and to be prepared to travel hard. He was to bring as many men as he could muster. Alexander MacDonald would receive a lesson in royal justice he would never forget—if he survived the king's initial wrath.

Cicely was not pleased. "Can you Scots not learn to live peacefully among yourselves?" she demanded. "I should have married a man like my father: rich and unimportant. One who did not have to answer a call to arms."

"Now, sweetheart," he attempted to cajole her, but she waved her hand at him.

"Nay, Kier, I do not like this constant fighting. What if I were with child again?"

"Are you?" he asked eagerly.

"Nay," she admitted.

"We shall have to do something about that," he teased her with a mischievous smile. "Johanna and Ian need another brother or sister."

"Most men would want another son," she replied.

"Aye, I do. But the lasses have their value too, sweetheart. Their marriages unite Glengorm with other families, who become allies. Did you think I was satisfied just to be my father's son? Aye, Sir William loves me, and I bear his name, but I am still his bastard. My bairns, however, are legitimate. And Glengorm is not a poor apportionment to have been given. You say in your anger that you should have wed a rich man. I intend being a rich man, Cicely. I don't yet quite know how I will accomplish this, but I will. I have not yet spent a penny of your dower. It remains in Edinburgh with the goldsmith."

She had not known this, and was encouraged to learn it. "My father made his wealth investing in trading voyages to the Levant," Cicely said. "You must be careful, of course, which ships and voyages you invest in, but 'tis no less risky than cattle or sheep, which can be stolen away. And you never put all your coin in one play, he advised me."

He nodded. "This could be a way for us to begin, sweetheart. Together we will build a legacy for our descendants."

"If you do not get killed fighting the king's war," Cicely responded tartly.

"I won't," he promised her, and he took her two hands in his and kissed them.

The king's call came in late winter, a time when no one would expect a military campaign to be mounted. But the days were getting longer now, and the chance of a blizzard growing less with every day. The buds had not broken upon the trees and the snows still clung hard to the bens when James Stewart, a large army at his back, crossed the River Tay and moved north into the Highlands. When word reached Alexander MacDonald he was astounded, for the king had come earlier than any of them had expected. The lord of the isles smiled grimly, but he admitted to those closest to him that he had a grudging respect now for James Stewart that he hadn't had before.

The MacDonald called forth the ten thousand men who had sworn fealty to him. Many came. But there were also those clans who, having been impressed with James Stewart after their meeting at Inverness—the Camerons, the Buchanans, and Clan Chattan—switched sides to fight for the king. The two armies met at Lochaber, and the lord of the isles was firmly defeated in a dreadful slaughter. The king would not be particularly merciful to those who had burned, killed, and looted Inverness.

Alexander MacDonald sued now for peace and forgiveness. His Highlanders fled deep into the mountains, attempting to avoid the king's wrath, because they knew the harshest judgments would fall upon them. James Stewart would need the lord of the isles to bring his word and calm to the region, but before then the king did a bit of burning and destruction himself in an effort to make his point with the northern families. He would tolerate no more rebellion.

In the borders spring had come. The snows were gone from the hillsides, which were now green and blooming as the weeks passed from March to April to May. Cicely was certain she was with child again, and was eager for her husband's return. This child would be born in December, and her instinct, even this early on, told her it would be a lad. Kier would be pleased, and she wanted him home so they might share their happiness together. She had received a letter from her father in response to one she had written to him almost a year and a half ago. While he was still frail of body, his spirit was stronger than it had ever been. Her stepmother had died after escaping her keepers, drowning in Leighton Water, a swift-moving small river that ran through her father's estates. Robert Bowen was saddened, but not unhappy. He and her half brothers would welcome a visit from Cicely, should she be able to come home, he wrote.

Cicely laid the missive aside. She would like to see

her father before he died, but she had obligations as the lady of Glengorm, and there were the children to consider. They were too young for so long a trip. She would write to her father, explaining, on the morrow, she decided, climbing into bed. But tomorrow she had to ride out and inspect the hay fields and her herb garden was finally beginning to look healthy, with its new growth. The lavender would be particularly bountiful this year, from the looks of the plants she had growing. And the chamomile was already budding.

On the beach by the loch two of the men left behind by Frang patrolled the beach from one end to the other, meeting in the middle now and again. Bethia crept from her cottage, keeping to the shadows so that no one would see her as she made her way to the shoreline. Seeing the first man-at-arms, she called softly to him, and, startled, he turned about.

"I've brought ye some whiskey, Roddie Douglas," she said, holding out a stone flask to the man. " 'Tis a chilly night for the middle of May."

"Aye," the man-at-arms agreed. " 'Tis kindly, Bethia, but I hope you're not looking at me for a second husband, for I'm not of a mind to wed."

"Nay, nay, and especially as you're futtering that widow at the end of the village," Bethia cackled. "I'm too dried up for a fine young lad like you, Roddie Douglas."

He chuckled and, taking the flask, drank down a good portion of the liquid. "Thank you," he said.

"I'll give the rest to your mate," she said. "Who is at the other end of the beach?"

"That will be Black William," Roddie replied.

Bethia sauntered off into the dusk, seeking the second man-at-arms. Finding him, she offered him the flask. He was happy to drink the remaining whiskey down. She left him and, returning to where she had left Roddie Douglas, she found him collapsed and snoring on the sand. With a smile of satisfaction she waited a few minutes, then sought out the second man-at-arms. Bethia found him in the same state as the first.

Walking back up the shore to where Roddie Douglas lay, Bethia picked up his dark lantern. She removed the shade from the lamp and the light exploded. Bethia raised the lantern and waved it slowly back and forth as she stood facing the water. A twinkle of light from across the small loch answered her. And then her sharp ears picked up the sound of horses entering the water, swimming, coming closer and closer. She was able to make out the form of her brother, Durwin, leading the raiders.

"Welcome to Glengorm, brother," Bethia said, grinning. "How may I be of service to you, Durwin, my kinsman?"

Durwin slid from his horse. "You are certain we can take what we want, that the laird's away, and their defense is scant? I am not of a mind to lose any men. The Douglases have severely decimated the ranks of the Grahames. We're going to be taking women from the village for concubines. Those we have can't produce bairns quick enough. You'll know those old enough to futter and produce. How many men left?"

"None of fighting age. Lads and grandfathers. The few fighting men are up at the house. But once they hear a commotion in the village they'll come running. When they do you can creep into the house and steal the lady. Futter her if you will, but she will actually be worth more in ransom," Bethia said.

"Agreed," her brother replied. "Now, as we have discussed, sister, take the wee boat on the shore here and row yourself across to the other side to wait for us. I've brought a horse for you. We'll bring the women we're stealing to you. If you say they're too old or too young we'll toss them in the water. If they can swim home they will have their lives. If not . . ." Durwin Grahame shrugged. "Is your husband with the laird?"

"The bastard is dead," Bethia said. "His old mother died first." She smiled evilly, and her brother knew Bethia had killed the woman in some manner. "I poisoned her. It was too cold, and the ground was frozen, so we cremated her. Then came the storm. It snowed for three days. I killed my man the first day. Then, while the storm raged, I cut him up into pieces. Some I burned. Some I fed to the dog. The rest I put in a sack with stones. I kept it in the snow behind my cottage, meaning to dump it in the loch when it opened up. But some wild beasts found the sack and ran off with it. I couldn't even find his bones."

"Get in the boat then," her brother said. His sister was a far more dangerous woman than he had imagined. He would have to kill her before they began their return over the border today. He couldn't spend the rest of his life wondering about when she would turn on him. She was a traitorous bitch who thought only of herself. Despite being married to a Douglas, and living with the Douglases for all these years, Bethia had betrayed them without so much as a single regret. She would betray him too, given the opportunity, but he would not give her that opportunity.

Bethia nodded to him, obeying, and when she was settled in the small boat he pushed it from the sandy shore into the loch. "I'll see you on the other side," he said. Then, turning, he mustered his men, who had been waiting silently. "We'll leave the horses here and go on afoot into the village," Durwin Grahame told them.

In her cottage at the end of the village nearest the path to the house, Mary Douglas lay sleepless. She never slept well when her husband was away. A dog suddenly sent up a bark. Then she heard a yelp, and for a moment it was silent before Mary thought she heard a scream. She got up and peered through the small window to see the dark shapes of men running through the village and into the cottages. Mary did not wait. Grabbing her dark cloak, she slipped out of the little door at the rear of her cottage and, using the trees on the hillside as cover, made her way up the hill to the laird's dwelling. The shrieks of frightened women had become more audible.

Reaching the house, she pounded upon the little kitchen door until the lad, Gabhan, peered out and, seeing her, opened the portal to let her in. "Bar the door, lad! The Grahames are upon us!" Mary cried. "Where is Frang? We must rouse the house!"

"This entry won't hold against an assault," Gabhan told Mary.

"Then quickly, wake Mab and the lasses and get upstairs," Mary told him as she hurried to climb the stairs into the hall. There she found Frang snoring in a bedspace. "Get up! Get up!" She shook him. "The Grahames are upon us, man!"

He was awake in an instant. "How? Where?"

"In the village for now, stealing women, but they'll be at the hall soon enough," Mary told him. "They came from the loch side, or they'd have had me. I couldn't sleep, and heard a noise, saw the shadows, and ran."

"I'll get the men, and we'll go into the village and settle this," Frang said.

"Nay! Nay! You mustn't leave the lady and her bairns unprotected. The ransom would be fierce, and 'twould beggar the laird. Besides, it appeared there were more of them than there are of us."

The door at the end of the hall opened, and Cicely stepped out. "What is it?" She saw Mary Douglas, and her brow lifted questioningly. She was wearing a long chemise.

"The Grahames are in the village," Frang said.

"Is the house secure?" Cicely asked him.

He nodded.

"Nay, the kitchen can be breached," Mary said. "Gabhan said so."

"Then we'll seal the entry from the hall to the kitchen stairs," Frang told them.

"Where are Mab, the lasses, and Gabhan?" Cicely wanted to know. "Get them upstairs immediately."

Frang hurried down into the kitchen, where he found Mab, her two helpers, and her great-nephew shoving the big kitchen table so that it blocked the outside door, which was also barred. It was a good strategy. He helped them to get it the last few feet, and then shooed them all up into the hall. Cicely had gone into the large bedchamber with Mary Douglas, and they pulled the outer wooden shutter closed over the chamber's single window. The window was now made of glass, but they had not yet dispensed with the inner wood shutters. They pulled them tightly and laid a wooden bar across them. Then they piled the trunks in the room before the windows. With great effort someone would be able to get into the chamber eventually, but all they needed was time.

"I want you, the bairns, the women in that chamber," Frang said. "You'll be safe unless someone manages to break in, and you'll have time to reach the hall if they do. You can then bar that door to gain more time for us."

"Can we send to Sir William or Ben Duff for aid?" Cicely asked.

Frang shook his head. "Their men are also with the king but for a few, my lady."

Cicely nodded. "Then we are on our own," she said. "Sine, go up. Wake the children and their nursemaid. Bring them downstairs. Where are Mab and her lasses?"

"Here, my lady," the old woman said. She held a large wooden rolling pin in one hand. Her helpers, Bessie and Flora, held wooden mallets used to tenderize the meat.

"You are well armed, I see," Cicely remarked. "Let us pray they cannot breach the house," she said, leading them into the enclosed bedchamber. But she kept the door open, and after she had quickly dressed Cicely went back into the hall to speak with Frang. Kate came downstairs with the two children. She was wide-eyed, but calm.

"What are our chances of avoiding a fight?" Cicely asked Frang.

He shook his head. "We'll try to hold out until either they grow weary of the game and depart with their booty, or offer decent terms for our surrender," he said. "And, of course, they could go away with what they have gained today, and return another day."

"I don't want anyone's blood on my hands," Cicely quietly told the captain of the men-at-arms. "I could not bear to lose any of you."

He gave her a warm smile. "We will do our best, my lady," Frang promised. But he knew that if the Grahames managed to reach the hall it would be a fight to the death. He crossed himself and prayed silently for a miracle. Then he sent one of his men up to the second floor to see what was happening, and relay it down to them.

"The village is burning," the man called. "I can see it from here."

Frang shrugged. "It was to be expected," he said sanguinely.

"The women are shrieking up a storm," the lookout said. "They are having quite a time containing them. I can see some of them running, being chased."

"Good," Frang said. "They may have to decide if they want the women more, or what's in this house more. If they can't control our lasses they can't storm the house."

Durwin Grahame was learning, to his annoyance, the truth of this as the women scattered about the village, evading his men, half of whom were chasing after them while the other half fired the cottages. "Leave that cottage at the end alone," he called to his men. "We'll pen the women in there with two of you to guard them. Then we'll go after the laird's wife and bairns for the fine ransom they'll bring us."

After several hours of running the younger women of Glengorm down, the raiders finally had them bound and incarcerated in Mary Douglas's cottage. The older women and the children they had let run off, for they weren't interested in them. And while the elderly had protested the destruction of their homes, the Grahames had waved them away threateningly, telling them they were fortunate not to be killed. There were some who might have killed them, and another time Durwin Grahame might have. Today, however, he was interested in only two things: women to bear Grahame bairns, and a fat ransom.

Their prisoners contained, the Grahames moved purposefully towards the laird of Glengorm's house. The sky was beginning to lighten now with the mid-May dawn. The air was filled with the scent of burning, but the day would be clear. Suddenly Durwin Grahame saw a herd of six fat cows, in a pen near the barn. His eyes lit up. He wanted those cows, whose udders were enormous with milk and cream right now. He pointed to three of his men. "Swim that group across the loch," he told them. "Then come back."

The trio went off to do his bidding as Durwin led the rest of his men to the house. They had almost reached it when a hail of arrows flew from the upper story of the building. The arrows found targets. Howls of pain from some of his men pierced the air. He signaled his men back far enough to avoid the arrows, and so he might think. He could see that the front door was heavy and bound with iron. There had to be another way to gain access to the dwelling. In the meantime he set several men to cutting down a tree, from which they would strip the branches, and then use the trunk as a battering ram. Another two he sent to walk about the house to find its weakness.

Fortunately none of his men had been seriously injured by the arrows, although their wounds were painful. Care would have to be taken that the wounds did not become infected. The arrows were all yanked out and cast aside, while the injuries were bound up. The two men returned to report that they had found another smaller door near a kitchen garden that might be breached. And there was a shuttered window in an extension.

"We will try the door first," Durwin Grahame said. "If it is the kitchen there will be access to the hall from there." But try as they might, they could not get in through that small door. Durwin began to wonder if the portal was iron instead of blackened old wood. "We'll try the shuttered window then," he finally announced.

Inside the bedchamber the women heard the outside shutter being dismantled. They were silent. Flora whimpered as they heard the glass window being broken. Cicely debated their course of action. She stepped into the hall, saying to Frang, "They are already through the outside shutter and glass. Once they destroy the inner shutter it is just a matter of pushing the trunks away. I think the children and the women should be upstairs now, Frang. We can be contained there. Here we are open to attack from two sides, I fear."

"You're right, my lady," he agreed.

"Quickly," Cicely called to the women in her bedchamber. "Get upstairs into the nursery chamber before these villains break through into the house."

The women hurried from the chamber, carrying the children, and rushed upstairs.

"You, too, my lady," Frang said quietly.

Cicely opened her mouth to protest, and then, seeing the foolishness of it, nodded. "Do not get yourself killed," she said.

He grinned at her. "I'll take a few Grahames with me for company if I do," he promised her.

Cicely ran for the stairs and joined the others upstairs. What if they fired the house? she wondered. Could they all get out safely? *Blessed Mother!* This certainly wouldn't have happened if Kier had been here. Was James Stewart's war with the MacDonald of the Isles more important than the survival of Glengorm?

She smiled wryly to herself. The answer to that question depended upon who was asking the question. She already knew both answers to her query.

Almost within sight of his home Kier Douglas and his Glengorm men saw the smoke. The laird of Glengorm raised his hand to signal a stop. From the hill they had just topped they saw the village alight. Kier heard the men behind him beginning to swear. His gaze moved to the house. It was being assaulted. He turned. "It would seem that the Grahames have come calling, lads. No mercy!" Then he spurred his horse down the road leading to his home, his clansmen riding hard behind him.

Durwin Grahame and his men had almost broken through into the main floor. They pushed and pushed at the inner shutters until they gave way. Then they shoved the trunks piled up, blocking them. As the trunks fell away Durwin Grahame, his men behind him, climbed into the laird of Glengorm's house. They gawked briefly at the room in which they stood, and then began their attempt to get through the chamber's door.

On the second floor one of the archers saw the laird and their clansmen spurring their horses down the hill road to Glengorm. He called down the narrow staircase to Frang, "God be praised, the laird is home! Open the doors to him, Frang!"

Frang ran to peep out through a shutter. He saw his master as the laird galloped up to the house, his clansmen behind him. Frang's eyes lifted skyward, and he whispered a quick thanks for the miracle they were receiving. Lifting the bar from the front door of the house himself, he flung it aside and opened the door to admit Kier Douglas. "This way, my lord! They have gotten in through the bedchamber, and are trying to break through into the hall," Frang said, gesturing and running ahead of the laird.

They reached the door at the rear of the hall. Frang looked to his master, who nodded. The captain of Glengorm's men-at-arms lifted the bar he had earlier placed across the door. He turned the key in the lock and kicked open the door. Surprised, Durwin Grahame and his men dashed through the opening, only to find themselves surrounded by Kier Douglas and his men. The Grahames stopped dead in their tracks.

"No mercy!" the laird shouted as he had earlier, and the battle was enjoined. It was quickly over, for although the Grahames were fighting for their lives, the clansmen of Glengorm fought not only for life, but for their women, their bairns, and their homes.

At the last minute one man escaped, however. Durwin Grahame did not intend to leave this earth without his sister, Bethia. They let him run. His defeat would make a stronger point than anything else they might do. The Grahame chief raced down the hill and through the village to the beach. Finding his horse, he leaped into the saddle and urged it into the loch. Reaching the other side, he found Bethia waiting for him.

"What has happened?" she demanded. "Three of your men swam some cows across the loch and kept going. Where are the women you wanted? And where are your men, brother?"

"Glengorm is surely blessed, sister," Durwin told her. "The laird came home just as we had broken into the house. All are slain but for me."

"You ran? God forgive you for a coward, Durwin," she sneered, and then she spit at him in disgust.

"I could not die yet, sister," he told her. *"Not yet.* Not until I had killed you!" And Durwin Grahame leaped forward, plunging his dirk into Bethia's heart, twisting it hard, and gaining satisfaction from the look in her eyes as she died on his blade. Yanking the dirk from her chest, he wiped it on her skirts, replacing it in its sheath. Seeing that she had a small stone flask attached to her belt, he pulled it off, jerked the stopper from it, sniffed, and poured the whiskey down his throat. A moment later he collapsed to the earth, a look of complete surprise upon his face. "Jesu!" he groaned. "I've been poisoned." They were the last words he spoke.

They found him several hours later, dead on the stony beach that edged the far side of the loch. Looking down at Bethia and Durwin Grahame, Frang said, "Jesu! I had forgotten that Bethia was a Grahame. Her husband took her in a border raid so long ago I didn't remember it. This man must have been her kin."

"She incapacitated the watch on the beach, which allowed her kin to attack the village and the house," the laird noted. "Bury them." Then he swam his mount back across the water and rode up the hill to greet his wife.

Cicely met him in the hall. "Welcome home, my lord. Your arrival was fortuitous, to say the least. It was all I could do to keep Mab from getting herself killed, for she had armed herself with a very dangerous rolling pin and was ready to fight the Grahames herself."

Without a word he swept her into his arms, and his mouth descended upon hers in a fierce, hot kiss. When he finally raised his head he said, his voice thick with emotion, "I could have lost you, Cicely. I could have lost you!"

She wrapped her arms about him, looking up into his face, almost breathless, and smiling. "Then you really do love me, my lord," Cicely said teasingly.

"Aye," he admitted to her. "I *really* do love you! You are my life, my strength, the reason my heart continues to beat, lass!"

"As you are my life and strength, my lord," Cicely told him. "I love you too! I always will. Now, Kier Douglas, I want you to promise me, no more running off to war! You have done your duty by James Stewart. Now it is the time for you to do your duty by Glengorm. For

Johanna, and Ian, and the bairn I'm now carrying. For our own Glengorm folk. I want my husband home and by my side. Kings may come and go. But the legacy you and I shall build here for our children and for our descendants will be a strong and solid one, my darling."

Kier bent, kissing her more gently this time. "Aye," he agreed, "we shall build a fine legacy for Glengorm that will last at least as long as the Stewarts are kings, sweetheart."

Johanna's little voice suddenly piped up near them. "Da is home, Ian!" she said excitedly. "Da is home!"

Kier Douglas bent down, lifting Johanna and Ian into the curve of his arm while his other arm wrapped itself tightly about Cicely. "Aye, my bairns, your da is home," he said, his eyes moist with his emotion. "And home he means to stay forever!"

"Hooray!" said little Johanna, happily clapping her hands.

And, their eyes meeting in perfect accord, Kier and Cicely Douglas laughed aloud.

And Afterwards

*J*oan Beaufort bore her husband six daughters: Margaret, Isabella, Joan, Eleanor, Mary, and Annabella. It wasn't until October of 1430 that Scotland finally had a male heir. The queen bore twin sons, Alexander and James. Alexander did not survive the winter. James, named after his father, came to the throne at the tender age of six, when his father was assassinated on February 20, 1437.

James I had been beloved of his people. His English queen, and the extreme youth of England's king, not to mention England's struggle to retain her French possessions, had helped him to maintain peace between the two countries. It allowed James to concentrate on improving the system of justice in Scotland, establishing trade, and stabilizing the currency.

Unfortunately he was unable to control the ambitions, the petty jealousies, and the rapacity of his lords. They had been used to years of weak kings who could be bought off and controlled. The first James Stewart had proved to be not that kind of a man. His grandfather Robert II, a widower, had made a second marriage to Euphemia Ross that had produced four children, in addition to the nine Robert II already had. Two were sons, and uncles to James I.

It was the adherents to this branch of the family, including former servants of the late Duke of Albany, who hatched a plot to kill James Stewart and replace him on the throne with Walter Stewart, the Earl of Atholl, the king's adviser, who was the younger son of Robert II and Euphemia Ross. The king and his family were staying at the Dominican priory in Perth on that cold winter's night when the assassins burst in. The queen and several of her women were injured trying to protect the king so he might have time to flee his attackers. Sadly he was caught and stabbed to death. But while her husband was being murdered, Queen Joan escaped to safety, sending word to Edinburgh to protect her son from any other conspirators.

These lords had unfortunately seen things only from their own perspective. In their mind's eye they had destroyed a despot. However, Scotland's people did not see it that way. Regicide was not popular, for kings were anointed by the Church. They were God's chosen. Joan Beaufort, daughter of royalty, great-granddaughter of Edward III of England, granddaughter of John of Gaunt, having escaped death and kept her son—now James II—safe, knew exactly what to do, and she did it.

Her husband's body, bearing its terrible wounds, was put on display for all to see. Joan played the role of tragic widow to the hilt, organizing her own coalition. The conspirators floundered about, having not quite considered what they would do after they killed James I. In the confusion that followed the queen grew stronger and stronger. The papal nuncio, Bishop Anthony Altani of Urbino, had been in Perth at the time of the assassination. He declared that James I had died a martyr as the king was being laid to rest in the Carthusian priory outside of Perth that James I had founded.

Having aroused the people's sense of outrage, the queen and her supporters now acted. James I's murderers were hunted down, arrested, and imprisoned. The queen personally supervised their three days of torture as the top three conspirators were put to slow and painful death. The Earl of Atholl, the king's uncle, who had dared to involve himself in the plot, was crowned with a burning band of red-hot iron. Engraved on this terrible crown was *The King of Traitors*.

Two years later, in the year 1439, the widowed queen, Joan Beaufort, married again. Her second husband was Sir James Stewart, known as the Black Knight of Lorne. She bore him three sons: John, who was created Earl of Atholl; James, Earl of Buchan; and Andrew, who became the bishop of Moray. Dying in 1445, she was buried beside her first and great love, James I.

Author's Note

In my previous novel, *Betrayed,* set in this time period, I have Queen Joan bearing a son, Alexander, earlier. Later research since then has proved the queen bore her only male children, twins, James and Alexander, in October of 1430. I apologize for any confusion this may have caused the reader.

About the Author

Bertrice Small is a *New York Times* bestselling author and the recipient of numerous awards, including the 2008 Pioneer of Romance Award from *Romantic Times* magazine. In keeping with her profession, Bertrice Small lives in the oldest English-speaking town in the state of New York, founded in 1640. Her light-filled studio includes the paintings of her favorite cover artist, Elaine Duillo, and a large library. Because she believes in happy endings, Bertrice Small has been married to the same man, her hero, George, for forty-three years. They have a son, Thomas; a daughter-in-law; Megan and four wonderful grandchildren. Longtime readers will be happy to know that Nicki the cockatiel flourishes, along with his housemates: Pookie, the long-haired greige-and-white cat; Finnegan, the long-haired bad black kitty; and Sylvester, the black-and-white tuxedo cat, who is now the official bedcat.

Read on for a preview of
Bertrice Small's next
Border Chronicles tale

The Border Vixen

Available now!

As the laird enjoyed his mirth, Maggie Kerr entered the hall. "I am told we have a visitor, Grandsire," she said, coming forward.

Fingal Stewart watched her come. She was dressed in woolen breeks, boots, and an open-necked shirt. A wide leather belt encircled her waist. The skin of her neck and face was damp with obvious exertion. The lass was more than pretty, he realized, but the confident stride as she walked, the open curiosity in her hazel eyes, the set of her jaw, told him she would be neither biddable nor easy. He stood politely as she came forward.

"The king has sent ye a gift, lassie," the laird chortled. He was truly enjoying this.

"The king? A gift?" She looked genuinely puzzled. "The king has never set eyes upon me. Why would he send me a gift?"

"Ewan Hay went to visit His Majesty. He told him ye needed a husband, lass," the laird cackled. "And so the king has sent his own kinsman to wed ye." The laird waited for the outburst that was not long in coming.

"Ewan Hay told the king I needed a husband? Why would that pox-ridden donkey's ass do such a thing?" Then her eyes widened. "God's balls! He thought to steal Brae Aisir out from beneath us, Grandsire, didn't he? He thought the king would order me to wed him, the imbecile!" Then her eyes fixed themselves on her grandfather's companion. "Who are ye, sir?"

"Lord Fingal Stewart, madam," Fin answered her.

"And yer the king's kin sent to wed me?" she demanded.

"I am," he replied.

"And what, my lord, have ye done to win such a prize?" Maggie wanted to know.

"I have been loyal, madam. The Stewarts of Torra have always been loyal to the Stewart kings since the days of James the First. The king knows he may trust me to do as I have been bid," Fingal Stewart answered her in a hard voice.

"Torra? *Of the rock?*" Maggie was curious in spite of herself. "Where do ye come from, my lord?"

"Edinburgh, madam. We are the Stewarts of Torra because our house sits below the castle rock itself," he told her.

"Ye have no lands then," she said scornfully.

"I have a house, a manservant, twelve men-at-arms gifted me by the king, some coin with Moses Kira, the banker, a modest purse of gold I've brought with me, and James Stewart's favor. Naught else," Fingal Stewart responded honestly.

Maggie had not expected a candid answer. She had never met a man before who was quite so direct. Usually men struggled to please her, to win her over—even that obnoxious simpleton Ewan Hay. "So ye've come to wed me for my wealth," she said, contempt tingeing her voice.

"I've come to wed ye because I have been ordered to it," he replied as insultingly.

"If ye think to wed me, my lord, ye will have to comply with the same rules all my other suitors have faced. And none has succeeded to date. I'll wed no man, particularly a stranger, whom I cannot respect. If ye can outrun me, outride me, and outfight me, I'll go to the altar willingly, but not otherwise."

"There's no choice here, lass," the laird told his grand-daughter. "This man has been sent by the king, and I tell you truthfully that I am happy to see him. Ye'll wed him, and that's the end of it. Will ye let a man like Ewan Hay dispossess ye when I'm dead? Make no mistake, lassie, without a strong husband to follow in my path, our neighbors will be fighting ye and one another for control of the Aisir nam Breug."

"But, Grandsire, if he does not compete against me, those same neighbors will rise up against the Kerrs for having imposed our conditions upon them, but not upon the king's kinsman," Maggie argued. "Ye swore before them that all suitors must conform."

"The lass is right," Fingal Stewart agreed. "If I am to have the respect of yer neighbors, my lord, I must accept the lady's challenge. 'Twill not be difficult to overcome her. I'm surprised this Hay couldn't."

Maggie suddenly grinned wickedly. "I can outrun, outride, and outfight *any* man in the Borders, my lord," she repeated, "and I will, I promise ye, outrun, outride, and outfight ye."

"I am not from the Borders," Lord Stewart reminded her with an answering grin.

"Ye can have yer contest, Maggie," her grandsire said, "but first I will have the marriage contract drawn up. Ye and Lord Stewart will sign it. When the contest is over, win or lose, ye must accept the marriage and have yer uncle bless it in the chapel."

She hesitated.

"Are ye afraid I'll beat ye?" Lord Stewart taunted her.

"I'm just concerned with having to live with a weak-ling," Maggie said sharply.

He laughed. "Madam, have ye ever been spanked?" he asked her.

She turned an outraged face to him. "Nay, never!"

"Ye will be, and soon, I have not a doubt," he told her.

"Lay a hand on me in anger, my lord, and I'll gut ye from stem to gudgeon," Maggie told him fiercely, her hand going to the dagger at her waist.

The laird's face grew grim at her combative words, but before he might admonish her, Lord Stewart laughed aloud.

"Marrying a stranger cannot be easy for either bride or groom, madam," he told her, grinning. "I can but hope this passion of yers extends to the marriage bed, for then we will suit admirably, and there will be no talk of murder, I promise ye."

Though Maggie was tall for a woman, he towered over her. She gasped and blushed at his blunt speech. No man had ever spoken so suggestively to her. For a moment she was at a loss for words. Then she said, "I'll sign the marriage contract, for in law that will make ye my husband. And I'm certain that will convince the greedier among our neighbors that the Aisir nam Breug's future ownership is settled. Particularly after they have met ye. Ye would appear to be reasonably intelligent and competent, my lord. But ye will nae bed me until ye have fulfilled my terms."

"Maggie!" Her grandfather almost shouted her name. "Ye cannot set the terms of this matter. The king has said ye will wed him, and ye will!"

"Aye, I will, Grandsire, but for the reasons earlier stated, he must best me," she replied. "The king said I must wed him—not lie with him."

"I will best ye, lassie," Fingal Stewart told her quietly. "Here's my hand on it." He held out his big hand to her, smiling.

She took his hand, watching almost mesmerized as his long thick fingers closed over her smaller hand, enclosing it completely as they shook. Then he shocked her by yanking her forward. An arm clamped about her waist, pulling her close against him. His chest was hard, and she could smell a mixture of male and the damp leather of his jerkin. A hand grasped her head, those same fingers wrapping themselves in her chestnut hair to hold her steady as his mouth descended upon hers in a fierce, quick kiss that left her breathless and gasping with surprise. He released her as quickly as he had taken her. Maggie stumbled back, but then, swiftly recovering, raised her hand to slap him.

The big hand sprang forth to wrap firmly about her wrist. "Nah, nah, lassie," he warned her softly. "I have the right now."

"Yer hurting me," Maggie said through clenched teeth, "and ye have no rights yet, my lord."

The laird watched the interaction between his granddaughter and Lord Stewart, fascinated. He would have to thank the king for sending him such a strong man to take on his responsibilities, not that he was quite ready yet to relinquish them. Fingal Stewart had a great deal to learn about the Aisir nam Breug. But he obviously was already skilled at handling a woman. Dugald Kerr chuckled.

"Are ye going to allow this ape to manhandle me, Grandsire?" Maggie demanded. She was utterly outraged. He had kissed her! Made her feel weak, and she wasn't weak. *She wasn't!* And her grandfather had done nothing to prevent it. Indeed, he had laughed.

"I'm going to call for David to come and meet Lord Stewart. I want yer marriage contract signed by the morrow. What date will ye fix for the challenge, lassie?"

"I'll sign the contract, for I have already given ye my word, but the challenge will have to wait, Grandsire. We are only just past Lammastide. We have late crops to harvest, and the fields must be opened for gleaning. When this is done, we will set a date, Grandsire," Maggie said.

"I am content with that," Lord Stewart quickly said, for he could see the laird was eager to have the matter settled and ended. "Send for the priest I saw in the village as we passed through, and let us make a beginning to it."

"Busby," the laird called. "Send for my brother to come to the keep immediately, and tell him to bring parchment and pen."

"I must go back to the yard, Grandsire," Maggie said. "I was training the new lads when I was told of Lord Stewart's arrival." Without waiting she made a quick curtsy to both men and hurried out of the hall.

"She trains the recruits?" Lord Stewart was surprised.

The laird nodded. "In archery, and other combat skills," he said. "Do ye now see why I have acquiesced to her demand that a husband be able to outrun, outride, and outfight her? She is beautiful, and she is clever, but she would rather be outdoors than in the hall. She has been that way since she was a wee lass. And from the moment I taught her how to use a bow, her pursuits were more those of a lad than of a lassie. She governs the house as well, for Grizel, her tiring woman, made her learn the things she must know to manage it. I pray God that you can overcome her, my lord, for Brae Aisir will be all the safer for an heir or two. I wish she were not so difficult, and I too old to control her."

Lord Stewart sat down again and sipped from his goblet. "She is a strong woman—she must be to survive here in the Borders," he began. "She has become formidable, I suspect, to protect ye and the Aisir nam Breug. The signing of the contracts on the morrow makes us legally man and wife. Beneath her brave heart and fierce will, yer granddaughter is still a woman. She knows she cannot escape the king's will, but she is afraid, though she would deny it. The moment my lips touched hers, I knew she had never been kissed. Let her have the time she needs to accustom herself to our marriage. Let us learn to know each other before I bed her. Ye need have no fear. I will beat her in whatever challenge she puts forth. And when I do, she will do her duty, for I know ye have raised her to accept her responsibilities."

"The king cannot possibly know the great favor he

has done for us in sending ye here, Fingal Stewart," the laird said. Then his brown eyes twinkled mischievously. "How much is it costing Brae Aisir?" he asked.

Lord Stewart laughed. "I see my cousin's reputation extends into the depths of the Borders," he replied. "He wanted half of the yearly tolls paid each Michaelmas in coin. I argued for a third. When the contracts for our agreement reach me, I shall ask they be paid on St. Andrew's Day beginning next year. I believe that is fairer as I have no idea what ye collect, although judging from yer keep, I must assume it is a goodly sum."

"It is," the laird said, but gave no further details.

"Perhaps tomorrow the lady will ride out with me so I may see the pass," Lord Stewart suggested.

"Aye, before the winter comes there is much you will need to see and learn about Brae Aisir. And tomorrow I shall send one of my own men to the king with my thanks for sending ye. If ye wish to write to him, my messenger can take yer letter too."

Father David Kerr, robes swaying, hurried into the hall, his servant behind him carrying the priest's writing box. "What is so important that I must come posthaste, Dugald?" he asked his older brother. The priest's eyes went to Lord Stewart.

"This is Fingal Stewart, Brother. The king has sent his cousin, Lord Stewart of Torra, to wed with Maggie," the laird began. Then he went on to explain.

The priest listened, nodding as his elder brother spoke. When the laird had finished he said, "'Tis as good a solution as any, Dugald." He held out his hand to Fingal. "Welcome to Brae Aisir, my lord." The two men shook. Then David Kerr looked back to the laird. "And what, pray, does my niece think of this? I saw her when I came into the courtyard working her lads hard. I think she is not pleased to be told what she must do."

"She will sign the marriage contract tomorrow when it is drawn and ready," the laird assured the priest.

"And the blessing?" the priest asked.

"He must fulfill the conditions any other suitor would before the blessing," Dugald Kerr said. "She is determined, and Lord Stewart says he can beat her fairly."

"You would let her have her way in her foolishness?" David Kerr asked Fingal.

He nodded in the affirmative. "Aye. She needs to feel she has some control over her life even if she doesn't. Some men might not care, but I want my wife to respect me. She will not if I cannot best her. And yer neighbors will not feel so slighted by this match when I do."

The priest looked thoughtful, and then replied, "Yer a clever fellow, my lord. And I think ye could be dangerous, given the opportunity. If yer willing to indulge the lass, then so be it. When will yer contest take place?"

"After the gleaning," Lord Stewart replied.

"Well, 'tis not so long to wait," the priest said. "I'm pleased to see yer a disciplined man."

"Remain here tonight, and draw up the contracts," the laird said. "I want them signed after morning Mass, Brother."

"Agreed!" David Kerr said.

New York Times bestselling author

BERTRICE SMALL

The Border Vixen

The newest novel in the Border Chronicles
series "reaffirms her standing as a
historical romance stalwart."*

Aware of the covetous interest in his land, the laird of
Brae Aisir announces that any man who can outrun,
outride, and outfight his headstrong granddaughter
"Mad Maggie" will have her as a wife—along with her
inheritance. His proposition causes more chaos than
resolution, especially when King James II sends his
cousin, Fingal Stewart, to compete for Maggie's hand.
The competition brings out the fire in both of them, and
it doesn't take long for the rivals to become lovers. But
there are those who will do anything to gain control of
Maggie's inheritance—even if it means getting rid of
Fingal Stewart and his border vixen.

*Publishers Weekly

**Available wherever books are sold or at
penguin.com**

S0138

BERTRICE SMALL

The Border Lord's Bride

Second in the Border Chronicles from the
New York Times bestselling author of
A Dangerous Love

New York Times bestselling author Bertrice Small,
"the reigning queen of the historical genre" (Romance
Junkies), continues her Border Chronicles with this
sweeping tale of an imposing laird forced to marry
the woman he rescued...never anticipating that she
could bring him the love of a lifetime.

**Available wherever books are sold or at
penguin.com**

New York Times bestselling author
BERTRICE SMALL

The Captive Heart

THE THIRD PASSIONATE ROMANCE IN THE BORDER CHRONICLES SERIES

The year is 1461, and the winds of war rage across England, uprooting Alix Givet, the daughter of Queen Margaret's physician, and the rest of Henry VI's court. Alix's plight becomes bleaker still when, out of duty to her queen, and to her ill, widowed father, she's locked into a loveless marriage to a cruel Northumbrian. But when her luck changes, Alix has another chance to flee— this time to save herself.

Escaping north over the border into Scotland, she throws herself at the mercy of a dark and brooding laird who might provide the everlasting love of her dreams—if she can warm his cold heart.

Available wherever books are sold or at penguin.com

S0136

New York Times bestselling author

BERTRICE SMALL

A Dangerous Love

An exhilarating new historical romance series begins.

Adair Radcliffe is only a child when her family perishes in the War of the Roses, so her real father, the womanizing King Edward IV, takes her in, honoring his promise to her mother. Once Adair turns sixteen, the king marries her off without her knowledge in a wedding by proxy.

But when tragedy leaves her a widow twice over, Adair realizes that her already tenuous social position has sunk even lower. Now, all she can do is hope that the Scottish laird to whom she is sold will have mercy on her. But little does master or servant suspect that love knows no rank.

Available wherever books are sold or at
penguin.com

S0137